THE DROWNING TREE

CAROL GOODMAN is the author of *The Seduction of Water* and *The Lake of Dead Languages*. After graduating from Vassar College, where she majored in Latin, she taught Latin for several years in Austin, Texas. She then received an M.F.A. in fiction from the New School University. Goodman currently teaches writing in New York City. She lives on Long Island.

ALSO BY CAROL GOODMAN

The Lake of Dead Languages
The Seduction of Water

The
DROWNING
TREE

Carol Goodman

arrow books

Published by Arrow Books in 2005

1 3 5 7 9 10 8 6 4 2

Copyright © 2004 by Carol Goodman

Carol Goodman has asserted her right under the Copyright, Designs and
Patents Act 1988 to be identified as the author of this work

Grateful acknowledgement is made to Sulphur River Literary Press to
reprint the poem 'The Language of Trees' from *Talk Between Leaf and Skin:
Poems* by Lee Slonimsky (2002). Reprinted by permission of Sulphur River
Literary Review Press, Austin, Texas

First published in the United Kingdom in 2004 by William Heinemann

Arrow Books
The Random House Group Limited
20 Vauxhall Bridge Road, London, SW1V 2SA

Random House Australia (Pty) Limited
20 Alfred Street, Milsons Point, Sydney,
New South Wales 2061, Australia

Random House New Zealand Limited
18 Poland Road, Glenfield
Auckland 10, New Zealand

Random House (Pty) Limited
Endulini, 5a Jubilee Road, Parktown 2193, South Africa

The Random House Group Limited Reg. No. 954009

www.randomhouse.co.uk

A CIP catalogue record for this book is available from the British Library

Papers used by Random House are natural, recyclable products made from
wood grown in sustainable forests. The manufacturing processes conform to
the environmental regulations of the country of origin

ISBN 0 09 946812 3

Typeset by SX Composing DTP, Rayleigh, Essex
Printed and bound in Great Britain by
Bookmarque Ltd, Croydon, Surrey

For Lee, beloved

ACKNOWLEDGMENTS

For their continued support and good advice I wish to thank my agent, Loretta Barrett, and my editor, Linda Marrow, who knew when to offer praise, when to offer criticism, and when to offer dessert. Thanks, too, to Nicholas Mullendore at Loretta Barrett Books and Arielle Zibrak at Ballantine Books for all their help.

Thanks, as always, to my loyal circle of first readers: Barbara Barak, Laurie Bower, Cathy Cole, Gary Feinberg, Emily Frank, Wendy Rossi Gold, Laura Lipton, Mindy Siegel Ohringer, Scott Silverman, and Sondra Browning Witt.

For their expert advice, I'd like to thank Dr. Robert Dicker, Evie T. Joselow, Ph.D., Julie L. Sloan, and Ray Clagnan at the Gil Studio, Inc. Any mistakes or liberties I may have taken with the facts are solely my responsibility.

I couldn't have written this book without the love and patience of my family. All my love and gratitude to Lee, Maggie, Nora, Mom, Bob, Larry, Nancy, Katy, and Andrew.

The
DROWNING
TREE

PROLOGUE

THE RIVER FEELS WIDER FROM THE SHALLOW BOAT, THE humpbacked hills of the Hudson Highlands looming like the giants Dutch sailors believed dwelled there.

"Just put the water behind you," he says.

I can't see the man in the boat behind me, and I don't want to risk my precarious balance turning to see him.

"You've been through the drill," he goes on.

And I have. Six weeks practicing in the indoor pool under the watchful eye of the kayaking instructor, tipping myself into blue chlorinated water and rolling up again, gasping, into the humid air, all in one long in-drawn breath. I've practiced it until it's become second nature, but it's one thing to turn over in the clear, warm pool water and another to imagine myself hanging upside down in the cold gray water of the Hudson, trapped in the currents. . . .

"This is where the current is most dangerous," the voice says. "The Dutch called it World's End."

"I know," I say, and then, because there's something

about the voice that has made the back of my neck prickle, I start to turn, searching the sweep of water behind me for the kayaking instructor—dark, long-haired Kyle, who coaches my daughter's crew team as well—and instead catching the flash of blond hair gleaming between the stone-gray sky and the glittering skin of water. In that moment before the sky and water switch places I see him, and I'm not afraid; I'm glad. *He's come back.* After all these nights of seeing him in my dreams, he's really come back . . . but then I'm under the water, hanging suspended from the boat.

I reach for the cord that attaches my spray skirt to the rim of the kayak to free myself, but my hand grazes, instead, something smooth and slimy—long tentacles that reach up from the bottom of the river and have swamped my little boat. The hands of all those drowned sailors reaching up from their wrecks to pull down one more shipwrecked soul. When I open my eyes I see it's only the broad-bladed zebra grass that grows at the bottom of the Hudson, but then, looking through the tangle of greenery, I see something else emerging from the depths, a face, haloed by bright hair. . . .

I awake, gasping in the dry air of my bedroom as if still drowning. Sun is streaming through the glass skylights above my bed, filtering through the pattern of green vines that I set into the glass, casting a snarl of green reflections onto the sheets. I can hear, from the next room, the sound of my daughter getting ready—she has an early crew meet today—and the sound of the dogs' nails on the tiled floors of the loft. Today is Christine's lecture, I remind myself, which is probably why I had the dream. Or maybe this dream of hanging upside down in the Hudson—this new variation of the dream I have every night—comes from my fear over Bea's impending summer rafting trip out west.

I swing my legs over the side of the bed, throwing the twisted sheets back, trying to shed, as well, the residue of the dream. *How long will they go on?* It's been thirteen years since I last saw Neil—and fourteen years since we both nearly drowned in the river—and I still dream about him every night, and because he told me once that he believed that we could visit each other in our dreams, I always have the feeling that that is what he's doing—coming to me in my dreams each night. And what really frightens me, I think as I look down at the stripes of green light that coil around my arms and legs, is that a part of both of us was left behind at the bottom of the river, where the zebra grass grows over the bones of shipwrecked sailors, at World's End.

CHAPTER ONE

I WAS LATE FOR CHRISTINE'S LECTURE.

I almost didn't go. I wouldn't have gone if she hadn't especially asked me to come. The force of her preference was as irresistible now as it had been nearly twenty years ago when of all the girls at Penrose College she chose me to be her best friend. So even though I'd made a vow to avoid the campus during reunion—and had managed to do so, so far—I find myself on Sunday afternoon rushing through the lengthening shadows toward the library, just as I had on so many Sunday evenings during college, making a last dash to catch up on everything I'd avoided doing all weekend.

Usually it was Christine herself who had lured me away from my work in the first place, who had unearthed me from whatever hole I'd buried myself in. "The Middle Ages can wait," she'd say, "but the Sargent exhibit at the Whitney is ending this weekend." She was always reading about some art exhibit that was just about to close. Carried along by her enthusiasm, I'd follow her to the train station, trying to keep up with her fast stride, in the wake of her long blond hair that streamed out behind her like the wings of a dove quivering on a current of air.

As I open the heavy library door I almost catch a glimpse of that hair, shining in a swath of sun behind me, but of course it's an illusion. Christine is inside, standing at the podium, miraculously transformed into this older, more constrained woman—a lecturer—her long golden hair tamed into a sleek coil.

"This is where you'd find me," Christine is saying to the audience as I slide into a folding chair in the back of the crowded hall—even the second-story galleries are packed with students sitting on the floor between the stacks—"after dinner Sunday nights, when the work I'd happily neglected all weekend finally caught up with me."

Rueful sighs stir the group seated beneath the stained-glass window. Clearly, I'm not the only one who'd been reminded, walking toward the library through the late afternoon sunshine, of those last-minute penitential pilgrimages. And this is where I *would* find her, already at work on some paper due the next day, somehow arrived before me even though when we'd finally gotten back to the dorm from the city she'd claimed she was going to her room to sleep. While the escapades she'd led me on left me tired and bleary-eyed, they somehow left Christine refreshed and inspired. She had managed to write through the night and the paper she'd turn in on Monday morning would be the one the professors would hold up as the most original, the most brilliant.

"When I approached the table here below the window I

always imagined that the Lady looked down at me askance," Christine continues. "'Oh, so you've finally seen fit to join us,' I imagined her saying. I believe I endowed her with the voice of Miss Colclough, my sophomore Chaucer professor." Christine pauses for another ripple of knowing laughter. Miss Coldclaw—as we called her—was legendary for her withering comments and draconian teaching methods. "In fact, over the years, as I studied below her I endowed the Lady in the Window with many roles—muse, companion, judge. But of course these were my own projections. What we've come to consider today is who she really is, what she has to tell us—the class of 1987—about ourselves, and why it's so important that we save her from decay."

Christine turns slightly and tilts her head up, meeting the gaze of the figure in the glass as if she had been passing on the street and recognized a friend at a second-story window. Throughout the lecture she turns like this to address the Lady as if they were contemporaries—and truly, even though Christine is dressed in a spare, sleeveless black shift (Prada, I think) and the Lady is robed in a medieval gown of embroidered damask (ruby glass acid-etched with a millefleur pattern and layered with white drapery glass), there is a kinship between the two women. There's something in the curve of their spines—Christine's when she leans back to look up at the window, the Lady as she arches her back away from her loom to look up from her labors—that echoes each other. They've got the same yellow hair. The Lady's by virtue of a medieval metal-lurgical process called silver stain, Christine's thanks to a colorist on the Upper East Side. The Lady's abundant Pre-Raphaelite locks, though, are loose, while Christine's long blond hair is twisted in a knot so heavy that when she bows her head back down to her notes her slender neck seems to pull against the strain. I realize, from that strain and from how thin she's gotten, what a toll this lecture has taken on her and instantly forgive her for not making time to see me these last six or seven months—the longest we've gone without seeing each other since college.

"No doubt we all heard the same story on the campus tour. The window was designed by Augustus Penrose, founder of the Rose Glass Works and Penrose College, in 1922 for the twentieth anniversary of the college's founding and it depicts Augustus's beloved wife, Eugenie. As we all know, Penrose College grew out of The Woman's Craft League, which Eugenie had created for the wives and daughters of the men who worked in her husband's factory."

A college born from a glorified sewing circle, is how Christine put it once, a bit too loudly, at a freshman tea. But of course she doesn't say that to this assembly of women in their tailored linen skirts and pastel silk blouses, their Coach bags and sensible Ferragamo shoes. Penrose College may have originated from a socialist dream of aiding women from the underclasses, but it soon became a bastion of East Coast wealth and privilege.

"But before we accept that the Lady in the Window is merely a celebration of the medieval craftswoman," Christine continues, "let's review the social and artistic background of Augustus Penrose. His family owned a glass works in England, Penrose & Sons, in Kelmscott, a small village on the Thames River near Oxford, which supplied medieval-quality glass for stained-glass designers, including William Morris, the Pre-Raphaelite artist who also happened to live in Kelmscott. Young Augustus was particularly influenced by the opinions of William Morris, who believed that integrity ought to be restored to the decorative arts. When Simon Barovier, a wealthy factory owner from the north, purchased Penrose & Sons, he encouraged young Augustus in his artistic pursuits—and so did Barovier's daughter, Eugenie, who fell in love with Augustus. As you know, the two married, and were sent by old Simon over to this country in the 1890s to found an American branch of the glass works. Augustus and Eugenie wanted to do more, though, than run a glass factory. Influenced by Morris's ideas, they were soon in the vanguard of the Arts & Crafts Movement . . ."

Now that Christine has moved onto the firmer ground of her expertise in art history I let out a breath I hadn't known I was holding. I realize how nervous I am for her—how much I want this lecture to be a success for her—a comeback.

Back in college, Christine had a sort of glow about her—a radiant energy that drew people to her. We all believed she would go on to great things—even when she eschewed a PhD in favor of a job at a New York gallery and freelance writing on the arts. We thought then that she'd write a brilliant book or at least marry one of the famous artists she was often seen with at gallery openings. By the tenth reunion, when none of these things had happened and she got so drunk that she passed out during the Farewell Brunch, that glow of promise began to fade. Her name disappeared from the class notes; when I ran into people from the college who had known her, they would ask after her with a solicitous edge of concern in their voices as if expecting to hear the worst. Sometimes, I suspected, *hoping* to hear the worst.

Many were surprised, then, when the programs for the fifteenth reunion arrived with the announcement that Christine would be delivering the lecture on the Lady window, which the class of 1987 had elected to restore as their class gift. I wasn't, though, because I'd seen Christine through rehab four years ago and urged her to apply for a Penrose Grant, which supported alumnae who wanted to switch careers ten to twenty years out of college (the "second-chance" grant we often called it, a perfect prize for Christine, who always managed to pull her act together at the last minute and shine brilliantly) so that she could go back to graduate school. I even suggested she make the window the subject of her thesis and when McKay Glass won the bid to do the restoration of the window—the first really big conservation project we've gotten since I convinced my father to expand into stained-glass restoration—I suggested to the college that Christine deliver this lecture. So you couldn't really blame me for being nervous for her.

While Christine's lecturing on the Pre-Raphaelites and Arts & Crafts Movement (material I've heard before), I let my mind wander and my gaze shift to the window itself— brilliant now in the late afternoon sun. The upper half is dominated by a large rounded window—a window within a window—which frames a green pool carpeted with water lilies and shaded by a weeping beech. The view of mountains in the distance is the same as the view we would see if the window were clear—the deeply wooded hills of the Hudson Highlands on the western bank—still forested because Augustus Penrose bought up all the land on that side of the river for his mansion, Astolat. When Astolat burned down in the 1930s he and Eugenie moved back to Forest Hall, their house on this side of the river. All that's left of Astolat are the water gardens that Penrose designed—the centerpiece of which was a lily pool similar to the one depicted in the window.

Although the window is executed in opalescent glass and uses techniques made popular by Tiffany and LaFarge in the 1880s, the Lady herself could well be from a medieval window. Of course, as Christine is explaining now, the Pre-Raphaelites were in love with the Middle Ages—and in love with beautiful women with long flowing hair and expressions of abandon. This one has just looked up from her work. As she arches her back you can feel the strain of the long hours she has spent bending over her loom. A flush of color—skillfully produced by sanguine, a hematite-based paint used since the sixteenth century to enhance flesh tones—rises from her low-cut bodice up her long neck to the plane of her high cheekbones. It makes you wonder what she's been dreaming of over her loom.

"What I always wondered," Christine is saying now, "is why she is looking away from the window and why she has such a rapturous expression on her face. Her expression suggests some kind of revelation. Who is this weaver supposed to be? Remember that Augustus rarely painted his beloved Eugenie just as *Eugenie*. As the Pre-Raphaelite painters he admired had before him, Augustus often chose to depict his model in the guise of a figure from literature."

Christine presses a button on the speaker's dais and a slide screen unrolls on the wall to the right of the window and fills with an image of a young girl bending over a lily pool, her cascading hair turning into heavy branches that trail into the water, a sheath of bark just beginning to creep up her slim legs. "In fact, the only other work without a known mythological source is this one, *The Drowning Tree*, which seems to echo the tales of transformation Penrose was so fond of. He painted Eugenie as Daphne turning into a laurel as she flees from Apollo—" *The Drowning Tree* fades and is replaced with the more familiar image of the running girl sprouting leaves from her fingertips, "—and as the nymph Salmacis merging in her sacred pool with Hermaphroditus, and Halcyone turning into a kingfisher with her drowned husband . . . "

Christine clicks through one picture after another, naming each mythological or literary figure as the image appears and fades. She goes so quickly that the faces begin to blur together until we are left with the impression of one face—one woman appearing in many guises. Which is, of course, the impression Christine has been trying to create. They are all Eugenie—whether frightened as

Daphne, lusting like Salmacis, or in the throes of shape-shifting like Halcyone. When the screen goes dark an image of that face—radiant, haloed by bright red-gold hair—seems to burn on the blank screen for just an instant, glowing like the face in the stained-glass window.

"WHO, THEN, IS SHE—OUR LADY IN THE WINDOW? WHY, AFTER all these tales of transformation, would Augustus choose to depict Eugenie as some anonymous weaver in his last known portrait of her? To answer that question I ask you to notice the 'window' at her back. Many people have assumed that the landscape in the window depicts a view of the Hudson Highlands where Penrose built his grand estate, Astolat. But if you look carefully at the arrangement of ridges in the landscape,"—the flickering red arrow of Christine's laser pointer skims over the ridgelines in the window—"and compare them to the arrangement of hills in the actual landscape"—a photograph of the view across the river appears on the slide screen—"you will notice that the ridges are actually reversed. This is not a window—it's a mirror reflecting a window.

"And in what medieval story is a beautiful young maiden condemned to look at life only in its reflection? Why 'The Lady of Shalott' of course, Tennyson's version of an Arthurian legend. You probably remember it from Miss Ramsey's Nineteenth-century Lit class."

What I remember from Miss Ramsey's class was having to memorize Tennyson's endless ode to friendship, "In Memoriam." But as Christine outlines the story, "The

Lady of Shalott" comes back to me: the enchanted maiden in her island tower, prohibited from looking directly at the world, weaving what she sees reflected in a mirror set opposite the window. . . .

I look at the river landscape in the window and then at the scene unfolding in the Lady's loom. If this were the Lady of Shalott, they would be identical, but they are not. In fact the loom is blank. She seems to be weaving plain, unfigured cloth.

Still, Christine makes a good argument for identifying the Lady in the Window with the heroine of Tennyson's poem. The name Augustus Penrose gave his mansion—Astolat—is an alternate name for Shalott. The pose of our Lady is similar to that of several Pre-Raphaelite Ladies of Shalott, as Christine demonstrates through a series of slides. She even has an explanation for why the scenes in the window and on the loom don't match. According to Eugenie Penrose's design notebook, the original painted panes for those sections were cracked during firing and had to be replaced by plain colored glass in order for the window to be ready in time for the library's dedication.

I make a mental note to ask Christine for a copy of Eugenie's notebook—it might come in handy during the restoration—and turn my focus back from the slides to Christine.

"If we accept that the Lady in the Window is the Lady of Shalott the next question you are probably asking yourself is why? Why choose a doomed medieval damsel as a subject for a window in a women's college? When Vassar has a window depicting Elena Cornaro, the first woman PhD, why is it we have a maiden *literally* trapped in an ivory tower? What was Augustus Penrose thinking?

"Eugenie Penrose left us only one clue in her notebook. Although more craftswoman than artist, Eugenie used her considerable skills as a draftswoman to turn Augustus's paintings into cartoons for stained glass. Under her own sketch of the window she has written: 'Here with her face doth memory sit.' It's a line from Dante Gabriel Rossetti— one of the Pre-Raphaelite painters much admired by Augustus Penrose. Why, though, would she say this about her own portrait? It suggests to me that the figure of the lady reminded Eugenie of someone else, and I believe that someone was her sister, Clare."

Here Christine pauses to catch her breath.

"Perhaps you didn't know that Eugenie had a sister; not many people do. Clare was her half sister, the child born out of wedlock when Eugenie's mother ran away from Simon Barovier, but taken back into the family when the mother died. Clare was eight years younger than Eugenie and had always been physically—and mentally—frail."

The screen to the right of the window fills with a sepia image of two girls standing in front of a river beneath a large shaggy tree—a weeping beech I think. I recognize the taller woman as Eugenie, but only because she's got the same severe hair style that she wears in every picture I've ever seen of our illustrious founder. The other woman in the picture is almost identical to her sister except for her hair, which cascades loosely around her shoulders. Something about the photograph seems familiar. At first I think it's because it's the same setting as the one in the painting *The Drowning Tree*, the tree in the background the same weeping beech, but then I realize it's also because the contrast between the two women in the photograph—one prim and reserved, the other ethereal with her flowing hair—echoes the differences I've been noticing between the Christine I remember from college and the woman who's delivering the lecture. And yet, as Christine tells the story of how Clare came with Eugenie and Augustus when they left for America, and how by the time the threesome arrived in New York, Clare was suffering from some sort of delusional hysteria, I can see that she's enjoying the story's shock value—just as the old Christine would.

"She was sent," Christine concludes, "almost immediately upon her arrival in New York, to the Briarwood Insane Asylum—just a little upriver from here, where she lived out the rest of her life."

It might be my imagination, but it seems to me that Christine meets my eye for a moment when she names Briarwood. We both have a personal connection to the mental institution: she grew up just down the road from it and members of her family have worked there for generations. My connection is more recent—my ex-husband was institutionalized there fourteen years ago. I wonder if this is what she meant when she told me on the phone several weeks ago that she had discovered something while conducting her research that might have an impact on me. I'm more worried right now, though, about the impact that Christine's revelation will have on the audience. Eugenie Penrose has always been held up as an exemplary figure and role model—the college's secular saint.

"Imagine what it was like for Eugenie to know that her sister was a mental patient just up the river from here. Did she fear she might follow in Clare's footsteps? Or that her children would suffer from an inherited malady? Remember, the Victorians believed that madness was hereditary . . ."

Christine bends her head down to look at her notes. Unlike her previous pauses, this one does not seem timed for effect. I see, for the briefest of moments, a look of confusion pass over her face. She's flipping through her note cards as if she'd realized that her lecture was running over and decided to skip something. It occurs to me, though, that she has another reason for skipping this part of her lecture.

"Let's go back to the poem," she resumes. "It's when the Lady of Shalott sees Lancelot in the mirror that she disobeys the rules of her enchantment and looks directly at the world, thus condemning herself to die. She is not content to die in the solitary confinement in which she's dwelled, however. She finds a boat and sets off on her death journey down the river so that by the time she has died she will have arrived in Camelot and the object of her affection, Lancelot, will witness what his love has wrought. It's not a passive death. The Lady of Shalott is the woman scorned who secures her revenge through her own death. She is the woman left behind, watching her unfaithful lover disappear over the horizon, Dido staining the night sky with her own funeral pyre—a beacon of recrimination to Aeneas's departing fleet—or Madame Butterfly singing her last aria.

"It makes no sense to cast Eugenie in this role. It makes perfect sense, though, if we accept that the lady in the window is not Eugenie, but her sister, Clare, who looked enough like Eugenie that most people would think the portrait was of her. Only Eugenie and Augustus would know the truth."

Christine pauses to allow this idea to sink in. The silence in the library feels charged, but whether because the audience is appalled at the notion that the window depicts not our beloved founder but her crazy sister, or because they are impressed by Christine's scholarly sleuthing, I'm not sure. I've encountered this ambiguity in reaction to Christine before when, in classes or at parties, she would come out with statements so shocking and forthright that for a moment her audience would sway between embarrassment and admiration.

"If we see the figure in the window as Clare, Augustus's message becomes clear. The window depicts the moment that the Lady turns from her loom to look directly at Sir Lancelot—the moment when she disobeys the rules of her confinement, the moment that seals her fate. She is not content to dwell in the cloistered realm of women's work and she pays a heavy price for her rebellion. She is the artist—as Tennyson said—caught between reflection and reality at the moment when love releases her from shadows into substance. I believe that Augustus imagined this figure as his sister-in-law finally released from the spell of madness, and that he designed the window as a tribute to her.

"I believe that Augustus Penrose was also thinking about the generations of young women who would sit beneath this window. And so we must ask what her message is to us. I believe that the Lady is the student waking up from the cloistered world of the academy into the demands of the real world. In other words, she is you and me."

I notice that the room has gone very still. There's no nervous ripple of laughter. The women lean forward in their seats, their pale clothes soaked in the bright colors from the window. Later they might carp at Christine's unorthodox interpretation of the window, but for now she has their full attention.

"When I look back at my time here at Penrose it is as though I lived in a sealed tower, aloof from the world. Some might say we were too sheltered—that we dwelled in a world of shadows and that for many the strong sunlight of the real world was too much."

Christine raises a hand into a gold beam cast by the sun shining through the Lady's yellow hair and twirls her fingers around as if she were grasping the light. *How in the world*, I wonder, *could she have planned that?*

"That like the Lady of Shalott the journey away from here too quickly became a slow drift toward death." Christine unfurls her hand and it's as if she has released the golden light into the room—a dove set free by a master magician. She pauses, allowing the silence to swell. Although there is little doubt that she is talking about herself now—about her own disappointments and failures—I sense that everyone in this room understands what she is saying. For whom of us has life turned out the way we imagined it would when we left here?

"But I don't believe that Augustus Penrose wished us to be afraid of the journey—no matter where it might lead. He wanted us to be ready to look up from our books and away from the shadows—no matter where our awakening would lead us. I believe he conveyed his message in the way he painted the Lady's face. Look at her—look at the flush of color that bathes her. It is the reflection of the sun striking her for the first time in her life. She might be bound for death, but in this moment— the moment in which she chooses life over shadow—she is more alive than she has ever been.

"Remember, too, that the window behind her is not a window but the mirror from which the Lady has turned away. In looking through the window she is looking at us, the women of Penrose College assembled here before her. We are her reflection, we are her future. She has broken the spell that enslaves us—it's up to us what we do with that freedom."

Christine has chosen the perfect moment for her conclusion. The glass in the river scene, which was lit up by the sun during the first part of her lecture, is now cool and shadowy. The light has moved through the Lady's yellow hair, down her face and bare throat, and settled into the bodice of her brocaded dress. Every woman here must remember the superstition—one of those silly campus legends women's colleges are famous for—that when the light shone through the Lady's dress it was shining through her heart. If you were touched by that red stain you would die young. Christine, standing in front of the window as the setting sun hits the glass, is bathed in the ruby-red light.

CHAPTER TWO

THE WINE AND CHEESE RECEPTION, WHICH IS HELD AT FOREST Hall, the president's house, is not as horrible as I expected. The food and drinks are laid out in the dining hall, the walls of which are hung with Augustus's collection of old world masters. Even though many of the paintings have turned out to be nineteenth-century copies, it's still a pleasure to look at them. Christine is too well surrounded by college dignitaries to talk to me, but she manages to lip-synch a request for me to wait for her and take her to the train station.

If anyone has been offended by Christine's lecture it's impossible to tell from the crowd gathered around her now. Everyone is smiling as Gavin Penrose, current president of the college and grandson of Augustus and Eugenie, holds up a glass of champagne to toast Christine. I'm struck by how good the two of them look together. At forty-five, Gavin's lost none of the boyish good looks that made him the idol of every girl at Penrose. I remember that during our sophomore year he dated a girl in our dorm and when he'd drive up from Wharton to visit her every girl in the dorm would contrive to drape herself over a chair in the study lounge. His dark curly hair and slightly olive complexion are a nice contrast to Christine's yellow hair and pale coloring.

The contrast in their coloring is echoed by the Titianesque blond Venus and dark, burly Mars they're standing beneath. After Gavin's toast, Christine gestures toward the painting and makes a comment that's greeted by another ripple of laughter within the group but not from Gavin, who looks, instead, slightly mortified. If I know Christine, she is probably explaining why Augustus Penrose should have known the painting was not an authentic Titian when he bought it. Since Augustus donated the house and all of his art collection to the college, it's of no personal moment to Gavin whether or not the work is original, but who wants to be told that their grandfather couldn't tell a fake from the real thing? I'm afraid it's just the kind of tactless comment Christine is wont to make—not out of malice, but because she has the habit of saying whatever occurs to her. Fortunately, Gavin seems more interested in the real-life Venus he's talking to than the painted one above him. In fact, his attention is so riveted to Christine that it takes several tries before Fay, his assistant, is able to steer him over toward a petite, faded blonde in a Chanel suit whom I recognize from the alumnae magazine as Joan Shelley, class of '77 and one of the college's richest trustees.

When Gavin finally turns to Joan, Christine catches my eye and raises a conspiratorial smile at Joan's obvious pique at being kept waiting. I head across the room to join her, but I'm waylaid by Robin Lindley, a girl I sat next to in Latin 101.

"It's June, isn't it?"

"Close," I say, "Actually it's . . ."

"No, wait! I remember. Juno. Juno McKay. Like the goddess. The Latin teachers loved that. Wasn't your mother Greek or something?"

"No," I say, "Italian. If she were Greek I'd be named Hera."

Her puzzled expression—I remember suddenly that she was one of those girls who kept asking why we had to study a *dead* language and who petitioned the college to drop mandatory Latin—is not half as bad as DeeDee Smith's, our class president, when I tell her I was unable to attend the reunion because of my daughter Bea's crew match upriver in Poughkeepsie.

"A daughter old enough to crew, why she'd have to be . . ."

Do the math, I'm tempted to say. I had her the week before our graduation—or your graduation, I might say—and so instead of celebrating my fifteenth college reunion this weekend I watched my fifteen-year-old daughter out-row Poughkeepsie Country Day. A pretty good trade, I'd said to myself earlier today catching a flash of Bea's red-gold braid, coiled between her taut shoulder blades. I'd read in the tension of her back muscles all her fire and enthusiasm, the way she leans into life, never away. A pretty good trade, I say to myself now, as DeeDee lifts a tennis-braceleted hand to smooth her already perfectly smooth hair.

"Beatrice," she murmurs. "Such a lovely name. Beatrice McKay."

"Beatrice Buchwald," I correct her, "Her father's name. We did get married—"

"Yes, I remember now. In the Rose Garden on May Day . . . didn't he go to Columbia?"

"—and divorced two years later."

"Honey," DeeDee says, laying her flawlessly manicured hand on mine, "half the girls at the club are divorcing this year. My best friend Elyse's husband left her for his twenty-three-year-old lab assistant. Men, they think with their *dicks.*" She lowers her voice on the last word, but just in case I don't get her point she crooks her little finger to illustrate the male organ of derision.

"I'm afraid that wasn't Neil's weakness . . ." I look over DeeDee's shoulder to see if there's someone—*anyone*—to distract her attention from me, but the only gaze I meet is the lascivious leer of a Raphaelesque Triton pursuing a naked sea nymph. Explaining what happened to Bea's father is not my favorite topic and in the interest of protecting Bea's privacy I've been known to lie about his whereabouts, but when I look back at DeeDee I can see from the wash of red—crimson as the hematite paint in the Lady window—creeping over DeeDee's tanned skin that she has remembered what happened to Neil.

"Oh my God!" she says squeezing my arm. "I completely forgot. I heard at our fifth reunion that he'd ended up in a mental hospital. In fact, wasn't it the one Christine just mentioned in her lecture—the Briarwood Insane Asylum? The same one that Eugenie Penrose's poor sister went to?"

Went to, I think, as if we're talking about where they went to college. Of course, Briarwood is one of those institutions—like MacLean or Austin-Riggs—so exclusive that it has almost the same cachet as a prestigious college or social club.

"Yes," I admit, desperately trying to signal to Christine to come to my rescue. "Only now it's called the Briarwood Institute for Mental Health. They dropped the 'Insane Asylum' part years ago. As far as I know he's still there."

DeeDee takes a quick look behind her—as if afraid that someone is about to seize her and force her into a mental institution—and sidles a step closer to me. "That's okay," she says, patting my hand, "at least you don't have to deal with *visitation*."

"No, SHE DIDN'T ACTUALLY SAY THAT!"

"I swear on my honor as a Penrose Girl, that's what she said. I was tempted to mention that given Neil's delusions I might have to deal with *astral visitation*."

Christine stops—we've been walking briskly away from the library toward my car—drops the overstuffed messenger bag she's carrying and grabs my hand. The last rays of the sun have laid a pattern like the spokes of a wheel across the smooth green lawn. Outside of their light the night is growing cold, but inside this last patch of sun I feel a warmth that comes more from the pressure of Christine's hand than from the sun's heat. The distance I'd felt from her during these last six months seems to evaporate, like fog burning away in the morning light.

"I'm so sorry, Juno, it's my fault. This never would have come up if I hadn't mentioned the asylum in my lecture."

"Don't be ridiculous, Christine, why do you think I avoided the reunion? That's all anyone could talk about at our fifth and I knew someone would eventually bring it up. It's not that I mind for myself so much, but the story has faded enough in the town that Bea rarely has to hear about it. I didn't want my presence at the reunion to revive talk about it."

Christine reshoulders her bag, flips up the collar of her thin leather jacket, and shivers. "Still, I should have told you what I found out about Clare Barovier. I tried not to dwell on it . . ."

"Yes, I noticed you cut short your talk on hereditary insanity. But honestly you didn't have to worry. No one could be saner than Beatrice."

"I know *that*, Juno."

"Look, it's okay. We ought to get you something to eat before you have to go back to the city. We could stop at Gal's and get you an amaretto cappuccino."

Christine smiles, pleased, I think, that I remember her favorite (nonalcoholic) beverage from college, but then the smile abruptly vanishes. "No . . . we'll end up running into people from the reunion and I wanted a chance to talk to you alone. Besides, I'm dying to see what you've done with the glass factory. I think it's amazing you're actually living there."

Anyone else would think living with your teenaged daughter in an old abandoned factory was sheer lunacy—and certainly I've heard that opinion voiced often enough—but it's clear from her tone that Christine is impressed. As I turn away from her to walk to the car, stepping out of the sun, I still feel warm, only now it's from the pleasure of her approbation.

BY THE TIME WE GET DOWN TO THE WATERFRONT THE SUN HAS dropped below the line of mountains on the other side of the river. Still, when I unlock the factory door there is enough residual light coming through the windows and skylight on the western wall that I don't need to turn on the overhead lights. In fact, it's brighter in here than outside.

"What amazing light," Christine says, crossing the empty space with her arms held out as if to embrace the space. Her boot heels click against the wide maple planks and echo in the high-ceilinged room. "Are these the original windows?"

"Except for the panes I've had to replace. Most of the broken windows were on the north side, which faces the train station parking lot. It used to be a sort of Rosedale High rite of passage to see who could smash the highest panes. Fortunately these windows front the Metro-North tracks; only the really stupid kids braved the tracks to get a shot at the windows and even then you can't really get far enough back to reach them."

Christine pivots on a tapered heel, and raises an eyebrow. "And you would know that because . . ."

"Let's just say that I told Mr. Penrose the window repair would be on me."

"So you're leasing this from Gavin?"

"Uh-huh. It's one of the few properties Augustus Penrose didn't give away to the college or some other socially worthy cause. I don't think industrial real estate is really Gavin's thing. He'd have unloaded this property years ago if he'd had a buyer. Now, though, it's becoming popular to turn these old factories into art spaces . . ."

"Like MASSMoCA in North Adams?"

"Right, and Dia is converting a factory up in Beacon into a museum . . . anyway, suddenly Gavin's interested in the space again. What I'm hoping is that instead of turning it into a cheesecake factory with cheap souvenir stores we can get some gallery space and studios for working artists. Actually, I thought you might be able to help me with the proposal to ArtHudson . . . Gavin's on the board and you seem to have his ear."

Christine turns on her heel so that she's facing the windows again. "Actually I could do with some cheese-cake at the moment," she says. "Where's that food you promised?"

"Right this way."

As soon as I open the door to the courtyard both dogs bound in, their nails scrabbling on the polished wood floor. They lap the room, their long dainty necks stretched out sniffing the air, and then come to rest against my hip, eyeing Christine with suspicion.

"Hey, you didn't tell me you got dogs."

Actually I did, but I don't remind Christine of that. Clearly all she's been able to think about the last few months has been the Lady window.

"Bea's been hounding me—pun intended—for a dog since she could talk, but we couldn't have one in the apartment over my dad's garage. We got these two from Greyhound Rescue three months ago."

"They're beautiful. What are their names?"

"Paolo and Francesca."

"Oh, are they Italian greyhounds?" Christine asks, smiling.

"No, just regular, overworked racing Greyhounds. Watch them for a minute and you'll see where they get their names." I nudge them off my hip and they do another circle around the room, Francesca on the outside, Paolo leaning into her in the tight curves.

It takes Christine a few minutes to remember the line from our junior year Dante seminar. ". . . *these two that move together and seem to be so light upon the wind.* That's how Dante describes Paolo and Francesca when he first sees them in the second circle of hell."

"Brava! Professor Da Silva would be proud—remember how much he loved that line?"

Christine tilts her head at me. It strikes me that with her pale coloring and long neck she looks a little like the greyhounds. "I remember it was Neil's favorite line, too . . ."

Although Penrose is a woman's college, Neil, a junior at Columbia, had petitioned the college for special permission to sit in on Umberto Da Silva's famous Dante seminar as an exchange student.

I look away from Christine's inquiring gaze into Francesca's adoring one. Paolo has his eyes closed, his head resting on Francesca's neck.

"The Greyhound Rescue lady told us they stay so close together because they were crated in a cage so small they couldn't both lie down. She thought they took turns leaning against each other for rest, and she wouldn't let me take one without the other. After that story I was lucky to get Bea out of there with only two rescued greyhounds."

"Talk about the ninth circle of hell," Christine says, still giving me that quizzical look, which I ignore by leading her through the courtyard, stopping to unlock the metal gate to the north wing of the factory. She wanders through the weeds and stops at the door to the east wing.

"What's that noise? It sounds like a wind tunnel," she asks while I wrestle with the rusted lock.

"The glass furnaces," I tell her. "We've got two glass blowers renting space. Ernesto Marquez, who also does window removal and installation for me, and a woman named Marina who trained at the Corning Museum and is exhibiting in Venice right now. She does amazing work."

"Isn't it a fire hazard to keep a furnace like that burning?"

"That's why all the hot glass work is kept in that wing. Notice that it's not joined to the other wings. It's a completely fireproof building made of concrete and steel— it's where the Penrose studios made the glass for his windows."

"Yes, now that I think of it, Eugenie talks about the furnaces in her journals—she compares them to the fires of hell. I don't think she liked that part of Augustus's work. She preferred the tapestry and pottery studios."

"Well, it was all here—like a medieval crafts work-shop—that was Augustus Penrose's ideal. It's rare for a stained-glass studio to make its own glass, but Tiffany did and so did Penrose so I figured, why not McKay Glass?"

I've finally gotten the door open and wave Christine into my studio. "Our apartment is just up here," I say, steering her toward the wrought-iron spiral stairs. "Let me get you something to eat before you have to get on the train . . ." But Christine has paused in front of the drawing on white vellum that covers the two-story-high wall opposite the stairs. It's a wax rubbing of the Lady window that we'll use as a guide for releading the window after it's been taken down.

"Are all those cracks places where the lead is broken?"

"Uh-huh," I say heading up the stairs, "this restoration is coming none too soon. Lead can start deteriorating after seventy years and the window is eighty years old. . . ." I pause at the top of the stairs to grab a bottle of Pellegrino water, half a loaf of sourdough bread, some fresh mozzarella my father brought me back from Poughkeepsie last week, and a jar of olives. Christine is still dawdling, halfway up the stairs, looking down at the studio. "But I keep forgetting," I yell down at her, "you're the expert on the window now. I bet your lecture convinced a lot of people to contribute to the restoration fund."

"But I wouldn't have even done the lecture if you hadn't steered me toward studying the window—or convinced me to apply for that grant . . ." She stops as she comes up the stairs and sees my expression—the same one she gives me when I try to thank her for the many times she's saved my life. "Anyway, I just reminded them they had an important piece of Arts and Crafts stained glass that they were letting rot—you told them what they had to do to save it. And you're the one who will save it—look at this place." She sweeps her hand over the view of the studio laid out below us. "Juno, I'm so impressed. You've re-created Augustus Penrose's dream of the medieval workshop!"

I've got to admit the place looks pretty good from up here. I've gotten the guys to clear up most of the smaller restorations—a few fanlights for houses up on the Heights, some lancets for a Presbyterian church down in Tarrytown—to make way for the Lady window. My dad has built a new light table and installed a wall of vertical shelves to hold the sheets of colored glass that Ernesto and my father have painstakingly blown to match the colors originally used in the window so we'll be able to replace any broken panes.

"I don't know about a medieval workshop. All I did was expand my dad's business. . . ."

"No affront to your dad, Juno, but he was repairing broken storefronts on Main Street and installing storm windows up on the Heights. You're really creating art here . . . did you do these?" She's moved now to the panels set into the French doors. I use the opportunity to open them and wave her out onto the rooftop garden, but only Paolo and Francesca respond to my hand gestures by sauntering side by side out onto the tarpaper roof.

"A little project I did with Bea before giving up on the idea that she had any interest in working with glass," I say, giving the glass panels a rueful look. The truth is I'd had to finish them myself while Bea made one excuse after another to get outside on the river.

"Well, they're beautiful." Christine traces with one finger the pattern of vine and leaf. "They look like real vines climbing up the outside of the building. . . ." She looks up, following the vine pattern up to the skylight. She looks away and then back again, noticing what it usually takes people a few times to notice. It looks, at first glance, as if the vines are growing over the metal frame of the skylight, but actually, the pattern of vine and leaf is one I've set into the glass panes.

"Wow, you did those, too? I like it even better than the piece you had at Urban Glass last year . . ." Looking back down, Christine notices that I'm awkwardly balancing the water bottle and glasses in my right hand, the bread and cheese in my left. "Here, let me take those . . ."

We put the food and water down on an old wicker table and I upend a lawn chair to brush away the soot that finds its way up from the Metro-North tracks. I offer to get a towel for her to sit on but Christine waves away the idea and sinks into the torn vinyl webbing, consigning her Prada dress to industrial grit and her expensive leather bag to the sooty tarpaper roof. I bend down to pick up the bag—I remember when she brought it back from Italy and showed me its fancy silk lining embossed with the logo of a trendy Italian luggage designer—but she waves me off, saying, "I have something in there I want to show you." Instead of taking anything out, though, she crosses her long slim legs, the leather of her boots making a sticky sound like a tape pulling off glass, and sighs at the view.

"Incredible—you'd pay a million dollars for a view like this on the West Side of Manhattan."

It is my favorite hour of the day—the stained-glass hour, I can't help but think of it as, when the sky cools down to an opalescent glaze and the trees darken into traceries of lead. I sit down on a rusted metal chair and pour the sparkling water into long-stemmed glasses, admiring how the bubbles turn into a faceted gem in the ruby red bowl of the goblet. I've never seen anyone do cut glass the way Ernesto does—as intricate as Waterford, but as delicate as Orrefors. They transform plain water into some exotic elixir—which is just the effect I was after. Since Christine gave up drinking I've tried to make a point of serving her nonalcoholic beverages in this ceremonial fashion.

Christine holds her glass up to the dark line of hills across the river as if saluting the last light lingering in the distant Catskills. A ray catches the glass, traveling through the red glass and casting a red stain on Christine's hand, like a bracelet of rubies dripping off her delicate wrist.

"Here's to the Lady in the Window," I say, leaning forward to strike the rim of my glass against hers. The chime they make is still resonating in the air when I sip my water. "The lecture was a success and now the window will be restored in time for the college's centennial celebration in the fall. You'll come back, won't you?"

Christine sets her glass down on the table and tears off a piece of bread. "If they'll have me. I have a feeling my talk wasn't quite what Gavin Penrose expected. He knew I was going to identify the subject of the window as 'The

Lady of Shalott' but I don't think he was happy about me bringing up Eugenie's sister, Clare."

"The research you did was amazing. I never even knew that Eugenie had a sister. How did you find out about her?"

"My aunt Amy told me about this woman Clare Barovier who had spent her whole life in Briarwood and I recognized the name as Eugenie's maiden name. Then I went over to Briarwood and did a little digging around—" Christine smiles mischievously. From my past experiences with Christine I know that "digging around" could mean just about anything, including actual digging. Once, when she was doing a paper on landscape design she sneaked into the formal rose gardens next to Forest Hall and dug up one of the borders to prove that the garden had originally been laid out according to a knot design copied from a fifteenth-century gardening book. The college trustees wanted her expelled, but when her paper was published in *Architectural Digest* they thought better of it. "—I thought Gavin would be interested in what I found out but I guess no one wants to be reminded of their crazy relatives . . . shit, I'm sorry, I didn't mean . . ."

"It's okay, Christine, you don't have to tiptoe around the subject." I wonder if this is why Christine's been so distant these last few months. Was she afraid that her discovery of Eugenie's crazy sister would remind me too painfully of Neil? "Of course I worry about Bea inheriting Neil's instability, but so far she doesn't seem at all like him. She's the most levelheaded kid I've ever met."

"You've done a remarkable job raising her."

"Bea's amazing, but I'm not sure I can take credit for

that. You remember what I was like after what happened with Neil—there were days when I was so depressed I couldn't get out of bed. I used to wake up and find Bea sitting on the foot of my bed pretending to read to herself. If you hadn't come and stayed with us I might never have gotten out of bed. After that I was so busy working for my dad during the day and going to night school that I had hardly any time for her. I look at her now—she's not afraid of anything, she hardly seems to need anything or anyone—and I don't know whether to be grateful for her independence or guilty that's she's had to be so strong to grow up with me."

"But you don't wish that you never had her."

It's such a wild suggestion, even for Christine, who has a habit of saying exactly what she's thinking, that I stare at her. Blood rises to her skin and fills the curve of her cheek, making her face appear fuller than usual. She looks away and then says, softly, "I mean, you had to give up a lot when you had her."

"You mean not graduating from Penrose or going abroad to study art the way I wanted to? Lots of people dream of becoming a painter and don't . . . who knows if I would have even if I hadn't had Bea."

"So you don't mind the loss of freedom?"

"No, not that kind of freedom, at least." I take a sip of my water, wishing it were wine, and look away from Christine, toward the river and the light on the boat landing in the park beyond the train station's parking lot.

"What I do miss is freedom from fear. Like right now," I say, half laughing, trying to ease the tension that has crept into our conversation, "I'm waiting for Bea to get home from the kayaking trip she took upriver today. She spent the morning rowing against Poughkeepsie, but she still couldn't wait to get out on the river when we got back. She should have been back an hour ago and I can't help worrying that she's tipped over and been dragged under by a current. The Hudson is full of treacherous currents—we're not far from what the Dutch called World's End. The current there tends to sink ships a whole lot bigger than Bea's little kayak."

Christine follows my gaze out over the water. Without the sun on it the river looks cold and forbidding, the current moving relentlessly to the sea. "I remember what World's End is, Juno," Christine says reprovingly.

"Well, then, you'll understand why what looks like a pretty view to you looks like a death trap to me. Trust me, it's not a pretty way to look at the world."

Francesca, hearing the tremor in my voice, rises to her feet and lays her long delicate muzzle in my lap. I stroke her silky ears, looking down into her large, liquid eyes to avoid Christine's gaze.

"I'm sorry, Juno. I know it's been hard raising her alone. Have you seen Neil at all . . . I mean other than those *astral visitations* we spoke of earlier?"

I laugh, relieved to hear Christine venture a joke even if it doesn't seem as funny as it did before when we were crossing the college lawn. "No, no visits in the flesh. As far as I know he's still at Briarwood," I tell her, "but you know, all kidding aside, I *do* dream about him—*a lot*. Sometimes I wonder if he isn't projecting himself into my dreams."

I look up at Christine, expecting her to appreciate the humor, but instead it appears she's taken me seriously. "And what is he like in your dreams? I mean, is he the way he was when we first met him—charming, funny Neil— the artist who did those incredible paintings . . ." She pauses for a moment, looking away from me toward the water, and then speaks in so soft a whisper I have to lean toward her to hear what she's saying. "Or is he the way he was at the end—the way he was out on the river that day?"

I stare at her a full minute before answering, shaken by the memory of that day. Maybe bringing up such an intimate memory is Christine's way of bridging the distance that's grown between us these last few months, but it has the opposite effect, making me pull back and retreat into an apparent chilliness I don't really feel. "Christine, I was just kidding, I don't really dream about Neil," I finally tell her, although the truth is I wasn't kidding. Neil has been invading my dreams almost nightly.

Christine nods and then sits up. Her hair, caught on the torn vinyl webbing of the chair, comes loose from its knot and cascades over her shoulders as she stands up. She bends down and takes a brush out of her bag and brushes it—a fan of dull gold that nearly reaches to her waist— and then briskly coils it into a rope and knots it at the nape of her neck. I can feel the weight of the lie I've told between us, closing off the possibility of her telling me something. I'm sorry for it, but I'm not willing to talk about those dreams or relive that day on the river.

"I'd better get going," she says, handing me her empty glass and picking up her bag, "or I'll miss my train."

CHAPTER THREE

I TAKE THE DOGS AND LET US OUT THE FIRE ESCAPE DOOR, DOWN an outside flight of rusting metal stairs—warning Christine which steps to avoid—to a narrow grassy alley in between the north wall of the factory and the fence surrounding the train station. We have to walk toward the river, over the train tracks, and past the waterfront park to get to the station, but it's quicker than going around by River Street—plus I get to take a glimpse at the landing beach where Bea should be coming in any minute. As we pass the park the dogs' ears prick up and they strain against their leashes.

Christine peers into the shadowy park toward the water and checks her watch. "I've still got a few minutes if you want to see if she's come in."

"You're sure you don't mind?" I ask, unable to disguise the relief in my voice—relief, not only at the chance to check on Bea's whereabouts, but also at Christine knowing so well that this is what I'd want to do. *There's still time*, I think, following Christine, who is in turn trailed by the two ecstatic greyhounds, *to mend the distance that's grown between us in the last six months.*

We pass the old boathouse, which was used in the twenties by guests at Astolat who paddled across the river and in my day by Rosedale high school students looking for a place to make out and smoke cigarettes. Now it's the headquarters of Hudson Kayak. I hear voices from the water and then the thump of heavy plastic on sand as two narrow-prowed kayaks nose up the beach. Paolo and Francesca strain toward the farthest kayak and I let go of their leashes.

"Hey," I hear Bea's voice as the dogs splash into the water, "what are you guys doing here?"

In the dim light from the boathouse I can just make out Bea's lanky figure unfolding itself from the low boat. The rubber and nylon spray skirt that kayakers wear to seal themselves into their boats makes her look like a Victorian lady with a bustle. She steps out of the plastic hull into ankle-deep water with all the grace of a titled socialite dismounting from a coach and four, but then ruins the effect by tumbling to the sand to wrestle with the dogs. This is what she's like these days—my fifteen-year-old— one minute a graceful woman, the next a gawky child.

"What's up, Mom?" Bea asks wiping wet sand from her lycra biking shorts.

"I'm just walking Christine to the station," I say, trying to sound casual, trying not to sound as if I'd been imagining her drowned for the last hour. Kyle, who runs the kayaking rental and tour operation, gives me a skeptical look as he drags his kayak up the sand. I recently confessed to him—over a bottle of Valpolicello—how nervous I am when Bea's out on the water.

"Hey, Aunt Christine." Bea straightens up and leans toward Christine to kiss her on the cheek, being careful not to drip on her. But Christine steps forward on the sand, teetering a bit in her high-heeled boots, and hugs Bea to her. When she steps away her hand lingers on the damp ends of Bea's long braid for just a moment.

"I'm sorry I missed your lecture, Aunt Christine, but we thought about you. We paddled across the river and up the Wicomico onto the grounds of Penrose's abandoned estate. There are all these cool statues underwater."

"The sunken gardens of Astolat," Christine says. "Penrose was inspired by the Sunk Gardens at Great Dixter, which he saw on a trip to East Sussex in the twenties. I didn't realize there was much left of them—or that the property was accessible."

"Yeah," Kyle says while motioning for Bea to grab the front end of the kayak, "it's private property but if you enter from the river no one stops you. You have to know what you're doing though. Some of the statues are half submerged. The first time I saw one I thought it was a dead body. Scared me half to death."

Christine turns toward Kyle, who's coiling a nylon towline. He's wearing lycra bike shorts and a Polartec fleece vest half unzipped over his bare chest. Beads of river water on his arms—deeply muscled from paddling and rowing—catch the light from the boathouse. It's hard to imagine him being scared off by a bit of garden statuary. "I'd love to see what's left of Penrose's landscape designs," Christine says.

Kyle tosses the coiled towline and gives Christine a more careful look. Even in this light, Christine's gold hair and sapphire blue eyes are striking. I can't blame Kyle for being drawn to her—men always are—or Christine for the flirtatious lilt to her voice. I've learned over the years that she does it without meaning to. It's like there's so much extra energy in her that she gives off sparks.

"You'd love it, Aunt Christine," Bea says. "Why don't you come up next weekend? I'm sure Kyle would take you . . ."

"We'd better get going or we'll miss your train," I say, making a mental note to lecture Bea later on the penalties for trespassing. "Bea, would you take the dogs home?"

Christine hugs Bea again and waves toward Kyle. As we're passing the boathouse I remember to ask about Eugenie's notebook.

"That officious secretary of Gavin's demanded I give the original back," Christine tells me. "I told her I still needed it for research and she said she would make me a copy, so I asked her to make you one while she was at it. *If that wasn't too taxing for her*. Make sure you get it from her."

I thank Christine, trying not to laugh at her aggravation. Fay Morgan is famously protective of Gavin and everything to do with Penrose College. We cross over the trestle to the southbound side—Christine already has her ticket so we bypass the station—and descend onto the brightly lit platform, where I notice that she's covered with wet sand.

"You're going to be miserable all the way back to the city," I say, batting at her damp dress.

"Tell me about Kyle," Christine replies, swatting my hand away. "Did I notice something going on there?"

"With Bea? Don't be ridiculous, she's fifteen, he's our age. . . ."

"I'm not talking about Bea."

I sigh and look up the tracks to see if the train is coming. "Bea's been dying for me to go kayaking with her so Kyle's given me a few lessons . . ."

"Lessons, hm . . ."

"And we've had a few glasses of wine afterward . . . he's really an interesting guy. He's been everywhere, reads a lot, knows everything about computers and the stock market . . ."

"Juno," Christine reaches forward and brushes back a strand of my hair that's come loose from the ponytail I wrangled it into before her lecture and tucks it behind my ear. *Pre-Raphaelite hair*, Christine always too-generously called my unruly masses of dark red curls. "You don't have to be a snob on my account. The man doesn't have to have a PhD or wear a business suit to be a great guy. It seems to me you've spent altogether too much time alone since Neil. You deserve someone wonderful."

"Nothing's happened yet. I mean with Bea around, I just didn't think it was appropriate."

"Come on, you've been a single mother for . . . what? . . . thirteen years? I know you date. What about that curator from the Frick?"

"I used to see him on weekends when Bea stayed with my dad, but he got a better job offer in Chicago and wanted me to move."

"And?"

"Well, I couldn't very well leave the glass business when I've spent all this time building it up and uproot Bea from her school . . . besides, I just didn't feel *that* much for him. Not enough to disrupt our lives."

"Have you felt that much for anyone since Neil?"

It's the second time she's brought up Neil tonight and I have to quell the desire to tell her to mind her own business. But if anyone has a right to ask me about Neil, it's Christine. When things fell apart—*when Neil fell apart*—it was Christine who stayed with me day and night until I was able to get out of bed and start taking care of Bea again. It was Christine who convinced me to move back in with my father, revive the glass business, and go to community college at night to get a business degree.

I shake my head. "No. To tell you the truth I'm not sure I ever want to feel that much for anyone again. You remember what I was like when I fell in love with Neil—it was like the rest of the world turned gray and he was the only part in color—like one of those windows that's all in grisaille except for the central figure. Sometimes I wonder now if that weird glow Neil gave off wasn't his madness."

"But what if Neil was well again, do you think . . ." I miss Christine's next few words in the blast of the whistle from the approaching train. When the noise subsides her head is bent and she's rummaging inside her bag and again I miss something she says because she's talking into the bag instead of to me. It sounds like she's saying something about the dogs.

"What about the dogs?" I ask as she straightens up. She's got her hand on a file folder, as if she's going to take it out, but then she seems to change her mind and slides it back into the satchel.

"No, I meant Dante's Paolo and Francesca," she says, "I was thinking of another line from *The Inferno*. Something Francesca says to Dante, 'Love, which absolves no one beloved from loving . . .' Do you think that's true? That if you love someone enough they'll have no choice but to return your love?" Christine has turned to face me in the open door of the train and I almost laugh at the absurdity of it—what a question to ask on the threshold of a departing train!—but when I see how serious she looks I don't laugh. I think for just a moment about how much I loved Neil, and how I hoped and believed that as long as I loved him that much everything would turn out all right. That my love would save him from going crazy. What can I say? The only truthful answer I have isn't the one she wants to hear.

"I'll have to get back to you on that," I tell her.

She smiles but I can see she's disappointed. She starts to say something but another commuter brushes past her and she shrugs her shoulders. "I'd better find a seat," she says.

When the door closes I move in the same direction on the platform that I saw Christine head in inside the train. During college we often saw each other off at this train station—on holidays when Christine went home to Poughkeepsie, or when I was going down to the city to visit Neil—and whoever was left on the platform would always wait and wave. "Just like in those old wartime movies," Christine would say, "when the heroine runs along the side of the train and the hero waves from the window." Would she remember now?

When I see her through the window I think she has forgotten. She looks suddenly very tired, like all the currents of energy that have kept her afloat today had drained out of her. This is the way she looks, I realize, when she doesn't think anyone is looking at her—as if it were the gazes of others that held her aloft. It frightens me to see her this way because I know that for Christine moments of excitement and triumph have always been followed by periods of desolation. She looks now as if a heavy weight has descended on her. Then she sees me and her brow smooths, her blue eyes ignite, and for a moment she looks as if that weight has been lifted. It's only for a moment, though. By the time she lifts her hand to wave to me her eyes are empty and unfocused, as if she were looking not at me, but at someone over my shoulder.

I wave to her and try to mouth a better answer to her question because I've thought of one that's not quite a lie, but then the lights flicker inside the train and instead of Christine I see my own reflection in the dark glass. Still, I stand on the platform, waving until the train pulls out, because even if I can't see her, I'm hoping she might still be able to see me.

CHAPTER FOUR

I SPEND MONDAY OVERSEEING THE REMOVAL OF THE LADY window. Usually Ernesto and my father handle this part on their own, but on a project this big I think it's a good idea for me to be there. I've also asked Robbie—a recent Parsons graduate who's apprenticing with us—to photograph the window before and after we take it down. Lead came that looks perfectly good in situ can deteriorate rapidly in the removal process. I want to make sure that when I present the bill to Gavin Penrose we have a detailed record of every stage of the restoration.

It turns out that we need all our hands just to dig the putty out of the stone slots holding the window.

"Man," Robbie says after a half hour applying hammer and chisel to the hardened putty, "they were making sure this window wasn't going *no place*."

"Augustus Penrose didn't do anything halfway," my father answers, his voice, even though he's on the scaffolding working with his back to me, ringing clear in the vaulted space. On the other side of the window is a watery shadow: Ernesto, who is working on the outside of the window removing the exterior putty.

"Dad, you're not wearing your mask," I say.

He swerves around so quickly that the scaffolding rocks on the uneven stone floor, and he grins at me. "How'd you know that with my back to you?"

I look up from the bottom edge of the window and smooth away a film of dust from the Lady's dainty red and gold slippers. "From your voice—it's not muffled."

"Would you listen to that, Robbie! She could tell from the sound of my voice! When she was little she knew from my footsteps on the front stoop whether I'd stopped off at Flannery's on the way home."

"You'd take off your work boots so as not to wake Mom when you'd been drinking," I say, striking the hammer until a plume of flesh-colored dust fans out over the glass. "If you don't care about your own health—" I point to the mask still dangling around his neck "—think of the bad example you're setting for Robbie here."

Dad starts to laugh but it gets stuck in his throat and turns into a cough. "There," he says, pummeling his chest with his fist until he's surrounded by an aura of putty dust, "there's your example for you, Robbie boy, wear your mask while working with this stuff if you don't want to end up a broken-down old man like me."

"You look pretty good, Mr. McKay, for a man your age."

"Mebbe for a hundred-year-old man," Dad grumbles, turning back on his ladder. I can tell he's pleased, though. He's vain about his appearance, my sixty-year-old dad, about his full head of hair that's still more black than gray—at least when it's not covered with putty dust—his good teeth and his arm and chest muscles still strong from a lifetime of lifting and installing heavy plate-glass windows. I only wish he'd take as much care of his insides as he does his outer appearance: he still isn't wearing the mask. "Which is how old I feel when someone calls me Mr. McKay. Call me Gil, son."

"Okay, Gil," Robbie replies, "did you really know Augustus Penrose?"

"Sure did. Now there was a man old as Methuselah. He was already in his eighties when I started cutting glass in his studio, but he still put in a full day of work. If he didn't like how you were doing something he'd take the cutter right out of your hand and do it himself. Going on ninety and his hands were steady as bedrock. Cool, too. He could stand next to a twenty-five-hundred-degree furnace and not break a sweat. Man had ice water in his veins. . . ."

"Robbie, maybe you ought to go outside and help Ernesto—" I start to suggest, anxious over what colorful Gus Penrose story my father might launch into, but Ernesto comes in through the side door at just that moment to tell us that he's managed to free all the exterior putty in the time it's taken the three of us to scrape out the interior putty. He's already got the wirecutters in his hand and is ready to cut the tie wires from the saddle bars supporting the window. I hold up my hand with five fingers splayed. "Give us five minutes," I tell him.

"Are we clear?" I ask my father and Robbie. Dad runs his chisel around the top and right-hand side of the window, Robbie checks the left-hand side and I swipe the shallow bottom groove with my gloved hand. All clear. I give Ernesto the thumbs up and he proceeds to cut the tie wires. The window shivers slightly with each cut and I look up at the Lady's face to check for any panes coming loose. That would be the hardest glass to replace—the finely painted portrait of Eugenie—or is it, as Christine suggested in her lecture yesterday, Eugenie's sister, Clare? *The mad sister*. For the first time today I look at the window not as a set of technical problems—of cracks and deteriorating lead came, bowing and crizzling—but as a portrait. The Lady's yellow hair spills over her shoulders more wildly than I recalled. Her left hand grasps a hank of the abundant tresses almost as if she were pulling her own hair. I've never noticed how firm that grip looks and now—with the window shaking in its setting—I have the impression that she's trying to clutch onto something. She does look a bit mad—or at least desperate.

When the wires are all cut we all prepare to slide the window into the deeper slot on the right side. She sticks at first, then makes a grating sound like a soft moan which, when the glass clears the left groove and Ernesto carefully tilts the window into the room and we lift her out of her stone setting, turns into a long sigh as a gust of warm air snakes in under her robes. I almost imagine that I hear her skirts rustling—and then I see that it's just some old newspaper that must have been stuffed in the grooves and sealed in the putty fluttering down to the floor. I let out my own breath as the three men lay her down gently on a plywood pallet and stoop to gather the shredded paper.

"We'll clean that up," my dad says. "Don't you have to pick up Bea from school?"

I look down at my watch and am amazed to see it's almost three. It's taken seven hours to release the Lady. "Damn, I don't even have time to go home and take a shower. I promised Bea I'd take her shopping . . ."

I look down at my clothes, which are covered with a fine dust that is mostly putty but also some lead from the decaying cames. I'm always lecturing the guys on washing up after handling lead. *If you don't want to end up brain-dead by forty.*

"Use the showers down by the gym," Ernesto suggests. "Don't you keep a locker there for when you go swimming?"

One of the perks of teaching a stained-glass class here at night is that I get to use the campus pool. "Yeah, that's what I'll do. I've got some exercise clothes in the car. Can you guys handle the rest of this?"

Ernesto and my dad exchange an amused look. Robbie is already sweeping the dust off the floor. I start to toss the papers in my hand into a loose garbage bag when I notice that in among the shredded newspapers are heavy cream-colored sheets folded into quarters. I unfold one and hold it in the light that's now flooding through the gaping hole in the wall. The light's almost too bright—bleaching the old paper clean—but I can just make out fine pencil lines, a sketch of a face, and an intricate tiny script running along the edge of the paper like a mouse scurrying along the rim of a baseboard.

"Look at these," I say, holding the pages out to the men.

"Looks like discarded sketches for the window—got jammed in with the putty—saw something like it in that window we did down in Irvington," Ernesto says.

"Might be a message," my dad says.

"A message?" I ask. My dad doesn't usually wax so mystical.

"From the previous craftsman," he explains, "to the restorer. Which would be you, Junebug. Medieval craftsmen did it all the time. Notes on how and when the glass was made, what kind of caming was used. Then when the window was restored they'd stuff some notes in on what they did so the next restorer would know what was original, what was restored."

"So these could be notes from Augustus Penrose, or Eugenie . . ." I gather up all the cream-colored sheets, counting twelve in all. Because they're covered in lead and putty dust I seal them in a garbage bag.

"Or just trash," my dad finishes my sentence for me.

"I'll have a look at them later," I say, checking my watch again. "If you guys can really handle the rest . . ."

"Go!" the three men shout at me.

So I do. Halfway down the hall, though, I turn back to look at where the window was. Through the stone arch I can see the Hudson and the long, sloping ridges of the Hudson Highlands. For a moment I wonder why anyone would ever want to hide that view with colored glass, but then, I remind myself as I turn away, I'd be out of a job if they didn't.

* * *

I STOP IN THE MIDDLE OF THE MAIN QUAD AND CALL BEA ON MY cell phone to tell her I'm running late. She says no problem, she'll head down to the gym and work out on the rowing machines. At her age I would have spent the spare time out in the woods behind the track smoking Marlboros with Carl Ventimiglio, the juvenile delinquent I dated my last two years in high school.

Old Gym—so called since the college built a multi-million-dollar field house on the edge of campus—is deserted. Finals ended last week and most of the students have already packed up and left for home. The pool, though, has been kept open for faculty members still finishing their grades. I run into Umberto Da Silva, my old Dante professor, who's now assistant to the president, on the steps coming up from the basement, his thin gray hair combed in damp strands across his forehead, his usual pipe tobacco and licorice mint smell mixed with chlorine.

"*Ciao Bella*," he says, leaning toward me to give me the traditional European kiss on both cheeks. I hold up a hand to wave him off.

"I'm covered with lead dust, *Professore*," I explain. He purses his lips and blows out a puff of air—*puh!*—a dismissive sound as if to say, *what's a little lead poisoning between friends*, but still I keep my distance.

"So you have taken the Lady away," he says. "She went willingly?"

I laugh. "Like Blanche DuBois on the arm of her gentleman caller."

"*Bene*. After Christine's lecture yesterday I dreamed bad dreams of her all night." *Of Christine*, I wonder, *or the Lady?*

But Umberto is already raising a hand to signal his departure—a gesture that is at once elegant and imperious: Augustus saluting the centurions. The professor comes from an old Italian family—like my mother—which is, I believe, the source of his fondness for me.

"*Ciao Professore*," I say, resisting an impulse to high-five his raised hand. "If you miss the Lady come down to the studio to visit—we'd both appreciate the company."

The women's locker room is cold and empty. I strip off my powdery clothes and seal them in the same garbage bag that holds the cream-colored pages. The shower floor is so cold on my bare feet that I decide, after rinsing off, to hop in the sauna for five minutes just to warm up and bake some of the soreness out of my neck and shoulders. Seven hours of chiseling and craning to look up at the window have taken their toll on my back. I stretch out on the hot wood of the top shelf and close my eyes. Splotches of bright color float across the inside of my eyelids—bright citrine yellow, ruby red, cobalt blue—lozenges of bright jewels, all the colors in the window I've spent the day removing. When I hear the click of the door and open my eyes to see who's come in all I can see are sunbursts of color hovering ghostlike in the dimness of the sauna.

"Oh, Juno, there you are. I wanted to have a word with you." It's Fay, Gavin's assistant, acting for all the world as if she'd found me in the president's waiting room instead of naked and sweating on a slab. I adjust my towel, which was not made to cover a five-foot-eleven-inch woman, and sit up. Fay, I notice, is wearing the kind of terry wrap that buttons at the side, the elastic puckering over her flat chest. Her fine silver hair—which I've only ever seen folded and clipped to the back of her head—is combed back wet from her high forehead, so thin in places I can see the shape of her skull.

She sits sideways on the bottom shelf, leans against the wall, and stretches her legs out in front of her. "Have you spoken to your friend Christine today?"

"No, I've been in the library all day. . . ."

"Because there are several pages missing from archival material she borrowed."

I wipe away the sweat beading up on my forehead and wonder if Fay turned up the thermostat control when she came in.

"You mean from Eugenie Penrose's notebook? Christine said you were copying it—"

"Well, I can't copy what I don't have, can I? Personally, I don't see why she was given the original source material in the first place and now look what's happened."

"I'm sure Christine would never be careless with a rare document. Are you sure the missing pages were there when she took the journal?" I'm thinking of the pages in the bottom of the garbage bag in my gym locker. For all I know they're the missing pages, torn out from Eugenie's notebook years ago. I'm afraid, though, that if I mention them to Fay she'll confiscate them immediately. "Are you sure that Eugenie's notebook was completely intact when you gave it to Christine?"

Fay purses her lips and rakes a hand through her hair, leaving whitish trenches where the scalp shows through.

"Unfortunately a full inventory has never been made of this material," Fay admits, "but I'm almost certain there were pages there that are missing now. You know what I think?" Fay leans forward, her thin shoulders hunched so that her towel gapes open and I'm treated to a view of her flat sternum. Before I can look away I notice a strip of pearly white skin—scar tissue—snaking across her chest. A mastectomy? I close my eyes and a vision of my mother's scarred chest after she came home from the hospital blooms in the darkness. I open my eyes, preferring Fay's censorious face to that vision. She's holding a hand to her chest now as if she's testifying at a Bible meeting.

"I think she's planning to write a book about Eugenie Penrose, and she doesn't want anyone else scooping her research. All that nonsense about Eugenie's sister, Clare, and awakening from the shadows. What do you think she meant by that? It was the oddest lecture I've ever heard at the college. It made me wonder if she'd come a bit unhinged. Wasn't she in a rehab clinic a few years ago for substance abuse?"

"She had a little drinking problem, that's all, but she's completely over that—"

"And wasn't she hospitalized during her senior year for a drug overdose?"

"That was an accident," I say a little too quickly. "She was taking pain pills after she broke her leg skiing spring break and she just messed up on the dosage." At least that's what we'd told people had happened. What had really happened was that Neil had dared Christine to climb up the tower of the library. We'd all been high on mushrooms, and Christine had fallen and broken her leg and cracked three ribs.

"You forget that I worked in the infirmary back then. I overheard the head nurse say she had taken over thirty Darvon—that's no accident. When she came into Mr. Penrose's office Sunday morning before the lecture she seemed quite agitated and she asked me for a glass of water so she could take a pill. She had one of those pill-sorters and it was *stocked*! And Mr. Penrose seemed concerned about her after the lecture. He asked me to place a call to her office this morning but she wasn't in. Don't you think she seemed depressed?"

I slip down off the shelf, holding my towel tightly over my chest. I'd like to deny it, but then I remember Christine's expression when I last saw her through the train window. And the lecture was a bit odd—all that preoccupation with madness and doom. And even though Fay is a bit officious for my taste, no one cares more about the fate of the college.

"I think she was probably just under a lot of pressure getting her lecture ready," I answer, turning my back to the door so that I can back out without exposing my towel's limitations. The sight of Fay's hand splayed over her chest makes me wince with the memory of her scar. "But I'll call her tonight to see how she's doing and I'll ask her about the missing notebook pages. I'm sure if she kept any pages it was an accident."

BY THE TIME BEA AND I GET HOME, THOUGH, IT'S TOO LATE TO call. When I picked her up, Bea had hesitatingly expressed

interest in a North Face backpack that she'd seen at the
outlet store in Harriman two weeks ago when she'd gone
there with her friend Melissa and Melissa's mother, Lisa.
When they'd dropped Bea off I'd noticed the back of the
Ford Escort crammed with bags from Coach and
Burberry's and Diesel and felt a pang remembering the
twenty-dollar bill I'd given Bea for the trip. Of course Bea
had expressed total indifference to Melissa and Lisa's
purchases. While most of the moms I know in Rosedale
have spent their daughters' high school years fending off
requests for Kate Spade bags I usually have to corral Bea
into trading one set of worn Nikes and Levi's for another.
She's always claimed complete disinterest in the trappings
of high fashion but I also suspect she absorbed early on the
true state of our financial circumstances (she knows, for
instance, that the only money I've ever taken from Neil's
family has been put into a college trust for her) and made
a pact with herself (Bea's always making pacts with
herself) never to strain them. So whenever she does
mention an interest in a material good I try to satisfy it.
Besides, I've only got another week of her before she'll be
gone for eight weeks—the longest we've ever been apart.

After getting her the backpack and a fleece jacket at
North Face I take her to an Italian restaurant on Route 9
and we linger over our cappuccinos and Italian cheese-
cake. How often do you get to linger with your fifteen-
year-old? Especially one like Bea, who's in accelerated
motion from the minute she opens her eyes in the
morning to the moment she crashes—usually with her
kayaking gear still on—on the floor of her bedroom. We

talk about the rivers she'll be rafting on, she tells me a story that Kyle told her about rafting down the Yampa River in Colorado (he's told me the story already but I act like I'm hearing it for the first time), and I try to pretend that the idea of my daughter whipping down a chute of churning water and sharp rocks doesn't fill me with dread. Driving home, I'm congratulating myself on the good job I did hiding my fears when Bea's sleepy voice startles me from the passenger side of the car.

"Someone told me in school today that Aunt Christine talked about that insane asylum up near Poughkeepsie during her lecture. Isn't it where Dad is?"

"Who at your school knew about the lecture?" I ask.

"Denise Levitan. Her mother was in your year at Penrose. Did you know her?"

I shake my head, but then sneaking a look at Bea out of the corner of my eye, see she's not looking at me. She's closed her eyes and I realize she's giving me a chance not to answer.

"Yes," I say, "Neil was at Briarwood, but I don't know for sure if he's still there. Since your grandma Essie died I haven't had any updates and that's . . . what? Almost three years ago."

"Oh." That's all she says. Then she lifts her hand to a curl of hair at her temple and begins twirling it around her finger. The same gesture she'd made as a baby when she was soothing herself to sleep.

"Do you want me to find out if he's still there?" I ask, my voice suddenly hoarse. The sound it makes in my throat reminds me of the moaning sound the Lady window made today when it scraped against its stone setting.

"I don't know . . . yeah, I mean I'd like to know where he is at least. Do you think he might have gotten . . . better? We learned in Health about all these new drugs they use for mood disorders. Maybe one of those would work for him."

I imagine Bea studiously copying down pharmaceutical names in her spiral notebook and making a pact with herself to bring up the subject with me. "I'll call your aunt Sarah tomorrow and ask her," I tell Bea. "I'll see what I can find out before you leave."

It's eleven when we get back to the loft. Bea heads straight for her room, but I sit out on the roof for a while, staring at the lights on the train tracks and the dark water of the river beyond them. Across the river the hills where Penrose had built his grand estate are dark, thanks to the fact that Penrose specified in his will that the property couldn't be developed.

Surely if there'd been any change in Neil's condition someone would have let me know, I tell myself. But who? Neil's sister, Sarah, who married an Orthodox rabbi the year after Neil's breakdown and has since refused to eat at her mother's house? Essie Buchwald, on her twice-a-year calls to me, had bemoaned her daughter's newfound religious zeal with almost as much drama as her son's mental incapacity. I'd dreaded those calls from Essie, but since her death I've missed them and I realize now that there is no one in Neil's family who would feel obliged to call me. For all I know, Neil could have been released from Briarwood a year ago.

I get up and lean against the railing at the edge of the roof. From here I can see the park and boathouse and the brightly lit Metro-North train platform. Christine had asked me an awful lot of questions about Neil. Had she heard something about him while researching Clare Barovier's confinement at Briarwood? Had she maybe even visited him? Christine had, I knew, a bit of a crush on Neil. It would be only natural for her to ask about him while she was at the hospital, but then wouldn't she have told me if there were any change? I remember suddenly the question she'd started to ask me: *But what if Neil were well again . . . ?* Had she asked because she knew he was well?

I check my watch: eleven thirty. Christine often stayed up late, sometimes working through the night when she was excited about a project. Maybe it wasn't too late to call after all. I go inside and dial Christine's number. When I get her machine I speak into it and give her a minute to pick up but she doesn't. After I hang up I notice there's a message on my machine. I hit the replay button, expecting that it will be Christine, but it's not. It's a man's voice that I don't recognize, identifying himself as Nathan Bell, a graduate student in Christine's program at Columbia.

"Christine gave me your number in case I needed to reach her over the weekend," he says, "and I was wondering if she were still there." There's a pause and I think the message is over, but then his voice resumes. "She didn't show up for her classes today. When I went by her apartment today to feed her cat it looked like she never came home."

CHAPTER FIVE

I TRY CHRISTINE'S HOME NUMBER TWICE BEFORE I GO TO SLEEP, but only get her answering machine. In the morning I try her again but when she doesn't pick up I call Nathan Bell.

"She missed a meeting with her dissertation adviser and her senior seminar," he tells me.

"That doesn't sound like her at all."

There's a silence that lasts so long I think we might have been disconnected, but then Nathan Bell asks me a question, "Look, you're her oldest friend, aren't you?"

It takes me a moment to answer. I've never put it that way to myself but I guess it's true. Christine never mentioned any friends from high school and although she seemed to know everyone in college, I was the only one you could really call her friend. Well, Neil maybe—but she'd met him at the same time I had during junior year.

"Yes, I guess I am," I finally answer. "Why? Do you think something's wrong?"

"I wanted to know if *you* thought there was anything wrong. How did she seem this weekend?"

"To tell you the truth we didn't get to spend that much time together. She was pretty much in demand all weekend—" I don't mention that I avoided most of the reunion events, "—and by the time we hooked up after her lecture we only had an hour before she had to catch her train."

"And how did the lecture go?"

"Great—you know Christine, she's a performer." I picture Christine standing in front of the window twirling her hand in the yellow light. Thinking about the window prompts me to wander down the spiral stairs to the studio, where the window has been laid out on the glazing bench, waiting to be dismantled. I notice again how the Lady's hand is tangled in her own hair and I realize that Christine's gesture with the light had echoed the Lady's pose. "It was like she had really absorbed her subject," I tell Nathan Bell. "I remember once when she was writing a paper on John Everett Millais's *Ophelia* and she read that he made Elizabeth Siddal pose for hours in a full bathtub. Christine decided to see how long she could stay in a bathtub. She managed five hours and came down with pneumonia."

Nathan Bell laughs. "Yeah, that sounds like Christine. When she talks about a painting it's like she's walked into that world and chatted with the subjects—whether it's one of Brueghel's villages or a de Chirico streetscape. It's part of her brilliance, but I wonder sometimes if she doesn't pay too high a price for that insight. In the last few months she's seemed possessed by that Penrose window. I wondered if you noticed a change in her or if there was anything in her lecture that struck you as odd."

"Well," I say, picking up a lead knife and sliding it under the came at the top edge of the window, "she identified the figure in the window as Eugenie's mentally ill sister Clare. I guess that's bound to be controversial. We've always been told that Eugenie was the model and that Augustus Penrose designed the window as a tribute to craftsmanship. Christine identified the iconography with the story of 'The Lady of Shalott' and drew an analogy between being stuck in an insane asylum and spending four years at Penrose. She ended her lecture by saying that the Lady is calling us to 'turn away from the shadows and face reality.' I think it's a brilliant interpretation but it's bound to strike some people as too radical."

I shift the phone to my other ear to ease the crick in my neck from cradling the receiver against my shoulder and miss the beginning of Nathan's response.

". . . anything about the Briarwood Asylum?"

The lead knife slips in my hand and nicks my thumb. When I draw back my hand a drop of blood falls on the landscape portion of the window. Fortunately, it's not a piece that's painted: In fact Penrose had used a technique called plating, in which he layered clear glass over the painted mountains to give an illusion of distance and depth.

"I'm sorry, what did you say about Briarwood?" I remember my promise to Bea to find out if her father was still at Briarwood, but of course I'd had to return Nathan Bell's call first.

"Christine said she had some more research to do up there and she mentioned an aunt who worked at the hospital who could get her in to see the head doctor—could she have gone up to Poughkeepsie instead of coming back to the city?"

"Well, I put her on the southbound train." I've put down the knife—I had no business using it while on the phone anyway—and look into the Lady's face, only it's like she's looking past me at something in the distance. How had Christine described the blush of color on her face? *It is the reflection of the sun striking her for the first time in her life. She might be bound for death, but in this moment— the moment in which she chooses life over shadow—she is more alive than she has ever been.* There is something in her expression that reminds me of my last glimpse of Christine before her train compartment's lights went out but I don't know what. Christine had looked more worried than radiant.

"She did seem preoccupied with something when I put her on the train," I tell Nathan. "Like she'd remembered something she'd neglected to do."

"Maybe it was something she wanted to research up at Briarwood. Are you sure she didn't get off the train?"

"Well, I stayed until the train pulled out." Waving at the blank window. When the train was gone I walked south, away from the station, toward the factory. "I suppose she could have gotten off on the north side of the stairs," I tell Nathan, "and gone up to the station and waited for a northbound train. Her mother still lives in Poughkeepsie. Even though she and Christine don't get on so well she could have gone there for the night. Why don't I call her and check?"

Nathan Bell thanks me and gives me his cell phone number. "Let me know as soon as you find out anything," he says. "I won't feel easy—"

His voice is drowned out by a high-pitched moan.

"What the hell is that?" I ask.

"Christine's Siamese," Nathan tells me. "I though I might as well bring her over here. She doesn't seem very easy about Christine's absence either."

I AM NOT ABLE, UNFORTUNATELY, TO PUT NATHAN BELL'S concerns to rest. Ruth Webb tells me curtly that she hasn't heard from *Chrissie* since Christmas although she had heard from her sister, Beth, who still works at Briarwood (Ruth had worked there in the kitchen before she'd injured her knee and retired on disability) that Christine had been nosing around up there last month. "You'd think she could have spared a minute to visit her mother."

I murmur something noncommittal—the alternative being to point out that fifteen years ago Mrs. Webb hadn't been able to *spare a minute* to come to Christine's graduation. Christine had graduated *summa cum laude* and *Phi Beta Kappa* without a single family member in attendance. Since I had just given birth—and Bea was still in NICU because she'd been born prematurely—she also missed having her best friend there.

I WISH I COULD SAY I SPENT THE REMAINDER OF THE WEEK trying to find Christine but although I was worried about her, I didn't really see what I could do. When I asked her mother if she would file a missing persons report she responded that Christine had vanished like this before and turned up *when she was good and ready to*. I could tell from her tone of voice that she assumed Christine must be drinking again. Maybe she was right. When Christine was drinking she would often disappear for days at a time. Nathan said that he would notify the police if she didn't show up in another twenty-four hours. In the meantime I had my own work on the window to start and Bea's end of school and upcoming rafting trip to think about.

Every time I looked at Bea I thought about not seeing her for eight weeks and I'd have to stop myself from saying something absurdly sentimental or hugging her, so instead I'd bring up the number of extra socks she was taking or how many protein bars she would need to subsist on her new vegan diet and we'd end up fighting. By Friday we were barely talking. I didn't want her to go away like that so on Saturday I gave in to a request she'd been making for almost a year.

"I thought maybe we could go kayaking together," I mention casually over breakfast (eggs and coffee for me; a protein bar and Japanese twig tea for her). "Kyle says I'm making a lot of progress."

Bea looks up from her mug of murky brown tea. "Really? You mean like out on the river?"

I shrug. "Water's water, right? Whether it's chlorinated pool water or Hudson River water—" I'm about to say *you can drown just as easily in both* but stop myself. "—it's the same drill flipping yourself back up. Besides, I hardly ever tip." This part is true. During the lessons Kyle has given me at the college pool he's had to push me to make me learn how to capsize and right myself. Otherwise I'm so rigidly still the minute I slide into the shallow boat that it would take a tidal wave to swamp me and, as far as I know, the Hudson is relatively free of tsunami.

Bea gets up from the table and heads barefoot out onto the roof with Paolo and Francesca close at her heels.

"It's a beautiful day," she calls to me. I get up and follow her, trying not to look quite as slavishly attentive as the dogs. Her palms flat to the railing, Bea leans out toward the river and sniffs at the morning air. Her red hair, loosed from its braid, fans out in the mild breeze. Francesca rises on her hind legs, paws on the railing, and muzzles Bea's hip. Above the hills on the western bank the sky is bright with only a thin line of clouds hovering over the Catskills. The river, which looks suddenly wider to me, is a shade of slate blue stippled with white caps.

"It looks kind of windy," I say.

Bea turns to me, her hands already working in her hair to braid it. For a moment she reminds me of Christine standing in the same pose last week twisting her hair up, but then I realize the similarity is more in their expressions: the same shadow of worry that I saw in Christine last week has fallen over Bea. She's worried I'll be too afraid to go out on the river because of the wind. She's right; I am.

"I've got an idea," I say, "why don't we cross the river and paddle up the Wicomico onto the old Astolat grounds? That way we'll only be on the open river for a little while and I can see the sunken garden you and Kyle were talking about." Bea's face brightens instantly. I'm not sure what pleases her more: the fact that I've agreed to go kayaking with her or that I'm willing to trespass on private property.

WE GO DOWN TO THE BOATHOUSE AND FIND KYLE GIVING AN intro lesson to three couples who have come up from the city to spend a day on the river. Standing with his back to the river he's inscribing figure eights with a red paddle in the bright air. He makes it look easy—a natural motion like the rise and fall of a dragonfly's wings. His audience, when they take up their paddles, bats the air clumsily, more like bees drunk on honey. He tells them to keep practicing and wends his way between their darting paddles over to us.

"Hey, I was afraid you were going to head out before dropping by to say good-bye." He's talking to Bea, but he manages to catch my eye and wink. He's supposed to come over tomorrow night after Bea leaves to make dinner for us.

"Mom's finally ready to launch out into the great outdoors," Bea announces. She looks so proud of me I'm instantly ashamed it's taken me so long to do this. "Can we have two boats?"

"Maybe one of the wider models," I say. The wider kayaks, though slower, are less likely to tip.

"Sorry, Juno, I've promised those to this crew, and frankly," he lowers his voice, "they need them more than you do."

We all look over just in time to see one of the men—
snappily attired in lycra shorts and tangerine fleece—
spade the dirt at his feet with his paddle.

"Don't you have seven of the wider kayaks?" I ask.

Kyle shakes his head. "I did. One was stolen last week."

"Stolen?" Bea sounds incensed. Although happy to
break rules that she sees as pointless, my daughter
possesses a fine sense of moral outrage against unkindness
to others. "Someone broke into the boathouse?"

Kyle nods. "I knew the lock was flimsy. They took two
kayaks, one of the reds—the wider kind—and a yellow.
Also two paddles, two aprons, but no life jackets."

"Serve them right if they drowned."

"Beatrice!"

"Well, Kyle's worked hard to get this business going. I
bet it was some rich kids from the Heights on a graduation
night dare."

"Actually it happened last Sunday night—but speaking
of businesses to get going, I'd better get this crew in the
water before they kill one another on land. You two can
tag along if you like."

Bea looks at me and I try not to look like I'd feel safer in
a crowd. "Actually we thought we'd head across the river
and up the Wicomico," I tell Kyle.

"Excellent. You'll love seeing the ruins of the water
gardens. Just don't run into any of those submerged
statues. . . ." Kyle's attention has drifted back to the
tourists and from them to the sky over the hills across the
river. Although it's still sunny, clouds have begun to
gather above the highlands, just where the Dutch settlers

believed an old goblin summoned thunderstorms to plague sailors. "And keep an eye on the weather," Kyle says. "We may get a storm late in the day."

By the time we've got our gear on and boats in the water it's after ten. The mouth of the Wicomico is a quarter mile south on the west side of the river. Bea sets a diagonal course across the river. "It'll only take us about fifteen minutes to cross going with the current," she calls to me, twisting to look at me over her shoulder.

Not so long, I tell myself. Although I've been practicing in the pool, I'm unprepared for how it feels to be out on the river. Riding low on the water, I feel as insignificant as the drowning boy in Brueghel's *Fall of Icarus*. The hills on the opposite shore, which have always looked as worn and comfortable as a broken old couch from my rooftop, now seem to loom over the water like giants. The grinning goblins of Washington Irving's stories. The Hudson River looks wide as a sea here and, in fact, it is still part of the sea—a tidal estuary all the way up to Troy. The spray that lifts off the whitecaps and washes over my face tastes of salt.

I try to breathe in rhythm with my paddling, and concentrate on how beautiful the river is and not on what it would feel like to find myself hanging upside down in it. That's what scares me so much about kayaking: the idea of being trapped in the boat, suspended in the water. I haven't always been this fearful. When I was Bea's age I'd hop the train tracks and take my dad's rowboat out into the river. When I first met Neil he said he loved my fearlessness. We went rock climbing across the river in the

Shawangunks—or the gunks, as rock climbers call them—and scaled every building on the Penrose campus. We climbed over train trestles and sneaked into abandoned Hudson River mansions, sometimes spending whole nights in the ghostly ruins of Gilded Age splendor. I'm not sure what changed me—whether it was having Bea or watching Neil descend into madness. Sometime during Bea's first two years of life I lost a tolerance for hanging over the edge.

"Isn't this great, Mom?" Bea calls back to me, turning her radiant face toward me.

"Beautiful," I tell her, wishing she'd face forward in her kayak. It makes me nervous to see her swiveling around in the narrow craft. "Absolutely beautiful."

And it is. Still, I'm glad when we turn into the Wicomico even though it's harder paddling against the stream's current. I'm happy to be held on both sides by green banks and more distracted by the creek's tamer charm than by the wild beauty of the Hudson. There'd been something in that beauty that had made my heart race. Here the meandering curves of the creek soothe. Wild iris and narcissi fringe the gently sloping banks, and water lilies carpet the water's surface. Even the great blue heron, which is startled into flight by our approach, rises into the air with unhurried grace. Nothing sudden or unexpected will happen here.

As we paddle farther upstream I realize that the tranquil effect of the stream has not been left to nature or chance. The trees that line the banks, trailing their long branches in the water like girls bending over the stream to wash their hair, have been planted there and so have the sedges and reeds, cattails and rushes that fringe the shore. I catch a glimpse of a pale figure crouched beneath a weeping willow and nearly cry out before realizing it's a marble statue half submerged in the water and covered in moss and creeping ivy.

"Do you see that one?" Bea calls, backpaddling her kayak to stop opposite the statue. I come up beside her and peer into the deep gloom of the willow's shade. The marble boy is perched on a stone ledge that might have once been on the edge of the bank but is now under a foot of water. His lips just touch the surface of the water, but it must have looked once as if he were staring at his own reflection instead of lowering himself to drink. He's surrounded by yellow daffodils.

"Narcissus," I say to Bea. "Look—" I use my paddle to point at another statue sitting a little farther along the bank—a slim girl sitting on a crumpled bit of stone wall, up to her waist in water. Her head is turned toward the self-absorbed boy, an expression of longing in what remains of her ruined face.

"That's Echo, right?" Bea asks. "She loved Narcissus."

"That's right," I tell Bea, glad that she's remembered at least a little of the mythological tales I used to read her at bedtime. "But he only loved himself."

"She should have gotten over him," Bea says, dipping her paddle into the water to push her boat away from the bank. "No boy's worth that grief."

"You can say that again." I push off from the bank and end up in front of Bea this time, and even though I prefer

to have her in front I paddle on ahead of her. I figure that
if my fifteen-year-old can show such good sense about
romantic entanglement I can summon up a little practical
bravery.

As we go upstream the creek becomes narrower and
darker. The light-limbed willows cede to the dense foliage of
weeping beeches. Several times I'm startled by fragments of
statuary submerged just beneath the surface. An arm
curving out of the water, like a swimmer in midstroke, the
crested head of a sea serpent and, most disturbingly, a
submerged face of a girl looking up through the water with
sightless marble eyes. I don't know if they've toppled into
the water or Penrose planned it this way—taking the idea
of a sunken garden one step further and placing even the
statues underwater. Christine would know if she were here.

I'm glad when the creek widens again into a deep pool
surrounded by stone walls, carpeted in water lilies, and
shaded by the long heavy branches of a giant weeping
beech. It's like entering the apse of a church that's been
glazed in green and yellow glass. Dappled with leaf
shadow and light, the water lilies glow like travertine
marble. This must be the water lily pool that Penrose
depicted in the Lady window. I'm loath to disturb the quiet
with my paddling, but when I rest the paddle across my lap
I begin to drift backward. I dip my paddle into the water—
remembering what Kyle always says: *Just put the water
behind you*—and pull myself forward through the curtain
of beech branches. For a moment the sunlight is so
blinding I can't see but then I make out the ruins of the old
mansion, Astolat: four ruined towers rising above terraced

ledges like a castle in a fairy tale. I've seen photographs of the mansion before the fire, but I've never appreciated how well its setting on the water echoes Tennyson's poem. *Four gray walls, and four gray towers, Overlook a space of flowers, And the silent isle imbowers The Lady of Shalott.* I'm about to share the lines with Bea when I hear a scream, followed by the sound of something slapping the water.

"Bea!" I start paddling on one side to turn the kayak around and nearly tip over.

"Bea!" I call again, barely righting myself.

"Mom, come here, quick—" I hear a sob in her voice, but at least I know she's above water. I try to concentrate on turning, but even when I've gotten the kayak pointed in the right direction I can't see anything because Bea's still under the beech tree.

"I'm coming, honey, don't worry." I paddle through the thick curtain of branches, moving quicker now that I'm going with the current. I nearly bump into Bea's boat. She's backpaddling to keep herself stationary, her eyes fastened on something near the bank. After the bright sunshine it's hard to see in the tree's shadow. I paddle closer to the shore and make out, wedged between a half-submerged boulder and stone wall, half hidden in a thick clump of water lilies, something long and yellow. The underbelly of a kayak.

"Maybe it's the one stolen from Kyle's . . . ," I begin, but then I realize that Bea is sobbing.

"I didn't mean it when I said that whoever stole the kayak deserved to drown."

I want to reach out and touch Bea but I'm afraid I'll tip us both if I get too close. Instead I move carefully toward the capsized vessel. As I do a breeze stirs the beech branches, parting the heavy curtain. A swath of sun cuts through the water between me and the upturned kayak. When I lean over the water I think, for just a moment, that I'm looking into my own reflection. Beneath the water a woman sits in a yellow kayak. Her hair, standing straight up from her scalp, is like a cartoonist's idea of someone scared out of her wits. Only that's not it at all. It's a woman suspended in the water, her long yellow hair swaying in the stream's current.

CHAPTER SIX

"Is she dead?" I hear Bea's voice from behind me. "Should we try to get her out of the water?"

I lean a little farther over to get a better look and see a white face, indistinct in the shadows, and a plume of yellow hair rising like smoke . . . no, not rising . . . I'm still reading the scene below the water as if it were a reflection of something above the water. In reverse. The woman's arms, hanging down toward the bottom of the creek, seem to be raised above her head as if she were fending off an attack. One white hand moves languidly in the current as if waving at the passing crowd of fish. Then I notice one of those fish delicately nibbling on the woman's fingers.

I jerk backward so quickly I nearly tip and have to slap the water with the flat of my paddle to right myself.

"I'm sure she's dead," I tell Bea. I've angled my boat so that I can look at Bea and, at the same time, block her view of the body. "There's nothing we can do for her and we probably shouldn't disturb the position of the body until the police come."

Bea nods. "It's one of Kyle's boats, isn't it? That means she's probably been in the water since Sunday, right?"

A sickening thought occurs to me and I look back at the mass of yellow hair swaying in the water. I bend down to look closer and suddenly I have a sense not so much of sinking as of the water rising to engulf me. When I look back up at Bea the sky spins and for a moment it's as if I'm the one hanging upside down under the water, the branches of the weeping beech like so much seaweed choking my path to the surface.

"Beatrice," I say, gripping the paddle to keep my voice from shaking, "it would take hours to hike out of here. I think one of us should stay with her . . . with the body . . . while the other paddles across the river to the boathouse to call the police."

"I'll go," she says quickly. "I can't stay here with that. But what about you? Why don't you come with me?"

I shake my head. As much as I hate the idea of Bea crossing the river alone I know she's more equipped to do it than I am. And even though it's clear that the woman trapped under the kayak is beyond help, I can't give in to my fears and leave her here.

Beatrice must see the pain on my face. Her eyes flick past me to the water lily bed. "Do you know who it is?" she asks.

Our boats have drifted close enough for me to touch Bea's hand. I reach out and squeeze her cold, callused fingers. "I think it's Aunt Christine."

As soon as Bea turns the prow of her boat downstream she's quickly gone, the current taking her under the curtain of beech branches and around the next bend in minutes. It won't take her long to cross the river and reach the boathouse, I tell myself. Still, the idea of spending another minute precariously perched on top of the water above a drowned body—a drowned body that might be my best friend's—is almost unbearable.

I scan the shore for a place to beach the kayak, but the banks here have been reinforced with stone walls that rise steeply from the water's edge. I paddle downstream, and then upstream, but this stretch of the Wicomico has been corralled between stone, the whole bucolic setting engineered from the water lilies to the weeping beech, from the statues lining the banks and lurking in the water to the sudden view of Astolat when you come out of the beech's shade.

Augustus Penrose was such a control freak—he had to orchestrate every detail of his surroundings. It's Christine's voice I hear, happily expounding on an article she'd read senior year about our founder. *He was into the whole total design thing from the British Design Reformation. Not only did he draw the plans for his faux-gothic castle, Astolat, he designed its stained-glass windows, its tapestries and furniture—even the china and glassware used to set its tables were designed and manufactured by the Rose Glass Works. He even had to design the gardens himself because he wanted them to look like the water gardens back in England.*

The voice in my head is so alive that I can't believe that

I may never hear it again in life. I paddle back under the beech branches and position my kayak as close as I can to the water lily patch and the overturned kayak, hoping I suppose that I'll see on closer inspection that this horrific tableau is just one more planned effect. But no, there's no mistaking the bloated figure beneath the water for a classical statue. And although I can't tell for sure if the woman suspended beneath the water is Christine, I have a strong feeling it is. What, though, would she have been doing here?

I run through in my mind watching her board the train and waving to her—or to the blank screen of her window—until the train left. Could she have possibly gotten off the train without me noticing her on the platform? It seems unlikely, but possible, especially if she walked to the north end of the train and exited on the other side of the stairs leading up to the station waiting room. From the station it was a short walk to the boat-house. . . .

When we stopped at the boathouse on the way to the station Bea had enthused over her trip up the Wicomico through the ruined water gardens of Astolat. Christine had been interested that so much of the sunken gardens remained and that you could reach them by water. She'd been fascinated with those gardens since she read about them senior year. Could there have been some piece of research she thought she could discover by paddling up the creek in the middle of the night? It seems crazy, but then I remember what Nathan Bell said about Christine seeming obsessed by the Penrose window. We'd laughed about Christine soaking herself in a cold tub to replicate Millais's *Ophelia*. . . .

I lay my paddle across my lap and wipe my eyes, forgetting that my hands are covered with salt from the spray off the Hudson. Immediately the stinging is so bad I can barely see. The stream is fresh, but I'm certainly not going to dip my hands in that water. I use some of the water from the bottle of Poland Spring strapped under a bungee cord across the prow of my kayak to wash my hands and flush my eyes and decide I can't afford to start crying now. If I give in to these images of Christine I'll be a wreck by the time the police come. I also notice that while busy with hand-washing maneuvers I've drifted downstream. I paddle closer to the yellow kayak and force myself to look at the whole picture.

Again I hear Christine's voice in my head. *You have to stick with what you see and follow where your eye leads you.* Advice she once gave me on writing art history papers.

My eye is certainly drawn to the bright yellow kayak— a strong diagonal slash in the bed of water lilies leading the eye to . . . what? There's a pile of rubble half-submerged beneath the water, part of the stone wall that's caved into the stream. The prow of the kayak is wedged between it and the part of the stone wall that's still standing. If Christine paddled close to the wall she might have struck the submerged rocks and flipped over. But why would she drown? Even if she was unable to flip her kayak up because it was trapped between the wall and a boulder she should have been able to release her spray skirt from the rim of the kayak and swim to the surface. Right on the front of the skirt there's a nice big bungee loop that you can pull to free yourself from the boat. I've gone over the drill in my mind dozens of times to assure myself that what has happened to Christine would never happen to me—or to Bea. Even if Christine didn't know about the loop a little struggling should have released her. Unless she was unconscious when she went over.

I let myself drift downstream a bit and then approach the lily patch closer to the wall, coming up behind the yellow kayak, and peer into the water at the collapsed wall, where I see a hand reaching out from the stone. For a horrible moment I think it's another body trapped under the rubble, but then I realize that the hand belongs to a statue that's been toppled headfirst into the water, probably when the wall caved in. I can just make out a marble leg and then, when a ray of sun creeps into the water, something metallic flashes like the bright gills of a carp. I bend over and see that it's a flat piece of bronze— probably a plaque identifying the statue. When I straighten up I'm so dizzy I nearly topple backward. Is that what might have happened to Christine? Had she paddled over here to look at the statue—at night? with a flashlight maybe?—and lost her balance and flipped over, her head hitting the rocks hard enough to knock her out? Trapped beneath the water she would have drowned.

I look down into the water, where the woman's golden hair sways between her white swollen fingers. It almost looks as if she's grasping her own hair—as if her fingers had instinctively grabbed for something to hold onto in her last conscious moments. It's the same gesture that the Lady makes in the Penrose window.

WHEN THE POLICE COME THE FIRST THING THEY DO IS HELP ME out of my kayak. Two uniformed officers take an arm each and yank me unceremoniously out of the boat—like pulling a cork out of a wine bottle—and deposit me on top of the stone wall, where I instantly sink to my knees. I have no feeling in my legs at all. Bea, who'd been hanging back by the patrol car, runs over and practically dives at me. I gather her close to me and we stay there—leaning against each other just like Francesca and Paolo—and watch the three policemen.

The two uniformed officers crouch on the edge of the wall while the third man, who's wearing gray slacks and a white button-down shirt, makes a call on a cell phone. Within minutes a police van arrives and three more men approach the shore holding diving gear and what looks like an inflatable raft.

"Ma'am, you'll have to move back now and clear the way for the recovery team. Do you need assistance moving?"

I look up at the plainclothes officer. In the shadow of the beech I can't see his face clearly. While he waits for me to answer he unbuttons his shirt cuffs and rolls his sleeves up over tanned forearms. I look up into pale gray eyes spaced far apart—the same silvery color as his short-clipped hair. His nose is slightly hooked. When I first moved into the factory I surprised a screech owl in the warehouse rafters with much the same steely expression.

"Ma'am? Do you need help getting up?"

I shake my head and, with Bea's help, struggle ungracefully to my feet. A little ways up the bank is a rustic bench. We sit there facing the water, but only I watch; Bea lies down, draws her knees to her chest, and lays her head in my lap. My legs are throbbing with pins and needles, but I stay put, stroking Bea's hair and watching the "recovery operation" under a darkening sky. The day that started out so clear is turning overcast. As the divers disappear beneath the beech tree I notice that the surface of the creek dimples with raindrops and realize that I'm already half soaked from the rain. Even though I'm pretty sure the woman in the water is Christine I'm hoping that maybe I'm wrong. By the time the men in wet suits have laid the grotesquely bloated form on the stone wall I'm praying that I'm wrong.

The gray-eyed officer comes back up the hill. I can make out his face better now and see that he's probably a good-looking man when he hasn't just had to look at a drowned corpse. He runs his hand over his close-cropped silver hair and cuts his eyes sideways to signal me to come with him. I nudge Bea off my lap and walk with the detective down the embankment toward the prone figure on the wall.

At first I think the body on the grass has been encased in black neoprene—like the wet suits the divers are peeling off—but then I realize that it's just that the black leather jacket and the dress beneath it have been stretched tight by the body's swelling, and the leather and cloth have taken on an oily sheen from algae.

"We're guessing she's been in the water a week, so you may not be able to identify her, but your daughter said something about you thinking the deceased might be her aunt. Would that be your sister?"

I shake my head, swallow, try to speak, and find my throat's a little dry. I try again. "Not my sister—my best friend." I remember what Nathan Bell said on the phone. "My oldest friend."

"Don't pay too much attention to the face," the detective tells me, "look for distinguishing marks—a birthmark, a scar. . . ."

I look away, not just from the face but from the body. I look straight up into the heart of the giant beech, where its branches spring from the main trunk like the ribs of a groined vault. A groined vault made of green glass. If Neil were here he'd already be halfway up the smooth-skinned trunk. He was able to find handholds and footholds on surfaces that looked unbroken to others; he could see where the hidden cracks were.

Look, he'd said to Christine and me the night he'd decided to scale the library tower, *can't you see it—like a ladder leading to the moon*. And up he'd gone, clinging to the side of the gray stone wall like a water strider skimming the surface of a moonlit pond. Christine had followed, but for once I hadn't. Looking up at the sheer wall had made me nauseous—everything had begun to make me nauseous. I hadn't known it at the time, but I was pregnant. I've wondered since if that was the reason

I didn't climb the tower with them that night—not just the nausea but because of some subconscious instinct to preserve the life growing inside of me. It's what I'd like to think, not that I could have done anything when Christine fell.

She landed on her side—if she hadn't it might have been her back and not just her leg she broke—one arm cradled under her head as if she were pillowing her cheek for a nap. I'd seen her sleep like that a dozen times on train seats and couches in the library. If not for the unnatural angle of the leg bent beneath her I would have thought she was just napping, but then she raised her head and I saw the blood dripping from her right temple.

The detective kneels and pulls out a pair of latex gloves from his pocket. When he's put the gloves on he touches a fingertip to the corpse's chin and gently tilts her face to the left. The hair—now sodden and colorless—falls back from her face. Embedded in the swollen skin is a long scar above the right ear.

"It's Christine," I manage to say clearly with only the slightest tremor audible in my voice. "Christine Frances Webb." I look up and the ribbed vault of the beech tree spins like a kaleidoscope filled with bits of green and yellow glass. Then I lean into the trunk of the tree and throw up on its knotted roots.

CHAPTER SEVEN

BEA ASKS ME THE NEXT DAY IF I WANT HER TO PUT OFF HER TRIP and stay with me. As much as I'd like to keep her close to me after catching a glimpse of my worst nightmare (drowning in a boating accident) turned into horrifying flesh, I know how much the trip means to her. I tell her to go. I drive her to the Wal-Mart parking lot in Poughkeepsie, where she boards a bus with twenty-five happy teenagers. She shoulders her backpack and turns to wave to me from the steps of the bus. Only the smudges under her eyes hint at the sleepless night we both passed.

She'll sleep on the bus, I think as I wave to the rear end of the Greyhound until it has pulled onto Route 9. *And I will not*, I tell myself firmly, *compare this leave-taking with saying good-bye to Christine last Sunday. Go home, sleep.*

When I park my car in front of the factory, though, I find the silver-haired detective—at some point yesterday I'd learned his name was Daniel Falco—standing in front of the main entrance. He's dressed in gray slacks and suit jacket, a pale blue tie loosened at his throat—church clothes—and he's standing with his hands on his hips, head back, looking up at the inscription carved in stone above the doorway. *Ars longa, vita brevis.* Art is long, life is brief. Not a particularly comforting sentiment after what we saw yesterday come out of the Wicomico.

"Good morning," I say, getting out the heavy ring of keys to unlock the door. "You're up early."

"I could say the same for you. I thought you might be sleeping somewhere in there, but there doesn't seem to be any way to rouse the lady of the manor."

"There's a service entrance on the side for deliveries," I explain, "and I don't get many unexpected visitors. I took my daughter Beatrice to the bus for her camping trip. You did say yesterday that it was okay for her to go."

I've gotten the door unlocked but the detective remains a few feet from the doorway, still looking up. Ignoring my reference to Bea's departure he jerks his chin at the stone carving above the door.

"I asked my dad what that meant once and he told me it was the names of the guys who built the glassworks. Artie Long and Vito Brevis."

I laugh but I'm so hoarse from crying all night that the sound comes out more like a bark. "Your dad had a sense of humor."

"Nah, he just didn't want to admit to his kid he didn't know something." He hooks a finger underneath the knot of his tie and pulls. The silk slithers under his collar, making a sound like running water.

"Your father worked for the Rose Glass Works?" I'm

surprised because I thought I knew everyone in this little town, especially anyone connected to the glassworks.

The detective nods, folds his tie and stuffs it in his suit jacket. "My father and his father. If it hadn't closed I'd probably have worked there, too, but when it closed down my family moved across the river to Kingston."

"Were they cutters or blowers?"

"Blowers. Descended from Venetian glassworkers—at least that's what my dad always told me."

"What did your father do after the works closed?"

"Sat mostly. At home in a La-Z-Boy recliner in front of the TV or down at the Italian-American club, where he and the other descendants of the great Venetian glassblowers drank grappa all day and sometimes played a little boccie."

"Sounds like my dad—if you substitute Flannery's and Jameson's whiskey. Oh, and hurling, only not to play, just to watch a couple times a year down at Gaelic Park in Riverdale. He started McKay Glaziers but his heart was never really in it. Storefront windows and mirrored foyers are quite a comedown after you've trained to work with stained glass. I've always wondered what this town would be like now if the Works had never closed down."

Daniel Falco looks at me for the first time this morning and then quickly looks away, turning left, then right, to survey the deserted street in front of the factory. I don't need to follow his glance to register the boarded storefronts and dilapidated houses—once grand Victorian houses now with sagging porches, peeling paint, and half a dozen mailboxes hanging crookedly from each porch for the tiny apartments that have been carved out of once-plush homes. Ironically, there are probably fewer people living in these houses now than when they were single-family homes. The projects just south of town have taken most of the welfare recipients and the neighborhood has too high a crime rate for anyone else. Still, beneath the cheap siding and bad paint jobs these houses could be beautiful—certainly as beautiful as the renovated houses in gentrified towns like Hudson and Cold Spring. It's not impossible, I think for not the first time, it could happen to Rosedale. I see in the detective's cool gray eyes, though, how improbable such a transformation would be.

"Yeah, and if I had balls, said the queen . . . but I hear you're at least putting the factory to some good again. It's not my idea of a great neighborhood to live in, but hey . . . how about a tour?"

"I'm happy to show you around, Detective Falco, but I can't help but think you've got better things to do with your Sunday."

"Like find out what happened to your friend?"

I nod.

Detective Falco runs his hand over his mouth and jaw. In the morning light he looks older than I took him for yesterday—closer to fifty than forty. The creases along the sides of his mouth are deeper, the shadows under his eyes darker. I realize he was probably up half the night filing reports on Christine's death but still he got up early to go to church. I imagine there's some elderly relative who counts on him to take her to church—his mother? a maiden aunt? I'm about to apologize for my remark when he smiles. "Who says that's not what I'm doing?"

I SHOW HIM THE OLD LOADING DOCKS AND WAREHOUSE AND, because of his family background, the furnaces where the glass was blown. If this tour is just an excuse to question me about Christine he does a good job feigning interest in the history of the factory and its possible uses for the future.

"You mean these arts organizations are really interested in using these old factories for museums? And the government hands out grants to do it?"

"The Dia Art Foundation is converting the old Nabisco factory in Beacon to house its permanent collection. MASSMoCA did it with an old mill in North Adams, Massachusetts, and it also houses working studios on-site. The Rose Glass Works is perfect—close to the train station, clean of any industrial contaminants, and just look at this light! We've already got several artists working here and more would come with government funding. It would be great for the downtown area. An influx of artists can really turn an urban area around; look at DUMBO in Brooklyn. That stands for Down Under—"

"The Manhattan Bridge Overpass. One of my class-mates from John Jay works in that precinct."

When I let him into the McKay studio he immediately heads for the unlit light table where a section of the Lady window—stripped of its lead caming and cleaned—lies in pieces like a giant jigsaw puzzle.

"How do you know how to put it all back together?" he asks, tilting his head to get a better look at the lady's darkened face.

"We do a rubbing first—" I point to the drawing on white vellum lying on the table. "—and then place the glass pieces on top of the rubbing."

"It looks like some of the paint has come away here and there," he says, laying a finger on the lady's lips.

"Yes, the enamel Penrose used wasn't very stable." I switch on the light box and the lady's face comes to life as if waking after a long sleep. The scratches in her cheeks and lips become even more apparent.

"So do you repaint those parts?"

"No. The new paint could cause further deterioration of the old paint. We might do something called plating, where we paint in the missing details on another plate of glass and place it behind the original." I pick up a piece that Ernesto has been experimenting with and slide it under the original glass. Instantly the lady's cheeks and lips glow bright red.

"Nah, now she looks tarty."

I laugh. "Yes, that's the problem; we can't have Eugenie Penrose looking like a streetwalker . . ."

"Even if she's not Eugenie Penrose, but her crazy sister, Clare?"

I look up from the window to the detective's face. He's still studying the figure on the table and I suddenly realize that this is just how he stood above Christine's body yesterday—and no doubt will stand above her body after it's been autopsied.

"Where did you hear that?" I switch off the light box—as if I could, by shielding the lady, make up for not being able to spare Christine's poor body from the inspection of strangers.

"From the college president, Gavin Penrose, and a few of the trustees I saw at St. Al's this morning—" *Ah, so he didn't get up early solely out of filial duty,* I think, "—and from Penrose's secretary, Fay Morgan. Although shocked at the news of Christine Webb's death they seemed equally shocked at the content of her lecture last week."

"It doesn't take much to shock the trustees. They're very protective of the college's reputation; that's what being a trustee is all about—they're entrusted with the college's welfare."

"Oh, is that what it means; I always wondered. Of course the one who seemed most put out with the lecture's content was Penrose."

"Really? I thought Gavin looked pleased with the lecture."

"According to his secretary he and Miss Webb argued about the lecture's content before she gave it."

"Fay's not always the most reliable of witnesses." I think about the strange conversation I had with Fay in the gym sauna and I'm about to tell the detective about it when he interrupts me. "She wasn't the only one who heard the argument. It was at a brunch at the president's house. Several of the trustees overheard President Penrose accusing Miss Webb of not having the college's best interest at heart. I spoke to Penrose this morning and he said he was *regretful* about having argued with Miss

Webb but that he'd been worried that some of the content of the lecture might distress the trustees. Apparently Miss Webb finally agreed to edit out some of the more objectionable parts."

I think of the moment Christine paused while flipping through her note cards. It was just when she'd mentioned the Victorians' belief that madness was hereditary. I'd thought that she was cutting out something in consideration of my feelings—knowing how often I've dwelled over the years on the chances of Bea inheriting her father's mental condition—but now I see that it's more likely she was trying to appease Gavin Penrose. After all, Clare Barovier was his great-aunt. While I've been distracted with this thought Falco has wandered over to the spiral staircase.

"Where do these stairs lead to?"

"To my living area—" I'm about to make an excuse about unmade beds and messes caused by fifteen-year-olds packing for eight-week camping trips but he's already halfway up the spiral stairs. He's greeted at the top by two sleepy-looking greyhounds. The dogs spent half the night trailing Bea around, eyeing her suitcases with deep suspicion, and have only now roused themselves.

"*Che Bella,*" the detective croons, scratching Francesca behind her ear. Francesca rubs her long muzzle against his leg while Paolo whimpers for attention.

"They're usually shyer around strangers," I say, edging past the greyhound lovefest and opening the rooftop door. I'd like to get him outside before he can notice the chaos left behind in Bea's wake. Not that I'm so proud about my housekeeping—it's just that I have a sudden aversion to having my private life scrutinized by those coolly assessing gray eyes.

It's not my laundry and unwashed dishes, though, that he's interested in. When we get out on the roof he immediately moves to the edge and points toward the boathouse.

"You mentioned yesterday that you and Miss Webb stopped at the kayak rental before proceeding to the train station, right? And you spoke to a—" he takes a small spiral-bound notebook out of his pocket and looks at it, "—a Mr. Swanson."

"Kyle Swanson. Yes, he runs the kayaking center. My daughter and I have both taken lessons from him."

"Your daughter had been out kayaking with Mr. Swanson . . . How old is your daughter, again?"

"Beatrice is fifteen. Kyle Swanson also coaches the girls' crew team at Rosedale High. We've known him for over a year . . . is there something wrong with that? Something I should know about Kyle?"

Detective Falco, ignoring my question, asks, "Did Mr. Swanson mention to you that there were two kayaks missing from the boathouse?"

I nod. "Yes, he did, but wait a minute . . . if there were something I should know about Kyle Swanson—a reason why I wouldn't want my daughter to be alone with him, you'd tell me, wouldn't you?"

"I'm not at liberty to give out that kind of information, Miss McKay. I would advise not allowing a minor to be alone with any adult you don't know very well. If we can return to the issue of the kayaks for a moment . . . we found the second one beached on this side of the river, which suggests to me that someone went with her and came back."

"But if someone was with her why wouldn't he or she help her when she tipped over?"

"Maybe Christine Webb tipped over, hit her head on the stone wall, and drowned before whoever she was with could save her. Maybe the other kayaker panicked and didn't want to be implicated in a drowning accident."

Falco pauses but continues looking at me. I can't see his expression because his eyes are still shaded by his hand, but I can sense the force of his attention and that he's waiting for something. It takes me only a moment to realize that he's giving me a chance to admit that I was the one with Christine that night.

I shake my head. "You obviously don't know me very well," I tell him. "I'd never go out on the river at night. Not even for my best friend."

"So you think it would have to be someone more confident in their boating skills?"

"You mean like Kyle Swanson? I can't imagine Christine asking him to go with her—or that he would agree."

I remember, suddenly, the questions Christine asked me about Kyle while we were walking to the train station. I'd thought she was just teasing me about my involvement with him but what if she were feeling out the situation because she was interested in him? It wouldn't be the first time we were both attracted to the same man.

"So you think Christine got off the train to take a moonlit kayak trip with a man she'd just met half an hour before?" I ask.

"I hadn't actually thought that Mr. Swanson was the main attraction. Your daughter said that she mentioned to Miss Webb that the Wicomico Creek afforded access to the Penrose estate—private property, by the way, but I'm sure you've spoken to her about trespassing—oh no, wait, I guess not, because you went back onto the Penrose property yesterday."

"*Back?*" I ask. "I've never been to the estate before."

"But you do know it's private property?"

"Are you planning to arrest me for trespassing, Detective Falco? Because if you are maybe I shouldn't be talking to you without a lawyer. . . ."

Falco raises a hand and then gestures toward the two lawn chairs where Christine and I sat last week. "No, no, not at all, Miss McKay. Please, I'm sorry if I gave you that impression. Can we sit down? I just want to figure out what happened to your friend. I imagine that's what you want as well."

"Of course I do," I say, swatting the soot off one of the chairs. Detective Falco has already sat down in the other one as seemingly unconcerned about the fate of his Sunday suit pants as Christine had been about her dress last week. "I'm just not sure how much I can help you. I know that Christine was interested in Penrose's water gardens but I can't imagine what she would have wanted to see so badly that she would paddle across the river in the middle of the night."

"You mean she wasn't the type to get that wrapped up in her research?"

Something in the way he phrases the question makes me pretty sure that the detective has already spoken to Nathan Bell and has heard about Christine's obsessive nature. Feeling like I'm being led into a trap I try to swerve in another direction. "Christine wasn't a 'type' at all, Detective Falco, she was unique. She cared passionately about the subjects she pursued and was rigorous in her scholarship. But she'd already delivered her lecture on the Penrose window. She'd uncovered some very interesting facts about Eugenie Penrose's younger sister, Clare Barovier," I say, sounding, I know, a little as if I'm a lecturer myself. "I thought she made a very convincing case for identifying the iconography of the window with the Lady of Shalott legend and connecting it to the story of Clare Barovier's mental collapse and confinement in a mental hospital. You see, the lady in the story is confined to a tower and forbidden to look directly at the world—"

"And then she sees Lancelot in her mirror and she just has to look at him and the spell is broken. 'Out flew the web and floated wide; the mirror crack'd from side to side. "The curse is come upon me," cried the Lady of Shalott.'"

I try to hide my surprise at the detective's command of Tennyson but I can tell from his grin that I have failed. "Freshman Comp at John Jay. I liked 'The Charge of the Light Brigade' better myself. Kind of a coincidence, though, when you think about it, that your friend died in the same way as the heroine of the poem she'd just been reciting in her lecture."

"The Lady of Shalott didn't drown," I say primly. *So much for your command of Tennyson*, I think.

"Your friend may not have either."

CHAPTER EIGHT

"How can you know that?" I ask. "Isn't it too early for you to have the autopsy results?"

Detective Falco tilts his head sideways and narrows his pale gray eyes. I have a feeling that the look he's giving me is pretty much the same one I gave him when he quoted from Tennyson.

"You're right," he says. "We don't know it for sure but the medical examiner's preliminary report says there's little or no water in the lungs—and we found this—" He pulls a plastic bag out of his jacket pocket and holds it up. Inside is an amber-colored plastic pill case—the kind with little compartments to store a daily dose. It's exactly like the one that Fay Morgan said she saw Christine take a pill from last Sunday. "—inside Miss Webb's jacket pocket."

"Pills? You think Christine took an overdose? She paddled up Wicomico Creek and then swallowed—what? How do you know what was in there? They could have been vitamins."

Falco gives the bag a sharp shake and I hear a rattle. I

lean forward to get a closer look. The early morning light turns the ordinary plastic into a surprisingly lovely shade of buttery yellow—not unlike the silver stain in medieval glass. I notice that all of the numbered compartments— enough for a month's worth of medication—are empty except for the last one, in which a pink oval tablet rests next to a round orange pill.

"The pink tablet is Luvox, an antidepressant, and the orange one is Klonopin, a tranquilizer that is also used as an antianxiety medication. I reached Miss Webb's physician last night and he confirmed the prescription for Luvox, but not the one for Klonopin. Did your friend ever mention to you that she was taking either one or the other of these pills?"

I lean back in my chair. "I knew about the Luvox but not the Klonopin, but then she might not have wanted me to know she was taking a tranquilizer."

"Why not?"

"She had a bad history with tranquilizers. She was given some to help her sleep after she broke her leg and she kind of got hooked on them."

"In fact she overdosed on them, isn't that right?"

"Did Fay Morgan tell you that? God, it's amazing how gossip lives on in a little college like Penrose. The overdose was an accident . . ."

"I didn't say it wasn't. Still it is a *history*, as they say. Was that time in college the only time she overdosed?"

I look away from the detective toward the river. It's still early enough that there's mist rising from the water, an opaque coating that reminds me of the white enamel paint I use on glass sometimes. I think of Christine lying beneath the surface of that water and feel cold in spite of the sun. I realize that my reluctance to answer the detective's questions comes from a desire to protect Christine, but clearly she is far beyond any need for my protection.

"No," I answer, "but you probably know that already. Four and a half years ago she was admitted to Bellevue because she overdosed on tranquilizers."

"Yes, in fact, Christine's mother mentioned it. Still, I'd like to hear it from you. How did the substance abuse problems begin?"

"Well, she probably had a drinking problem as far back as college, only we all drank a lot then, so I didn't really think about it. Then six or seven years ago she started taking pills, too. It started when she was writing regularly for an art journal and she said she was having trouble making her deadlines. She took Ritalin, because she said it helped her focus, and some other kind of amphetamines to stay awake. Then she would need tranquilizers to help her sleep . . . she mentioned she was taking Halcion once. She told me about it because she thought I'd get a kick out of the mythological reference—" I pause to see if Falco's Greek mythology is up to his Victorian poetry but he's shaking his head.

"You Penrose girls! Never at a loss for the literary reference."

"I'm sorry—I know it sounds silly. It's not important . . ."

"No, no, I'll never rest now unless I hear the story. Can I have the Cliff's Notes version though?"

"Sure. Halcyone was the daughter of Aeolus, god of the winds, and she was married to Ceyx, son of Hesperus, the evening star."

"A match made in heaven."

"They *were* very happy together, but Ceyx decides to go on a sea voyage and Halcyone has a presentiment of doom. She begs him not to go, or at least to take her with him, but he goes anyway. If he's going to die, he figures, he'd rather she be spared."

"Big of him."

"Yes, well Halcyone's fears prove grounded. Ceyx's ship is caught in a storm. In his last dying moments he begs the gods to bring his drowned body home to Halcyone so that she can bury him."

"That's what I never got about these Greek myths—if he could ask for that why couldn't the gods just save him?"

I laugh. "I know. My ex-husband always explained it by quoting his favorite literary source, 'You can't always get what you want—'"

"'But if you try sometime, you just might find, you get what you need.'"

"Tennyson *and* the Rolling Stones. I'm impressed, Detective Falco."

"Yeah, call me Mr. Renaissance Man," he says. I notice that he hasn't asked me to call him by his first name. "So go on. Ceyx's body comes back to his poor grieving widow?"

"Well, not at first. Halcyone keeps praying to Juno to bring her husband back . . ."

"Your namesake."

"She *is* the goddess of marriage. It bothers Juno, though, to go on hearing these prayers for a dead man—she feels it defiles her altars—so she sends Iris to the god of sleep, Somnus, who sends his son, Morpheus, in a dream to Halcyone to let her know that Ceyx is dead."

"Quite a chain of command there."

"The gods are big on delegating," I reply, getting into the spirit of the story. For now I have forgotten why I am telling it. I am back in college telling it to Neil, who loved it so much he did a series of paintings based on the myth. He especially loved the part where Morpheus visits Halcyone in the guise of drowned Ceyx.

"Halcyone believes the dream because her husband appears to her not as he was in life, but pale, naked, and dripping in seawater. In the morning she goes down to the shore and there, floating out in the water, she sees Ceyx's drowned body. As she reaches out to him she's trans-formed into a bird and when she touches Ceyx he, too, is changed into a bird."

"So they get to live together as birds?"

"Yes. And for seven days during the winter when they're sitting on their nest—which floats on the ocean—Aeolus reins in his winds. Hence the term *halcyon days*—a time of peace and tranquility."

"Or a drug to make you feel that way. Who knew the pharmaceutical companies were so literary? And you say this was why your friend Christine called up to tell you she was taking these pills? Because she thought you'd appre-ciate the mythological reference?"

"My ex-husband, Neil Buchwald, did a series of

paintings based on the Halcyone myth. She said she thought it was ironic—that if Neil had *taken* Halcion instead of *painted* Halcyone he might not have ended up in a psychiatric hospital . . ."

"Wait a second, back up. Your ex is in a psychiatric hospital?" For the first time this morning I see a look of genuine surprise on the detective's face.

"You mean none of the Penrose gossips you spoke to this morning mentioned that? The story's usually hauled out any time something goes amiss at Penrose. You see, Neil was admitted to the college as an exchange student during my junior year. The college was experimenting at the time with the idea of going coed. After I got pregnant and Neil had a rather spectacular mental collapse the plans for coeducation were ditched."

"A *spectacular* mental collapse?"

I get up and walk to the railing. Only a few patches of mist remain, leaving streaks of white against the blue as if a layer of enamel has been scratched away to reveal the colored glass beneath. That's what Falco's questions have been—a scratching away to reveal some pattern in the glass.

"There was one incident senior year, but the real clincher is what happened the next year. Neither of us was attending Penrose at the time so it shouldn't have concerned the college but still it was here in Rosedale . . ."

"Why don't you just tell me what happened, Miss McKay?"

"He took a boat out on the river and tried to drown himself."

"I see."

"No," I say, turning back to the detective. "You don't. He took me and Bea along with him. He tried to drown us as well."

DETECTIVE FALCO GIVES ME A FEW MINUTES TO COLLECT MYSELF before asking his next question. "Did you and Christine discuss the incident with your ex-husband—the drowning attempt—last Sunday night?"

"We didn't discuss it, but she did allude to it. I told her that I sometimes dreamed about Neil, and she wanted to know which Neil I dreamed about—the sane Neil or the crazy one, the Neil we knew when we first met him or the Neil that took me out on the river that day."

"And?"

"I didn't tell her. I lied and said I really didn't dream about him at all." Falco looks away from me when I confess my lie, as if to spare me the embarrassment. I think of the things he must have heard people confess to and try to believe that my little lie to Christine must seem slight in comparison, but then I remember the closed look that had come over Christine's face when I lied to her. Had she brought up the incident on the river because she was already thinking of killing herself? If I hadn't lied would she have told me what she was planning? And if she had, could I have stopped her? Could I have helped her any more than I'd been able to help Neil?

I expect that these are the questions going through Falco's mind, but his next question takes me by surprise.

"But you do dream about him—like Halcyone dreams of Ceyx. So who does Morpheus send in your sleep? Sane Neil or crazy Neil?"

I can't imagine what bearing my answer could have on his investigation, but I tell him just the same. Maybe to make up for not telling Christine. "Neither. The Neil who shows up in my dreams is dead. It's as if he succeeded that day and drowned. He comes to me, just as Ceyx came to Halcyone, like a drowned man."

I LET DETECTIVE FALCO OUT THE SIDE DOOR AND WATCH HIM GO down the fire stairs, hoping he doesn't notice the rusted-out spots and cite me for some code violation. When he gets to the bottom step he lifts a hand up in farewell but doesn't turn around. Instead of turning toward River Street where he left his car he turns left and heads toward the boathouse. I wonder if he has more questions for Kyle, but when he gets to the boathouse he veers right, toward the landing beach. When I lose sight of him behind a stand of willows on the edge of the water I go back inside.

The sight of the mess left in the wake of Bea's departure does nothing to cheer me and even though I'm exhausted I know that if I lie down I won't be able to sleep. So instead I start collecting the piles of laundry that lie scattered around the loft and stuffing them into a black garbage bag. I move quickly, not even stopping to find a tissue to wipe my eyes, but no matter how hard I work I can't keep at bay the image of Christine hanging upside down in the clear water of Wicomico Creek. The thought that she got there by her own hand is unbearable. How could I have let her get on that train? I knew something was bothering her and with her *history*—as the detective put it—I should have known not to let her leave alone. I also know, though, that the minute she started talking about Neil I was ready to see her go. Had she brought up Neil's drowning attempt because she was already planning to kill herself that way? Would she have asked me to go with her if I hadn't lied to her about the dreams?

And is that what Detective Falco thinks happened— that I went along with Christine on her suicidal mission and fled the scene when her kayak capsized? If only I *had* been there.

I pick up the bag I've just stuffed as well as the bag that still holds the dust-covered work clothes I wore last week and haul them both down the side stairs. I'd usually take the car with this much laundry, but today I seem to crave the backbreaking labor of dragging the heavy load down River Street—like some medieval penitent flogging himself through the streets of plague-ridden Europe. A homeless man wheeling his shopping cart full of tattered possessions, and the tolling of bells from St. Aloysius's help complete the image for me.

At the laundromat I sort the regular laundry into light and dark loads and then dump my work clothes—after covering my mouth and nose with a clean bandana—into one of the oversized machines. I set the dial for hot. I'm just about to pour in detergent when I notice some papers sticking out from under a pair of jeans. As soon as I reach in and touch the thick, rough pages I remember what they are—the discarded sketches we found in the stone groove during the removal of the Lady window.

Cursing at myself for forgetting about them, I pull the wad of folded paper out of the washing machine and tap them against the edge of the tub to shake the dust off them. *Some conservator*, I think, *about to use industrial-strength cleaning solvents on fragile archival material.*

When I've pumped in enough quarters to start all the machines I stick the pages in my bag and walk down the street to Cafe Galatea, or Gal's as the locals call it, an Italian bakery that's one of the few surviving downtown businesses. Housewives and society matrons from the Heights still stop off at Gal's after dropping their husbands off at the train station, to pick up cannolis and biscotti for bridge luncheons and Italian cheesecake and tiramisu for dinner parties. In an hour, when late mass lets out at St. Al's there'll be an after-church crowd, but for now there are only two old men playing chess at a corner table and a teenage boy who, between sips of black espresso, is stealing glances at the beautiful girl behind the counter.

"Ciao, Portia, Come stai?"

"Bene, Zia Juno." I'm not really Portia's aunt—I think we're second cousins actually. After my mother died my father avoided her family, and most of them repaid the favor. Because Portia's just a few years older than Bea, though, I've stayed more in touch with her and her mother—who was my mother's favorite cousin.

"Any news from Penrose?" I ask. Portia shakes her head and sighs. She'd been wait-listed at the college a month before. I know it's her first choice and I can't help thinking that if only I had graduated I might have more pull in getting her in.

"*E tuo amico? Chi e?*" I ask after ordering an amaretto cappuccino and a hazelnut biscotti to go.

Portia rolls her lovely almond-shaped eyes up toward the stamped tin ceiling and tells me, in Italian, that he's a new kid in school and that her English teacher assigned them to do a project together on *The Merchant of Venice*. "*E' sempre qui.*"

I glance over at the poor love-struck boy. It's obvious why he's here all the time. He's smitten with Portia. The patches of red streaking his acne-pitted skin, though, must be coming from more than his proximity to his beloved. I notice that's he's reading *La Vita Nuova* in the original Italian and guess the cause of his blushes. I quickly scribble on a Cinzano coaster, "I think he understands Italian," and slide it across the bar to where Portia's lowering the press to make my cappuccino.

"Shit," Portia says in English and loudly enough to draw the attention of the two chess players.

"*Scusi, Zii, mi sono bruciato il dito sul macinino da caffe.*" Portia points to the offending machine and holds up the supposedly burnt finger. I notice, as I leave, that the boy is grinning into his Dante.

I take my coffee and biscotti to a bench outside facing the river, remembering only after I sit down that I haven't washed my hands since handling the lead-contaminated clothes. Fortunately, Portia's put the biscotti in a bag so I put it aside and take out the coffee, being careful not to touch the rim of the blue and white to-go cup with its stylized rendering of the Parthenon. I take a sip, savoring the combination of rich, bitter espresso beans and the sweet almond amaretto. Christine told me once that she was forever ordering amaretto lattes from Starbucks and forever being disappointed because they never got the combination right like Gal's did.

I push away the thought of Christine and take out the folded pages from my bag—figuring I might as well handle them now before I wash my hands. The first page—the one I looked at in the library last week—is covered with sketches of a woman's face. I remember that Ernesto thought they were probably discarded sketches for the window, and the face depicted does resemble the face of the lady of the window even though none of the details of costume or setting are the same. Still, the curve of her cheek, the way her head tilts to one side, even, in one sketch, the way the woman's fingers trail through her own hair, all recall the image in the window. So I'm surprised when I turn the page sideways and see that the writing there is dated June 21, 1892—three years before the Penroses came to America and thirty years before the window was installed at Penrose. Could the window actually be based on sketches that Augustus Penrose did thirty years earlier when he was still in England?

I hold the page up to the light to make out the minute handwriting. The overall effect of the penmanship is of some intricate embroidery pattern. Even though it's small, each letter is precisely rendered—as if the writer had just taken a class in calligraphy—and I'm able, once I stop looking at it as decoration, to make out what it says.

Today we went boating on the river with Augustus Penrose, son of the owner of the glassworks which Papa has bought. He drew these sketches of Clare. He said she was his very ideal of a character in a poem which he recited by heart and is called "The Lady of Shalott" by Alfred Lord Tennyson. I thought it a morbid poem and wasn't sure I liked my sister being compared to a sorceress who lost her wits for love of a stranger, but Mr. Penrose just laughed and said it was obvious we were both sorceresses to have so enchanted him and made him lose his wits. Then he asked if Clare would consent to pose for a painting of The Lady of Shalott. I began to answer that we'd have to ask our father, but Clare—ever impetuous Clare!—was already accepting and having the man write down the directions to his studio. I was sure Papa would object but instead he said that because he was connected in business to the young man's family he supposed it would be fine. He said that as long as I chaperoned Clare he didn't see any harm in us going. Clare was ecstatic and we spent the rest of the day altering my good white muslin dress for her to wear because, as she says, "I have nothing suitable to lose my wits in!"

At the last line I shiver despite the warm sun on my back. What a chilling presentiment of Clare Barovier's future madness! I can't help wondering if it was some hint of that madness that caused Augustus Penrose to see her as the perfect model for his Lady of Shalott.

I turn to the next page to see if the entry is continued

but find a new date—several days later—at the top of the page. I flip through the rest of the pages and find that they're densely crammed with Eugenie's small, precise handwriting—the only sketches are those on the first page. What I've got here are pages from Eugenie Penrose's diary from the day she met Augustus Penrose through the first weeks of their acquaintance—courtship, actually, because even though this first entry gives no hint of it (she makes it sound as if Clare were the object of Penrose's interest) I know from what I've read about the Penroses that they married only three months after they met and left almost immediately for America. The only journals that the college has, though, date from after the founding of the college. These pages—which I very nearly destroyed!—represent an incredible find for the college archives. I suppose I should be excited, but all I can think about is that the person who would have been most interested in Eugenie Penrose's girlhood diary is dead.

CHAPTER NINE

IN MY DREAM I HEAR SOMEONE COMING UP THE STEPS FROM THE river. I think it's Neil—it's always Neil—but when I open the door I see it's Christine.

"We have to talk," she says. She's wearing the same slim black sheath, leather jacket, and knee-high boots she wore to give her lecture.

"Of course," I say, following her out onto the roof. She sits down in the torn vinyl lawn chair and I start to drag the rusted metal chair toward her but she holds up a hand.

"I need something to drink first."

So I go into the loft and retrieve a bottle of water from the fridge but when I look for glasses I see that they're all dirty. Dozens of Ernesto's long-stemmed goblets are bobbing in dirty dishwater.

I hold one under the spigot, delicately sponging away the gray water, but just when I've gotten it clean the glass shatters in my hand. I fish another one out of the murky water but it, too, implodes under the lightest pressure from my fingertips. One after another, each glass crumples in my hands until I've gone through a dozen of Ernesto's lovely goblets and the gray dishwater is tinged pink with my own blood.

Finally I open the cabinet above the sink and take out two jelly glasses decorated with faded Disney characters: Ursula from *The Little Mermaid* and Maleficent from *Sleeping Beauty*. I fill the stubby glasses with sparkling water and take them out to the rooftop. Christine has let down her hair and I notice that she's intertwined long green-and-white-striped ribbons through the damp locks. I hand her the Ursula glass and sit down next to her. She turns to me but just as she begins to talk we both hear someone knocking on the side door.

"He must have followed me," she says.

I turn back to tell her that he can wait but already the dream is fading, the long green ribbons in her hair—no, not ribbons, but grass, long strands of the striped zebra grass that grows at the bottom of the Hudson—are melting like glass canes twisted in the furnace. I reach out to touch her arm and her skin shatters like Ernesto's goblets. I find myself in my own bed in a tangle of clean laundry and inert greyhounds—Paolo nested in the crook of my knees, Francesca curled up at my ankles—listening to a pounding in my head.

I lie perfectly still, eyes closed, willing myself back into the dream to hear what Christine had come to tell me, but though I can see her face it's like an image on a videotape that's been paused. It has no power to speak. The only thing I hear is the pounding—which I realize now is actually someone knocking at the side door.

When I lift myself out of bed I see that the sky is a pale overcast lavender that could be dawn or dusk. I can't remember when I went to sleep or what day it is. All I remember is that Christine is dead.

I open the metal door a crack, half expecting to find one of the drowned apparitions of my dreams, but it's only Kyle carrying a sack of groceries tucked under one arm and a bottle of wine in the other.

"I didn't know if you'd still feel up to dinner but I figured you could use the company," he says. "Were you working downstairs?"

"No, I was sleeping. I didn't get much sleep last night. What time is it?"

Kyle tries to turn the hand that's wrapped around the grocery bag, but it's obvious that he can't see around the bag to the watch. It's equally obvious that I should be stepping back to let him in, taking the bag, or at least the wine, out of his hands, and then moving forward to . . . what? Kiss him on the cheek? On the mouth? I'm as confused about what stage we are in as I am about the time and the day. For the last few weeks Kyle and I have been hovering on the edges of romantic attraction. We've brushed up against each other at crew matches, gotten drunk after Bea's gone to bed, and once, after one of my lessons at the college pool, made out in the sports equipment closet. I think we both expected this to be the night we'd end up in bed.

"I'm sorry," I say, "I completely forgot about dinner . . . the house is a mess and I didn't get a chance to go shopping—"

"Juno," he cuts in, "your best friend just died. I'm not here to be entertained; I'm here to take care of you."

I meet his gaze and see nothing but innocent compassion there. I could be looking at Francesca or Paolo when they want to be taken for a walk. He's wearing a Creedence Clearwater Revival T-shirt, and his dark, shoulder-length hair falls loosely forward as he leans toward me. *A boy*, I find myself thinking, even though he's the same age as I am. It's only because I had Bea so young that men—and women for that matter—my own age often seem so much younger.

I take the bottle of wine from him and lean forward to press my cheek against his, catching as I do a sweet earthy smell that reminds me at first of the river until I recognize it as marijuana.

"I got some organic mesclun at the farmer's market," he says, setting the grocery bag down on the kitchen counter, "and three kinds of wild mushrooms for soup. Have you ever had kombu?"

I shake my head and start rummaging through the silverware drawer for a corkscrew. Of course I realized before this that Kyle smoked pot and it's not as if I hadn't indulged in plenty of illegal substances in college. It's just that with Bea to raise I've tried to stay away from any drugs stronger than a glass of wine and the occasional Advil. *How else*, I've asked myself over the years, *could I tell her with a straight face—literally—to "just say no"*? And given what happened to Bea's father under the influence of drugs, I think it's a pretty good idea for Bea to stay away from them.

"It's seaweed," Kyle tells me when I find the corkscrew, "harvested off the coast of northern Japan and sun-dried right on the beach. I'm going to use it to make a dashi—a stock for the soup. It's excellent for digestion and the immune system." Kyle opens a plastic bag and pulls out something that looks like a dried plant stalk bent in half. He holds it up for me to inhale its sweet, low-tide smell.

"You have to take care of yourself when you're grieving, Juno," he says, laying the flat, broad blade of seaweed into a bowl of water. "Christine was very important to you."

"I think if I hadn't met Christine I would have spent my four years of college in the library or in my dorm room," I say turning the screw in the cork. "After my mother died I retreated into this hole. Christine pulled me out of it. She'd lost a parent, too. Her father died when she was little and her mother's always been a miserable person—shit, *Christine's mother*. Detective Falco said he was notifying her, but I should call to find out what she's doing about a funeral . . ."

Kyle takes the corkscrew—which I hadn't even realized I'd pulled out of the bottle—and folds my hand in both of his. "Take it one step at a time, Juno. The police probably won't release the body for at least another week."

"Did Detective Falco tell you that when he questioned you this morning?"

Kyle's hands on mine feel suddenly cool and damp. He gives my hand a final squeeze and lets it go to reach for a knife. "He told you that he talked to me?" he asks, turning back to the cutting board and starting to chop the mushrooms.

"Yes, but it's not like he said you were a suspect or anything . . ."

"A suspect!" His voice sounds surprised but he keeps chopping in the same, even rhythm. "A suspect in what? Don't they think she killed herself?"

"Did Falco tell you that?"

"No, but I remember you told me that she was a little unstable—didn't you say she had a lousy childhood and a drinking problem? And that she was on antidepressants?"

What he says is perfectly true and no doubt I did tell him, over a few glasses of wine, all about Christine's awful, near Dickensian, childhood—how the family worked in Briarwood and the only picnics they ever went on were with the patients and how no one understood why she wanted to go to college and study art history. I probably concluded that it was no wonder she ended up with a drinking problem and hadn't been able to settle into a real relationship for years. I'm sure I told her story with compassion and real regret that *things have been so hard for her* but the thought, now, of dragging Christine's problems out in front of a man I hardly know leaves me with a bad taste in my mouth. It reminds me a little too much of the way Fay talked about Christine the other day in the sauna.

"So what's the difference between taking anti-depressants and smoking pot? At least prescription drugs are legal." The words are out of my mouth before I even know I thought them. In fact, I'm not sure I do think that prescription drugs are better than pot. Kyle has stopped chopping now, the silver blade poised over the pile of finely minced brown flesh.

"Juno? Do you have a problem with me smoking? I mean, I knew you wanted to keep it hidden from Bea, but I thought you said you wouldn't mind getting high after she left for her rafting trip."

Did I? It sounds like something I might have said after a few glasses of wine.

"I'm not sure that doing anything illegal would be such a good idea with the police around . . ."

"Exactly what illegal activities did you have in mind?"

I'd only been thinking about the pot, but something in the way Kyle's avoiding eye contact with me makes me wonder if there's something else he's not telling me. "I don't know, Kyle," I say, "is there something you want to tell me about?"

Kyle turns to me slowly, the knife still in his hand. "That detective told you about what happened in Colorado, didn't he?"

"Detective Falco didn't tell me anything, Kyle." I look down at the point of the blade trembling in the air between us and he, following my gaze, lays the knife down on the counter. When I look back up at him I see tears standing in his eyes. "What happened in Colorado?"

"It wasn't my fault. There was an accident on a youth hostel rafting expedition I was leading and when the police came in a couple of the guides had some pot in their backpacks . . . it wasn't like we were getting high with the kids or that had anything to do with the accident . . ."

"What kind of accident?"

Kyle sighs and runs a hand through his dark, shoulder-length hair. I notice when he pulls the hair back that there are silver strands mixed in with the black. "I didn't want to tell you because I knew it would freak you out about Bea's trip. A kid was killed. He capsized and hit a rock. He broke his neck."

"Shit, Kyle. How could you not tell me a thing like that?"

"Yeah, well, I guess it's a little like you not mentioning that your husband tried to drown you and Bea."

I close my eyes and take a deep breath to steady myself and instantly I'm on the river that day in the boat with Neil and Bea. We've rowed out to the middle of the river where the currents are most dangerous. World's End, the Dutch called it, because of the confluence of currents that wreaked havoc on ship navigators. Neil loved going there. He said he could feel the spirits of shipwrecked sailors calling to him from the bottom of the river. He'd been up for days trying to finish a series of paintings for his first really big gallery showing. I'd been up, too, nursing eight-month-old Bea through whooping cough—Neil had refused to have her inoculated because he believed the vaccination program was a government plot to compromise our immune systems or control our dreams—I can't remember which.

He had become obsessed with his dreams. I remember that. Ever since I told him the story of Halcyone and Ceyx he'd been convinced we could visit each other in our dreams. *Try*, he'd whisper in my ear before I fell asleep each night, *to visit me tonight and hold something in your hand—don't tell me what—and I'll tell you what you were holding in the morning.* I'd go to sleep imagining that I held a feather, a rock, a blade of grass. A surprising number of times he guessed right in the morning, but the morning he took us out in the boat he said I'd come to him in his dream carrying a knife and that I'd slashed his paintings. *But you didn't even sleep last night,* I'd pleaded with him.

It's that you don't trust me anymore, he said, ignoring the truth of what I said. He asked me to come out with him in the boat. He said it would prove I trusted him. I pleaded that Bea was still too sick. I suggested we at least drop her off at my father's house, but he said he had to know I trusted him with our child's life. I knew that since Bea was born he'd felt like I had withdrawn from him, that I'd become too protective—too timid. I wasn't the girl who'd scaled heights with him and rowed across the Hudson in a summer storm. And what about him, I'd wanted to scream, was he the same boy I'd sat next to in Dante class? The gentle artist who'd sketched my face and made me feel more beautiful than I ever imagined myself? The boy who'd recite the cantos to me in Italian while we made love? No, he wasn't the same boy, but still I didn't believe he'd hurt us.

"Who told you about that?" I ask Kyle, my eyes still closed.

"Bea told me. She said it was the reason you didn't like to go out on the river."

I open my eyes and I'm looking down into a bowl filled

with fat green slugs, swollen things smelling of brine and drowned bodies. Even when I realize it's the seaweed, not slugs, I'm already gagging. Kyle snatches the bowl away, slopping poisonous green water on the counter. The dead sea smell rises up like a noxious gas as Kyle pours the bowl into the sink and the bloated seaweed slithers over the lip of the bowl like a live eel. I can feel the bile rising in my throat. It's how Bea and I both smelled when the Coast Guard fished us out of the river—a brackish odor that lingered in our hair and on our skin for days and lingers still in my dreams.

KYLE STAYS FOR ANOTHER HOUR OR SO AFTER THE SEAWEED incident. While I heat up a can of Campbell's tomato soup he makes us grilled cheese sandwiches. To his credit, he doesn't say a word about preservatives or the evils of dairy. In return, I don't ask him any more about the boy in Colorado, but he tells me anyway. How he knew the instant he saw the raft overturn that the boy had been killed—*I was ten feet behind him and even over the roar of the rapids I heard the crack of his head against the rocks*—but still he risked his own life diving into the water and dragging his body to the shore, where he performed CPR on him until the ambulance came.

"Could the same thing have happened to Christine? Could she have hit her head on the stone wall when she capsized?"

Kyle shakes his head. "I can't see the impact being hard enough to kill her in a slow-moving creek like the

Wicomico. Although I suppose it might have been hard enough to knock her out. Then—if she were alone—she might drown."

"Or if the person she went with was ahead of her at the time and didn't see her capsize he—or she—might not get to her until it was too late."

Kyle looks up from his mug of soup and smiles. "Sorry, Juno, Falco already tried that trick on me—giving me a chance to confess that I was there. He even told me that they found a pill container in her pocket so I'd feel less guilty if I had been there. But I wasn't. Besides, if I had been crazy enough to take her out on the river at night I'd have stayed behind and kept an eye on her the whole time. So unless you believe I deliberately killed your friend . . ."

"I don't, of course I don't believe that, Kyle. Falco presented the same scenario to me. I guess he thinks it could have been me in the other kayak."

"It makes more sense. The other kayak was wider. It'd be the one you'd pick if you were going out on the river at night."

"Do you see me doing that, Kyle?"

He grins. It's the first time either of us has smiled since he got here. I try to return the smile but it feels like I'm posing for a picture instead of responding to another human being.

"No, I don't," he says, lifting his hand to stroke my cheek. I feel the muscles of my face relax out of the false smile at his touch. It occurs to me that there's still a chance that Kyle and I could come out of this okay—that the suspicion and mistrust we're both feeling doesn't have to be the end of whatever was beginning between us. "Not with your fear of the water—especially now that I know why you're so afraid of going out on the river."

Kyle moves closer and pushes his hand through my hair, his callused fingertips kneading into my scalp and then down into the knotted muscles in my neck. I let my head fall forward, easing into the weight of his hands, and my hair falls in front of my face like a curtain between us. He brushes back my hair and tucks it behind my ear. It's the same gesture Christine made on the train platform when she asked me about Kyle. What had she asked me? *Have you felt that much for anyone since Neil?* Kyle ducks his head to kiss me. I have only to lift my head to meet him halfway, but instead I'm remembering how I answered Christine. *I'm not sure I ever want to feel that much for anyone again.*

I don't move away, but I don't move toward him either. I feel curiously frozen, trapped in the moment like a bubble inside a glass paperweight. I've watched Ernesto make those bubbles. You stick the tip of your pincers into the hot glass and then twist. The glass closes over the pocket of air, trapping it forever. When Kyle moves away from me it feels like the space he's left between us has been sealed over with something harder than cooling glass.

He doesn't stay long after that. When he leaves, I try to go to sleep but I toss and turn so much that even Paolo and Francesca grow disgusted with me and retreat to Bea's bed, where they curl up together, nose to rear, like a monotone yin yang. I turn on the light, determined to read myself to sleep, but the books on my night table might as well be in Sanskrit for all the interest they hold for me. Then I remember Eugenie Penrose's journal pages and get up to retrieve them from my bag.

The second entry is dated June 27, 1892. Five days after the first entry.

> *Today we went to Augustus Penrose's studio. Clare wore my white muslin, the hem much taken up to fit her. She complained bitterly of her "diminutive stature" as I cut off a good six inches of the bottom ruffle.*
>
> *"It's not fair you should get all the height," she said with her usual petulant—yet adorable—pout. "Was my father all that much shorter than Papa Barovier?"*
>
> *"I suppose he was," I answered, forgiving her for forgetting that I was only eight when Mama ran away with my drawing master. How could I remember his height? And why would I want to remember anything about the awful man who took Mama away?*
>
> *We walked the rest of the way along the footpath by the river in silence. Clare in white, me in my plain blue serge. Not a dress to "lose your wits in" at all—but sensible and not likely to show dust, which I was grateful for when I saw the state of Mr. Penrose's studio. It's in an old boathouse shaded by a giant beech tree and so near the river I could feel the damp in my bones. I at least had a shawl, but Clare, who sat in a boat upon the hard cold floor, had nothing but her thin white dress and her own hair—which Mr. Penrose insisted she let down loose around her shoulders.*

I brought some needlework to keep me busy while Clare posed but I must confess I got very little work done. Positioned as I was, behind the easel, I was able to see Mr. Penrose at work on his preliminary sketches, which I found most interesting to observe. Between watching his progress and listening to his comments—he is a great admirer of William Morris and had much to say of interest about the value of honest workmanship—I was surprised that the three hours passed so quickly—less quickly, I'm afraid, for poor Clare, who was quite stiff and frozen in her boat by the time we remembered about her. I'm afraid she was quite cross with me on the walk home. I wonder if the whole undertaking is not a mistake. Whether poor Clare really has the stamina to pose for long periods of time. She has, like many of the artistic temperament, a delicate constitution which I imagine she inherited from her father. But when I ventured to suggest we abandon the scheme she flew into one of her fits and I was all afternoon trying to soothe her. Best to proceed as we planned, I suppose. Nothing so upsets dear Clare as a change in plans.

Or having her older—and taller—half sister usurp her in a young man's affections, I think, laying the journal pages down on the bed by my side. Could Eugenie really have been so blind not to see that Clare's fit (*one* of her fits, she'd written; how often did she have these fits?) was caused by jealousy over Penrose's attentions to herself? Perhaps she simply couldn't imagine anyone preferring her to her prettier, more vivacious (albeit volatile) younger sister. Or was that prim, self-effacing tone a ruse meant to conceal even from herself her own burgeoning interest in Augustus Penrose? Whether genuine or sham, Eugenie's narrative accomplishes one thing—it's taken my mind off Christine's death for the moment. I close my eyes and see not the awful image of Christine below the water but instead two sisters walking home along the path by the river in their long Victorian dresses in white and blue. An image that sees me into a deep—and dreamless—sleep.

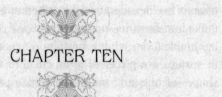

CHAPTER TEN

I SLEEP LATE THE NEXT MORNING AND AWAKEN TO THE SMELL of lead solder. Coming down the stairs I see Ernesto at the light table bent over a tray of glass, and Robbie at another workbench soldering a crack in one of the ruby-red folds of the Lady's dress. From my vantage point on the steps I can see that Robbie's solder line is smooth and even, a perfect silver band, as delicate and shiny as scar tissue. Robbie has a steady hand, patience, and a great eye for color; he'd make an excellent stained-glass conservator. I know, though, that his real ambition is to be a painter. This is just a summer job between semesters at Parsons. When he graduates he plans to share an apartment with three or four other students over in DUMBO or Williamsburg, paying the rent with graphic arts jobs while hoping to be discovered by the art world. I wonder whether if we could get funding to turn the factory into an art center—with studios and stipends for working artists—young artists like Robbie would stick around Rosedale.

"Good work," I tell Robbie, walking by him to the coffeemaker. He doesn't lift his head but I can see the edges of his Plexiglas mask lift as he smiles. I don't want to make him nervous so I take my cup of coffee over to the light table to see what Ernesto's doing. Spread out on the lit surface are pieces of glass cut into the low curving shapes of hills and mountains. Each piece is a slightly different shade of green, blue, or purple. Assembled together they make up the hills in the inset window—or mirror, if Christine was right in her interpretation—above the Lady's head. The landscape's the most complicated part of the restoration because Penrose used a plating technique to create the illusion of depth, layering separate sheets of glass on top of one another so that the lily pool appears bottomless, the branches of the weeping beech dense and shadowy, and the mountains seem to recede into a misty distance of sky and cloud. Of course we numbered and diagrammed each piece before taking them apart, but I notice that Ernesto's not looking at the blueprint I drew up. Instead he's moving the pieces around on the table with the intent focus of a kindergartner assembling a picture puzzle.

"I think they got this wrong," he says when I sit down on the high stool next to him.

"Who got it wrong?"

"Mr. Penrose . . . or whoever he paid to put together these mountains. They got it backward."

"You mean because they're not in the same order as the real mountains on the other side of the river? My friend Christine said in her lecture that was because it's actually a mirror reflection of the window. See, if you rearrange them—" I try to arrange the mountains the way Christine had suggested they should go, but when I'm finished they don't look at all right. "Anyway, it's not supposed to be a photo-perfect rendition of the Hudson Highlands, just a suggestion of the landscape across the river . . ."

Ernesto shakes his head. "Then why is this piece in the back—" He holds up the plate of green glass. "—green?"

The thick glass he's holding up in the light from the window is streaked through with a number of colors— iridescent swirls of purple and plumes of peacock blue— even a wavy line of palest aqua, but it is predominantly green.

"Uh . . . because the hills are forested and trees are green?" I suggest. The truth is I have no idea what Ernesto's getting at. Although a loyal employee and a brilliant hot-glass worker, his English is a little shaky and some of his ideas can be a bit fanciful.

"All these hills got trees, girl," he says, shaking his head. It could be the opening line of a spiritual. *All these hills got trees, girl, all God's children's got* . . . "But it's only the closest one where you can see the trees. The ones farthest always look blue—" He holds up another mountain. There's still some green in this glass, but more blue, mostly dark blue except for another wavy line of pale aqua. "—and the really far away ones look purple." He holds up a darker piece of glass, peaked in the center and hued a rich shade of grape. "So why'd he put the green mountains in the back?"

"He did?"

Ernesto nods and takes his eyes off the glass for the first time to wink at me. "There's something more. You see these wavy lines of water blue at the ends of these mountains and in the middle of this purple one?" Ernesto picks up another piece of glass and traces a wavy line of pale glass with his long delicate finger. Most of us who work with glass have a million tiny scars on our hands but Ernesto's hands are immaculate. "That's dichroic glass, girl."

"Dichroic? What's that?" I hear Robbie's voice ask. He's put down his solder gun and come up behind me.

"Mr. Tiffany invented that and liked to use it in his lamps, but Mr. Penrose copied it off him. See, you put this glass down on the table and turn off the light. "Now you see it—" Ernesto points to Robbie to switch the light box off. "Now you don't." The wavy aqua line is gone.

"Cool," Robbie says. "It's like a secret message in the glass." He says it like a boy who's just found a decoder ring in his Cracker Jacks.

"I sat under this window for four years," I say, "I never noticed a dichroic pattern."

"'Course you didn't, girl, because someone messed up on these mountains. See, here's how they were." Ernesto sets to work layering the glass according to the blueprint of how they were assembled when we took the window down. When he's done he motions for Robbie to switch on the light box but still there's no sign of the wavy line. "The light can't shine through because there's all these dark pieces over the pattern. Turn that light off again, Robbie boy." Deftly, Ernesto rearranges the glass mountains with the green mountain in front, then the blue one, and then the rest of the mountains receding into the distance. When he's done he's created a landscape of mountains tapering down into a valley in the middle. Ernesto takes a step back and then makes a few minute adjustments to the position of the glass. "See, now you got a valley, but it's like a valley in a drought, no water flowing through it. But then the light come—" Ernesto lifts up his hand with the grandeur of an Old Testament prophet and Robbie reaches down to switch on the light box. "—and the light set the rivers to flowing."

Where the foothills of the mountains had a moment ago been cloaked in darkness a stream now appears—a snaky line of pale blue leading the eye from the water lily pool toward the purple mountain in the distance. It's as if the light had uncovered a secret passageway leading into the heart of the distant hills.

AFTER ERNESTO'S DISCOVERY I DECIDE TO PAY GAVIN PENROSE a visit. The excuse that I formulate driving up the hill toward the college is to tell him about the dichroic pattern Ernesto's discovered in the landscape panel—but what I'd really like to know is how the college plans to handle the news of Christine's death and whether there will be a memorial service on campus. Driving up College Avenue is a little like watching a home repair show in accelerated motion. The shabby Victorians that surround my neighborhood neaten up: sagging porches straighten out, gaps in gingerbread trim are filled in, and faded paint grows bright. Perhaps a shade too bright. The faculty members who have bought and refurbished these old houses seem to think they're in San Francisco. They also seem to have been seized by a mania for flags so that I feel as I approach the college gates as if I were part of a parade. When I pass under the gates—beneath the wrought-iron motto "Spectemur Agendo"—"Let us be judged by our actions"—the transformation from decaying factory town to the hallowed groves of academia is complete. The grass on this side of the gate is actually greener, the sun that bathes the red bricks of Forest Hall and the clean gray granite of the library's gothic tower seems to shine a little brighter—it's almost as if the very air were different. Sharper. And while that air has always made me feel a little light-headed—still the townie trespassing on private property—I know that to Christine it was the elixir of life. She loved the college. Coming to Penrose transformed her life. She would want a memorial service here, not at a dour funeral home in Poughkeepsie.

I park in a visitor slot in front of Forest Hall, right next to a pale green Jaguar which I recognize as Gavin's, and enter the stately, tiled foyer. When Augustus Penrose designed the house for Eugenie and himself he also envisioned it as a showplace for his art collection and a communal gathering place for artists. When I went to Penrose College, students were invited in for a weekly tea, a tradition most of my classmates regarded as hokey and boring. Christine, however, loved it and compelled me every Friday to put on a skirt and go with her. It occurs to me as I enter the tiled foyer that it would be the ideal location for Christine's memorial service—better than the chapel even—because it was, after all, Christine's favorite place on campus.

It's not hard to see why. Although eclectic in its architecture and decoration—combining Gothic, Moorish, and Japanese features—the cruciform design with its open courtyard at the center creates a harmonious whole. The central courtyard is paved with a pale green marble that matches the green leaf pattern in the domed skylight and the ceramic capitals of the columns that support the skylight. The floral design in the capitals—a mixture of water lilies and wild irises—is echoed in a pattern of water lily pads that surrounds a large glass vase at the center of the fountain. The vase itself is a pale iridescent lavender etched with irises. Water rising up from the center of the fountain slowly seeps over the edge of the glass vase and spills into a narrow canal that leads from the fountain down the main hall—the Forest Hall, as it's called— which gives the building its name.

Passing the dining hall, where I watched Christine bask in the success of her lecture a little over a week ago, I follow the narrow stream of water down that hall toward Gavin's office. It's called the Forest Hall because of the series of paintings on the wall—all of which are set in a deeply wooded forest. The first paintings appear to be nature studies of a forest of widely spaced trees but, as you go farther down the hall, the trees crowd together, their leaves darken, their branches knot and twist like fingers clenching and reaching out.

Walking down the hall I feel as if someone is shadowing my steps in the painted wood. It's more than just my morbid imagination. Penrose painted the trees anthropomorphically so that you'd feel you were being followed even before you saw hints of figures hiding in the trees: a wisp of drapery snagged on a branch, a hand resting on the boll of a giant beech. Soon the forest is populated with figures from Greek mythology who, for one reason or another, were turned into trees. There's Baucis and Philemon, the elderly couple whose reward for their hospitality to Zeus is eternal life intertwined together as two trees, and Daphne at the moment when the River God, her father, grants her wish to turn into a laurel to evade Apollo's embrace.

After Daphne comes a series of paintings that have always simultaneously repelled and fascinated me. In the first one a woman crouches at the edge of a pool, holding a baby in one arm and reaching for a flower floating on the water with her other hand. Another woman sits on the shore watching. In the next painting, the woman reaching for the flower has drawn back her hand, which is covered with blood. There's a look of horror on her face that I've always found frightening. In the next scene you see why she is so horrified: as a sheath of bark creeps up the woman's body she tries to suckle the baby to her breast, but the baby's mouth touches only smooth, impermeable bark.

Gross! is what half the girls at Penrose say when they happen to pass by this tableau. Christine loved it, though. "The one nursing the baby is Dryope. She's being

punished because she picked a forbidden lotus flower,"
Christine told me. "The one with her arms around her is
her sister, Iole. Dryope begged her to take her baby to raise
and always warn him to 'beware of pools and never pick
blossoms from trees'! Sound advice we should all follow."

I can very nearly picture Christine shaking her finger
as she delivered this last bit. When I asked her why all the
women in the paintings—even Dryope and her sister—
looked alike she said because they were all portraits of
Eugenie. But then the Lady in the Window was supposed
to be Eugenie. If Christine's right about the lady in the
window, might some of these other portraits also be of
Eugenie's sister Clare? I look closely at the faces of Dryope
and her sister, and wonder if the one imprisoned in the
bark might be Clare, and the one watching her sister's fate
might be Eugenie.

"There you are! I was just calling you." I'm startled out
of my examination of the painting by a voice from behind
me. When I turn around I see it's Fay, her thin gray hair
held back on her head by a phone headset. For a moment
I think she must be talking to someone on the phone
instead of me because there's no reason why she should be
expecting me, but then she grabs my elbow and steers me
toward the president's office at the end of the hall.

"Mr. Penrose has been asking me to get in touch with
you all morning. Your assistant at your studio claimed
you didn't have a cell phone where I could reach you. Is
that true? You really ought to have a number where you
can be reached at all times." I'm about to explain that I
don't get many stained-glass emergencies, but Fay's still

talking, her words keeping time with the sharp click of her heels on the tiled floor as we fly past the thickening trees in the paintings. "What if the school were trying to reach you because something had happened to Beatrice, for instance, or your father had a heart attack or fell off a stepladder while installing a window . . ."

I'd like to think of some way of halting Fay's litany of disaster but I can't think of any. She's right; I guess I should have a cell phone, but she won't even let me get a word in edgewise to tell her I agree with her. Soon enough, though, we've come to the sliding screens at the end of the hall. Panels of thorny vines and roses embroidered on pale green silk are set into frames of honey-colored oak. One of Eugenie's patterns, no doubt. The forest has turned into the overgrown thicket surrounding the bower of Sleeping Beauty. Fay slips her hand into a recessed groove to slide open a panel but then turns to me, her back to the screen and lowers her voice. "I just want you to know," she whispers, "that when I said all those things about Christine the other day I had no idea she was already dead. I feel very strange about the whole thing."

"You couldn't have known, Fay; none of us did."

"Yes, but it was almost as if I had a presentiment of what was to come. Remember I told you about the pills she was taking? If I had taken them from her maybe she wouldn't be dead now."

"I know how you feel," I tell Fay, "but there probably wasn't anything any of us could have done."

"Yes, I'm sure you feel the worst of all of us—since you

were the last to see her alive and her best friend and all. If anyone could have saved her . . . well, as you say, there was probably nothing you could have done. I wish you'd tell Mr. Penrose that—he's been beside himself since he got the news yesterday after morning services. I can't help but think it was a bit tactless for that policeman to track us all down at church yesterday morning, especially since it's most likely a suicide—"

"I'd like to talk to Gavin," I interrupt. Although the chances are that the suicide theory is right, I find I'm tired of hearing it from Fay. There's something almost gloating in the way she brings it up. "That's why I'm here. Can I go in now?"

"Let me just tell him you're here," she says. She slides the screen open just wide enough for her to step backward through the narrow space and slides it closed again so quickly I'm unable to catch even a glimpse of the inner sanctum. I'm left staring at the pattern of thorns and roses until another panel—not the one Fay went through—opens and Fay slips halfway out.

"Mr. Penrose will see you now," she says, gesturing for me to enter through the side panel.

I go in and hear the whisper of the oak-framed panels sliding closed in their grooves. If the hallway felt like a path through the woods, this room is the sacred grove in the heart of the forest. The furniture is simple and unobtrusive—a mission-style library table for a desk, two Morris chairs, and a low settee upholstered in the same thorns-and-roses pattern as the screens, only here on green velvet instead of silk. Painted on a wide panel beneath the windows is a frieze of Sleeping Beauty drowsing on a bed of thorns. The glass in the windows above her is thick and greenish, stippled with delicate bubbles, and unfigured except for a narrow panel of falling leaves on either side. I've been in this room a half dozen times—including the time when I was asked by the president (Gavin's father, Arthur Penrose) to take a voluntary leave of absence while I had Bea—and I've always found it a peaceful place. Even on that occasion, I was lulled into a sense that the college really had my best interest at heart (*you don't want to be studying for finals in your condition*) by the soft palette of green and gold and the subtle hints of decaying foliage everywhere. The light, filtered through the antique glass, is gentle, but when Gavin rises from behind his desk to greet me I can see even in this dim light how haggard he is.

"Juno," he says, coming around his desk and reaching for my hand. "I still can't believe she's gone." To my surprise he takes my hand and pulls me into his arms, where he holds me, tight against his crisp white shirt, for several long moments. Although I've known Gavin Penrose since I was in college here I've never so much as kissed him on the cheek.

After several minutes—long enough for me to inhale the sandalwood in his cologne and admire the Morris pattern in his tie—he takes a step back and holds me at arm's length.

"You must be devastated," he says, "Christine told me how close you were. She said you were like the sister she never had and better than the mother she did have."

I nod, unable to trust myself to speak. It's Gavin, though, who looks devastated. His pale olive skin has turned sallow, the shadows under his eyes are deep as bruises. I remember now that I wondered last week if he and Christine were romantically involved.

Something in how I'm looking at him must suddenly make Gavin feel uncomfortable, because he drops his hands from my arms and turns from me, gesturing toward the low couch.

"Please, sit down, let me ring Fay for some tea; you must be exhausted. I know I haven't slept."

I take the seat but turn down the offer of tea, guiltily remembering that I actually slept well last night—no more drowned visitors for a change—and ate two of the French crullers Ernesto had brought. Gavin, slumped next to me on the couch, is the one who looks like he hasn't slept or eaten.

"I guess you spent a lot of time with Christine while she was researching her lecture," I say, feeling oddly ill at ease with the evidence of Gavin's grief. I don't know whether I should be treating him like something more than Christine's last boss.

"Yes, she was very thorough; once she got an idea she was like a pit bull, she wouldn't let go." *Thorough* and *pit bull* don't sound like terms of endearment but the way Gavin says them, with a fond smile and slight shake of the head, I suppose they might be. "That's why I feel so bad. You see, we argued that morning before the lecture."

"But I saw you with her after the lecture, talking about that Titian painting in the dining hall. You didn't seem to be arguing then."

Gavin runs a hand through his hair—thick, dark hair with a buoyant wave and only a touch of gray at the temples—and bows his head. I've heard lots of people compare his looks to John F. Kennedy Jr., but to me he's always looked more like the pictures of Mario Lanza on the records my mother used to listen to.

"Oh that! You know that's not a real Titian. Christine was explaining to me how my grandfather should have known it was a fake."

I smile, remembering that that was exactly what I had assumed she was doing.

"Thank God we'd made it up by then," he says, "and I got a chance to tell her what a remarkable job she'd done. And to thank her for sparing my family some of the less savory details . . ."

"You mean about Clare Barovier's time in a mental hospital?"

Gavin hesitates for a moment and then nods his head.

"Yes. There were some details about my great-aunt's internment at Briarwood that I felt would reflect badly on the family and, by extension, the college. Did you notice how she paused when she got to the part in her lecture about Briarwood? I think that she'd decided to leave out the details we'd discussed." I remember thinking that she'd paused to spare me some unpleasant memories. Maybe she was protecting both of us. Gavin lifts his head out of his hands and reaches across the few inches between us on the couch to squeeze my hand. "You of all people must understand. You don't want Bea to live under that shadow."

"Did you know that your great-aunt Clare had been institutionalized?"

"*Know* is perhaps too straightforward a word for how information travels in my family. I always suspected there was something, some secret the grown-ups were trying to keep from us. There were whispers and hints about *hereditary madness* and innuendoes of insanity. And my mother was always extremely overprotective of me—although that may have been because she'd lost two children in infancy before she had me. When I told her that I wanted to take a year off between college and graduate school to live in Paris and paint she warned me that there was a strain of madness in my grandmother's family that could be set off by *delving too deeply into the artistic side*."

"God, how archaic!" Even as I shake my head in disapproval, though, I'm picturing Neil standing in front of his last portrait in the Halcyone series, scraping paint off with his palette knife until he pierced the canvas. Would he have had that last episode if he hadn't pushed himself so hard?

"Did you have your year in Paris?"

Gavin smiles ruefully—it makes him look younger and I remember him driving up to the dorm in his sports car. He looked like he was leading the perfect life—not some proxy life he'd been pushed into by the family. How could you ever really tell if people were happy? Or so desperately unhappy that they might want to die?

"I went for the summer but my mother had done her job well. The specter of 'Crazy Aunt Clare' hovered over my canvases like some spiteful incubus. I came back in the fall in time to start Wharton. No loss to the art world, I'm sure. I still paint a little for my own amusement, but I'm glad I don't have to make a living at it."

I'm not sure what to say. I've never seen any of Gavin's paintings so I can't really offer a judgment. It seems sad for him to have been diverted from his artistic pursuits, but looking at him, healthy and sane if a little sleep deprived, and imagining the life Neil's lived half an hour up the river at Briarwood, I can't help but wonder if Gavin's mother wasn't right.

"But enough of my faded dreams, eh? We've got Christine's memorial service to think about. That policeman said her body should be released by the end of the week, so I called her mother this morning and told her that I would make the arrangements for her to be moved to a funeral home in Poughkeepsie. I've already arranged for flowers to be sent from the college and diverted the check Christine was owed for her lecture to her mother—not strictly legal, but I figured the poor woman could use help with the funeral expenses while Christine's estate is pending—I understand the family's not well off."

"No, they're not. Christine's father died when she was only four and Mrs. Webb had an accident and went on disability not long after that. I'm sure Mrs. Webb appreciates all you're doing, but . . ."

"It's the least we can do. I thought, too, that when the window's done in the fall we could have a little ceremony in Christine's honor. Something private—I think Christine would have liked that."

I'm about to say that what Christine would really like is a memorial service here at the college. The last place she'd want to end up—dead or not—is back with her mother in Poughkeepsie. But Gavin is already standing up and walking toward the screens that Fay, as if she heard us coming, has slid open. I'm out in the hall, in the painted forest of trees, before I realize that I didn't even get a chance to tell him about the pattern Ernesto found in the window.

CHAPTER ELEVEN

IF I HAD HAD ANY THOUGHTS, THOUGH, OF GOING BACK INTO Gavin's office, Fay's stance in front of its entrance would have dissuaded me. After sliding the screen closed she stands, her rigidly straight back to the embroidered screen, and folds her arms across her flat chest. An image of that long scar snaking out from beneath her towel in the sauna flashes through my mind and I take a step back. I can tell Gavin about the dichroic pattern in the glass some other time—it seems profane, at any rate, to talk business while Christine's body still lies at the morgue. Fay, though, must see my hesitation.

"I hope there's nothing else you need to bother Mr. Penrose about this morning," she says, stepping past me toward her own small office just off the main hall. "This tragedy has taken quite a toll on him. I try to absorb the worst of it, but there's only so much that I can do."

"I'm sure he values your—" I stop because the word that I'd been about to use was *interference* and I'm not sure what other word to use for the fierce protectiveness she has for her boss. Cerberus at the gates of hell is what comes to mind. "I'm sure he values all that you do," I finish lamely, following her into her tiny office. It's hardly more than an alcove recessed off the main hall behind another sliding screen (like many designers of the Arts & Crafts movement Eugenie and Augustus were heavily influenced by Japanese art)—this one embroidered with a pattern of falling leaves to fit in with the forest mural. Fay sits down behind a desk piled high with orderly stacks of papers and, looking up, gives me one of her rare smiles.

"It's little enough after all Mr. Penrose has done for me. Do you know that last year when I needed my operation the college's insurance provider refused to pay for it?" Fay lays the edge of her hand against her breastbone, her hand curled into a sickle shape. "Mr. Penrose personally called up the insurance company and threatened to change the entire college to another provider if they didn't pay for my surgery."

"No, I had no idea. That's shocking that they wouldn't pay for breast cancer surgery . . ."

"Oh, I didn't have cancer. I found out last year I have the gene for it. The surgery was prophylactic. The insurance company would have had me wait to get the cancer when it might be too late."

"Wow." I remember well from my mother's experience how physically devastating that surgery was and I'm stunned at the thought of opting to have it . . . how had Fay put it? . . . *prophylactically*. It seems either extremely brave or slightly insane. "I didn't know you could find that out . . ."

Fay, who had begun to sort some papers from one pile to another, looks back up at me. "Didn't your mother die of breast cancer?"

I nod. "She got it when she was only forty, but I don't think anyone else in the family had it . . ." My voice trails off as I realize that I've had so little contact with my mother's family since she died that I really don't know that for sure.

"Well, you should find out and be tested right away. Here, let me give you the card where you can go." Fay opens the top drawer of her desk and out of a jumble of pens, erasers, paper clips, breath mints, tea bags, and Post-it notes extracts a business card. Under the name of a hospital in Poughkeepsie I read: Division of Medical Genetics.

"Well, I'll think about it," I say, tucking the card into the outside flap of my purse. What I'm really thinking, though, is that this is the last thing I feel like dealing with now. Fay lets out a long sigh that ends in a little tsk. I can tell she's gearing up to tell me all the reasons why I should immediately call the number on the card, backed no doubt with statistics and case studies that will scare the hell out of me. It's the last news I want to hear right now so I try desperately to think of something to divert her. Casting my eyes over the piles on her desk I notice a large album covered with embroidered silk just to my right.

"I recognize this pattern," I say, a bit inanely. "Isn't it one of Eugenie's?" I run my hand over the silk, feeling, where the cloth is worn, the cardboard underneath. The colors have faded but I can just make out a pattern of olive-green water lilies floating amid trailing copper branches on a violet background.

Fay is staring at me as if I were crazy, but then I think of something that will make at least a little sense out of my rambling. "Is this the notebook that Christine used for her lecture? The one you were supposed to copy for me?"

Something shuts down in Fay's face and I feel sorry for it. She was trying to give me lifesaving advice and I've put her in her secretarial place.

"I've *tried* to photocopy it, but it's not so simple. You can see for yourself how fragile the document is. I can't just hand it over to photocopying and let some work-study student *splay* it out on the copying machine." Fay fairly sputters on the word *splay*, giving a force and violence to the word that horribly calls to mind what's being done to Christine's body in the morgue. "And the ink Eugenie used has faded to near invisibility. Augustus was experimenting with handmade vegetable dyes at the time and this was one of his less successful attempts." Fay carefully opens the album to the first page. At first I think the page is blank but then I notice a faint pattern of wavy lines—subtle as a fingerprint—on the cream-colored paper. In fact, it's the same pattern of water lilies and branches that's on the cover. Peering closer, I notice that the branches, as they twine around the water lilies, turn into snakes. I pull back, as startled by the hidden snakes in the design as if a real one had crawled out of the clutter on Fay's desk, and laugh nervously at my own response. Fay looks at me as if I'd lost my mind.

"These sketches could be extremely useful in restoring the Lady window," I say in an attempt to restore my dignity.

"I already told you, I can't make an adequate copy."

"Then I'll take the original. I promise I'll be careful."

"That's what your friend said and look what happened."

For a second I think she means that Christine's death was somehow a result of her taking the notebook, but then Fay opens the book to the middle and points to a ragged edge close to the spine. "These pages have been torn out recently. You can't tell me Eugenie Penrose did it. It was Christine Webb."

I shake my head. "Christine would never . . . ," I start to say, but then I remember how far Christine was willing to go when she wanted to know something. "You're right," I tell Fay, "I can't expect you to take the responsibility for letting such valuable archival material out of the office. I'll have to ask Gavin if I can borrow it."

I have only to angle my body in the direction of Gavin's office for Fay to concede. "That's entirely unnecessary." She comes out from behind the desk to hand me the notebook, placing herself between me and Gavin's office. "Just make sure you take better care than your friend did," she says, following me into the hall. Again Fay's warning seems to suggest that Christine's drowning was somehow a direct result of her bad treatment of Eugenie's notebook. I'm about to tell her that she needn't worry, that I have no plans to mistreat the notebook *or* go kayaking by myself when I notice a blank spot on the wall next to the painting of Iole and Dryope.

"Isn't that where the painting of *The Drowning Tree* used to be?" I ask.

I can tell from her expression that Fay would like to

accuse Christine of making away with the painting as well as the missing notebook pages, but instead she looks embarrassed as she's forced to concede that the painting's absence has nothing to do with Christine.

"President Penrose sent it down to the city to be cleaned. You wouldn't believe how filthy some of these paintings are."

I think she's referring to the subject matter—naked nymphs and breast-feeding trees—but then she swipes a finger along one of the picture frames. "It's because of the candles they use during parties. President Penrose thinks it's romantic, but it's just plain dirty."

I spend the rest of the day with Eugenie's notebook spread open on the light table. To gain some time and quiet—and because we've still got bills to pay—I send Ernesto and Robbie out on a job to reinstall a fanlight up on the Heights.

I turn on every light in the studio, but still I find it almost impossible to read Eugenie's writing in the margins of her sketches. It's as if the free-flowing script she employed in her youth had contracted and become brittle—like an old woman's bones—as she grew old. After a while I give up trying to read and let her pictures tell the story. The pen-and-ink sketches are faint, too (I could curse Augustus Penrose for his damned homemade ink) but beautifully intricate. Studying them, my hand itches to be drawing and I find myself doodling on scraps of the white vellum paper we use for rubbings. I find it helps me make sense of the designs to draw them, to see how one thing turns into another in Eugenie's exotic menagerie of plant and animal life. I recognize many of the patterns that she used in her line of domestic textiles, but I can't imagine that some of these designs ever made it out of the sketchbook and onto the loom. They're not exactly what the turn-of-the-century matron would use to upholster her parlor settee and chairs. Sea serpents swallowing carp, bloated octopi ensnaring dainty sea horses. There's an undercurrent of violence in the sketches that I never noticed in the textiles. She's linked pieces of the design together by having one *devour* the other. Or transform into the other. There's a whole series of designs—none of which I have ever seen rendered in cloth—of women turning into birds or trees or, sometimes, water, wind, or just pure swirls of chaos. I know that Augustus Penrose often used Ovid's *Metamorphoses* as a source for his painting, just as J. W. Waterhouse, another second-generation Pre-Raphaelite, did. I picture Augustus and Eugenie reading Ovid together, selecting the stories of Baucis and Philemon and Iole and Dryope, for the Forest Hall. Perhaps that's where Eugenie got the idea for these *metamorphic* tapestries that then proved too complicated to weave into cloth.

Halfway through the notebook, Eugenie stops drawing patterns and starts working on sketches for the Lady window. I wonder if Augustus put her to work on the window plans to give her a rest from designing textiles. Maybe he had found some of her recent fabric patterns disturbing—or, at least, unmarketable.

The first sketches of the window are rough cartoons. A generalized figure of a woman bent over a loom—not looking up as she does in the completed window, the details of the room around her only vaguely suggested. The window above her head is at first empty. Then, in subsequent sketches, trees and shrubbery appear, a few clouds stray into the sky. The surrounding room becomes more detailed. Bolts of cloth appear, then stacks of books, a table with a vase of flowers . . . a cross between a lady's sewing room and an artist's studio, much like the textile studios in Forest Hall. These interiors are lovingly detailed—far too detailed for representation in stained glass. Augustus must have pointed that out to her because I find, turning a page near the center of the book, a drawing with the interior scene roughly crosshatched out. Scrawled across the drawing in black ink that has not faded with time are the words, "You've turned my muse into a seamstress!" The handwriting's nothing like Eugenie's—young or old—it's clearly Augustus's verdict on his wife's work.

In the drawing on the next page the interior has been simplified: The lady has looked up from her loom, and mountains have risen in the window behind her. A shaggy beech tree looms over the lily pool like a beast about to leap through the window and devour the lady. When I turn to the next page I see I've come to the place where the page has been torn out. The next page shows the completed drawing for the window, the glass sections blocked out and numbered according to a number key in the margin.

"If you get any closer to that drawing you'll fall into it."

I pull my head up and feel a sudden twinge in my back from bending over the table so long.

"Dad, you startled me. I don't mind you using your own key—but give a person some warning when you come creeping up on them," I say, closing the notebook.

"Ha! This from a girl who used to hear me light up a smoke from two blocks away. I hollered twice," he protests. "These sorry excuses for guard dogs certainly heard me."

Paolo and Francesca look up from either side of my dad's legs, their large liquid eyes full of rebuke. Obviously they'd scampered right past me and I hadn't noticed.

"I'm sorry, I guess I was preoccupied . . ."

"You were drawing." My father moves closer to the table and takes one of the scrap sheets I've filled with sketches from Eugenie's notebook. "I haven't seen you draw like that since before you went to college. Reminded me of how you were after your mother died. Remember? You'd draw your pictures from morning to night. Your teachers complained that you drew pictures on your homework and in all your class notebooks. I told them to let you be. It was like you were drawing the pain out of yourself."

I smile at the thought of my father facing down the teachers at Rosedale High but then the smile fades as I see the look of concern on his face. I can see he's trying to think of something to say about Christine—that he's connected this fit of drawing with my current grief. And who knows? It's true I've drawn little except designs for windows in the last fifteen years.

"I can't even remember what I drew back then," I say.

"Oh, all sorts of things—unicorns and dragons, fanciful things and places that looked like they came out of fairy tales. Beautiful princesses—all with your mother's face. Here—I've still got one."

My father pulls out a worn leather wallet that's been molded to the shape of his hip and extracts a grayish piece of newsprint folded into quarters. When he unfolds it I see it's a pencil sketch of a woman's face. Beneath the fanciful crown and even more fanciful hairdo I recognize my mother's face, forever frozen at forty-four, the age she was when she died.

"Wow, it does look like her, doesn't it?"

My father looks at the picture and nods. Then he carefully folds it and puts it back in his wallet.

"You had a lot of talent. I never understood why you gave it up."

Because I got pregnant at twenty-one and my husband cracked up and I had to take over your glass business to make a living, I could say, but then, none of that was his fault. He helped me the best he could after Neil was taken away.

"I'm better off," I tell him, meaning it. "I'd hate to be in Robbie's shoes—living hand to mouth—hoping someone will notice my paintings. I'm happy bringing other people's works of art back to life."

Dad nods but I notice he is not looking at me. Instead he's looking over my shoulder at the sketches I've drawn. They're doodles mostly, sea creatures and aquatic flowers—not so different from the unicorns and dragons I drew as a child—strung together in a swirling pattern of seaweed. The swirls cascade down the paper, turning into a stream flowing between two hills. Alongside the stream is a curving path on which I've drawn two women walking arm in arm under a weeping beech tree. One woman has already gone under the tree, her abundant hair radiating out in serpentine coils that intermingle with the foliage, while the other turns her face to the side. The features I've sketched bear a crude likeness to the lady in the window and like the lady in the window she's smiling because she is finally free from her imprisonment. She's woven the landscape she glimpsed in the mirror and, instead of dying, escaped into a world of her own creation. A happy scene until you notice that, influenced by my visit to Forest Hall this morning, I've sketched a face on the tree—a woman's face that has the same features as the lady in the window, only crying instead of smiling. The cascading branches of the weeping beech have intertwined with the hair of the woman who's gone under the tree as if they were getting ready to drag her into the water.

CHAPTER TWELVE

THE NEXT WEEK, WHILE WAITING FOR CHRISTINE'S BODY TO BE released from the morgue, I find that I can no longer cut glass. It's something I'm generally quite good at. My father taught me the summer I was sixteen when he corralled me into working with him as a glazier's apprentice instead of attending the summer art institute at the Rhode Island School of Design.

"It's not like anyone can really teach you how to draw," he'd said, his callused hand on mine guiding the glass cutter over a smooth pane, "but a trade like this . . . well, you gotta get it from someone who's got the touch, like I learned it from my father. The McKays have been cutting glass for generations. I can see already you've got the knack for it, just press a little harder till you hear a scratching—" The cutter made a sound like sand makes when it's caught between your teeth. "—but not so hard so you see white coming off your blade, and always make sure your cutter's freshly oiled, and never go over a score twice."

It had seemed like a million things to keep in mind at once—impossible to remember—and it was only when I stopped listening to his words and let my hand go limp under the steady pressure of his hand that I had learned to make a perfect score. Then he showed me how to break the glass along the score line by gently rocking the plate between my thumbs. The first time the glass snapped free along the curving line I'd drawn was like a miracle. "See," my father had said, "I told you it was in the blood. You'll make a fine glass cutter."

The only blood I see this week, though, is my own, as plate after plate of expensive handblown opalescent glass shatters in my hands in crazy jagged patterns that refuse to follow my score lines. The glass explodes in showers of splinters that lodge in my fingertips and under my nails, and spray far afield so that hours later I'm still picking out miniature daggers of ruby and emerald from my socks and hair. I wake up in the middle of the night to find crushed cobalt glass, like a dusting of frost, sticking to my damp skin.

By Thursday Ernesto bans me from the studio. "The boy and me can cut the replacement pieces—why don't you call your friend's mother and see if she knows when the funeral is yet?"

Ruth Webb is the last person I want to talk to but Ernesto is right—I can't put it off any longer. As I dial the number, which I still know by heart from the many calls I made to Christine during vacations, I tell myself that at least I called the week before when I first knew Christine was missing. Still, there's no evading the aura of disapproval that emanates from the silence on the other end of the line when I tell Mrs. Webb how sorry I am.

"I'm sure you are, June," she says, refusing as always to acknowledge my real name, which she once told Christine was *heathen*, "but it's a bit too late for *sorry*, isn't it?"

Only Ruth Webb could turn an expression of sympathy into a confession of guilt. I have no idea of what I'm supposed to be guilty, but I've always known that Ruth doesn't like me and that she held me somehow accountable for Christine's problems. First because I indulged her daughter's foolish ambitions to pursue an academic career (as if anyone could have swayed Christine from her chosen course once she'd made up her mind) and then for Christine's abandonment of that career and her subsequent slide into drug use. Even when I helped get Christine into a rehab center, Ruth refused to help pay for it, insisting that it was *coddling* her. *All she needs is a little willpower, not a country club to loll around in. It's like the patients at Briarwood—half of them would pick themselves up if their families didn't pay for them to wallow in the lap of luxury.* That was another favorite theme of Ruth's—the special treatment received at Briarwood. To hear her talk you'd think she was jealous of the patients there.

"Well, I'm sorry for your loss, just the same," I say now, knowing better than to try defending myself, "for what we've all lost in Christine. She was a remarkable woman. I wish you could have heard her lecture. I think Christine was really putting her life back together."

"Apparently not or she wouldn't have committed a mortal sin and taken her own life."

"Mrs. Webb, have the police determined that as the official cause of death?"

"I don't have to wait for the police to tell me what I've known in my bones since that girl was born. She was always unhappy. Always crying for no reason. Nothing ever good enough for her. She couldn't go to the community college just down the road like all her cousins or work at Briarwood during summers when I got her a job there. She had to go to Penrose and then live in New York City, but nothing ever made her happy."

I could argue, but listening to Mrs. Webb's disparaging dirge half makes *me* want to jump in the river. What must it have been like to grow up with a mother so out of tune with your nature? I was luckier losing a loving and supportive mother at sixteen than having one like Christine's.

"Have the police said yet when they'll release the body?"

"Tomorrow. The funeral's set for ten AM on Saturday. I told that Italian police officer that we had to bury her over the weekend because her aunts and cousins can't miss work what with Briarwood laying off so many people right now."

I almost smile imagining Detective Falco's response to being given such a directive from the deceased's mother.

"Do you want me to go to the morgue to . . . to ride up with her . . ." I falter thinking of all the times I'd given Christine a ride home over the years. My dad would let me borrow the van so we could pack up all Christine's stuff—although truthfully she never had that much. We liked taking the van, though, because we could pull over and smoke a joint in the back. Often, as we approached her house she would suggest we pull over again and we'd just sit in the back talking, clearly putting off her arrival home. The idea of bringing her back home now, for all eternity, is almost more than I can stand.

"That won't be necessary," Mrs. Webb says, "that man from the college said he'd go to the morgue and ride up in the hearse with her."

"You mean Gavin Penrose, the college president?" I remember Gavin saying he'd take care of these arrangements, but I'm surprised to learn that he's personally accompanying Christine's body from the morgue to the funeral home—and guilty at the sense of relief I have that I don't have to do it.

"Yes, I know what his job is. I expect he feels bad about encouraging Chrissie on that fool's errand poking into his family's dirty laundry . . ."

"Christine was thrilled when Gavin asked her to give a lecture on the window."

"Well, I'm sure she was . . . any notice from that college . . ." For a moment Mrs. Webb's voice falters and I'm reminded that beneath the constant stream of criticism and carping at her daughter's lifestyle she must have really loved her—at least, I've always hoped that was the case.

"Mrs. Webb, if there's anything I can do to help . . ."

I'm expecting a curt dismissal of my offer, but Ruth

surprises me. "I do have a job ahead of me getting this house ready for the wake afterward, what with my knee and all."

Thirty years ago—when Christine was seven—a patient at Briarwood slammed a steel tray into Ruth's right leg and shattered her kneecap. She'd been able to retire on full disability, but had always been bitter that nothing had been done to punish the patient. *She was happiest in the days of insulin shock treatment and lobotomies,* Christine always said.

"Well, do you want me to stop at Grand Union and pick up anything on the way?"

Ruth responds with a shopping list the length of my forearm. I write it all down—the liters of soft drinks, jumbo packages of chips, hot dogs, hamburger meat, Miracle Whip and Sara Lee cake—all of which sounds more like a supply list for a Fourth of July picnic than a wake—on a scrap of paper I steal from the studio. Only afterward do I notice that I've written the shopping list on the back of the drawing I did earlier in the week of the two Barovier sisters walking on their riverside path.

THE SILAS B. COOKE FUNERAL HOME IS IN DOWNTOWN Poughkeepsie, not far from the train station, in a neighborhood that feels even more run-down than where I live. Looking at Poughkeepsie always makes me feel discouraged about the prospects of reviving Rosedale. No matter how much federal aid is pumped into the town— and at one point in the eighties Poughkeepsie was receiving the most federal aid of any city in New York State—the town continues to look hopelessly dreary and borderline dangerous. The funeral home itself was nearly burned down a few years before by a gang of teenagers. Two of the front windows are still boarded up and someone has scrawled a *d* at the end of Silas's name on the front awning—boasting that Silas Be Cooked.

Inside, under the cloying smell of wax candles and flowers, a charred aroma still lingers. Clearly the Cookes haven't been able to afford to renovate since the fire. In addition to the boarded-up exterior windows there's a wall of stained-glass windows between the anteroom and the chapel that have obviously suffered serious fire and smoke damage. The panels are landscape scenes similar to ones that Tiffany made popular for use as memorial windows in churches and mausoleums in the early twenties. Called "The River of Life" or "End of Day," these landscapes were supposed to evoke religious significance, but I've always thought Tiffany just loved creating flowers and streams with glass. Although they're probably not Tiffany's, these windows are actually quite lovely. I move closer to get a better look and see that soot has gotten between the layered plates of glass and that there are erratically curved cracks in many of the panels. *Internal crazing.* It happens when glass is heated quickly to a high temperature and then rapidly cooled. The tension between a cooling exterior and hot interior creates delicate, bright cracks, like phosphorescent spiderwebs. It's almost impossible to restore glass damaged like this, but I did recently read in a conservation textbook of a process in which the cracks were infused with epoxy and then reassembled. I make a mental note to talk to the owner of the funeral parlor and head into the chapel.

I'm relieved to see, when I enter the main chapel, that the room feels full, mostly because Ruth Webb's family takes up five or six pews on the right side. Ruth Webb has four sisters and they all have three or four children apiece. I had remembered that the aunts, like Ruth, tended to fat, and I can't help but notice that their children have followed suit. It's always amazed me that Christine, reed thin even during freshman year when we all put on ten pounds from late-night pizza and keg parties, came from such a corpulent family. Of course I never met her father, who died when Christine was only four, but his two sisters, whom I notice now sitting a little apart from Ruth's family, are also quite large.

One of the Webb aunts—Amy, I remember just in time—greets me as I come down the aisle with such a warm smile that I feel instantly guilty for obsessing about familial obesity at a time like this. I recall as she grasps me in a sweaty embrace—it feels as if the fire that cooked poor Silas is still raging somewhere below us—that she had been Christine's favorite aunt.

"Juno, thank you for coming, Christine was just telling me not a month ago what a good friend you've always been to her."

"You saw her last month?"

"She was doing some research at Briarwood and I got her an appointment with Doctor Horace," Amy says, lowering her voice. "Ruth's still upset she didn't get in touch with her when she was up at the hospital. If I'd known I'd never have mentioned seeing her . . ." Amy takes a quick look around—the nylon fabric of her navy and white polka-dot dress making a rasping noise as it moves over some under layer of fabric—and then leans forward to whisper in my ear under the cover of kissing me on the cheek. "I have an idea why she didn't want to see her mother . . ."

Before Amy can finish her sentence we both notice Gavin Penrose striding purposefully toward us. He's quite a startling sight amid the nylon print dresses and floral wreaths crafted of carnations dyed in colors not found in nature. He's wearing a charcoal gray suit with a subtle chalk stripe and a silk tie in yet another Morris print. Even though the suit is wool he appears to be the only one in the room not sweating.

"Juno, everyone from the college is sitting over here," he gestures toward the left side of the chapel. "Let Fay know if you feel up to saying a few words—I'm going to, but don't feel obliged."

"Oh, that would have meant the world to Christine," Amy croons into my ear. She's still standing close enough that I can feel the heat radiating off her and smell her Jean Naté body splash.

"I don't have anything prepared . . ."

"Just a few words from the heart—that's all I'm doing. Come and tell Fay, though; she's keeping a list."

Gavin takes my arm and I reluctantly leave Amy. "We'll talk later back at the house," I say, hoping she doesn't forget what she'd been about to tell me.

Gavin leads me to the front pew on the left side of the chapel and seats me between Fay Morgan and Joan Shelley, the petite blond trustee who I saw at Christine's lecture last week. I'm touched that a woman of Joan's social standing—I read in the alumnae magazine that she's used her considerable fortune to found a number of art organizations—would come to Christine's funeral. After we've exchanged greetings—and Fay has written my name down on her "list" of speakers, which only contains my name and Gavin's—the two women resume their conversation, leaning forward to talk across me, about college budget cuts. I turn in my seat to look back and notice, in the very last pew, Detective Falco mopping his forehead with a white handkerchief. He catches my eye almost the instant I turn, waves at me and then, when he sees he's waving the white handkerchief, quickly pockets it and blushes.

I turn back in my seat and smile, oddly pleased at the detective's discomfiture, and then remember where I am and why and stop smiling.

The service is delivered by a minister of uncertain denomination who clearly never met Christine. For one thing he keeps referring to her as "Chris" in a pathetic attempt to sound familiar, but it's a nickname that Christine loathed. He praises her fine academic career at *Vassar* (Gavin Penrose groans audibly at the mention of Penrose's rival) and bemoans the loss to the world of a talented artist (apparently not having grasped the difference between an art historian and artist). I glance over at the family pews to see if Mrs. Webb is taking umbrage at this misrepresentation of her daughter's life but she is placidly fanning herself with the funeral program. Artist, art historian; Vassar, Penrose—it had probably all seemed equally far-fetched to her.

"Let us pray that Christine finds peace with the ultimate artist, He who fashioned us from clay, our creator," the minister concludes. "Amen."

Gavin is up before we've finished echoing the minister's amen. I'm relieved that he's going first until I realize this means that the responsibility of the last word is mine. What in the world can I say, I wonder, as Gavin unfolds two sheets of white typescript—his *few words from the heart*—and begins to speak.

"Christine Webb was the epitome of everything Penrose College stands for," he says, laying heavy stress on the words *Penrose College*. "She's the kind of girl Eugenie Penrose had in mind when she founded the Woman's Craft League and when she and her husband, Augustus Penrose, broadened the scope of the Craft League by founding Penrose College." I wonder if Gavin really wrote his speech this way or if he has altered it to get in as many references to Penrose as he can to extinguish the lingering echoes of *Vassar* in the overheated chapel.

"Augustus and Eugenie Penrose wanted to elevate women's work to give girls from humble beginnings a chance to do honest work and create lasting beauty. Christine Webb was *not* an artist—" I peek to see if the minister, sitting to Gavin's left, has any reaction to Gavin's correction of his elegy, but his eyes are closed in prayerful contemplation—or perhaps heat-induced stupor.

"—She didn't create beauty. Instead she looked for beauty in the world around her so she could uncover it and show it to the rest of us. She wasn't the stained-glass window—" Gavin half turns to indicate the stained-glass window behind him—a reproduction of Tiffany's "The River of Life" mounted on a light box, not lit by natural light. "—she was the light shining through it. She spent her life and her great talent and her intellect *illuminating* the truth because Christine believed, with Keats, that *Beauty is truth, truth beauty*."

Gavin stops. Looks down at his notes. Looks up and then folds the pages neatly in quarters and slips them into his breast pocket. A little dramatic gesture I suspect he planned as carefully as the Keats quote.

"Sometimes I think that Christine was too relentless in her search for the truth—that she shined her light into corners that should, perhaps, have remained in the shadows. That she spared nothing and no one—least of all herself—from the full force of her scrutiny. I could wish now that she'd been a little easier on herself, but I know that my grandmother, Eugenie Penrose, would have admired Christine. She would have considered her a worthy successor to the dream upon which she founded the college. Because, as Christine and Keats believed, she, too, believed that truth is beauty and *that is all ye know on earth, and all ye need to know*. Wherever Christine is I hope that she knows now what she needed to know and that she rests easy with that knowledge."

There's an uncomfortable stirring as Gavin walks down from the podium and I get up to take his place. I can hear the pews creak as the aunts shift their weight and a dry rattle as they fan themselves. My mind is sadly blank when I turn to face the little assembly. It's more than I can bear to meet anyone's gaze, so instead I look over their heads at the smoke-damaged stained-glass windows at the back of the chapel. I can just make out the figure of a man on the other side of the panels, a shadow moving behind the cracked glass that comes to rest near the entrance to the chapel but doesn't come inside. Instead of thinking about Christine I am remembering, stupidly, Keats's poem, "Ode on a Grecian Urn"—the one Gavin quoted from—and picturing the scene Keats describes on the urn, of a young man pursuing a young woman. I can even remember the lines (another legacy of Mrs. Ramsey's Nineteenth-Century Lit): *What men or gods are these? What maidens loth? What mad pursuit? What struggle to escape?* and I picture, suddenly, my last glimpse of Christine's face in the train window and realize that the look I'd seen there was of someone pursued. But by what? Or by whom?

"Gavin is right that Christine sought out beauty. She saw it in places no one else would notice it. In the angle of light in a smoky bar, in a brick wall of an old factory, or in an eighteen-year-old college freshman who had stopped seeing any beauty in the world."

I take a deep breath that shudders only slightly and go on. "I remember the first time I met Christine. It was a few months into our first year at Penrose. She was studying in the library at the table in front of the Lady window and for a moment I thought the figure in the window had stepped down from the glass and turned into flesh. The girl at the table had the same long blond hair and she was wearing an embroidered tunic with bell-shaped sleeves that looked like the Lady's medieval dress. It turned out to be an Indian kurta—a cheap gauzy thing that she'd bought in a thrift shop in the East Village, but it didn't matter; Christine looked like a queen in it.

"'I bet you've heard the superstition, too,' she said when I sat down at the table. When I asked her what she meant she told me that any paper written under the Lady window would get an A. I told her I could use the help. Unlike a lot of my classmates at Penrose I hadn't gone to a fancy prep school. It wasn't just that the work was hard for me, but that the teachers and other students seemed to speak a language I didn't understand. I'd just gotten back my first art history paper and gotten a C– on it.

"'You have to stick with what you see,' she explained to me, 'and follow where your eye leads you.' She spent the rest of the evening showing me not just how to rewrite the paper but how to really *see* the paintings we were supposed to write about. I found out later that she had a paper due the next day, too; she ended up writing it between two and four that morning and still got an A on it. When we left the library at midnight, though, she didn't rush back to the dorm to work on her paper. It had started to snow for the first time that year.

"'I believe it's an old Penrose tradition to climb to the top of the library tower and watch the first snow fall over the valley,' she told me. And so that's what we did. I'll never forget what the view of the Hudson Valley looked like from up there."

The figure behind the stained-glass windows turns away as if disappointed in my elegy for Christine. *What more can I say?* I want to call to the retreating figure. Instead I finish up with the only thing I can think of, raising my voice a little as if calling after my unknown listener in the anteroom.

"Christine had the gift of showing you what the world could look like from the highest heights and uncovering depths inside yourself you never knew you had. In losing her I've lost more than a friend, I've lost that part of myself that she saw in me."

The man behind the glass walks away, crossing behind the heavy leaded joints of the window like a man slipping behind the trees of a forest. I can't see his face, but something in his posture, his loping gait, suddenly reminds me of someone. Only it's impossible for it to be him.

CHAPTER THIRTEEN

IN MY HASTE TO GET OUT TO THE LOBBY I NO DOUBT CONVINCE Christine's mother that I am as rude a heathen as she always thought me to be. I know it's insane—that the figure behind the glass couldn't possibly be Neil—but I have to know for sure.

The lobby is empty of everything but that faint whiff of smoke still hanging in the air. It's a little fainter now than it had been before, as if the outside door had recently been open. It's impossible to see the street because the outside windows are boarded up, so I move toward the front door, which opens in just as I reach it. I nearly run into a slender young man in a crumpled black suit and skinny tie. As it is, the man treads on my feet with his pointy-toed black cowboy boots.

Who would wear cowboy boots to a funeral?

I look up into a face so young he could be Beatrice's age. Or maybe it's just his red swollen eyes that make him look like a child.

"Am I late? Did I miss it? The train was delayed and

then I walked from the station and got lost. This is where Christine Webb is—I mean, where her funeral is?"

"Yes. You're Nathan Bell, aren't you?" I say, having recognized his voice from our phone conversation. I hold out a hand to shake his and then, thinking better of it when I see him use his hand to mop his perspiring forehead, pat his shoulder instead. The black cloth, I notice, is covered in white cat hair, reminding me that he still has Christine's cat. I can also feel through the thin fabric that he's drenched. It's a good mile to the station and he's breathing as if he had jogged it.

"I'm Christine's friend, Juno. We spoke on the phone last week. I should have thought to call you and ask if you needed a lift from the station."

"Oh, no, I didn't want to be a bother and Mrs. Webb told me it was only a few blocks. Have I missed the service?"

"I'm afraid so, but honestly, you didn't miss much. The minister wouldn't have known Christine if he'd tripped over her." I look back guiltily over my shoulder to see if anyone's overheard me, but the congregants are only now slowly filtering out of the chapel into the lobby. I notice that Ruth is walking next to Amy, leaning heavily on her sister's arm. Detective Falco comes up beside her and offers her his arm as well, but she waves him away. Then he leans over and whispers something in her ear. I see Ruth's skin, washed out already, turn whiter and then flush pink. *Something to do with the autopsy report?* I wonder. But what bad news could there be left to tell? I step forward, trying to get closer to them, but they're surrounded by Ruth's sisters and other Webbs. Besides, I've still got Nathan Bell, who's stepped forward with me, glued to my side and shifting uneasily from foot to foot in those damned incongruous cowboy boots. What could he have been thinking? But then I realize that he's probably a poor graduate student and they might be the only pair of black shoes he owns.

"Christine was cremated so there's no burial," I say to him, abandoning my efforts to get closer to Detective Falco and Ruth. I can always find out later what the autopsy results have revealed. "But everyone's going back to Mrs. Webb's house. I can give you a lift."

He looks so grateful I feel bad that I've made the offer half grudgingly. The truth is that I'd like to take the drive myself so I can think more about that apparition behind the stained-glass windows. "By the way, when you came in did you happen to pass someone going out—a young man . . ."

I falter, unsure of how to describe Neil, whom I haven't seen in over ten years. Would his hair still be that shade of blond that turned to gold when the sun hit it? Did he still have that spray of freckles across the bridge of his nose— the same configuration that sprawls over Bea's face—and hazel eyes that turned blue or green depending on his mood and sometimes didn't match? Or had fourteen years in a mental hospital—even one as expensive and elite as Briarwood—washed all those colors out of him?

Nathan is still waiting.

"Did you see anyone leaving as you came in?" I ask.

"No," he says, "only you."

* * *

ON THE DRIVE TO MRS. WEBB'S HOUSE I DECIDE THAT WHOEVER I saw through the funeral parlor windows—if anyone was there at all—couldn't be Neil. It was an undertaker, or a shadow—some trick of light in the distorted, fire-damaged glass. Still as we drive out of downtown and turn onto the wooded road that leads to Christine's childhood home I find myself scanning the edges of the woods as if looking for some fugitive shape flitting between the trees.

"Webb Road," Nathan says, reading the road sign. "Any relation—?"

"They're all relations," I answer. "Almost everyone on this road is a cousin of some degree. Even Christine's mother was a Webb before she married Mr. Webb—a third or fourth cousin."

"I didn't know the area Christine grew up in was so *rural*." The way Nathan says *rural* I know that what he's really thinking is *white trash*. From his accent and the Star of David I can see now that he's loosened his tie, I place him as a nice Jewish boy from Long Island or Queens. Although only two hours from New York City this rural pocket must seem as remote to him as backwoods Georgia. "I'd never have found my way on these back roads—maybe we should have followed the other cars."

I take my eyes off the side of the road long enough to flash what I hope is a confident smile in Nathan's direction. "Ruth wanted us to go on ahead because I've got some groceries I picked up for her, but don't worry, I know these roads pretty well. It happens to be the road to Briarwood as well."

"The psychiatric hospital? Christine said she lived just down the hill from it. Her mother worked there, right?"

"Until she was injured. Her aunt Amy and aunt Beth still work there. Their mother was head cook there for thirty-five years. It's kind of a family legacy to work at Briarwood."

"They must have a lot of sympathy for the mentally ill."

I turn my head sharply in Nathan's direction to see if he's joking but he looks perfectly sincere. *How well had he known Christine, anyway*, I wonder. Certainly, she'd never mentioned him to me. "Christine used to say it gave them someone to feel superior to, but whenever I heard Ruth talk about Briarwood it was more as if she envied the patients. She always spoke as if they were all lollygagging around some country club, faking their symptoms of insanity so they didn't have to *put in an honest day's work*. 'I'd have me a nervous breakdown, too,' she'd say, 'if I thought it'd get me breakfast in bed and bubble baths for the rest of my life.'"

"Do the patients really get breakfast in bed?"

"Only when they're being force-fed through their nasal passages. As for the bubble baths—I know that years ago they practiced a kind of hydro-shock therapy by dunking patients into ice-cold tubs. It's no Club Med, but the buildings and grounds are beautiful. Look, you can just see the rooftop of the main building from here."

We've come to a split in the road where the private drive to the hospital proceeds uphill through two massive stone pillars, and the county route plunges downhill into a scraggly hollow flanked by an auto repair shop and a home hair salon called Shear Beauty. I pull the car over to the dirt shoulder and point out a turreted tower just above the tree line.

"It looks like a castle in a fairy tale," Nathan says.

"Yeah," I say, pulling back onto the road and heading downhill, "the evil witch's castle."

EVEN THOUGH WE LEFT BEFORE THE REST OF THE WEBBS, they've managed to beat us back to the house.

"I thought you'd never get here with the food," Ruth says by way of greeting after Nathan and I have hauled all the grocery bags up the quarter-mile driveway from the road (the driveway is blocked by three vehicles—a rusted-out gold Duster, a Pacer, and a pickup truck sitting on concrete blocks—that don't appear to have been moved since Christine's college days). When I glance into the front sitting room on my way to the kitchen it doesn't look like anyone is in danger of starving. Two aunts and several young people who I recognize as Christine's cousins wave forks laden with coffee cake in our direction as Nathan and I take turns bringing in the bags. In the kitchen we find an array of Corning casserole dishes that would have turned Augustus Penrose green with envy that he'd failed to follow his competitor, Corning Glass, into household dishware. If he had, Rosedale would be a thriving town right now.

When we've finished unloading the food I look around

for Ruth again, but find, instead, Amy sitting on a back porch that's been converted into a TV room. She pats the spot on the love seat beside her and I remember that I still haven't found out from her why Christine didn't see her mother when she came to visit Briarwood last month. I sit down next to Amy and instantly sink into a deep hollow in the old sofa. I'm hauling myself up onto a firmer perch when Nathan comes out of the kitchen holding two plates of food and, seeing me, rushes to my side like a drowning man swimming to shore. He squeezes himself onto the love seat, which was hardly big enough for me and Amy, and hands me a plate full of potato salad, doughnuts, and hot dogs wrapped in Pillsbury dough.

"Christine's aunt Beth said I *had* to try a little of everything," he says with a desperate look in his eyes. "She made me take two plates. You'll eat some, won't you?" He's holding up one of the doughy blobs and looking at it as if it might explode. From the bright yellow mustard stains on his skinny tie I guess that his fears aren't unwarranted.

Amy reaches over me and takes both plates out of our hands. She manages to extricate herself from the viselike love seat with surprising grace for such a large woman. "I'll just take these to the front room where Beth's children are watching TV. You two young people want to talk among yourselves."

"But I thought he was Chrissie's young man," Aunt Beth says, coming into the room with another platter of pigs in blankets to replace the plates Amy has removed. Guiltily, Nathan takes a bite of the hot dog still in his hand.

"Though I must say you look a hair young to have been taking Chrissie out."

"I wasn't—" Nathan stammers through a mouthful of hot dog. A jet of mustard—bright as cadmium yellow paint—squirts out of the pillowy dough as if it had been secreted there under high pressure. Nathan futilely tries to intercept the fallout with a paper napkin so thin (it looks like the kind sold in bulk to institutions and I suspect it's come to the Webb household courtesy of Briarwood's supply closet) it instantly dissolves as if bathed in acid.

"But then I read in *People* magazine that older women have started going after the younger men because all the ones their own age have been taken already," Beth says, taking Amy's vacated place on the love seat. Nathan has turned such a bright red that along with the spots of French's mustard dotting his shirt and pants he looks like he's contracted some kind of exotic jungle fever since entering the Webb household.

"That's what comes of taking so long to finish school and putting off getting married. I never did understand why Chrissie needed to go to school for so many years and if she were going to go back to school again why she couldn't have gone for a certificate in something she could get a job in. Like my Alice has gone for her occupational therapy license so she can get to the next pay level uphill . . ."

"Uphill?" Nathan whispers in my ear.

"Up at Briarwood," I explain, trying to keep my voice low, but Beth can't help but hear me since she's practically sitting in my lap.

"Did you see it on your way in?" Beth asks, straightening her spine and patting her teased and lacquered hair.

"Yes, Juno pointed it out to me. It's quite an impressive building. Gothic revival, I would think . . ."

"It was built by Frederick Clark Withers," Beth answers proudly. I can see that Nathan is surprised to hear the name of the famous English architect come out of the same mouth that just swallowed three pigs in blankets whole. He's made the mistake many do on first meeting Christine's family of underestimating them. They're not stupid—just uninterested in anything outside of a five-mile radius of the little hamlet that surrounds the hospital. They are experts, though, on anything to do with Briarwood and the luminaries connected to it. I once heard Amy, for instance, compare the benefits of insight-oriented therapy to reality-adaptive psychotherapy on schizophrenics—the subject of a research study that Briarwood had participated in during the eighties. (*Neither did them any good,* she'd concluded, *there's nothing you can do for those poor souls but keep them clean and out of harm's way.*)

"And Calvert Vaux designed the grounds," Beth continues, "the same fellow as worked on Central Park." As she pronounces the landscape architect's name to rhyme with "sew" I can feel Nathan, who's slipped down into my hollow on the couch, tense and murmur the correct pronunciation, which rhymes with "fox." Before he can say it again more loudly (the aunts hate to be corrected on anything to do with Briarwood) I put a hand on his bony knee.

"You know, Nathan really ought to see the grounds while he's here. Can you still get onto the bridle path through the side gate?"

Beth nods. "Yes, as long as you stay on that path no one will bother you and the boy ought to see it if he's interested in architecture. New York City's not the only place to see famous buildings."

By the time I've gotten us free of the love seat's bony grip and declined Beth's offer of packing us a picnic lunch for "our hike" I feel as if I've busted out of jail. The air outside, although warm, feels like balm after breathing in the aunts' Lucky Strikes.

"The path's a quarter mile up the road. I hope you don't mind an uphill hike."

"Are you kidding? After all the pork fat I've consumed? Do you think those doughnuts were fried in lard? And were those actually pork rinds? I didn't think anyone ate those north of the Mason-Dixon Line. And what were those crunchy things in the potato salad . . . no, never mind, I don't want to know. It's not that I'm kosher, but I've actually never seen that many pork products at one meal before. God, do I sound like a horrible snob?"

Nathan stops so abruptly that I bump into him and nearly shove him into the path of an oncoming SUV. The shoulder is narrow here because of the ten-foot-tall brick wall that surrounds the grounds of the hospital.

Before I can think of a kind way to answer Nathan's question he answers it himself. "I do, don't I? I'm making fun of Christine's family at her own wake."

"It's okay. Christine would be the first to join in." I put

my hand on Nathan's elbow and steer him off the road toward a gate in the brick wall that's so overrun by vines and bramble I almost missed it. It's obvious that the bridle path hasn't been used in years. "She couldn't stand her family."

"I know it sounds awful to say, but I can't imagine someone as refined as Christine coming from this kind of background. Is it possible she was adopted?"

I laugh. "Christine admitted that it was a cherished childhood fantasy that she didn't really belong to the Webbs. But then in the fifth grade her class learned about blood types and she found out she was AB negative—which is pretty rare. She asked her mother what *her* blood type was and found out it was the same. Then when her mother figured out why she was asking she lifted up her shirt and showed Christine her caesarian scar and told her, '*Don't you ever think I didn't give birth to you after what you did coming out of me.*'"

"Lovely." Nathan bats at an encroaching vine that has reached out to snag his shirt cuff. Poor Nathan. Now he's got blood as well as mustard on what is probably his one good shirt.

"Yeah, well to give Mrs. Webb some credit it must have felt crummy to know your own daughter would prefer not to be related to you. I don't think Ruth knew what to make of Christine—she must have seemed like a changeling." The word, with its fairy tale connotations of demon offspring swapped at birth, makes me shiver. Or maybe it's just that it's cold here in this tunnel-like path hidden from the sun. The overgrown state of the path makes me realize how much time has gone by since I walked here with Christine and that saddens me, too. It's as if the past we shared together has already been encroached upon by her death.

"You'd think she'd have a little more sensitivity considering she worked in a psychiatric hospital." As if the words had summoned up the place, the path opens up to a clear knoll from which we can see, across a sloping green lawn, the rambling brick building that's the main ward of the hospital, and the Hudson River below it. There's a bench here where Christine and I used to sit and where I came after my last visit with Neil. *In memory of our mother, Elizabeth "Binky" Soames* reads the plaque set into its slatted back. I point it out to Nathan as we sit down.

"Christine called it the Binky bench. She always said you couldn't blame the woman for ending up uphill when everyone called her Binky."

"Ending up uphill?"

"That's what her mother and aunts said when someone was institutionalized here. They'd ended up uphill. Christine said it was kind of a childhood threat, her family's version of the boogie man. Any sign of eccentric behavior—like drawing or daydreaming or talking to yourself—and her mother would say *if you keep that up you'll end up uphill*. I don't think working here made the Webbs sensitive to the victims of mental illness. You probably have to be a little callous not to go crazy yourself. But for all their hardness, I suspect the things they saw here scared them. Unfortunately, it just made Christine afraid that she really was crazy. She told me once that that was the thing she feared most—losing her sanity."

"Do you think she would kill herself if she thought that was happening?"

The question, coming so suddenly, startles me. And yet it's what everyone at the funeral and down at the Webb's house must be thinking. I suspect it's the conclusion Detective Falco shared with Ruth at the funeral and that it's what Amy was going to tell me at the funeral—that Christine avoided her mother because she was having some sort of breakdown.

"I don't know, maybe. There were times—four years ago before she went into rehab and for a period back in college—that she seemed almost infatuated with the idea of suicide. She and my ex-husband Neil had this sort of running joke where they'd compete over who was the most likely to end up killing themselves."

Nathan winces.

"I know, but they had a literary precedent. Sylvia Plath and Anne Sexton used to argue over martinis at the Ritz Hotel about who was most suicidal. When Plath killed herself Sexton wrote a poem accusing Sylvia of *stealing* her death from her. Neil and Christine loved that."

"So what happened to your ex-husband? If you don't mind me asking."

I lift my chin in the direction of the gothic pile of brick. "He's here at Briarwood. At least, I think he still is." I think again of that fleeting shadow I saw through the windows at Silas B. Cooke's. What would Neil make of Christine's death? Would he remember that grudge match they had

in college? But looking at the hospital—at its barred
windows and gated doors like some medieval castle sealed
off from the world—I can't imagine how he would even
hear about her death, and before Nathan can ask me what
I'm sure will be a series of prying questions about Neil I go
back to Christine. After all, this is her day. I'll have time to
think of Neil later.

"But I don't see why Christine would have committed
suicide now. She seemed like she was getting her life back
together. She almost had her degree . . ."

"You know she'd switched concentrations again."

"I know she switched from medieval art to nineteenth-
century painting last year."

"She'd just switched again—to early-twentieth-century
decorative arts. She said it was because of researching the
Penrose window."

"But that would have set her back at least another
year."

"It's not that unusual. People take decades to get their
doctorates. But there was something so intense in
Christine when she was focused on something that it was
unsettling when she switched gears so abruptly—"

I knew what he was talking about. Neil had been like
that, too. One minute you'd have his complete attention,
and the next he had disappeared, gone to work on a
painting.

"—her thesis adviser confessed that he was worried
about her. She'd missed appointments with him over the
last few months and she wasn't keeping up with her
teaching responsibilities. He said she was in danger of

losing her scholarship money if she didn't get her act together."

"He said that to Christine?"

Nathan nods, his gaze on the river and the hills in the distance. "Just last week."

"Damn. It probably sounded to Christine like one of her mother's threats. '*If you don't shape up you'll end up uphill.*'"

"Maybe that's what she thought her choices were."

"What?"

Nathan lifts his chin toward the sprawling brick building just like I did a moment ago to indicate Neil's abode. "Look at the two things she grew up with that had any beauty—a psychiatric hospital—" He turns his head toward the river. "—and the river. Maybe she decided to choose the river because she thought that otherwise she might end up in the hospital."

CHAPTER FOURTEEN

ON OUR WALK BACK DOWN THE BRIDLE PATH NATHAN AND I lapse into silence. It feels appropriate after the conversation we've just had about Christine as a way of honoring her in the chapel-like stillness of the woods. At least I hope that's what Nathan's doing. I, regrettably, have gone back to thinking about Neil.

The reason the glimpse of the shadow behind the windows at Cooke's made me think of him, I've realized, is that it's so much like the first glimpse I ever had of him.

I usually tell people that I met Neil the spring semester of my junior year in Professor Da Silva's Dante class, but that isn't precisely true. I met him—or perhaps I should say, caught my first sight of him—during Christmas break that year at the Cloisters museum in Manhattan. Christine had called me the first week of the new year and begged me to meet her on the southbound train on what turned out to be the coldest day of the year.

We got off at the Marble Hill station and walked across the 225th Street bridge and down Broadway toward Fort

Tryon Park. It was a good two-mile hike through icy city streets, and it began to snow as we entered the park. I'd been to the Cloisters once before on a school field trip on a muggy day in June but I'd found it hard to lose myself in the feeling of being in a medieval monastery. There'd been too many high school kids making lewd jokes about the grotesque demons and beasts carved into the column capitals. But on that day with Christine, trudging across the snow-covered terrain of Fort Tryon Park on cold, tired feet, I could imagine, when I caught sight of the stone towers, that Christine and I were two of Chaucer's pilgrims looking for sanctuary at the monastery.

We had the place pretty much to ourselves. Christine was disappointed that the Cuxa Cloister—the largest cloister at the center of the museum—had been glassed off against the cold weather, but I loved the way the sun came in through the glass panes, warming the mottled pink Carrara marble. While Christine paced around the square, I settled against a column in the northwest corner of the arcade and took out my sketchbook. While I drew she kept up a running commentary on the figures carved into the marble capitals, pointing out particularly grotesque demons.

"Have you ever wondered," she asked from the far end of the arcade, "why the most religious people are most fascinated with hell?"

I shrugged. It didn't seem like the kind of conversation to shout across a public space, even though we appeared to be alone in the cloister.

"I'd like to ask Professor Da Silva that when we take Dante this semester. Why does Dante have to go down into hell to find his way again—just because he lost his way in the middle of his life? Do you think that means that when you're at your lowest you have to go lower? To face your demons?"

I looked up from my drawing. Christine was standing in the north arcade, hands buried in the pockets of her hooded Penrose sweatshirt, gazing up at the leering face of a monkey-demon. Even though she was wearing the same college sweatshirt as I was the effect on her was medieval. Her hair, loose under the sweatshirt, fell in smooth loops on either side of her face. She could have been an abbess, a dethroned queen in monastic exile, Guinevere pacing the stone arcades of Almesbury. I flipped a page in my notebook and started to draw her, lengthening her sweatshirt into monastic robes and turning the casual disarray of her hair into a medieval coiffure. When I came to filling in the background of columns in the east arcade I noticed that the protective glass panes on that side had frosted over so that the columns looked blurry. I imagined a painting of Guinevere, looking out into her cloistered garden and seeing figures from her past rising out of the mist, Arthur, Lancelot . . . and then I noticed that there was, indeed, a figure in the mist. Someone was sitting in the archway directly across from me, leaning against a column, a sketchpad resting on bent knees. For a moment I thought I was looking at my own reflection, but then the figure rose and walked south along the east arcade.

"What is it?" Christine asked.

I put a finger to my lips and waved her over with my

other hand. When she was closer to me I pointed to the figure walking past the pink columns on the other side of the cloister. Just as I did the figure passed behind the last column and vanished. Christine and I looked at each other and then, when we looked back, he reappeared two arches back.

"How . . . ?"

"He must have crept back under the stone bench," I whispered. "He knows we're watching him."

By now the figure—he was wearing a hooded sweatshirt much like ours so all we could tell was that he was tall and slim—had passed out of sight into the southeast corner of the cloister.

"Let's follow him," Christine said. "He must have gone into the Unicorn Tapestries room."

Clutching my sketchpad to my chest I followed Christine south along the west arcade into the Nine Heroes Tapestry room and from there into the room that housed the museum's most famous exhibit—the sixteenth-century tapestries depicting the hunt and capture of the unicorn. The room was empty except for the hunters in their plumed hats and their fine-boned greyhounds wandering through a heavily flowered wood.

"There he is," Christine said, pointing toward the windows facing out into the cloister. I glanced out the leaded glass windows and saw the hooded figure walking west along the south arcade. "Come on."

Christine headed back out into the Cuxa Cloister, but I lingered a moment in front of the last unicorn tapestry, the one that shows him collared and trapped beneath a pomegranate tree. The image had always disturbed me, even after our medieval art teacher assured us that the red stains on the unicorn's milky white skin were pomegranate juice, not blood. What bothered me the most, I suppose, is that I'd admired the image for years—my mother had hung a framed print of it in my room when I first showed an interest in unicorns—without knowing I was looking at a dead creature.

When I came out into the covered walkway Christine was standing at the entrance to the Early Gothic Hall on the west side of the cloister waving to me. When I followed her in I expected to find our mystery man cornered there but instead Christine was standing by one of the unglazed lancet windows overlooking the Gothic chapel, leaning so far over I was afraid she might fall and break her neck on the stone floor below, joining the entombed nobility whose stone coffins lined the chapel floor. When I joined her there I saw what she was pointing at. Someone had propped a sheet of cardboard on the folded hands of a tomb effigy and drawn a red arrow pointing east.

"He's pretty sure of himself," I said. I expected that Christine would suggest we call off the chase, but she seemed intrigued.

"I wanted to see the exhibit down there anyway," she said, heading down the stairs to the lower level of the museum.

We passed through the Gothic chapel (Christine retrieved the arrow placard from the tomb of the medieval knight) and into the Glass Gallery, which was empty except for a guard at the end of the hall.

"We could ask the guard if he saw anyone come through here," I suggested to Christine. But Christine shrugged and wandered over to a display of ivory diptychs. "I guess we'll find him when he wants to be found."

While Christine looked at the display cases, I walked along the wall of windows. Set into the leaded glass were roundels of silver-stained glass. If he'd given me a chance, I thought, I could have impressed that boy by explaining how the yellow color was produced by applying a solution of silver nitrate to the clear glass and that the process was discovered in the fourteenth century. Instead I was left admiring the way the patches of yellow stood out against the bleak white and gray of the winter sky outside like the first daffodils coming up through the snow. I loved the way the yellow was the only color in the muted grisaille panels and stopped to get a closer look at the intricate painting that had been done on the glass when I saw another patch of yellow. A shock of sun-bright hair in the courtyard outside the window. The boy was sitting on the far side of the little Bonnefont Cloister, his back to the George Washington Bridge in the distance. He was smoking a cigarette. When he saw my face pressed up against the window he lifted a hand and waved.

I turned back to tell Christine that I'd spotted him, but she was at the far end of the gallery talking to the guard so instead I went in the opposite direction to the door that led outside. I was sure he'd still be there but when I stepped outside I was alone in the cloister. A cold wind rattled the dry leaves of the espaliered pear trees, and I could still smell the smoke from his cigarette, but he was gone. I walked through to the Trie Cloister and then back into the glass gallery just in time to see the bottom of his sneakered feet disappearing up the stairwell. Christine was still talking to the guard, but when she saw me head up the stairs she followed me.

"Did you see him again?" she asked as we arrived on the main level.

I shook my head, not because I meant that I hadn't seen him, but because I was so befuddled by the chase, but she took it as a negative. We went into the Campin room at the head of the stairs and Christine walked over to a fifteenth-century triptych of the annunciation.

"What a tease!" she said, looking at the virgin but meaning, I suppose, the boy.

As usual I gravitated toward the windows—even though these were clear hexagonal leaded glass and not stained—and sat down on a stone ledge beneath them. I felt tired and disappointed and hungry and cold. Like a pilgrim who'd come looking for sanctuary but been turned away at the monastery gate. Outside through the falling snow the blond-haired boy was loping down the steep cobblestoned driveway with nothing but his hooded sweatshirt to protect him against the snow. I breathed onto the glass and drew my initials in the steam from my breath. That's when I noticed the folded paper wedged in the wood frame of the window. Prying it out I unfolded the paper and found that it was a sketch of a woman seated beneath a columned arch. She wore a long medieval robe, her face half hidden in the folds of its hood. As in my sketch of Christine he'd turned the prosaic college sweatshirt into a romantic garment, but this picture was of me, not Christine. He'd turned me into Guinevere pining for Arthur and Lancelot in the convent of Almesbury.

In the lower right-hand corner of the picture there was a tiny drawing of a tree. I didn't know then that it was a symbol Neil used to sign his paintings—a beech tree because his name meant beech forest in German. *Or book forest*, he told me later, *only that wouldn't make any sense.*

I turned the drawing over and was disappointed to see that he hadn't signed his name or written his phone number. I assumed I'd never see him again, but I was wrong. On the first day of spring semester I walked into Dante class and found our Cloisters Phantom (as Christine and I had taken to calling him) sitting in the back row. Later he told me that he'd heard Christine and me talking about the class in the Cuxa Cloister, figured out where we went to college from our sweatshirts, and applied to spend his junior spring semester as an exchange student at Penrose and then signed up for the Dante class. I'd spent that day at the Cloisters feeling like the pursuer, but in the end it was Neil who'd hunted me down. I'd never felt as wanted before—nor have I since.

NOR HAVE I EVER FELT AS LOVED AS I FELT BY NEIL IN THE YEARS we spent together before he began to lose his mind. *Beloved*, really, *adored*. When we were in a room together he never seemed to take his eyes off me. He was always drawing me as one figure from romantic mythology or another: Beatrice, Guinevere, Halcyone, Isolde. I should have wondered why he never simply drew me as myself, but by the time I understood that what he loved was something inside his own mind—and that when his mind cracked so would his image of me—I was addicted to being loved like that. No wonder I still dreamed about him. No wonder I had imagined him as the indistinct figure behind the glass at Cooke's today.

Even here, walking under the arched canopy of twisted branches with Nathan Bell, I've got half an eye out for a sight of him behind the thick, overgrown foliage even though these woods are so dense—as lushly green and rich with wildflowers as the millefleurs tapestries at the Cloisters—that a dozen Neils could be passing by us ten feet off the path and I'd never see them. That thought sets my skin prickling, but whether from fear or excitement I'm not sure. *How would it feel to see Neil again after all these years?*

When we turn into the final curve of the bridle path I get an answer of sorts. A figure steps out of the shadows into a patch of sun at the bottom of the path and for a moment the sun makes a halo of his bright hair. When he steps toward us, and into the shadows again, I see it's Detective Falco, but for just that moment when I thought it was Neil I felt something take flight inside me that wasn't fear.

"Miss McKay, Mr. Bell." The detective nods at me but extends his hand to Nathan and introduces himself. "Amy Webb said you'd be on this path. I thought I'd catch you before you got back to the house and have a word with you both alone. There's not much opportunity for privacy at Mrs. Webb's house."

"No, Christine always said the same thing," I say.

"Do you want to talk to both of us at the same time . . . or should I go back . . . ?" Nathan takes a step down the hill and points one arm toward the road, the other toward the detective, flapping his arms up and down like a giant crow. I notice dark half-moons of sweat beneath his arms on the shiny fabric of his suit jacket that could well be from walking in the heat or from the nervousness I hear in his voice.

"I thought as Christine's closest friends you'd both like to hear the results of the autopsy together. It's not an interrogation. If you have time we could walk up the path a bit. I think there's a bench overlooking the river . . ."

"I have to get back home to feed the dogs before dark," I say. It's a lie—I've asked Robbie to feed and walk Paolo and Francesca—but one view of Briarwood is enough for one day. "I don't mind standing."

Nathan checks his watch. "I've got to catch the 6:16 back to the city," he says, "I'm sure Juno could fill me in on whatever I need to know . . ."

"You've got plenty of time; I'll drive you there myself. That way if I have any further questions I can ask them on the way. Meanwhile, it will save time to tell you this together. Kill two birds with one stone, so to speak." He smiles as if to disarm the expression of its implicit threat, but it has the opposite effect. It strikes me that for a man concerned with saving time he's spending an awful lot of it in preamble.

"You've ruled it a suicide, right?" I ask. "You wouldn't be telling us together if it were still a homicide case."

Detective Falco cocks his head to one side in a gesture that makes *him* look like the bird now, but not the fragile kind that could be killed by a stone, more like the bird his name suggests—a bird of prey.

"We haven't ruled out homicide but it does *look* like it could have been suicide. The lab results indicate that she had a combination of drugs in her bloodstream that together could have killed her and there was very little water in her lungs. It looks like she took an overdose of pills, passed out, and then capsized. Her respiration at that point was so minimal she hardly breathed in any water."

"And the drugs in her system?" I ask.

"They're consistent with the pills we found in the container in her pocket. Fluvoxamine, an antidepressant sold under the brand name Luvox, and benzodiazepine, a tranquilizer and antianxiety agent sold under the brand name Klonopin."

"So could it have been an accidental overdose," Nathan asks, "since these were drugs she was taking regularly?"

"You mean, did she feel sort of depressed after her lecture, take twenty to thirty antidepressants and then worry she wasn't going to be able to sleep on the train ride home so she took fifteen to twenty tranquilizers? And then, after washing all those pills down with a couple of cups of coffee—which we also found in her system—she decides to take a little kayak trip across the Hudson and up the Wicomico?"

"I was just asking," Nathan says, sounding a bit peevish. I can't help but feel sorry for him. First he misses the funeral, then the aunts assume he was Christine's boyfriend . . . I look from Nathan to Detective Falco and wonder if that's why the detective's being so hard on him. Does he think Nathan was Christine's lover? Does he think Nathan did something to drive Christine to kill herself?

"I don't understand that last part at all," Nathan continues, straightening his spine and raising his voice, which, unfortunately, just makes him sound shrill. "If she wanted to take an overdose of pills why not do it in the comfort of her own apartment? Why paddle up a stream in the middle of the night?"

"That's what I was going to ask Miss McKay here. You knew Christine the best. Any reason she'd stage a suicide like this?"

"I still don't—"

Detective Falco raises his hand. "I know—she was feeling much better these days, she'd gotten her act together and was starting over—but you do admit she'd been suicidal in the past. Let's just assume, for argument's sake, that it was a suicide. Why do it like this? Why the boat?"

"I guess to make a statement," I say reluctantly. "Back when she and Neil would talk about famous suicides they discussed different methods—how the method made a statement more clearly than any note did. Virginia Woolf stuffing her pockets with stones, Sylvia Plath sticking her head in the oven . . . By dying in a boat and having her body drift down the stream to be found she could have been imitating the Lady of Shalott. She said in her lecture that the Lady of Shalott was one of those women whose deaths are a recrimination to the men who betrayed them, like Dido throwing herself on the pyre or Madame Butterfly singing her last aria. Even though she's not a suicide *per se* the Lady of Shalott seals her fate by looking directly at Lancelot, and then she writes her name on the boat and makes sure it'll drift down to Camelot so Lancelot can see it . . . but Christine's boat didn't make it down the Wicomico."

"Well, she didn't know it would flip over. I guess hanging upside down in the water wasn't the picture she was trying to draw."

I wince at the image, remembering Christine's long blond hair waving in the clear creek, the bright yellow of the kayak reflected in the water . . .

"Did you look at the kayak?" I ask. "Was there anything written on the boat?"

"No. If she did write anything it washed off."

"But in order for it to make sense . . . for the whole scene she was setting up to make sense . . ." Nathan stops and starts again. "You're saying she was trying to send a message to someone—a lover who spurned her. But who? As far as I know she wasn't involved with anyone. Did she mention anyone to you, Juno?"

"Not exactly, but I had a feeling that she was holding back something from me. She asked me a lot of questions about whether I was seeing anyone . . ." I notice Detective Falco's eyebrow raised inquisitively but choose to ignore it. ". . . and about whether I was ever sorry about . . ."

Falco sees my hesitation and nods his head. "Yes?"

"She wanted to know if I ever regretted my choice to have Bea," I say, remembering how Christine had blushed when she asked the question and the way the color had made her face appear fuller. It only takes me a moment longer to put the rest together. "That's what you found in the autopsy," I say, "and that's why Christine wouldn't see her mother when she came up here last month, because she knew Ruth would have guessed."

"Guessed what?" Nathan asks, looking from me to Falco.

"That she was pregnant," Falco says to Nathan. "She was four months pregnant."

CHAPTER FIFTEEN

"BUT SHE DIDN'T *LOOK* PREGNANT," NATHAN SAYS, PULLING A handkerchief out of his suit jacket pocket and mopping sweat off his forehead. I can't help but feel sorry for him. Clearly Falco is trying to get him to admit to being the father of the child or at least knowing something about the pregnancy. But why then, I wonder, did he go out of his way to tell him with me here?

"When *was* the last time you saw Christine?" Falco asks Nathan.

"The Friday she left the city. We had lunch at the Oyster Bar in Grand Central and I saw her to her train."

"Really? Christine didn't mention . . ." the words are out of my mouth before I can help myself. Now I understand why Falco wanted me here—to see if Christine had said anything to me about a relationship with Nathan Bell. Well, it's worked. I couldn't be more surprised at the possibility that Nathan might be the father of Christine's unborn child. It's not just that he's probably ten years younger than Christine. I can imagine Christine having an affair with a younger man, but in my imagination the man would look more like, well, Kyle or Neil when Neil was that age. Christine has always gone for the *bad boy* type—slightly dangerous men in torn jeans and motorcycle jackets, not pale, gawky aesthetes like Nathan Bell.

"And you got a good look at her then? I mean, close enough to be sure she wasn't four months pregnant?"

"If you're implying . . ." Nathan's voice warbles on the last word; he's close to tears. I steal a look at Falco to see if there's any remorse in his face but his eyes are as coldly assessing as those of the bird he's named for—a hawk circling its prey looking for subtle movements in the grass.

"We weren't in a relationship, if that's what you're implying." Instead of quailing under Falco's assessing gaze Nathan has, surprisingly, pulled himself together. "And I don't appreciate being questioned in front of Miss McKay."

"Then why don't I give you that lift to the station," Falco suggests. "If you weren't in a relationship with Christine Webb perhaps you have an idea of who was. At least you can provide me with a list of possibilities at Columbia—other students, professors . . ."

Nathan's turned pale again, no doubt at the idea of informing on his peers and superiors.

"Why is it important?" I ask, partly to get Nathan off the hook, partly because I'm genuinely confused. "If you think Christine killed herself why does it matter?"

"As I mentioned earlier, we haven't ruled out homicide. What I said was that it *looked* like it could have been suicide. That might be because someone wanted it to look like suicide, someone who knew that Christine took Luvox and Klonopin. There was quite a bit of coffee in her bloodstream as well; did you give her coffee at your place?"

I shake my head. At Falco's instigation we've started back down the path toward the road. When we reach the road we have to proceed single file on the narrow dirt shoulder. Nathan goes first and Falco waves me to go on ahead of him.

"No one at the reception after the lecture remembers her having coffee either. Now, it's possible that Christine purchased a large coffee to go at the cafe across the street before heading over to the boathouse to steal a kayak—or that someone met her at the station, or the boathouse, with a thermos for their boat trip up the Wicomico. Remember, there were two missing kayaks. What confuses me is if Christine were alone and she used the coffee to wash down a few dozen pills, where's the coffee cup?"

"You're saying that a paper to-go cup couldn't go missing in the Wicomico? Or in the Hudson if it floated downstream?" I ask, turning my head back and raising my voice to be heard over a couple of motorcycles revving their engines down Webb Road.

"Maybe—but I don't like that we haven't found one. That area where you found Christine is in a protected curve of the stream. Not much current. A paper cup would have floated and gotten snagged in the water lily bed where Christine's kayak was overturned. Same for a glass thermos . . ."

"But not one of those metal thermoses," Nathan says without turning his head. I'm surprised that he's been able to keep up with the conversation as far ahead as he's been.

"True, but then it would have sunk to the bottom and our divers searched that whole area. All we found were some pieces of an old statue that had toppled in the water."

We haven't quite made it back to Ruth Webb's house but Falco stops at a dark blue Chevrolet Caprice parked on the side of the road and calls to Nathan to stop.

"I thought I'd just go back and pay my respects to Mrs. Webb . . ." he says, turning in the road.

"I'm sure Miss McKay can convey those sentiments and explain that you didn't want to miss the train. Right?"

Nathan looks at me so imploringly that I'd like to think of a reason to keep him out of Falco's grasp but then I wonder why I should be so anxious to protect him. What if he did have something to do with Christine's death?

"So this person in the other kayak—you think it could be the father of the baby?" I ask.

Detective Falco holds out both hands, palms turned up. "I'll be honest with you, Miss McKay, I don't have a lot to go on besides Miss Webb being pregnant. Some guys might not take that kind of news so well. Especially if they're married—you're not married, are you, Mr. Bell?"

"No!" Nathan says so adamantly you would think the idea of marriage had never occurred to him.

"Or engaged?"

Nathan shakes his head.

"Ever read a book called *An American Tragedy?*"

Nathan's been so set on denying any question put to him that he starts to shake his head at this one but then jerks his head up. "You mean the one by Dreiser?"

"I don't know of any other—but then I only took three or four Lit classes at John Jay. It was all I could fit into my schedule what with the demands of a double major in police science and forensic psychology."

"Well, you did better than I did," Nathan says, smiling. I suppose he means the smile to be congratulatory but it looks to me—and no doubt to Falco—condescending. "The art history major at NYU kept me so busy I could hardly fit in any literature classes. What I did take had to be tied into medieval art so I'm afraid I never got much past Dante . . ."

"That's a shame; you shouldn't neglect American literature. How about you, Miss McKay? Ever read *An American Tragedy* by Theodore Dreiser?"

"Yes," I say, amused in spite of myself. "In freshman English. Because it takes place in upstate New York, Penrose College considered it part of our 'regional heritage' along with *The Last of the Mohicans* and Washington Irving."

"Care to give us the Cliff's Notes version?"

"Promising young man has affair with factory girl but then has a chance to date the boss's daughter. When the factory girl gets pregnant he doesn't want to marry her so he takes her out rowing on a lake and drowns her."

"Well, I'm not engaged to anyone and I'd hardly think of Christine as a poor factory girl . . ."

The effect of Nathan's little speech is unfortunately ruined by the sight of a car full of Webb cousins cruising slowly by in a rusted-out Plymouth, plump elbows sticking out the rolled-down windows. As they pass us one of them flicks a lit cigarette out the window, which lands at Falco's feet. The detective steps on the cigarette, grinding it out under the heel of his black shoe, and opens his car door for Nathan, confident that he's not going to finish his sentence. The fact is, for all her apparent refinement, Christine could be second cousin to the girl in Dreiser's story.

AFTER DETECTIVE FALCO LEAVES WITH NATHAN I GO BACK TO the house determined to find Amy and talk with her. Although I've guessed that what Amy noticed last month was Christine's pregnancy, I want to know for sure. I search the downstairs rooms without finding her until one of the cousins tells me she's upstairs in Christine's old room "packing up some of Chrissie's old stuff for the Good Will."

I'm amazed, while climbing the narrow back stairs to the attic room I remember as Christine's, that Christine would have left any of her old stuff here, but even more amazed when I enter the slope-ceilinged room to find it almost unchanged since I last saw it fifteen years ago— two weeks before Christine graduated from Penrose. The same threadbare quilt on the same narrow, cast-iron bedstead—Christine had found the headboard at a flea market in Rhinebeck and painted it white—and the same art prints of Augustus Penrose's early paintings tacked to the walls, which she'd collected over the years on visits to the Met and the Museum of Fine Arts in Boston and the Penrose College Art Gallery.

"Aren't you going to take these?" I'd asked on that last visit. I'd stretched myself out on the bed, becalmed by the heat of the attic room and the weight of pregnancy.

"I've kind of lost my taste for all this mawkish Pre-Raphaelite stuff," she said. "I want to study the real thing now—medieval art, not what some effete Englishmen made of it to fulfill their wet dreams. Penrose wasn't even a real Pre-Raphaelite, or even a second-generation one like Waterhouse, he was just a bad Victorian painter with an infatuation for prepubescent nymphomaniacs."

I remember I'd felt somehow betrayed by her dismissal of these wan, long-haired girls in their watery bowers. The picture I approach now is *The Drowning Tree*. I've wanted to have another look at it since Christine mentioned it in her lecture, but I haven't had a chance because it was taken down from the Forest Hall for cleaning. . . . *follow where your eye leads you*, I hear Christine's voice say in my head. My eye is drawn to the cascade of golden hair that falls from the head of the girl bending over the lily pool. Intertwined in her hair are beech leaves, some green, some turning yellow, and then, as her hair trails into the pool the ends begin to writhe as if the water had brought them to life. I follow these snakelike tresses deeper into the water where they loop around the face of a girl—the reflection of the girl bending over the pool. Her mouth is distended in horror as she witnesses her own transformation into something not human.

I sink down on the bed, which creaks under my weight, feeling the same heaviness and nausea that I had the last time I was in this room—only then it was because I was pregnant. I remember feeling that I was transforming as stealthily and irrevocably as these frightened nymphs caught in the moment of metamorphosis—that my body was not my own. It had been taken over, first by Neil, and then the baby. The plans I'd made for after college had been derailed—the trip to Europe Christine and I had planned to take together after graduation, the months I'd planned to spend drawing in the great museums, and maybe art school afterward . . . but then I'd gotten pregnant and Neil had wanted me to have the baby and marry him. Had *begged* me to have the baby and marry him. And Christine had left me behind to go off to Oxford to study twelfth-century Psalters and Burgundian tapestries. She'd left me behind just as she'd left all these lovesick, shape-shifting nymphs.

The window at the foot of the bed is swollen shut but after a short struggle it opens and lets in a little stale air. Leaning against the wall, I rest one elbow on the ledge much as I imagine Christine must have for many hours in her childhood. Because the room's so high up I can just make out the brick towers of Briarwood and a glimpse of the river beyond.

"Oh, my goodness, you looked so much like Christine for a moment you half scared me to death."

Amy is standing in the doorway, one hand to her heaving chest, the other clutching a box of trash bags.

"I'm sorry, Amy," I say, sliding toward the edge of the bed. Before I can get up, though, she sits down beside me. "I didn't mean to startle you. I came up looking for you actually and then . . . I didn't know that Ruth had kept the room like this."

"Ruth said she had no other use for the room because it got so hot in the summer and so cold in the winter, but when Beth asked once if her youngest, Doreen, could stay over here, Ruth flat out said no. I think she wanted to have a place for Christine to come home to."

"Did Christine understand that? Because she never mentioned it to me."

"I know Ruth didn't seem like a very loving mother but she did love Christine. She just didn't know what to make of her. Did Christine ever tell you much about her father?"

I shake my head. "She said he died too young for her to remember him—she was only four, right?"

"Did you know he killed himself?"

"No, I had no idea. I'm sure Christine said it was a heart condition."

"That's what we all agreed to say. Ruth was so ashamed. She came home one day from working uphill and found him in the woodshed. He'd hanged himself. You of all people must know what she had to go through—being left with a four-year-old and that kind of knowledge."

Amy pauses long enough for this thought to sink in: that Ruth Webb and I have something in common.

"I think she was always afraid that Christine had inherited her father's black moods—that's what she called them. I'm not saying she handled it right, but I believe she did the best that she could, raising that girl on her own, working overtime up at Briarwood to make ends meet until she had the accident."

"Did Christine ever find out how her father really died?"

"I'm afraid she might have. When she came up here last month she went to see Dr. Horace up at Briarwood. She asked me to set up the appointment. She said it was for some research she was doing on that window down at the college."

"It was part of her lecture. Eugenie Penrose's sister was apparently an inmate at Briarwood around the turn of the century."

"Clare Barovier. I remember her—she was an old woman when I came to work there in the early sixties."

"You mean she was still in Briarwood after all those years?"

"Oh my, let's see, I went to work at Briarwood in '64 and I believe Miss Barovier died two years later. She must have been over ninety and she'd been there since she was just a young woman. Many of our old-timers spent their whole lives at Briarwood. That used to be more common back before they came up with all these new drugs and the insurance companies stopped paying for such long stays—not that most of our patients needed the insurance. Most of them had wealthy families that didn't mind paying to keep their crazy relatives out of sight."

Like Neil.

"Clare Barovier was something of a legend at Briarwood," Amy continues. "I grew up hearing stories about her. You could tell she had been a beauty, and unlike most of the poor souls there she hadn't lost her looks entirely. She had a tower suite all to herself and private servants, and was even allowed to go out on her own for picnics and boat trips down the river."

"She went out boating by herself?"

"Oh, not all by herself—I just meant she didn't need an escort from the asylum. A relative of hers would come with his yacht and take her out. When I was little it was something of a family story that sometimes she invited children along on the boat to draw their portraits. The place is full of her sketches and watercolors of the river."

"She was still painting?"

"Oh, yes, Dr. Peabody, Dr. Horace's predecessor, encouraged artistic expression as therapy. She even taught drawing to the younger patients. We've always had an artistic set."

She sounds proud—as if she were talking about a country club or a girls' finishing school.

"So Christine went to Briarwood to research Clare Barovier. Why do you think she found out about her father's suicide?"

"Because Dr. Horace knew that Edward killed himself and I think Christine asked him about her family history. She was suddenly very interested in hereditary traits—"

"Because she was pregnant?"

Amy nods, seemingly unsurprised that I know about Christine's pregnancy. "Yes, she asked me so many questions about where in England the Webbs came from and who had what diseases and what color hair that I finally told her she sounded like she planned on having a baby and the poor thing burst out crying and confessed she was. She made me promise not to tell anyone— especially Ruth—and said that was why she didn't want to see her mother. She knew Ruth would figure it out the moment she laid eyes on her."

"I don't know why—a month later I didn't notice a thing."

"You don't think you'd notice if your Beatrice was pregnant?"

"Bite your tongue, Amy! Bea's fifteen."

Amy smiles and pats my hand. "You know what I mean. A mother knows these things."

Would I? I wonder. I've always been able to tell by looking at her eyes when Bea was coming down with a cold or if someone had teased her at school. I'd watched her body change from a child's to a young woman's over the last few years and been amazed at the metamorphosis, seeing in the filling curves of her hips and breasts echoes of my own body. The night she got her first period I woke up with cramps of my own. There *was* an eerie physical bond between mother and daughter that I'd sensed, inchoately, in the first few weeks after she was born when I would watch her flail her tiny limbs and feel for a moment that I was watching my own body move. It made sense in a way. If amputees experienced feeling in their phantom limbs, why couldn't a mother sense something in this piece of flesh that had once been joined to her own? I just hadn't ever thought of the bond between Ruth and Christine as being of that nature.

"You said she cried. Was she unhappy about being pregnant?"

"I think she was scared."

"Did she say who the father was?"

"No—I told that policeman she wouldn't tell me—that she said there were *issues*. That's how she put it. But she wasn't despairing. I don't believe she would have ended her life—and her unborn child's—over it."

"But if she'd also just learned that her father killed himself? They say that knowing a parent committed suicide opens up the possibility for the child—makes it an option. Why would Dr. Horace tell her such a thing?"

"I don't know, dear, she must have asked in a way that he couldn't not tell her the truth. He's always been a stickler for the truth, even when a gentler approach might be called for."

I nodded, remembering my own meeting with Dr. Horace after Neil was first admitted to Briarwood. He'd told me that Neil had been diagnosed with a borderline personality disorder with manic-depressive features. I'd clung, at first, to that word *borderline*, thinking that it meant that whatever Neil had wasn't really that bad— that his condition was somehow *marginal*, perhaps *verging* on something more serious (the *mania* suggested by the second part of Horace's diagnosis) but still well on the side of curable. I thought *borderline* meant *not yet*, *not completely*, *not really*. In my mind I saw Neil straddling a grassy path on the edge of a cliff—on one side was sanity, on the other the howling abyss.

"So he's on the border of being really sick," I'd said to

Dr. Horace, "but it's not that bad yet. You can still make him better."

Dr. Horace had been quick to disabuse me of my misunderstanding.

"I'm afraid that borderline personality disorder doesn't refer to that kind of border," he said, not unkindly. I could imagine him, though, storing away my misunderstanding of the word for an anecdote with which to open up a paper at a conference. "It's not like he's in Germany and we can yank him over into Switzerland. Borderline, in this case, refers to an inherent instability—a condition that manifests itself in self-destructive behaviors like substance abuse and suicide. I'm afraid we don't have a lot of success with borderlines. We can try treating the manic-depressive illness with lithium—although even that has varying levels of success—but I'm afraid that borderlines often require long-term hospitalizations—many times becoming career mental patients."

I'd seen, then, that it wasn't that Neil was on one side of a line or another, but that he was inside the line—in a sort of limbo like the one Dante describes at the gates of hell.

Dr. Horace probably thought he was doing me a favor by being so blunt, but I've often thought I could have done without the phrase "career mental patient" seared into my brain. I wonder what he might have said to Christine about her father, about her own chances for inheriting the blackness that had driven him to suicide.

"Do you think Dr. Horace would talk to me?" I ask Amy, who's moved off the bed and is kneeling at a dresser, pulling out old faded clothes—gauzy Indian shirts and flowing tie-dyed tunics that I recognize as the shirts Christine wore her first year of college before she'd developed preppier, more subdued tastes—and stuffing them into a black garbage bag.

"I don't know if he'd be so keen on talking to you about Christine—what with the police investigating her death," Amy says without turning around. "But I think he'd see you if you said it was about Neil. I'll call, if you like, and set it up. He's probably not too busy on a Saturday to see you."

Of course, I realize, Amy hadn't forgotten for a minute that Neil was at Briarwood; she'd only been too kind to bring it up. But she'd known what all this talk about Briarwood would lead back to.

I glance around at the pictures on the walls, at the pale girls rising from dark water, holding their arms out as if welcoming me back, and wonder what Christine made of them when she came home. Although she'd dismissed them as sentimental Victorian art she'd kept them and eventually thrown over medieval art to write her thesis on one of their sisters—the Lady in the Window. I notice for the first time a hint of triumph in their smiles—as if these lascivious water nymphs and amorous water gods have had their way at last. They've finally dragged Christine down into their watery lairs.

CHAPTER SIXTEEN

FOR THE SECOND TIME TODAY I ENTER THE GROUNDS OF THE
Briarwood Institute for Mental Health—formerly known
as the Briarwood Insane Asylum. Driving through the
stone-pillared gate and up the wide curving drive under
the dappled shade of stately sycamores is quite different,
though, from slipping in the back on the bridle path. And
even though I know that the landscape here has been
designed to be soothing (the paths graded to slope gently,
the trees planted at regular intervals to give a sense of
natural order) its effect on me is quite the opposite. The
serpentine turnings and low grade of the drive create that
sensation I've had in dreams of running in place and not
getting anywhere.

Even so, I've driven around the building and reached
the river-facing front entrance far quicker than I'd like.
When Amy made the call I thought it was unlikely that
Dr. Horace would agree to see me on such short notice,
but according to Amy he'd agreed immediately. I could
have still backed out, but it seemed rude after putting Amy

to the trouble. Besides, I'd promised Bea I would find out how her father was doing and I wanted to be able to report, when she called this week, that I'd made some progress in that direction. And so I'd thanked Amy—and made her promise to call me when she went down to Christine's apartment in the city to clean it out so I could help—and driven to Briarwood.

I park my car in the visitor's parking lot to the left of the circular drive, turn off the engine, and sit for a moment looking up at the redbrick six-story building with its green-patinaed mansard roof and gothic crenelated towers. If not for the metal grates over the windows it could be an expensive hotel or college. The sun, setting over the Catskills on the other side of the river, sets the old bricks to glowing, and glances off the copper roof and glass windows, saturating the whole building in vibrant, almost surreal, color. The effect of all that color, though, isn't cheerful. It reminds me of the Technicolor hues of a 1950s movie. There's something flat about it and I have the uneasy sensation that when I walk around the circular flower bed—planted with huge dahlias in shades of burnt orange and coral pink—and knock on the front door I'll find that there's nothing there but a two-dimensional facade.

I close my eyes and wonder, not for the first time, if they didn't lock up the wrong person fourteen years ago. What scared me most about Neil's breakdown was that up until the very last moment before he capsized our boat on the river, his manias didn't seem so very different from my own. Even when I read the American Psychiatric

Association's official criteria for Neil's mood disorder, the symptoms seemed different from my own in degree rather than kind. I'd often envied the way Neil could paint for days without sleep or food. I'd sampled tastes of that absorption when hours would pass in front of the easel like minutes and I'd feel as if something outside of myself was guiding my brush. I'd even felt, at times, that the forms and colors were already there on the canvas like in one of those watercoloring books my mother used to buy that had invisible dye in the paper so all you had to do was stroke your wet brush across the paper to release the hidden color.

When I open my eyes the sun has sunk below the mountains across the river, releasing the building from its spell of light and me from my inertia. It's not as if insanity were catching, I reassure myself as I get out of the car and walk up to the front door.

DR. HORACE'S OFFICE IS, AS I REMEMBER IT, IN THE CENTER OF the building on the second floor, a large well-lit room facing southwest, its windows perfectly aligned to frame the curving river and the Hudson Highlands to the south. Because Briarwood faces southwest and the glass factory where I live faces northwest the view from this window takes in, albeit from a different angle, the same shoreline I see from my loft. It's far and away the best view from either location because it includes the grounds of Astolat. Dr. Horace, when he rises and comes out from behind his desk to shake hands, is also much as I remember him: tall, slim, and silver-haired. He's wearing a seersucker suit and a pink bow tie that matches the pink flush in his cheeks, an outfit very much like the one he wore to our meeting fourteen years ago and that I found, then as now, somewhat *aggressively* cheerful for the director of a psychiatric hospital.

"Juno McKay, I'm so glad to see you. You're looking very fit."

I suppose *very* fit is a high compliment from the head doctor of a psychiatric hospital. I just wish I could dismiss the idea from my mind that he's taking my pulse while grasping my hand and measuring the dilation of my pupils as he gazes intently into my eyes.

"So are you, Dr. Horace. You look great."

Dr. Horace pats his perfectly flat waistline as he sits back down. "I've got the best job in the world. I jog the carriage trails to work every morning and go out rowing every day at lunch. We put in a new state-of-the-art exercise facility last year and suicide rates have dropped by 28 percent. Some of our worst bipolars have been able to cut their lithium doses by half."

"Wow," I say, "just from exercise. Who knew?" I remember, though, that when Neil was in one of his manic phases he'd run for miles at the Penrose track in the middle of the night or bicycle to Albany and back in a day. No amount of physical exertion could put a dent in his energy level. But when he crashed he could lie in bed for days not moving, so tired, he once told me, the sheets felt too heavy to lift off his body.

"And you," Dr. Penrose says, "I hear you've got a

studio in the old glass factory down in Rosedale—" I think he's going to ask me about my stained-glass business and I straighten up in my chair, preparing to tell him about the Penrose window restoration and my plans for converting the glass factory into gallery and studio space, but apparently my riverfront locale has other significance to him. "—I'm friendly with the guy who runs the kayaking outfit at the park across from there—Kyle Swanson? We've gone kayaking together a number of times."

I open my mouth to tell him that I know Kyle Swanson but he's swiveled his desk chair so that he's facing the river, and he's looking at the opposite shore so wistfully I feel guilty for keeping him landlocked on this beautiful summer evening. In fact, even though I swore off kayaking forever after finding Christine, I find myself longing to be on the river, skimming over the water's purple-blue skin in a fast, low boat, riding the current seaward. I'd like, at any rate, to be anyplace but here when Dr. Horace drags his gaze back to mine and says, "Well, I suppose you're here to ask about Neil's progress, not listen to my boating plans."

I'd like actually, at this point, to talk about anything but Neil, but I launch into the subject gamely. "My— our—daughter, Beatrice, has been asking questions about her father. It's only normal at her age—she's fifteen now—when she's wrestling with her own identity issues to wonder about her father's mental instability. I feel I owe it to her to find out more about Neil's . . . status."

Although everything I've just said is true I sound to myself like a parody of a mother on some made-for-TV movie. It's how I often feel at PTA meetings and teacher conferences. Maybe it's because I had Bea so young that being a mother in public often feels like a charade even when there's nothing false about my feelings for Bea.

"Of course, of course," Dr. Horace murmurs. He leans back in his chair, his back firmly to the window now as if shutting off the temptation to look outside, and presses the tips of his fingers together. "I'd have thought Neil's family would have kept you informed."

"His mother, Esther, kept in touch but she never liked to tell me too many details. She always acted embarrassed around me—as if it were her fault Neil had gotten sick. I suppose she thought it was. People of her generation always blamed the mother when something went wrong with the kids."

Dr. Horace continues looking at me but says nothing. I recognize his silence as a therapeutic technique and resent it immediately.

"But as far as I could tell, Esther was a wonderful mother," I go on. "She was generous to me and Bea and it's because of the trust she set up that Bea will be able to go to college. But since she died the family's been distant. I never got on with Neil's sister."

I pause, expecting Dr. Horace to fill in the silence with some comment about Sarah Buchwald (now Cohen-Levy), but he merely lifts his chin a fraction of an inch and presses his fingertips together more tightly.

"So, here I am," I conclude, not willing to give him any more, "and I'd like to know how Neil is doing."

Dr. Horace is quiet for another few minutes and then,

still without speaking, he swivels his chair around to face a filing cabinet to the right of his desk, opens a drawer, and begins leafing through the tightly packed manila folders. It seems to me that he could have retrieved this file before I got here—but then I calm myself by remembering that he took this appointment with very little advance notice. I'm surprised, though, at how *irritated* the delay makes me, the anger I feel bubbling just below the surface. I try taking long breaths—yoga breaths, Bea calls them—and tell myself that my nerves aren't Dr. Horace's fault. It's waiting to hear what he'll say. I know that if Neil had killed himself I'd have been told—*at least I think I'd be*—but he could have been catatonic for the last half a decade, tied to his bed and drooling, and I wouldn't have known because I said thirteen years ago that I no longer wanted to know.

Dr. Horace finds the folder, flips it open, barely looks at the first page, and then closes it. The whole process of retrieving the folder *has* been a delaying tactic.

"You'll be happy to know that Neil has made tremendous progress," he says. "We don't like to use the word *recovery* in bipolar illness. Instead we speak in terms of remission. He's responded extremely well to a new medication and hasn't had a manic episode for well over a year. In fact he's done so well he's been released to The Beeches—our outpatient facility across the river."

"Released? You mean, he's free to come and go as he pleases?"

"Patients at The Beeches are strongly encouraged to check in daily with their doctors and follow a routine of outside work and recreation approved by a supervisory board—but yes, essentially he's as free as you or I am."

I look past Dr. Horace toward the river and the darkening hills to the west. The river bends before it reaches the sharp curve that marks World's End—the deepest spot in the river and the most dangerous, and I can almost feel the confluence of river currents and ocean tide and whirlwinds that sweep down from the highlands pulling the broad calm river into its maw. It's the spot Neil rowed to that day—where he capsized our boat.

"But you said—fourteen years ago you said there was very little chance of him ever leading a normal life. I believe the term you used to describe his prognosis was 'career mental patient.'"

If Dr. Horace registers the anger in my voice he doesn't show it. I suppose he's used to patients using stronger language than I've just employed.

"Yes, well, arriving at an accurate diagnosis is always a bit more art than science. Neil's case was always a complex one. In addition to his depressive and manic episodes he exhibited borderline personality traits. His idealization of you, for instance, and then his devaluation of you when you failed to live up to his expectations was classic borderline behavior. We saw the same pattern in his relationships with his father, professors at Columbia, and doctors here on staff. However, a few years after his admittance here those symptoms became progressively less evident."

"You mean they went away?"

"Not entirely. Neil still has a tendency to idealize

caregivers and entertain unrealistic expectations of behavior, but he's done a lot of work toward integrating his concepts of good and evil. At this point I would not diagnose him as a borderline."

"So you were wrong fourteen years ago?"

Dr. Horace smiles and taps his index fingers together. "Adolescent identity problems often present as borderline personality disorder."

"So you mean he grew out of it. What about the manic depression?"

"There's no doubt in my mind that Neil is suffering from bipolar disorder—what we used to call manic-depressive illness—but fortunately we've been able to control it with medication."

"He was on lithium when I saw him thirteen years ago. If you got the manic—the bipolar disorder—under control with lithium why has it taken this long to release him?"

Dr. Horace leans forward in his chair but at the same time looks away from me, sideways toward the river. As if he were simultaneously trying to confront and avoid me. For the first time since I came into his office I have the sense that he's unsure of himself.

"There were problems with the lithium—side effects Neil didn't tolerate well—and like many bipolars he fought taking it. He felt it deadened him and made it impossible for him to paint. Unfortunately, Esther Buchwald supported him in his *experiments* with going off the medication. I'm afraid she was of that generation that believes mental patients can get better as an act of will.

The results were always disastrous, though. Every time Neil went off his lithium he accelerated into a manic state. He would start out painting a few hours a day, but soon he would spend all day painting and then all night. We always knew he was reaching a crisis point when he started painting mythological and allegorical scenes."

Dr. Horace pauses, perhaps expecting me to exhibit surprise at this unusual detail, but I don't. I had firsthand knowledge of Neil's obsession with Romantic and classical mythology. I'd practically introduced him to it.

"He was fascinated with figures from Greek mythology and Romantic poetry," I say, "especially stories of doomed lovers who die together. I'm surprised he was still painting those subjects, though. He told me when I visited him the last time here that figurative art was dead." And then he'd added *As long as your face is dead to me, Juno, I won't paint another face*.

"Yes, that was one of the peculiarities of his manias. You'd expect his painting to become more abstract as he became more manic, but instead they became clearer, more ordered, classical in their composition, the figures he painted radiant—" Dr. Horace smiles at his own enthusiasm. "—if you couldn't see what a wreck the painter was you'd say they were the work of a man seeing clearly for the very first time."

I look away from the doctor's rapt expression toward the window. It's grown so dark outside by now that the glass blurrily reflects the shape of the room and the people in it. Dr. Horace and I appear only as blobs of color. What I see in my mind, though, is Neil standing in front of a canvas touching paint to the lips of a beautiful woman who bends down to embrace her drowned husband, both figures shining like gods. Neil, though, is barefoot in paint-spattered jeans and torn T-shirt, dark rings under his eyes, his hair so dirty it's no longer blond, his skin milk white as frosted glass, all the color leached out of him and soaked into the figures in the painting. Like Dorian Gray in reverse, all his beauty went into his paintings, leaving him a dried-out shell.

"You could understand," Dr. Horace is saying, "why it was so hard for him to give that up."

"But he did finally—is that what you're saying? He's staying on his medication and that's why he's well enough to be out?"

"Sort of." Dr. Horace is grinning. "He's on a new medication—one that's still in trial stage—that evens out the manias and depressions but leaves him lucid enough to paint. Not that his paintings have quite the same intensity of his past work, but they're arresting in their own right. Here, I'll show you." Dr. Horace gets up from his chair and comes around the desk holding an arm out toward the door as I get up. "I can show you what he was working on last year. He's taken away most of his recent work for the show next week—"

"A gallery show?"

Dr. Horace screws up his face, as if sorry for letting out that information. "Yes, in New Paltz. I can show you the opening notice before you leave today but I suppose we should talk about whether or not you should attend."

I nod, too stunned to think of any other response. The

idea of Neil preparing for a show chills me to the bone. His worst episodes always preceded openings. I want to ask Dr. Horace how he can possibly think this is a good thing, but I don't want to sound as if I begrudge Neil some good luck after all he's been through. So instead I search for a safer question. "This new drug," I say, "would I have heard of it?"

"Not yet, but you will soon. As I said it's still in trials, but our preliminary results have been so favorable that the *Times* is mentioning it in an article they're running on new drugs for mood disorders next month." Dr. Horace has lowered his voice to a confidential whisper. "When the FDA approves it, Pieridine will become as common a household name as Prozac."

"Pieridine? Why . . . ?"

"C'mon, you of all people should know your classical mythology. The Pierides?"

It only takes a moment for me to remember. The muses. The Pierides is an alternate name for the muses.

CHAPTER SEVENTEEN

"IT'S NOT SO ODD WHEN YOU THINK ABOUT IT," DR. HORACE tells me as we ride the elevator up to the sixth floor. "Psychologists and psychopharmacologists have always been fond of mythological references. After all, the name for our profession comes from the mythological personification of the soul, Psyche. Freud used figures from Greek literature to name his Oedipal and Electra complexes. Morphine was named for the Greek god of sleep and Halcion for the spell of calm induced by Poseidon upon the sea."

The elevator doors open and we walk out onto a broad landing with windows facing the river. The landing is more dimly lit than Dr. Horace's office so I can make out the dark shape of hills in the distance and the gleam of water. "It's not Poseidon—" I say, but Dr. Horace is already striding down the corridor. I can hear that he's still talking as if I were by his side, no doubt listing more mythological references in the world of psychology but I've been becalmed here at the window as if touched by the hand of Aeolus, who's the god—not Poseidon—who

calms the seas during the halcyon days. From here the
dark river looks as peaceful as those sedated seas,
untouched by current or tide or the winds that come
down from the steep hills on the opposite shore. Those
winds were so treacherous that Dutch sailors gave the
hills they came from names like Thunder Hill and Storm
King. It strikes me that the Dutch were doing just what the
Greeks did when they personified the unpredictable forces
that swoop down and ransack our lives. We're still doing
it—classifying the emotions that derail our reason as
psychiatric disorders. No wonder we name the drugs that
counter these disorders after gods, because who else but a
god could do battle with such unreasoning powers?

I walk to the end of the corridor without finding Dr.
Horace or coming across any open doors so I turn right
and head into the west wing. It's unnerving to be alone in
a psychiatric hospital. I imagine snarly-haired mad-
women—like Bertha Rochester in *Jane Eyre*—leaping out
of their attic aeries to scratch my face and pull my hair. Dr.
Horace explained, though, that the sixth floor is reserved
for patients who are considered trustworthy, low security
risks. Hence the lack of bars on the windows. Neil, he said,
lived here for the last four years before he was released a
few months ago.

At the end of the corridor there's an open door leading
into what appears to be a spacious sitting room, but before
I can reach it Dr. Horace pops his head out of an open
doorway on the left side of the corridor.

"There you are," he chirps. "I thought I lost you. Can't
afford to lose track of visitors. Come along, come along."

I'm walking as fast as I can but still Dr. Horace taps his fingers against the doorframe as if hoping to speed my pace by setting a marching rhythm. It strikes me that Dr. Horace himself is rather manic.

"I've kept Neil's paintings in his old suite."

I approach the room with some trepidation, still expecting some specter from a B-movie version of a crazy hospital to jump out. "Is anyone living in it now?"

"Oh no, it's . . . uh . . . vacant right now. Not that many patients qualify for the sixth floor and those who do are quickly released. Frankly, the drug companies will soon put us out of business."

"And would that be such a bad thing?" I ask, walking past Dr. Horace into the spacious, well-appointed bedroom. The room is large enough for a king-sized bed on one end and a full-length couch and several club chairs at the other. There's an easel set up near the window and original oil paintings on the walls. I walk over to one hanging above the mantel of a working fireplace. At least the basket of wood and iron poker and tongs would seem to indicate that it's a working fireplace, although I'm amazed at the idea of allowing psychiatric patients, no matter how trustworthy, access to matches and dry tinder.

"If every one of my patients could be cured of mental illness forever I'd be happy to retire, buy a Swan sixty-footer, and spend the rest of my days sailing around the world. But the truth is that no drug will work one hundred percent of the time for one hundred percent of our patients, and no drug works at all if the patient is unwilling to take it. It's taken years of therapy for Neil to accept the necessity of controlling his manic episodes."

"Nearly drowning his wife and baby wasn't reason enough?" I'm cowardly enough to keep my back to Dr. Horace as I say this. He doesn't answer me right away so I study the painting above the mantelpiece. It's a landscape of the Hudson River flowing between steep hills. Although the water is calm and sunlit, the sky in the right-hand corner of the canvas, above the jutting promontory on the west shore of the river, is darkening with rain clouds. The shadow of the storm has just reached the river, sending cat's-paw ripples across the placid water.

I move to the next painting on the wall. It's the same scene only the storm has moved farther into the river, darkening the water and combing the current into stiff-peaked whitecaps. The leaves on the trees along the eastern shore in the foreground have flipped over, showing their white underbellies. In the next picture the sky is black, the trees bent to the ground, the water churning into whirlpools. A small boat has appeared in the mouth of the channel between the mountains.

When I turn to face Dr. Horace he's got his hands spread out, palms up, gesturing toward the paintings on the walls. Every painting in the room depicts the same riverscape at some stage of a storm. "Nearly drowning his wife and child," Dr. Horace begins, carefully echoing my words, "was reason enough for him to attempt suicide six times over the last fourteen years. I said he wouldn't stay on his lithium because it made painting impossible, but that isn't the whole truth. I don't think he believed that he *deserved* to be well after what he did. When the lithium returned his reason he realized what he had done and he'd stop taking the lithium because he couldn't face that guilt."

"So how is this new drug any different?"

"As I said, it's not just the drug, it's the years of therapy helping Neil to understand that what he did out on the river wasn't his fault. His pathology drove him to see you as a betrayer and the baby as a threat and something that took your attention away from him. His psychosis was so advanced at that point that he believed the three of you would drown only to be reborn in some other form."

As birds. Or trees. Or pure water. Who knew Neil would take the *Metamorphoses* of Ovid so literally?

"When Neil finally understood that *and* he started taking the Pieridine, he was able to work out his pain at what had happened between you by painting it. I believe that many cyclothymic artists work through their cycles of depression and hypomania by creating—by painting or composing or writing. The Pieridine doesn't totally cure Neil of his disorder but it lessens it to a manageable level while leaving him capable of using his art to work through milder cycles of depression and mania. Most of the paintings you see in here were done while we were regulating the dosage of the Pieridine. The storm, you see, represents his mania—a force always hovering on the horizon threatening to overtake him. The symbolism may be a little trite . . ."

"But the paintings aren't," I finish for him. I find I can't bear to listen to Dr. Horace apologize for Neil's paintings.

They don't need any apology. Looking from one to another I'm struck by their beauty, by how the simple elements of landscape—a river, two mountains, a few trees and some weather—can evoke such a spectrum of emotions.

"Does he always paint this stretch of the river?" I ask. "It's not what you would see from here."

"No, it's not. He wanted to paint the area around Storm King precisely because it was where your accident took place—"

"Actually, the *incident* took place south of the area in the paintings—World's End is just around this out-cropping—" I point at one of the paintings. "—which is called Martyr's Rock."

"I suppose he wanted to paint the *approach* to the actual location." Dr. Horace sounds impatient with my geographical nit-picking. "At first he did it from memory and then, as he got better, I offered to take him on boat trips down the river. Frankly, I had to field quite a bit of opposition from the board, but our outings were not without precedent. Our other great artist-inmate was taken on frequent sketching outings, as I'm sure your poor friend Christine must have mentioned to you before she died."

I'm startled by his mention of Christine. I've been so engrossed in his tale of Neil's recovery that I'd nearly forgotten that half my purpose in coming here today was to find out more about Christine's visit here last month.

"So you know about Christine's death?"

"Of course. I would have gone to the funeral but one of

my patients committed suicide last night and I had to notify her parents this morning." Dr. Horace shakes his head. "A very sad business," he says, and then, drawing himself back to Christine's case, continues, "I recognized, of course, that Christine's heightened interest in Clare Barovier had many of the signposts of a hypomanic episode, but I understood that she was under a psychiatrist's care and was taking an antidepressant. I wouldn't have predicted that she'd commit suicide, but then there is the family history."

"So you told her about her father?"

Dr. Horace sighs, the energy that's buoyed him up throughout our talk suddenly seeping out of him. "Yes. I thought she knew. It came up when we were discussing Clare's work."

"But how?"

"That's difficult to explain. Perhaps we should sit down." He motions to the two club chairs positioned on either side of the window. Sinking into the well-upholstered chair I realize how tired I am. It's been a long day; I can hardly believe it's still the day of Christine's funeral.

"As I imagine her aunt Amy already told you, Christine came here . . . oh, sometime in May. I remember it was soon after the Phystech conference in Bermuda—that's the drug company that manufactures Pieridine. She said she was researching the Lady window at the Penrose library and that she believed the window depicted not Eugenie Penrose, but her sister, Clare Barovier. I told her I thought she was right."

"You do?"

"Absolutely, I've thought so for some time. Of course, I never met Clare Barovier because she died in the sixties, a decade before I took over here, but I've seen pictures of her in our archives and she bears a striking resemblance to the woman in that window."

"But so does Eugenie Penrose. After all, they were sisters."

"True, and painting on glass is not as effective in creating a likeness as a sketch—or oil portraiture. I imagine that's why Augustus Penrose thought he could get away with doing a portrait of his wife's sister right in front of his wife. She couldn't say for sure that the portrait wasn't of herself, but I bet she had her suspicions."

"'Here with her face doth memory sit,'" I say.

"I beg your pardon?"

"It's from a poem by Dante Gabriel Rossetti. Eugenie wrote it in her notebook under her preliminary sketches of the window. Christine quoted it in her lecture as evidence that the portrait called to mind her sister."

"I can't imagine that it would have been a pleasant reminder to Eugenie. She never visited her sister once in all the years that Clare was here."

"Not once? How can you be sure?"

"My predecessor, Dr. Peabody, kept excellent records."

"Poor Clare. Her own sister," I say, wondering if it's what people said when I stopped visiting Neil. *Poor Neil. His own wife.*

"Well, she didn't lack for visitors. Augustus Penrose visited her once a week until the last months of his life."

"And you told Christine that?"

"Well, that's the thing; she not only knew that Augustus visited Clare, she also had the idea that he took her out on weekend excursions to Astolat which, I told her, was very unlikely."

"Where'd she get that idea?"

"From her family. Remember, the Webbs have worked here for generations. Someone told Christine that when her father was little he was invited on board Penrose's yacht and that he told everyone he'd been taken to a 'marvelous palace' on the river with a beautiful woman."

"Amy said something about a family story in which Clare Barovier took children along with her on her boating trips to sketch their portraits."

"That's probably how the story got started. I think she did sketch pictures of children of the staff members, but I doubt she and Augustus took them on trips down the river. I guess it was one of those stories that get passed around and become part of family lore. One of Christine's aunts—I'm not sure which one, but I don't think it was Amy—said that Edward bragged about that boat trip all his life until it became several boat trips as the years went on. Christine thought it was proof that Augustus was taking Clare to Astolat. I told her that under the circumstances she shouldn't put too much stock in a secondhand story from her father."

"And then she asked what circumstances."

"Exactly. That's when I realized she'd never been told that he killed himself. I tried to evade her questions, but you know Christine. Once she saw I was keeping something from her she was like a pit bull on a poodle."

Dr. Horace grins. I've heard Christine compared to a pit bull recently—by Gavin Penrose—but I still don't think it's an apt analogy. She was much more like one of my greyhounds, both in looks and how she'd lean into a thing until it yielded to her gentle but persistent pressure. Dr. Horace, however, with his pink cheeks, wispy silvery hair, and pink bow tie, does look a little like a poodle. I almost feel sorry for him, but then I remind myself that his careless slip might well have led Christine to take her own life. It strikes me that Dr. Horace is altogether too cavalier about his responsibilities. Maybe running an antiquated private hospital like Briarwood isn't such a plum position in the psychiatric field. Maybe it's the kind of job where socializing with the Briarwood trustees and the rich families of his patients—families anxious to keep their addlebrained relatives safely out of sight—is a more highly valued skill than psychiatric finesse.

"So you told her that her father was a suicide," I conclude. "She must have been shocked."

"She became very quiet, but then she said that actually it explained a lot of things."

"Did she say what she meant?"

"No. She was suddenly very anxious to go. I thought she wanted to be by herself to process what she had just learned. I suggested she stay and discuss the impact of her father's suicide on her, but she declined my offer. She said she had a lecture to prepare—oh, and that's when she asked if I could put her in touch with Neil."

"She did? But why?"

"She said she wanted to discuss Clare Barovier's

paintings with him. After all, he'd lived with them for years. She talked quite a bit to poor Daria Cohen, as well, because she was living in the suite then . . ."

"Daria Cohen? Who's she?"

"The woman who had this suite . . . I mentioned her earlier . . ."

Dr. Horace looks flustered. It takes me a moment to put together the "suicide" he mentioned earlier and "poor Daria" and realize that we're sitting in the room of the woman who killed herself just last night. It's worse, in a way, than the wild-haired specter I'd been imagining.

". . . but Christine was more interested in Neil," Dr. Horace goes on, anxious to be off the subject of *poor Daria*, "because it was obvious that his own paintings were influenced by Clare's."

"They were?"

"Yes, do you want to see them?" Dr. Horace is out of his chair before I can answer, glad, I think, to switch the conversation to yet another art tour. I'm not quite ready, though, to let him off the hook. I stop him at the door to the adjoining room by laying a hand on his seersucker sleeve.

"Don't you think it was a little irresponsible to give her Neil's number? I mean, she'd just learned that her father killed himself and then you hook her up with someone as unstable as Neil—"

"Oh, I'd never give out Neil's phone number. It's my responsibility to protect the privacy of my patients—even former patients. I offered to give her number to Neil."

Dr. Horace swings open the door and gestures for me to

go in ahead of him, apparently unaware that his answer seems worse to me than my original accusation, but I'm not ready to go into the other room yet. "And you did? You gave Christine's number to Neil?"

"Yes. He seemed pleased that she was willing to speak with him. The poor boy feels like a pariah to all his former friends."

"Maybe that's because he could be a threat to those friends," I say, thinking more of Bea than of myself.

Dr. Horace looks at me with an expression of deep disappointment. "Do you honestly think that I would have signed Neil's release papers if I thought that were true? That's just the kind of attitude, though, from which I wish to protect Neil."

"Protect Neil!" I say a bit more vehemently than I'd intended, but I can hardly believe that Dr. Horace's priority is protecting Neil from me and Christine and not vice versa. Although I hadn't decided on asking for Neil's number the idea that he might not give it to me is infuriating. "Do you mean to say that if I asked for his number—or for that gallery show notice—you'd refuse? Even though it was Neil who almost killed me and my daughter?"

"Well, with that attitude I certainly would, but—" Dr. Horace furrows his brow as if he might be relenting. Perhaps he's thinking of possible lawsuits in case something does happen to me or Bea. Perhaps it's occurred to him—as it has to me—that the last person whose phone number he gave to Neil has ended up dead. "—the gallery show *is* a public event. I'm sure you could find out about it if you wanted to." His fingers dip into the pocket of his suit jacket, where they flutter against the fabric for a moment like a trapped moth. "I'd have to let Neil know that you might come—and I'd hope that you'd act maturely."

I sigh, half in exasperation, half because I'm tired of fighting. "The last thing I want to do is confront Neil in a public place. I just want to see for myself that he's really better—so I can tell Bea."

Dr. Horace gives me a long clinical look—that pupil-measuring look again—and then nods. He pulls from his pocket a postcard and hands it to me. I look down at the picture and have the impression that the scene depicted on it is a place I've been to before. A stream flows through mountains and then pours itself into a still, green pool, darkened under the shade of a weeping beech, white water lilies glowing like stars on the velvety water.

"I've seen this before—" I start to tell Dr. Horace, but he's walked into the suite's living room ahead of me so I follow him. For a moment I think that I've stepped back into Christine's bedroom with its walls plastered with Augustus Penrose's prints only all the figures, the nymphs and water gods—have disappeared, leaving only the lily pond and the weeping beech, the stream and the mountains. It's the same landscape painted over and over again—the same as Neil's painting on the postcard—and the same scene that's laid out in pieces of glass back at my studio.

CHAPTER EIGHTEEN

IT WAS TO THOSE PIECES OF GLASS THAT I TURNED MY ATTENTION in the days following Christine's funeral and my visit to Briarwood. We'd dedicated the light table to the landscape section of the window because it was the part of the restoration that was giving us the most trouble. The rest of the window was relatively simple to reassemble because Penrose had, for the most part, used only a single layer of glass in the figure of the lady and the furniture of her room. The landscape in the window, however, was composed of many layers of glass.

"He was jealous of Tiffany," Ernesto concluded when he laid out all the pieces on the light table.

"Oh, he hated Tiffany," my father concurred. "He claimed that Tiffany stole the idea of this landscape from him."

"But it's such a simple landscape," I pointed out, "a stream flowing through some mountains into a pool . . ."

"If you look at Tiffany's memorial windows he often used the same image." Robbie, who had been hanging on the edge of the conversation, came over with an art book held open to a picture of Tiffany's window "Magnolia and Irises," which I'd seen a dozen times at the Met. He flipped forward a few pages to one called "Autumn Landscape." In both windows there are mountains in the distance, and a stream, although in "Magnolia and Irises" there's no pool and in "Autumn Landscape" the stream seems to start at the base of the mountains instead of transversing the mountains. "According to this book, the passage of the river through the mountains and into a pool is supposed to stand for the life of the dead person that the window is commemorating, and it says Tiffany used plating to create depth and three-dimensionality."

"Yeah, Penrose wanted to do the same thing, only better and with more layers of glass," Ernesto said, "and he wanted to create a dichroic pattern just like Tiffany did in his lamps only on a bigger scale." Ernesto pointed to the section of the mountain landscape in our window that he reassembled last week to produce a stream flowing through the mountains. The problem was that if we reassembled the rest of the landscape by following the blueprint of how it had been originally assembled the stream died out just below the mountains before it reached the lily pool.

"It looks like it just dries up," Ernesto complained. "That can't be how it's meant to be."

The area where the stream "dried up" though was in among the rocks and boulders that led to the lily pond. It was built out of hundreds of tiny pieces of glass, and when I started trying to rearrange them they threw off the rest of the composition.

"I say we put it together the way it was," my father suggested. "No one will be the wiser. You said you never mentioned the dichroic pattern to Gavin Penrose."

"No," I agreed. "I forgot to. But still, I'd like to try to see if I can figure out how it was originally laid out. If I can't do it, we'll put it back the way it was."

So for the next couple of days, while Ernesto and Robbie work on copper foiling the lady's dress, and my dad works on her hair, I sit on a high stool at the light table shifting through pieces of glass, some no bigger than my thumb, looking for a pattern that only shows up under light. I can't help remembering that the elements of the landscape I'm working on are not only similar to those Tiffany windows in Robbie's book, they're also almost identical to the scene in *The Drowning Tree* and the sketches I saw in Clare Barovier's room at Briarwood. The pool itself, with its water lilies and reeds and weeping beech, recalls to me the place where I found Christine. And so, as I lift up rippled blue shards, which turn dark in my hand away from the light, I picture Christine paddling her boat through the black water of the Wicomico and wonder why she went there and whether she really went there to die. Plucking a creamy petal from its green oval pad I think of her pregnant and remember that last question she asked me at the train station—whether I agreed with Dante's line: *Love, which absolves no one beloved from loving.* Was Christine in love with someone— the father of her child?—who had abandoned her to have the baby by herself? What had Detective Falco said— someone who was married and so wouldn't welcome the news? Is that why Christine had asked me all those questions about raising Bea on my own? And what had I told her? That you were never free of fear once you were a mother.

I try, while rearranging the mottled gray and purple rocks that border the pool, to imagine the moment when she pulled her pill organizer out of her pocket and began swallowing one pill after another until she felt her blood begin to thicken and slow—*Till her blood was frozen slowly and her eyes were darkened wholly* . . . was how Tennyson described the Lady of Shalott's death drifting down the river—but I find it hard to believe she would take her life and the life of her unborn child just because she was afraid of being alone.

Besides, the Lady of Shalott had at least written her name on her death-boat so that Lancelot would know her. Why hadn't Christine left any message for me? Or for her unfaithful lover, the father of her child? Or had she? Maybe she'd crafted a message out of her own lifeless body as Dido had, as Christine said in her lecture, *by staining the night sky with her own funeral pyre*.

I idly sift the smooth green beech leaves through my hands like so much sand. *Suicide*, I say to myself, pouring them into one hand, *accident*, into the other hand, *murder*, I spill them out on the lit table and study the pattern they form for clues like a gypsy reading tea leaves in the bottom of a cup. If the father of Christine's child was married—or engaged to marry some rich woman like the character in Dreiser's book—he might be threatened by Christine's pregnancy, especially if she'd gone to him and demanded he marry her. It's a role, though, that I have trouble picturing Christine in, but then I remember what Fay Morgan said about Christine and Gavin Penrose arguing before her lecture. Could Gavin be the father of Christine's child? But Gavin isn't married, and although it would probably be a fruitful source for gossip at the college, the news that he'd gotten an alum pregnant probably wouldn't be worth killing someone to keep secret.

Several times a day I think of calling Detective Falco, but what would I tell him? That the place where Christine died resembles a picture drawn by a crazy woman who died fifty years ago? I can only hope that the evidence he's sorting through is more substantial than the bits of colored glass I'm playing with. By the end of each day all I have for my questions is a sore back from leaning over the table and, when I close my eyes and press the heels of my hands into my eye sockets, the colors from the glass shards I've been handling swirl in my head like treacherous eddies and form a cool pool I'd like to dive into.

The heat doesn't help. In the week after Christine's funeral we have a spell of hot days unrelieved even by the summer squalls that roll down off the Highlands and, more often than not, knock out the power. By late afternoon it grows so close and hot in the studio that I tell Ernesto, Robbie, and my dad to go home and then I climb the spiral staircase to my loft, where the rain lulls me into a deep sleep. Sometimes when I awake the sun has come out for a brief appearance just before setting, catching the raindrops on the skylights so that my high-pitched roof seems to be glazed in a glass blown from diamonds instead of silica and soda.

Without Bea, the evenings feel as empty as the loft. The clicking of the dogs' nails on the hardwood floors as they trail me from room to room echoes in the cavernous space. They eye me hopefully for a walk but I don't want to go out in case Bea calls. Instead, I let them out in the courtyard and then I eat dinner standing at the kitchen counter, idly rearranging items on our bulletin board. I've tucked the postcard advertising Neil's show next to Bea's crewing schedule and the college's pool hours and take-out menus and dentist checkup reminders—as if Neil's show were one more detail in our busy suburban lifestyle. I've also tacked up the genetic counselor's card that Fay Morgan gave me and toward the end of the week I actually call to make an appointment so that I can feel like I've accomplished *something*.

The genetic counselor tells me, in a heavy Eastern European accent, that luckily she's just had a cancellation for tomorrow at one o'clock. Can I make it? In other words, can I take time off from my busy schedule of playing tiddledywinks with stained-glass pieces and pacing the loft each night? In fact, when I consult my calendar I see that the only conflicting "event" for tomorrow is Neil's opening, which is from 2:30 to 5:00. Although I hadn't decided whether or not to go, I realize now that I've been thinking about the show with dread. I can still tell Bea that I found out her father is out of the hospital and doing better and then let her decide if she wants to see him. I take Neil's card down and toss it in the garbage and write the appointment on the calendar. When I tell the genetic counselor I can make it she says that she'll fax me a list of questions about my family history that I should fill out and bring with me. The phrase *family history* reminds me that the last time I heard it was when Dr. Horace referred to the history of suicide in Christine's family. The idea that you could carry something like that inside you all your life—a propensity to suicide or a gene that incites your cells to riot into cancer—is so depressing that when I hear the fax machine come on downstairs I grab a bottle of wine and go out onto the rooftop.

I stretch out in one of the torn and sagging lawn chairs and read the diary pages I found in the stone grooves of the Lady window until the light fades from the western sky. The voice of the young Eugenie Barovier—measured, proper, and a little stiff—is oddly soothing even as the thread within her daily narrative of endless rounds of calls and teas and charity visits to factory girls is the increasingly volatile behavior of her willful younger sister.

July 3, 1892. Went to call on the Markhams. Clare wore her yellow silk and tea-green bonnet. I wore the plain muslin that I'd hemmed for Clare, but to which I have now added a border as she's grown tired of it. Miss Markham complimented Clare on her artistic sensibility in choosing colors and Clare responded, "Art isn't about choosing a dress—it's about caring enough for what you choose to risk everything."

July 16, 1892. Went walking along the banks of the river with Mr. Penrose. He sketched Clare sitting by the lily pool and told us the story of Syrinx, the nymph whom Pan pursued and who prayed to be turned into a reed to escape him. I commented that if the Greek gods would behave themselves better these poor girls wouldn't have to keep turning themselves into trees and vegetables. Clare laughed at me and said at least Pan would always remember Syrinx because he chose the reed to fashion into his pipe. "She became a vehicle for his art," she said. Mr. Penrose was kind enough to say that there were many ways to serve art, which I took as a compliment to my labors as he has, of late, entrusted me to mix his colors for him.

It's a curious dance these three performed along the banks of the Thames (clearly the model for the setting in so many of the paintings). A dance choreographed by Ovid, Dante, and Tennyson. Each *role* that Penrose chose for Clare to model seemed to say something about his feelings for her—at least she must have read it that way. Finally, he asked Eugenie to pose.

August 15, 1892. Today Mr. Penrose asked me to pose! I was not sure at first that I could bear to be stared at for so long, but he wants to do a series of paintings of Dryope and her sister, Iole, so he really does need the two of us. At first I was to be Iole, but then he felt that I ought to be Dryope because I'm the taller and when Iole clasps her sister as she turns into a tree the composition demands that Dryope be the taller of the two.

All this made perfect sense, but I could see that Clare was annoyed to be chosen as the secondary figure, but then Mr. Penrose pointed out to her that Iole is the one telling the story. That seemed to appease her.

Then he told us the story so we could understand our parts (and to keep our minds off our aching limbs, no doubt!).

"Dryope and her sister—half sister, actually, just like you two—go down to a pool, Dryope carrying her year-old baby. She picks a water lotus to give to her son, but as she plucks it Iole sees blood dripping from the blossom. She learns from some peasants that the flower is actually the nymph Lotis who was transformed to avoid capture by Priapus.

"Again, if only the gods would leave these nymphs in peace . . ."

"Please, Miss Barovier, I'm doing your face now; you'll have to be quiet," he said. I noticed that Clare smiled at that because I had so often told her she ought not to keep talking while Mr. Penrose was painting her.

"As I was saying . . . although she prays for the nymph's forgiveness it's too late. She begins to turn into a lotus tree herself as her sister looks on helplessly. She's still holding her baby to her breast as the bark engulfs her, but she tries to suckle it nonetheless. Finally, she knows she must hand over her baby to her

sister before the transformation is complete or else the baby will be smothered inside the bark. That's the moment I want to paint. The moment she gives the baby to her sister. Her parting words of advice to Iole are to warn her young son, 'Let him beware of pools and never pick blossoms from trees, but fancy every bush a goddess in disguise.'"

I thought the story a bit sordid, but I said nothing because I was not supposed to talk while posing.

Clare would barely speak to me on the walk home but would persist in greeting every piece of shrubbery on the path as "a goddess in disguise."

I laugh out loud at this last bit, which I've just barely been able to make out in the fading light. I find myself liking Clare. She reminds me, perhaps not surprisingly, of Neil. Greeting every bush as "a goddess in disguise" was the kind of thing Neil would do. When we'd walk around the campus—often at dawn after he'd thrown pebbles at my dorm room window to wake me up—he'd lay his hand on the trunk of a tree and press his ear against the smooth bark.

"You can hear the beat of the tree's heart," he'd say.

Or we'd sit in the middle of a pine grove and listen to the sound the wind made moving through the trees. "Can't you hear them whispering?" he'd ask. "If only we could understand what they're saying."

"Maybe it's just that they speak a different language," I said once. After that he drew pictures of trees with human faces, bark lips pursed to tell their secrets to one another.

Then he wrote a poem called "The Language of Trees," which went

You told me trees could speak
and the only reason one heard
silence in the forest   •
was that they had all been born
knowing different languages.

That night I went into the forest
to bury dictionaries under roots,
so many books in so many tongues
as to insure speech.

And now, this very moment,
the forest seems alive
with whispers and murmurs and rumblings of sound
wind-rushed into my ears.

I do not speak any language
that crosses the silence around me
but how soothing to know
that the yearning and grasping embodied
in trees' convoluted and startling shapes
is finally being fulfilled
in their wind shouts to each other.
Yet we who both speak English
and have since we were born
are moving ever farther apart
even as branch tips touch.

Beneath the poem he drew the little tree he always used to sign his paintings, only this time he drew a book under the tree, the roots springing from its pages. *You see, it does make sense,* he told me, *my name means both* beech forest *and* book forest.

The poem won the college literary magazine's poetry contest even though Neil was only a visiting student. I loved the way Neil made the inanimate world come alive. It wasn't until the morning when I found him under my dorm window with dirt-caked and bloody fingernails holding fistfuls of torn pages that I began to wonder how much he really believed the fanciful images in his poems and paintings. That was just before he was asked to leave the campus because he'd stolen dictionaries in a dozen different languages from the library and planted their torn-out pages under every tree on campus.

NOW READING THESE OTHER TORN-OUT PAGES—PIECES FROM A diary written a hundred years ago—I'm haunted by how close the images of poetry and art seem to the delusions of madness. How the world that Ovid created, and Penrose painted, has the same fluidity of form—one thing shifting into another, beauty turning into its opposite—as the worst manias that Neil suffered from at the end, when he came to believe in the stories he was transposing on his canvas and to identify the characters in those stories with the model he drew from. In other words, me. Reading the diary, I find myself putting off going inside to bed. I stay out on the roof, lulled by the sound the river makes lapping against the banks, until I fall asleep in the lawn chair.

The sound of the water enters my dreams and carries me to a still pool beneath a weeping beech, where I float, weightless, surrounded by tall reeds, borne up on a bed of water lilies. At first it's peaceful. The trailing branches of the beech sweep over me, caressing my skin like long fingers. The wind whistles gently through the hollow reeds. Beneath me I can feel the water lilies gently kneading my back. But then I understand that there's someone beneath me in the pool. I thrash out in the water, but my hands sink into the fleshy white flowers, which turn bloody at my touch, and then the reeds begin to scream.

I wake up with my face pressed into the nylon webbing of the chair, the Metro-North whistle shrieking in the distance. When I stumble back inside into the bathroom and stare at myself in the mirror—to see that I'm still me, not a flower or a tree—I find myself indeed transformed, metamorphosed, my skin ridged like bark, a veinlike pattern of leaves webbing my face. It takes me a few minutes to realize it's only the imprint that the nylon lawn chair has left on my flesh.

In the morning I oversleep. When I come downstairs Ernesto is at the light table shifting sections of glass in the landscape. I stand behind him, sipping a cup of Bea's twig tea because I've run out of coffee, and watch his long brown fingers graze the surface of the glass; he seems to be operating more on touch than sight.

"Why don't you have the light table on?" I ask.

"Hurts my eyes this early in the morning. Besides it would ruin the surprise."

"Surprise?"

"Uh-huh."

Since he's obviously not going to tell me anything else I wander over to my desk and stand looking at the bulletin board at our job schedule for next month, which I've kept mostly empty while we work on the Lady window. I see, though, that my dad has penciled in a few jobs for August. Someone—Robbie probably—has tacked up a notice for a lecture series on stained glass at the Cloisters and a flier for a band playing next weekend in Woodstock. When I take the flier down to read the reverse side, a postcard that must have been tacked underneath comes loose. A card with a green landscape of pond and mountains glides to the floor like a green-winged dragonfly.

"How'd this get down here?" I ask, stooping to retrieve the card advertising Neil's show. "I thought I threw it out . . ." but Ernesto isn't paying attention and I realize that of course it can't be the same card I threw out. Robbie, no doubt, picked it up somewhere and tacked it up, thinking someone would be interested in going. He'd have no idea that Neil was my ex-husband.

"I think I've got it," Ernesto says. "Come stand over here. I want to try something."

Ernesto grabs my hand, his fingers cool from handling the glass, and pulls me up to the third step of the spiral staircase. From here I'm looking directly down on the light table, the glass dark against the unlit surface.

"Now watch," he says.

Ernesto switches the light on and the glass comes to life. The purple mountains recede into the distance, the beech tree spreads a deep canopy of shade over the water, the water lilies in the green pool glow like stars and, linking all these together, a diaphanous stream zigzags through the mountains, tumbles over rocks, and cascades down into the still pool.

"You did it, Ernesto. I can't believe it was assembled incorrectly the first time."

"Wait, that's not all. Penrose designed it so you'd see the stream in the light but also so that when the light shifted behind the window—say when clouds pass over the sun—the pattern would move. Watch."

Ernesto turns the light on and off again, on and off again, quickly fluttering the switch so the fluorescent bulbs beneath the plastic tabletop flicker and stutter and the clear pattern in the glass begins to waver and sway, to flow, in fact, like water, as if the stream had, at just that moment, sprung out of the mountains and begun its journey into the pool. The mirage of movement brings the whole scene to life and forces the eye to follow the stream down into the depths of the pool and back again into the mountains to find the spring's source.

"What a genius," I say.

"Yeah, that Penrose was one smart man with the glass."

"No," I say, coming down the stairs and squeezing Ernesto's shoulder, "I mean you."

Ernesto smiles but keeps his gaze on the landscape, which glows steadily now in the light. I look down at the card in my hand at a scene that's almost identical to the one in the window. Looking at it, I feel as if I'm being drawn across the river—which, if I pretend we're a little farther north, would be to New Paltz, where Neil is having his show. I slip the card in my pocket. It occurs to me that there'd be plenty of time to make it to the show after my appointment in Poughkeepsie, which is, after all, just across the river from New Paltz.

CHAPTER NINETEEN

THE QUESTIONNAIRE FROM THE GENETIC COUNSELING OFFICE asks for more detailed information than I'd anticipated. In addition to the medical histories of my grandparents and great-grandparents, I'm supposed to know what their siblings died of and when, where they all came from, and whether any of them were of Ashkenazic descent.

"Jews from eastern or central Europe," Robbie says when I ask out loud who the Ashkenazis were. "Like from Poland or Germany. They probably ask because there's supposed to be a higher incidence of breast cancer in Ashkenazic Jews. Two of my father's sisters had it."

"I didn't realize you were Jewish, Robbie," I say and instantly realize the comment sounds like the old *you don't look Jewish*. Robbie, however, doesn't appear to be offended.

"My dad's family are Russian Jews, but my mom's not Jewish so I wasn't brought up with anything."

"Like Bea," I tell him. "Her father was Jewish, and I was christened a Catholic, but I haven't raised her with any religion. Does it bother you?"

"Nah. I figure most of the worst wars in history were waged in the name of religion. I do yoga and meditate. That's enough spiritualism for me."

I look over to see if Ernesto and my father, both Catholics, have anything to add, but they're so engrossed in figuring out how to assemble the rest of the landscape section—the trunk of the beech tree is especially giving them problems—that neither of them have been paying attention to our discussion on religion.

"Hey, Dad, any Jews on your side of the family?" I ask.

That does get his attention. "As a matter of fact my cousin Margie married a Jewish guy from Coney Island. I think they moved to Great Neck—"

"I mean blood relatives."

"Oh, now, let me see." My father tilts his chin up and stares at the ceiling as if looking for long-lost Irish-Jewish ancestors there. "No," he says finally, "I don't believe so, but I'm not sure about your mother's side."

"Well, Mom's family was Catholic . . ."

"Plenty of Italian Jews converted over the years. You never know."

"And you don't remember any cancer on your side of the family?"

"No, the McKays mostly had strokes or drank themselves to death."

"Well, that's encouraging. *That's* something to look forward to."

"If you ask me the whole thing's crazy. Testing your genes to see what might kill you. I'll tell you this—your mother never would have sat around worrying about such nonsense. Even after she knew she had the cancer she enjoyed every moment she had coming to her. That's what matters—making the most of the time you're here, not trying to measure it out with a yardstick."

My father turns away and lays down a pair of grozer pliers on the light table so hard that the table shakes and all the bright shards of glass shiver. He wipes his face with the back of his hand. I'm more than sorry to have brought him to this. He's right, of course, about my mother. Every memory I have of her is a happy one. Even after she was diagnosed with breast cancer when I was nine I never saw her cry. Never even saw her lie down in the middle of the day. When she lost her hair to chemo she said she'd always wanted to be a redhead and bought a wig the color of Hawaiian Punch. She was so alive that up until the moment she took her last breath I didn't believe I would lose her. For a while that insistent cheer made me angry. She should have warned me, I felt, should have gotten me ready for losing her, but now I realize that she'd given me a childhood free of fear and death and so full of love that no matter how bad things have ever gotten for me I can feel something steadying deep down in my core—like a smooth, round stone at the bottom of a pool radiating out rings of strength.

"I'm sorry, Dad, I didn't mean to upset you, it's just that I think of what would happen to Bea if anything happened to me, so if there's anything I can do . . ."

"You're right," he says, "it's a terrible thing for a girl to lose her mother."

And be left with just a father to raise her. He doesn't have to say it for me to finish the thought for him. Again I've said the wrong thing, but I can see that he's not angry. Instead he nods and tells me I should go down to Cafe Galatea and ask my mother's cousin, Annemarie, any questions I have about my mother's family. What we're both thinking is that as unequipped as he had been to raise me, Bea's father would be a worse choice—really no choice at all.

I'M HAPPY TO GO DOWN TO GAL'S BECAUSE BEA'S TWIG TEA HAS failed to keep my caffeine deprivation headache at bay. Half a block away I can smell the aroma of dark roasted coffee beans mingling with the smell of the river. The cafe's door is propped open and half a dozen old men are sitting on the front porch sipping from gold-rimmed demitasse cups and reading American *Oggi*. Portia is standing behind the high counter, her long arms folded over the cool, green marble, her cheek pillowed on her arms. She looks up and smiles dreamily at me.

"The usual?" she asks, drifting languidly toward the espresso machine.

"*Certo*," I tell her, "and put in an extra shot of espresso." I'm about to suggest she make herself one while she's at it, but then I study her carefully—her secretive half smile, the tilt of her hip, the tune she's humming—and realize that the adolescent languor she's fallen into isn't likely to respond to a double or even a triple shot of coffee.

"Is your mother in the back?" I ask.

"Uh-huh. She's making a cake for some big engagement party we're catering tonight." Portia hands me my coffee. She's forgotten the extra shot and she's also forgotten the amaretto, but I don't say anything as she drapes herself back over the countertop. As I'm walking past her into the kitchen, though, she lifts up her head and pulls a piece of folded paper out of her apron pocket.

"Oh, Aunt Juno, can you help me translate something?"

"*Certo, bella.* Something for school?"

"Not exactly." Portia's skin, which is as clear and delicate as milk glass, turns bright pink. She glances down at the paper without handing it over to me.

"You took Latin, right?" she asks.

"Four years. It was mandatory at Penrose back then."

"Then can you tell me what this line means?"

She holds out a piece of paper that's been folded so intricately it's like an origami crane. The purpose of these folds, apparently, is so that only a few lines of pale blue handwriting show. It would be easier for me to take the paper from her, but clearly she doesn't want me to read anything but the few lines in question.

"*Da mi basia mille,*" I read.

"I get that part because it's like Italian. It says, 'give me a thousand kisses,' right?"

I nod, keeping my eyes on the page to spare poor Portia any further embarrassment. She's blushing so violently now that it's like some foreign presence is moving under her skin trying to get out. A pink-plumed bird about to erupt from her long white limbs.

"*Deinde centum, dein mille altera, dein secunda centum,*" I read aloud.

"A lot of numbers?"

"That's right. I remember this poem from sophomore Latin. Catullus is asking his girlfriend to give him a thousand kisses, then a hundred, then another thousand, and then a second hundred—"

"In other words, a lot of kisses."

"Yeah, that's his basic point."

"Then what's this word—*conturbabimus?* It's not something dirty, is it?"

I laugh and am immediately sorry. Portia seems to be in actual pain. "No, not at all. He says that when they have made many thousands of kisses they'll mix them all up, so that they won't know how many there are and no bad person will be able to know and be jealous that so many kisses exist."

"Oh. That's kind of sweet, really." Portia draws the folded paper back into her lap and holds it there with both hands as if frightened it might stretch out its little paper wings and fly away.

"Uh, is this from the boy I saw in here a few weeks ago? The one from your English class?"

Portia nods and, leaning closer to me, whispers a name, "Scott Heeley." I remember the tall, awkward-looking boy with his copy of Dante and imagine him copying out poems in Latin for the pretty Italian girl in his class. I remember the last time someone wrote down a poem for me. I take a sip of the bitter coffee, scalding my tongue, and tell Portia that yes, it's really very sweet indeed.

* * *

ANNEMARIE IS UP TO HER ELBOWS IN FLOUR, DUSTING A complicated-looking cake pan and knocking the excess out on the wooden counter. She holds her hands up, like a surgeon who's just scrubbed, and gives me a kiss on the cheek. Her cheek against mine feels soft as velvet and when she steps back I find myself looking into eyes the same gold-flecked brown as my mother's. She's the same age that my mother would be if my mother had lived.

"*Cara!* I heard about your poor friend, Christina. What a horrible tragedy. Do they really think she took her own life?"

I sit down on a stool and brush away some flour from the edge of the table. "That's what it looks like, only I don't know . . . I find it hard to believe."

Annemarie shakes her head, scrapes a mixing bowl full of yellow batter into the cake mold, and slides the pan into a hot oven. I notice that there's a pile of crumbled cake on the breadboard. "Who can ever imagine such a thing? A young woman, with her whole life ahead of her. What could have driven her to such despair?"

"She was pregnant," I say.

"*Dio mio,*" she says, crossing herself and leaving dabs of flour on her forehead and on either side of her full bosom. "That's even worse. It's not like fifty years ago when a girl had to crawl away in shame. Look at you! How well you've done raising Beatrice on your own!"

I tell Annemarie that I appreciate her condolences for Christine's death, but that I've got to ask her a few questions before I go to this doctor's appointment in Poughkeepsie.

"You're not sick," she says, pressing her floury hands to my forehead.

"No, no, nothing like that. I've just decided to have this test for the breast cancer gene—because of Mom—and I need some information about the family."

Annemarie moves a hand from my forehead to my cheek, her eyes pinned to mine. The coronas of gold around her pupils seem to expand like little solar flares. "Tell me the truth, *cara*, have you found something—" she touches her other hand to her breast, "—a lump?"

"No, no, I swear, *Zia*, nothing. A woman at the college told me she had the test and that there are things you can do to prevent getting cancer if you have the gene. I thought I ought to find out—for Bea's sake. I probably don't even have it. No one else in the family's had breast cancer, have they?"

Annemarie drops her hand from my face and wipes it on her apron. She moves over to a large steel sink and washes and dries her hands. Then she sits down with her clean hands folded in her lap. I notice that there are half a dozen molds waiting to be filled with cake batter. It must be some complicated cake she's cooking up for tonight, but the way she sits there you would think she has nothing to do but to tend to my problems.

"Well, my mother's sister, Angela—so your great-aunt—had a lump removed when she was fifty and she said it was nothing, but my mother said she thought it might have been cancer. Angela died when she was sixty-three and no one ever said what from. You see, my mother's generation didn't even say the word cancer without making the sign for the evil eye. They just didn't talk about it."

I take out the questionnaire from my purse and fill in the information about Angela—such as it is—in the space for maternal grandmother's siblings. "This is going to sound funny," I say, feeling as shy as Portia with her love poem asking this question, "but do we have any Jewish relatives?"

Annemarie shakes her head. "Not that I've ever heard."

"Okay, anyone else with cancer?"

"My mother-in-law's cousin—but that's no blood relative to you. No, most of the women in our family live pretty long. It was a shock to everyone when your mother passed so young."

I look up at Annemarie and see that her soft brown eyes are shiny with tears. She's the second person I've made cry today and it's not even noon yet.

"I'm sorry for bringing up bad memories, *Zia*, I know how close you were to my mother. She always said you were her favorite cousin."

Annemarie lifts a corner of her apron up to wipe her eyes. A timer goes off and she moves to the oven to remove a large round pan. When she upends the pan the cake that slides out is shaped like a giant flower. The other molds, I now notice, are shaped like leaves. "It's all right, cara," she says, filling one of the leaf pans with the smooth yellow batter, "you have to ask your questions. I just hope that the answers you get bring you peace."

DRIVING TOWARD POUGHKEEPSIE I KEEP HEARING ANNEMARIE'S last words, but instead of applying them to the medical questions I've answered for today's appointment I think about the questions I have about Christine's death. Would their answers give me peace? Would knowing why she died the way she did make it any easier to do without her?

For the first time since I recognized Christine in that figure floating in the water, I feel the full weight of losing her. *My best friend.* In many ways, my only friend. Although I'm friendly with a number of the mothers of Bea's friends, most of them are at least ten years older than I am. There was no one I thought to call to come with me to this appointment. If she were alive, I would have called Christine and she, after telling me I was over-reacting and worrying too much, would have gotten on the next train to go with me. She'd gone with me when Neil was first admitted to Briarwood and to the ER with me when Bea got a concussion from falling off her bike when she was seven. I'd gone with her when she decided to get an AIDS test eight years ago and when she'd gone into rehab. So why hadn't she called me when she found out she was pregnant?

I glance across the highway toward the shining strip of river and the hills on the other side. Beyond those hills I can just make out the cliffs of the Shawangunks, an area famous for rock climbing. Neil had taken both of us several times and always Christine had been fearless. I can't imagine what would have made her so afraid to tell me that she was pregnant—unless she'd been afraid to tell me who the father was.

THE GENETIC COUNSELING OFFICE IS IN A MEDICAL OFFICE building adjacent to a shopping center on Route 9 just south of the Mid-Hudson Bridge. When I check in the receptionist collects the questionnaire I've filled out and tells me the geneticist will have to review it before seeing me. Then she asks if I want to put this on my insurance. I've already retrieved my insurance card, but the way she's phrased the question gives me pause. It hadn't occurred to me to wonder what my insurance provider's reaction might be to the news that I have a gene predisposing me to breast cancer.

"You don't have to decide now," she tells me when she sees me hesitate, "you can discuss it with the counselor. Help yourself to tea or coffee and have a seat." She gestures toward a tray set up with two silver urns and a plate of pastries and bagels. Helping myself to a cup of chamomile tea (I'm a little jumpy from the espresso), I sit down on a couch upholstered in a green and lavender chintz that matches the wallpaper and lampshades. The carpet is a restful shade of pale green and so plush that I'm tempted to slip out of my sandals. In fact, settling into the deep, soft cushions, I'm tempted to take a nap. The faux-Victorian decor has obviously been designed to lull nervous women into a soporific trance. Even the framed Alma-Tadema prints of scantily draped women lolling around on cushions suggest that we are here to join a seraglio instead of waiting to have our blood taken and our genes scanned for fatal imperfections. Or our babies' genes. I notice that three out of the four other women in the waiting room are pregnant.

I sit and read a story in an old issue of *Rosie* about the actress Fran Drescher's bout with uterine cancer. Bea and I used to love watching *The Nanny* and I have to restrain myself from asking everyone in the waiting room if they know how the actress is doing now. Then I read an essay in *More* about a woman whose best friend has breast cancer, which sends me sniffling to a Kleenex box covered in a crocheted tea cozy. Everything here feels cushioned, as if to blunt the blow of potential bad news. Finally I decide I'm better off checking in with the Barovier sisters than reading any more magazine stories.

August 28, 1892

Mr. Penrose is working now on a second copy of the Dryope triptych, which he's been commissioned to paint on a screen for one of his patron's drawing rooms. I think Clare was shocked to hear that he would interrupt his real art for such a project.

"We should never denigrate the decorative arts," Mr. Penrose told Clare. "Remember that William Morris himself said that the most important production of art is a beautiful house."

On our way home that day I remonstrated with Clare for embarrassing Mr. Penrose. I reminded her that he's not a wealthy man. After all, the glassworks were failing when Papa bought them from the Penrose family and

*most of the money Augustus's father got from the sale
went to pay off his debts.*

*"Mr. Penrose will have to make his own way in the
world and if that means creating beautiful interiors for
homes, I say that is a noble endeavor. Think of how a
mood is changed by our surroundings—how more
harmonious is the life lived among beautiful things . . ."*

"Miss McKay?"

I look up, startled out of Eugenie's little lecture on
interior decorating, at a woman who, in a lavender smock
and flowered dirndl skirt, could have walked out of
Eugenie's journal. Her long black hair, pulled back into a
loose braid, and large dark eyes could belong to one of the
Pre-Raphaelite models.

"I'm Irini Pearlman. We spoke on the phone. I'm sorry
to have kept you waiting, but I'm ready for you now."

As I rise she puts out her hand to shake mine but as I
place my hand in hers I stumble a little in the thick
carpeting and she enfolds my hand in both of hers to
steady me. I imagine for a minute that she's going to hold
my hand all the way into her office, but she lets go after
gently squeezing my hand and gestures for me to walk in
front of her down a corridor lined with more Alma-
Tadema prints—these of girls lounging on a marble
terrace above the sea.

Irini Pearlman's office is slightly less frilly and feminine
than the waiting room. The prints here are tasteful water-
color botanicals. The drapes and the two upholstered
chairs in front of her desk where we sit are plain cream-

colored linen—a fabric that reminds me, for some reason, of that muslin dress Eugenie altered for Clare and then realtered for herself.

"I've reviewed your family history and drawn up a quick chart showing the genetic risk factors we would be testing for," Dr. Pearlman says, indicating a sheet on a clipboard that she holds out for me. "Obviously, the major cause for concern is the presence of early breast cancer in a primary relation—your mother—" She points to a circle she's drawn and inked in. "And then we have the great-aunt—" she points to another circle, this one half-darkened with a question mark above it, "—but we're not even sure whether the lump she had removed was malignant or benign . . ."

"No, and as I wrote down there's just not a whole lot of information on that side. My mother's cousin, Annemarie, said the women could barely pronounce the word cancer without making the sign for the evil eye."

"Yes, in my family, too, the aunts would spit and say a prayer against the *kaynohara*. Not an uncommon attitude in the old country, but it makes my job a little harder. I have to say, though, that from this it doesn't seem like you have much to worry about—"

"Really?" I notice I'm leaning toward her, ready to fall into her reassuring dark eyes.

"But of course, whenever there's a parent with the diagnosis there's cause for concern, especially here because your mother was fairly young. I can understand why you would consider having the test. Let me explain a little about the factors you should keep in mind . . ."

I lean back while Irini Pearlman explains my statistical chances for getting breast cancer with or without one of the two genes that have been identified in "family clusters" with breast cancer, BRCA1 and BRCA2. Although I'm pretty bad at statistics and my mind starts to wander when too many numbers get bandied about, Dr. Pearlman's very good at her job. If I've got one of the genes, I have an 85 percent lifetime risk of developing breast cancer compared to a 10 percent lifetime risk for women without either of the genes. More disturbing is the news that if I have the BRCA1 gene I have a 40 to 60 percent chance of developing ovarian cancer compared to a 1 to 2 percent chance in the general population.

"Wow, that's pretty high," I say, "especially since ovarian cancer's so deadly."

"Yes, there's no reliable screening for it, which is why many women who test positive for the gene elect to have their ovaries removed. Of course, that isn't a decision to be made lightly if you'd planned to have more children . . ."

Dr. Pearlman pauses, leaving a hole like one of the blank spaces in her questionnaire for me to fill in, but I'm already too dazed by the onslaught of information I've received to even pretend to know whether I'd planned to have more children or not. I remember Christine asking at the train station, *have you felt that much for anyone since Neil?* It's hard for me to imagine ever caring enough for anyone again to even think about having another child.

"There's no reason to get too far ahead of ourselves," Dr. Pearlman says as if she can hear the questions roiling around in my brain. "We like to bring up the prophylactic measures available because without their existence there'd be very little reason to pursue this line of inquiry, but as I said, the chances are you don't even have the gene. There's also no reason to decide today whether or not you want to have the test. Perhaps there are family members you wish to consult . . ."

"No," I say, "I want to have the test. I might as well get it over with while I'm here . . . or do I have to go to a lab?"

As answer, Dr. Pearlman gets up and retrieves a hypodermic kit from a filing cabinet behind her desk. I'm a little surprised that she's the one to take my blood, but also a little relieved. Because I have narrow veins, giving blood is never easy for me. There's something extremely soothing in her voice though, as she talks to me while swabbing the underside of my elbow and flicking my arm to raise my veins. She tells me the results will take three weeks and that I'll have to come in for an appointment and I'm not to expect to receive any information on the phone. She also tells me that it's probably safe to use my insurance—that they haven't had any cases of people losing their insurance with a positive diagnosis—but that I'm welcome to pay out of pocket if I'd like. Although it's expensive, I tell her I'll pay for the test myself.

I look away when the needle goes in and Dr. Pearlman asks me inconsequential questions about what I do for a living and how old my daughter is and where we live—all to distract me from the needle in my arm.

"We get a lot of people from Penrose College," she says.

"Oh yes, that's how I was referred—"

"From that poor woman who died?"

I turn my head just as Dr. Pearlman pulls the needle out of my arm and presses a cotton swab hard into the crook of my elbow. "You mean Christine Webb? She came here?"

"I'm sorry, I shouldn't have said anything . . ." Dr. Pearlman gets up to dispose of the needle and comes back with a Band-Aid for my arm, avoiding my eyes while she replaces the blood-dabbed cotton with the adhesive bandage. "Everything that happens here is confidential."

"But if Christine came here you should at least talk to the police. Here—" I take out one of the business cards that Detective Falco gave me, "—this is the number of the detective who's handling the case. I'm sure it's important, especially if it had anything to do with the baby . . ."

Dr. Pearlman looks up at me and quickly looks away, but not so quickly that I don't catch a look of pity in those dark eyes so heartbreaking that I feel certain Christine came here because of her unborn child—and that the news she got wasn't good.

CHAPTER TWENTY

Detective Falco had given me two cards; I kept the one he'd written his cell phone number on. I dial the number from a pizzeria across from the medical center. He answers on the third ring.

"It's Juno McKay," I say, "do you have a minute?"

"Of course, Miss McKay, what can I do for you?"

"Well, I just had some tests done at a genetic counseling office in Poughkeepsie—"

"Anything wrong?" he asks, interrupting me.

"Oh no—well, at least let's hope not." I try laughing but it comes out more as a gasp. "Just checking something out. The reason I called, though, is that the genetic counselor mentioned that she knew a friend of mine from the college. I thought at first that she meant Fay Morgan—"

"Why did you think that?" he asks, interrupting me for the second time.

"Because Fay referred me to her." I pause, expecting another interruption, but Detective Falco is silent. "Anyway, it wasn't Fay—it was Christine. She came in for

278 · CAROL GOODMAN

some testing about a month ago. Around the same time she would have been up here visiting Briarwood."

"Did the counselor say what she was being tested for?"

"She wouldn't tell me anything, but I gathered it had something to do with the pregnancy and that the news wasn't good. I gave her your card and she said she'd call, but I thought I should give you her name and number as well."

"Absolutely," he says, "good work."

I give him Irini Pearlman's name and number and the address of the genetic counseling office and he thanks me. I can tell he's ready to get off, but I detain him another moment. "I guess bad news about her pregnancy could have been a motive for killing herself—"

"And it could tell us who the father was," he says, interrupting me for the third and last time. Then he thanks me again for my "good work" and hangs up. I'm not sure why, but the thought of Detective Falco homing in on the identity of Christine's lover makes me feel a little queasy, almost as if I'm the prey that's being circled. Or it could just be the loss of blood that's making me feel light-headed. I buy a slice of Sicilian pizza and head across the river.

IT'S BEEN YEARS SINCE I'VE BEEN TO NEW PALTZ, NOT SINCE Neil and Christine and I used to drive through on our way to rock climbing in the Gunks. Sometimes we'd pick up bagels on our way in—the only decent bagels north of the Bronx, Neil used to say—and stop at one of the bars on our way back. New Paltz had a lot more going for it as a college town than poor run-down Rosedale.

It still feels like a seventies college town. If anything Main Street seems to have gone back in time since I last saw it. Tie-dyed shirts and bright Indian kurtas hang in the windows, long-haired men and sandaled young women—many with babies in Indian-patterned slings—walk along the main street.

When I check the directions on the opening notice again I realize that the gallery is just outside the town, over the bridge that crosses the Wall Kill, in an old stone building—in fact, it's called Stone Gallery—by the side of the stream. The sight of the full parking lot brings me such a sensation of relief that I realize that my nervousness hasn't all been over seeing Neil again. It's the old anxiety I always felt when he did a show—the fear that if it were too sparsely attended or if too few paintings sold or sold to the wrong people or he overheard a callous comment or it was badly reviewed or not reviewed at all, Neil's manic high that preceded the show would dissolve into crippling depression. It took me a while to realize that it didn't really matter how the show went, that there was no amount of success that could staunch that downward flow from elation to despair—a process as inevitable as water flowing to the sea.

I park and walk up a flight of stone steps to an arched doorway flanked on either side by blue flags emblazoned with the show's title—River Light—and Neil's name and proceed down a narrow stone corridor. I wonder if the building is one of the original Huguenot buildings the town is famous for. It feels ancient, cool as a tomb, the wide planked floor worn and sloping ever so slightly downward so that I'm surprised that the room I emerge into is not some dark underground cavern. It is, rather, spacious and filled with color and wavering light.

I'd been expecting to see something like the river landscapes Dr. Horace showed me at Briarwood, but the canvas that fills the wall facing me could only be called a landscape in the most elemental sense. There is water—a great expanse of dark purplish water at eye level as if the viewer were swimming in it or skimming the surface in a low boat—and a towering rock face tinged with indigo and violet, and striped by wavering bands of pale mauve light that seem to be moving. In fact, the light is moving. The entire room is filled with reflected light coming, I soon figure out, from narrow rectangular copper basins lining the walls. I step over to one of the basins and look down through clear water to a tumble of smooth rocks at the bottom that nearly camouflage the underwater light fixtures. When I take another step forward the water vibrates, making the light bands on the paintings and walls jitter and shake.

"The basins are mounted on high-tension springs," says a woman who's come up behind me, "so that the pattern of light responds to the presence of viewers in the room. The artist is commenting on the Heisenberg uncertainty principle—the theory that there is no way to make an observation without affecting that which is observed." I stare at the woman to see if she's having me on, but she stares back with a straight face, as if

explaining art via obscure physics theories was everyday
stuff to her. Maybe it is. The woman is tall and slim, her
silver hair cut boyishly. She's wearing an ankle-length
coat woven in a multicolored geometric pattern that looks
vaguely Aztecan and chunky amber earrings the size of
cherries. She looks like she could be a physics professor or
an Aztec priestess. When I look down to see the springs
under the water basins I notice that she's wearing lavishly
impractical sandals of blue satin, the strap between her
toes encrusted with a rhinestone dragonfly that appears
to have just alighted on her foot.

"Do you work for the gallery?" I ask.

She smiles down at me from the height of her dragonfly
heels and I can't help but feel that I've offended some
Aztecan deity with my question. "*My* gallery is in
Manhattan, but I'm also on the board of ArtHudson,
which funds this gallery, and I'm volunteering as a docent
for this show. I believe in supporting local artists whose
work reflects the indigenous landscape. Buchwald's pieces
combine references to Hudson River school painting and
more modern sources—for instance, Dan Flavin's light
installations. Flavin lived for a while across the river in
Garrison and collected Hudson River school paintings . . ."

"Yes, I saw an exhibit of those recently at the Vassar
College Art Gallery." I'm lying. I saw the announcement of
the exhibit and meant to go. Something about this woman's
elegant bearing and well-meaning tutelage makes me want
to assert my own knowledge and credentials. I remember
this about art shows—the temptation to say something
pretentious and disingenuous. I'm wondering how to

escape the talkative docent when she spots someone more interesting over my shoulder and hurries away without saying good-bye.

I stand for another moment in front of the canvas and read the little card affixed to the wall by its side, which explains that the painting's title, *Water Lightning*, comes from a term used by Cambodian fishermen for the patterns of light reflected on the trees that stand in the drowned forests of Tonle Sap Lake. The next two paintings, following the same theme, are called *Drowned Forest* and *Dancing Trees*.

The gallery has been partitioned with alternating panels so that foot traffic moves through the space like a meandering river. In fact, the paintings in the next space are titled *Bend in the River I, II*, and *III*. Not only are they tonally bluer than the first painting, but the reflected light waves that play over their surfaces are slightly bluish. The lights in the water basins must be tinted.

There's only one painting in the next space and it's called *World's End*. Blue water tinged with green fills the entire canvas. Looking at it has the dizzying effect of staring into a whirlpool and I back away as if it might suck me into its maelstrom. I start to retrace my steps back to the front of the gallery, not sure if I'm disappointed or relieved that I've gone through the whole show without running into Neil, when I notice a small sign pointing down a short flight of stairs. NOT THE END, it reads. So *World's End* isn't the end. I recognize Neil's love of wordplay and his fondness for *the last word*: he always loved codas and epilogues, afterwards and envoys.

The steps lead to what must have once been a porch that is now glassed in. One whole wall is a window overlooking the Wall Kill. The paintings in this room are smaller and less finished—delicate oil sketches of pond life: water lilies, reeds, wild irises, fish swimming underwater. Many of them are signed with the little tree insignia that Neil used to use as his sign, but it's become an abstract, almost calligraphic insignia. Instead of rectangular basins lining the walls there's a round basin—its copper gone green with corrosion—at the center of the room, filled with water lilies and live carp. The lights at the bottom are either tinted green or turn green as they shine through the delicately veined lily pads.

Moving from painting to painting, I'm so mesmerized by the detail and the finely nuanced shades of light and color in each gemlike study that I barely notice the couple who have come in behind me. At least until I recognize the voice of the tall docent comparing Neil's works to Frederick Church's oil sketches—part of the same exhibit at Vassar I lied to her about attending.

When I've come full circle I turn back to take in the whole room: the steady green light pouring upward from the central basin like a fountain scattering not droplets but these exquisite emerald paintings. *This* is what comes after World's End—a still, green pool at the bottom of the river. I want to shout at the docent that it doesn't matter if the work reminds her of Flavin or Church. What matters is that it's beautiful and calm and, above all, *sane*. But I don't shout because as I turn, the man with her turns, as if we were caught in the same current, and I see that it is Neil.

* * *

HE LEAVES THE TALL DOCENT IN MIDSENTENCE AND STRIDES across the room toward me. I have just enough time to notice that his hair has darkened from pale straw to a more ordinary light brown and that his face is rounder, flesh filling the hollow shadows that used to lurk beneath his eyes and cheekbones. But his eyes are the same arresting blue green, and he walks with the same loose-limbed gait that I noticed the first time I saw him at the Cloisters—and that I thought I recognized in the figure behind the window at Cooke's.

He stops a few feet away from me and says nothing, only looks at me—really looks at me, in a way that, I realize now, no one ever has except for him—as if he knew everything about me in an instant but still thought there was more to look for. The way someone might look at a view of the ocean.

Then he nods as if I'd just said something he agreed with. "I'm so glad you came, Juno. I've been hoping you would since Dr. Horace told me you came to Briarwood."

The old Neil would have said *I knew you would come.*

"I'm glad I did. Your paintings—the whole exhibit—is amazing. They've taken my breath away." The last bit is not an exaggeration; I find I'm having trouble breathing. I stop and gulp air as widemouthed as the carp in the copper basin.

Neil looks around the room as if he's just remembered that he's at his own show and smiles. "Thanks. Thanks a lot." Another surprise—Neil used to greet praise with a scowl and a litany of queries: "What do you mean? What exactly do you like about it? Doesn't it bother you that—?" And then he'd list all the flaws he saw in his work and in himself and in the world in general. "I was lucky to get this space and ArtHudson's support to do whatever I wanted with it."

At the mention of her organization's name the tall docent, who's been mooning around the copper basin like a lovesick nymph, wanders over toward us. "How could we not when your ideas were so brilliant," she says.

"Juno, this is Regula Howell. Reg, this is my . . . an old friend of mine, Juno McKay."

Regula, a queen. The name fits her.

"McKay? Isn't that the name of the firm that's doing the restoration on the Penrose Window?"

When I tell her it is she tells me that she's a Penrose alum—class of '77—and that she's heard from Gavin Penrose that I'm one of the "best glass conservators in the valley."

"Well, we're still a pretty small operation . . ." I'm about to list all our liabilities, but instead I take a cue from Neil's gracious acceptance of praise, ". . . but growing. We've got a brilliant glass artist from Mexico—Ernesto Marquez—and a new commission for an installation at the Beacon train station."

"Juno's a very talented glass artist," Neil says. "She had a piece in the juried show at Urban Glass last year."

I stare at Neil, speechless. I'm not sure what stuns me the most. The fact that he knows about the Urban Glass show or that he's put the words *glass* and *artist* together in the same sentence. He used to condemn my forays into glassblowing and stained glass as *reversions to craft*— a waste of the time that could be spent painting. Fortunately, my silence is covered by Regula launching into a paean on the glass artist Dale Chihuly. "Have you seen the ceiling of the Museum of Glass in Tacoma?"

"No," I tell Regula. *I haven't managed to jet out to Washington State yet.*

I look at Neil to see if he'll surprise me on this one, too, and reveal that he's made the trip but no, he tells Regula, he hasn't, but he did read about Chihuly's "Seaform Pavilion" in the *Times* and had agreed with Chihuly's ideas that the boundaries between art and craft have blurred since the 1960s and that artists now choose the medium that best suits the ideas they want to express. "I think that glass is an amazing medium for exploring notions of flux and instability because it's not truly a solid or a liquid and it's always in motion."

Regula Howell is nodding away eagerly at Neil's comments, seemingly unaware that Neil has been steadily maneuvering us all over to the sliding glass doors at the far side of the room. With one hand on the door, he points to a man and woman across the room. "Aren't those the curators from Dia:Beacon you wanted to speak to?" he asks.

Regula swivels her head in the direction Neil's indicated, her amber earrings swaying like fruit in a wind-tossed tree, and Neil opens the door and propels me out onto the deck in one fluid movement. He steers me toward the buffet table, where he hands me a tumbler of red wine and takes a bottle of Pellegrino water for himself and a handful of almonds and dates. "Let's go down there," he says, pointing to a bench beneath a willow tree on the banks of the Wall Kill, "or we'll never get any privacy."

When we're seated on the bench I take a sip of my wine. "How'd you know I still drink red wine?" I ask. "The same way you knew about the Urban Glass show?"

Neil blushes and I realize it sounds as if I've just accused him of stalking me. It's the type of comment that in the past would have infuriated him, but now he looks more embarrassed than angry. "Yes, actually. I found out both from Christine. I'm so sorry, Juno, that she's gone. I know it must be a devastating loss for you."

I look away toward the slow-moving stream and picture what we must look like—a man and a woman sitting under a willow tree like a Victorian tableau representing mourning. "That was you at the funeral, wasn't it?" He nods. "Why didn't you come into the chapel?"

"I didn't think it would be fair for you to have to deal with seeing me for the first time at Christine's funeral. But I knew I had to go because I feel responsible."

"Responsible? For Christine's death?"

"Yeah."

"But why?"

He doesn't answer right away. Instead he leans down and picks up a flat stone from the ground and flicks it out over the creek, where it skips three times over the calm water before sinking. I'm terrified that he's going to tell me that Christine's baby was his and I realize that it's what

I've been afraid of since learning Christine was pregnant and that she'd been to Briarwood.

I close my eyes and remember a day the three of us spent hiking on the Mohonk Preserve not far from where Neil and I are sitting right now. It was during spring break, three months after Christine had broken her leg climbing the library tower with Neil and just after the cast had come off. I knew by then that I was pregnant, but I hadn't told Neil or Christine yet. Because Christine's leg was still healing we'd settled on a leisurely stroll around the Mohonk trails instead of rock climbing in the Shawangunks. I thought Neil would be frustrated by the slower pace and tamer terrain, but instead he was unusually solicitous of Christine and offered her his arm on some of the steeper paths so that I trailed behind them feeling like a dowdy governess chaperoning a courting couple (I'd been reading Jane Austen for British Lit that semester). I'd known before that day that Christine was attracted to Neil but it had never bothered me that much. On that day at Mohonk, though, the sight of them together started a fluttering inside my abdomen that, even when I realized it was the baby moving, still felt like a warning. A sign that it was too late to lose Neil to anyone—even to my best friend.

"Because of the way we used to talk about suicide back in college," Neil says. For a minute I've forgotten what question he's answering, I'm so pulled into the memory of Christine, limping but alive, on that day at Mohonk. "Like it was a sport or competition."

I open my eyes and I'm looking into Neil's, which seem, at the moment, filled with the green of the willow tree, and the stream, and the thick fringe of reeds growing on the water's edge.

"Did she talk about killing herself when you saw her?" I ask, wanting, really, to ask *when did you see her*? Dr. Horace said he'd given Neil Christine's phone number in May—only a month before Christine's death. If that was the first time he saw her, he couldn't be the baby's father.

"No, all she wanted to talk about was Clare Barovier and what I'd learned about her living in her old suite at Briarwood—what nurses and orderlies said about her and what I thought about the paintings. I asked about you, of course, and about Beatrice—"

It's the first time either of us have mentioned our daughter's name and I can't help but notice how soft and hoarse his voice is when he says her name—and that he still pronounces it in the Italian manner.

"—she told me Beatrice was going white-water rafting this summer and it actually scared me. After all the reckless and stupid things I did when I was her age! It made me realize what it must have been like for you all these years having to be a parent on your own. You don't know how sorry I am, Juno. About everything . . ." His voice breaks then and before I can think about it I lay my hand over his on the bench. He turns his hand palm up and grips mine and wipes his eyes with the other hand. I look away, not so much ashamed by his tears as by what I'm thinking: that the rafting trip was a last-minute thing because Bea knew I'd object. She waited until the day before the application deadline to tell me about it and when I realized how scared she'd been to ask me I said yes right away. We'd sent in the check only five weeks ago and I called up that same night to tell Christine that I was making great strides overcoming my possessiveness. It must have been right before she went to Briarwood and asked Dr. Horace to have Neil contact her. Christine would have already been pregnant by that time. Of course, Neil could have seen her before that, but for the time being I take it as a sign that Christine's baby wasn't his.

Neil lifts my hand and draws it into his lap and I look back toward him but keep my eyes on our hands as he turns mine over to study my palm. "You know what the hardest thing about getting better is?" he asks.

I almost laugh. It's such a Neil thing to say—not *the hardest thing about going crazy*, but *the hardest thing about getting better*. But I don't laugh because what I'm thinking is: *He is better, he is better*.

"No, what?"

"It's not knowing which parts of you are still you and which were your illness. Like being able to paint or feeling like you could fly or thinking you can leave your body at night and visit people in their dreams. For years I've wondered where loving you belonged. Were my feelings for you part of my 'idealization' problems? Were you an illusion of my madness? Could anyone be as beautiful as I remembered you?"

I look up from our hands and see myself reflected in Neil's eyes. Two Junos swimming in two pools of green. A double version of the dream I had last night.

"But the minute I saw you today I knew that everything I ever felt for you was real," he says. "It still is."

CHAPTER TWENTY-ONE

NEIL AND I SIT ON THE BENCH BY THE WALL KILL FOR ANOTHER half hour. I tell him everything I can think of to say about Bea and show him some pictures from her last crew meet.

"God, she looks so much like you," he says, staring hard at a picture of Bea smiling triumphantly after her victory over Poughkeepsie, her arms wrapped around two crewmates. "She's got your hair and your smile." He looks up from the picture to me. If he notices the gray that's crept into my hair or the lines around my mouth and eyes he doesn't say.

"She's got your eyes," I tell him, "and your build."

Neil picks up a flat stone and lobs it into the Wall Kill, where it sinks straight to the bottom. All this parsing of Bea's gene traits can't hide the fact that no matter what she's *gotten* from him, what she's never had is *him* in the flesh.

I notice Regula Howell standing on the deck talking to a man and a woman—both wearing identical square-rimmed eyeglasses—but looking over their shoulders in our direction. As soon as I make eye contact with her she waves and heads down the steps toward us.

"I guess I'd better get back," Neil says. "Reg went to a lot of trouble to put this thing together."

I nod, unable to speak. For all that we've said in the last half hour neither of us has said one word about seeing each other again. *Is this it?* I wonder, watching Regula Howell stop to take off her high-heeled sandals because they're sinking into the damp ground. *Do I want more than this? Does he?*

"Juno," Neil says when Regula is less than twenty feet away, "I wouldn't blame you if you didn't want to see any more of me. I wouldn't blame you for hating me."

"That's not how I feel. I've never hated you." I speak quickly, trying to cram fourteen years of ambiguity and confusion into the seconds we have left. "I've never stopped thinking about you. I still dream about you."

"Really?" he asks, grinning. "I dream about you all the time." Then his smile abruptly fades and I know he's remembered that last dream he told me about—the one in which I slashed his paintings. I see the color drain from his face and—with Regula Howell ten feet away—I come to a quick decision.

"Why don't you call me next week and we'll get together." I say it like we're old friends making a lunch date. "You could come over and see the studio and the factory—"

Neil breaks in just before Regula reaches us, "I'd love that, Juno." He squeezes my hand, which I'd forgotten he was still holding, and then lets it go. "I'll call you next week—Dr. Horace gave me your number."

"Congratulations, Neil," Regula says when she reaches the bench. I move over so she can sit down but she leans against the willow trunk instead, bending one knee and resting her bare foot against the smooth bark. The blue satin sandals dangle from one finger like expensive Christmas ornaments. "The show's quite a success. The curators from Dia:Beacon want to meet you. They'd like to run your show in a gallery in Beacon near the museum when it opens next May."

"That would be incredible, Neil. Dia:Beacon's going to be a major museum."

Regula Howell gives me a little condescending smile and I suddenly remember where I've seen her name before—in an article in the *Penrose Alumnae Magazine*. She'd started out in the early eighties working at a gallery in SoHo that handled artists as renowned as Basquiat and Haring. She has her own gallery now and it's rumored that she supports young fledgling artists out of her sizable private income. *What an amazing connection for Neil to make*, I think, trying not to be jealous.

"So, if you can spare him for a minute, June—"

"Juno," Neil corrects her, "like the goddess."

"Of course." Regula smiles, *queen to goddess*. "It's just that I've got a party to get to across the river. Perhaps you're going there as well, Juno, it's at Forest Hall."

I shake my head. "I'm not all that involved in the college outside of the window restoration."

"Oh, I just thought since you knew Gavin Penrose." Regula gives the sandals a little swing and the jeweled dragonflies wink in the pale watery light. "It's his engagement party. Didn't you know? He's marrying one of my classmates, Joan Shelley."

DRIVING BACK ACROSS THE RIVER I THINK ABOUT *An American Tragedy*. When Detective Falco first brought up the scenario from the Dreiser novel I thought it sounded too melodramatic to have anything to do with what happened to Christine. Handsome rake seduces poor, working-class girl and then tosses her over for rich heiress. And then what? Drowns her when she shows up pregnant demanding that he marry her? I can see Gavin Penrose in the role—he even has a good name for a rake—but I have trouble fitting Christine into the role of damsel in distress. As much as her looks suited her to her study of nineteenth-century painting—hadn't I noticed during her lecture how much she resembled the lady in the window?—her character didn't. She'd never marry for propriety or convenience; she'd raise the baby on her own.

But what if there was something wrong with the baby? What if she needed money badly? Would she have gone to Gavin Penrose? Could he have been so worried about saving face in front of his new—wealthy—fiancée that he took Christine out on a little prenuptial kayaking trip, fed her her own pills in a thermos of coffee, and then swamped her boat? As preposterous as it seems, I can't dismiss the odd coincidence that Gavin Penrose is suddenly announcing his engagement one week after Christine's funeral—an engagement no one knew about.

Or maybe I'm the only one who didn't know about it and I'm just piqued that I wasn't invited to the party.

I don't have much time to pout Cinderella-like in my sooty old factory, though. When I get home I find a faxed invitation along with a copy of an envelope addressed to me with UNDELIVERABLE stamped across the address. There's also a message on my answering machine from Fay Morgan explaining that my invitation came back to her just today and that when she showed it to him, Mr. Penrose insisted she call me right away and tell me he *especially* hoped I would be able to *come share in his joy in this time of grief*.

Fay pronounces the last words like someone reading from a script. Her own natural inflections return with her parting comments, "You really ought to talk to your mail carrier and clear up the confusion regarding your mail delivery."

The fact that she's right (it's not the first time my mail has gone astray) doesn't stop me from feeling peevish as I rush into the shower and pull out the same blue linen dress I wore four weeks ago to Christine's lecture—the only thing I own good enough for a reception at the president's house. *I'll add it to the list, Fay*, I say to my reflection in the mirror, *after cell phone purchase. You've already gotten me to a geneticist and given me three weeks of hell waiting for the results of that blood test.*

As if she heard me the phone rings and when I let the machine pick up it actually is Fay again—reminding me that the invitation includes a *plus one*. "Perhaps you'd like

296 · CAROL GOODMAN

to bring that nice man who works down at the kayaking shop if you're still seeing him."

Jesus, I think, *as soon as Bea graduates I'm out of this little town. How in the world did she know about Kyle? We barely even went out.*

But even my ranting can't disguise the real source of my annoyance. Who *can* I call for my *plus one?*

Then I know exactly who to call.

"HONESTLY, MISS MCKAY, I'D HAVE TAKEN YOU OUT FOR dinner without the cloak and dagger pretext," Detective Falco says when I meet him half an hour later in front of the factory.

I don't say anything for a moment because I'm so taken aback by the transformation wrought by his well-fitting tux. He couldn't have gotten a rental so soon. I wonder what kind of social life he leads that requires a more extensive dress-up wardrobe than my closet's meager offerings.

"You're certainly dressed up," I say.

"You look lovely yourself," he says, turning my grudging comment into an exchange of compliments.

I adjust my shawl over my shoulders. At the last minute I traded the dress's matching linen jacket for a velvet devore shawl that Bea bought for me from the Metropolitan Museum gift shop last year. Although it's hardly a designer item, the iridescent wisteria blossoms complement the blue in my dress, and the silk and velvet against my bare shoulders feels luxurious. I just wish I had Regula Howell's blue satin dragonfly shoes instead of my scuffed black sandals, but then I'd probably be taller than the detective . . . I stop this train of thought by reminding myself that this isn't a date and to remind him I say: "I just thought you'd be interested in knowing that Gavin Penrose is engaged. You're the one who brought up the whole *American Tragedy* scenario."

"Actually, I already know about his engagement to Joan Shelley. He told me about it in our first interview when I asked him what he was doing the night Christine died. He said he was driving Miss Shelley back to her apartment on East End Avenue in Manhattan—an alibi she confirms. Besides that, there are a couple of reasons why I don't think Gavin Penrose is the father of Christine's child—"

"Any you'd care to share with me?"

Detective Falco smiles and tugs at his black silk bow tie. "Not at the moment—but thanks for the lead to the geneticist." He holds the car door open for me. "You sure you're okay?"

"Absolutely," I say, putting on my seat belt.

He gets in the driver's side but doesn't start the car. "You don't have to tell me what you went there for," he says. "I know we don't know each other very well."

We don't know each other at all, I think, surprised that he should be so . . . what? . . . *concerned*. And why did he accept my invitation if he had already ruled out Gavin Penrose as a suspect? Maybe it's just that he's in the habit of ferreting out missing information or maybe he really is worried about me.

"It's to check for the breast cancer gene," I tell him when he's given up waiting and started the car. "My mother had it. Fay Morgan suggested I do it. She tested positive for the gene last year and had a prophylactic mastectomy."

"Really?"

"Yes. She said Gavin Penrose went to bat for her with the insurance company."

"Huh. No wonder she's so loyal to him."

"Yeah."

Detective Falco shifts the car into reverse, then back into park, and then half turns in his seat to face me. "Just your mother?"

"Maybe a great-aunt as well."

"That's not a lot. You probably don't have it."

"Probably not."

He puts the car back in reverse and pulls out of his parking spot and heads up College Avenue. Neither of us speak until we've pulled up in front of Forest Hall. A uniformed valet approaches the car, but Falco puts up his hand and signals for him to wait. He takes off his seat belt and turns around in his seat to face me, seemingly unconcerned about the Jaguar and two Mercedes waiting behind us.

"Look, I probably shouldn't tell you this and you've got to promise to keep it to yourself—okay?"

I nod. *Who am I going to tell*, I think.

"Christine went to the genetic counseling office because her unborn child had tested positive for Tay-Sachs."

"Tay-Sachs? Jesus—that's fatal, isn't it?"

"It's a nightmare. The child usually dies within its first three years."

I close my eyes and picture Christine standing in front of the Lady window, her neck bent down under the weight of her own hair. Overlaid on that image is a picture of her standing on the train platform asking me whether I thought if you loved someone well enough they would return that love. Was she thinking of the baby? Or of the baby's father?

"Poor Christine," I say, "It must have killed her—it might really be what killed her . . . but wait, aren't most people who get Tay-Sachs Jewish?"

"Yeah. According to Dr. Pearlman you're a hundred times more likely to be a carrier if you're of Eastern European Jewish descent. Christine might have been the rare exception of a non-Jew with the gene or she may have had a Jewish ancestor she didn't know about."

"The Webbs? That family has interbred up there on Webb Road for the last two hundred years. It doesn't seem all that likely."

"No, it doesn't, and the other thing is that both parents have to have the gene for their child to contract the disease."

"So the father would most likely be Jewish. Is that why you don't think it's Gavin Penrose?"

"Well, that and the fact that he has an alibi for the night Christine died. Of course he could be the father and not have killed Christine. Maybe she came to him and told him about the baby and he responded so harshly that Christine decided to kill herself. He wouldn't have committed any crime, but I'd sure like to know if that's what happened."

"So would I."

"But, it's a pretty big stretch to imagine that both carriers would be individuals without any known Jewish background. Especially when there are possibilities who are Jewish . . ."

"You mean Nathan Bell."

"Yes, there's Nathan Bell. And at least one other. Your ex—Neil Buchwald."

THE COLUMNS OF THE CENTRAL COURTYARD HAVE BEEN wrapped with hundreds of tiny white lights, and white gardenias are floating in the fountain. Four marble urns, one in each corner of the courtyard, are filled with lilies, white lilacs, and white roses. The drinks table has been set up in the dining hall near the glass doors leading to the terrace so I head there because I really need a drink. Detective Falco follows close on my heels.

"I didn't mean to upset you," he whispers in my ear as I try to decide between a White Russian, a white wine, or a White Mojito. Apparently Joan and Gavin have opted for a white theme to celebrate their impending nuptials. The dining room chairs have been slipcovered in white muslin (which to my mind makes them look as if they'd been straitjacketed) and the painting frames have all been festooned with white tulle—some of which has slipped over the frames onto the paintings themselves.

"It probably has no bearing on this case," he goes on in

a low voice—but not low enough for me to ignore. "As you yourself said, the news itself might have pushed Christine to suicide. It might not matter who the father was."

"But you're still going to find out, Detective Falco."

Falco shrugs. "Well, yeah, if I can."

"Will you tell me if you do?"

"Okay, on two conditions. First you tell me when you get back your test results. And you start calling me Daniel."

"It's a deal," I say, clinking my White Mojito against his White Russian. "I guess it was pretty useless for you to come here."

"Oh, you never know what you might pick up at a thing like this. Why don't we just relax and have fun."

Sure, I think, *right after you tell me my ex-husband—who I saw today for the first time in over a decade—might have impregnated my best friend.* I take a long sip of my drink. The conversation Neil described having with Christine couldn't have happened more than five weeks ago. Why didn't I ask him if that was the first time he saw her? Why had I been so anxious just to believe that he hadn't seen her before that? Because I'd let myself hope that Neil was better enough that there might be a second chance for us. I didn't want a little detail like the thought of him and Christine together ruining that. But if Neil was the father of Christine's baby, I'd better find out, and Detective Falco—*Daniel*—might be my best source of information.

"Okay, Daniel," I say, finishing my drink and picking up another one from the bar, "although you've obviously never been to one of these college functions before if you think *fun* is what they're about. Half the people here are worrying that they won't get tenure, the other half are worried that their departmental budgets will be cut, or if they're spouses they're worried that their wives or husbands are cheating on them with their young and beautiful students."

"No dancing?"

I laugh in spite of myself. "Maybe later on the terrace. Academics are a pretty reserved bunch."

"So what do people do at these things?"

"They trade gossip and recent honors—book deals or journal publications, grants and fellowship awards." I look around the room and notice Professor Da Silva standing in front of a painting of Virgil leading Dante into the underworld—a school of Lorraine work—and instantly regret my glib dismissal of academia. Many of these people are real scholars and—like Professor Da Silva—real friends. I realize that the line I'd just taken was Christine's and even she had stopped complaining about academia when she'd gone back to grad school. "There are the paintings," I say. "They're worth seeing."

"Great. Tell me about these." Falco gestures with his glass toward the closely hung paintings. "I don't know much about art but these look dark and dreary enough to be worth a fortune."

"They do need cleaning, in fact—" I squint past the festoons of tulle and notice a few blank spots. Maybe that's the real purpose of the tulle—to disguise the blank spots. "It looks like a few have been removed. I think it's part of

Gavin's campaign to spruce up the college for its centennial along with the restoration of the Lady window. Not that these paintings are really all that valuable. Augustus and Eugenie collected them on their various trips back to Europe, but unfortunately, most of them turned out to be fakes. Take this one for instance of the Muses on Mount Parnassus. Penrose thought it was by Mantegna, but it's really a nineteenth-century copy. And this one of the three graces—"

"Now this looks familiar, wait, let me guess, I did take one art history survey class at John Jay . . . Botticelli?"

"Very good—only it's not. If Christine were here she would explain how you can tell it's not a real Botticelli."

"So are they all fakes?"

"Not all of them. Occasionally Penrose got lucky, or, as Christine believed, he followed Eugenie's better judgment and picked out an authentic work. There's a real Ingres here and a Rubens . . ." I start looking for the voluptuous flesh of some minor goddess by Rubens, but if she's here she's well hidden by the tulle.

While I'm looking for the plump goddess I see instead the queenly Regula Howell through the French doors leading to the terrace. She's exchanged her long Aztec coat for a full-length ivory chiffon off-the-shoulder gown with tulle wrap. She looks like an amazon warrior, her height accentuated because she's standing next to tiny Joan Shelley, who's wearing a wispy little white dress that looks like the costume Bea wore in her third grade ballet recital. I guess I missed the part of the invitation that said wear only white.

"Maybe it's one that's been removed for cleaning. Why don't we go look at Penrose's paintings," I suggest to Falco. "At least we know who painted those." It's also occurred to me that if we run into Regula she might say something that will reveal to Daniel Falco that I saw Neil today, something I neglected to mention when Neil's name came up earlier.

We walk through the central courtyard and turn down the Forest Hall with its paintings of mythological characters turning into trees.

"Daphne and Apollo, right?" Falco points at Penrose's rendition of the myth. Unlike most versions I've seen— Bernini's sculpture, for instance—instead of looking over her shoulder at her pursuer she's looking at her own outstretched hand, which is beginning to sprout leaves. The look of horror on her face is haunting.

I nod. "You're pretty up on your mythology Detec— Daniel."

"I took Latin for six years at Our Lady of Perpetual Help and read some Ovid—that's where most of these stories come from, right?"

"Yes. His early subjects usually came from medieval folklore and Romantic poetry, but like J. W. Waterhouse and other second-generation Pre-Raphaelites he turned back to classical mythology. He especially liked stories about nymphs."

"If you ask me he was looking for an excuse to paint young naked girls."

"Well sure, but if you look closely some of these young girls aren't so beautiful while they're being turned into trees. I think Augustus Penrose was fascinated by meta-morphosis—one thing turning into another. Maybe it was because he watched his sister-in-law go crazy."

We continue walking down the hall until we're standing in front of the second painting in the Iole and Dryope series. Dryope's just noticed a drop of blood on her fingertips and her expression is one of dawning horror.

"Wait, don't tell me, let me guess which myth this is."

I try to keep from smiling—I seriously doubt that Falco will know the story of Dryope and Iole—and move closer to study the painting myself. I know from Eugenie's journal that the portrait of Dryope is really Eugenie and that Iole is Clare. While Falco rubs his chin, no doubt wracking his brain for the allusion—*it's really not fair*, I think, *Dryope is a pretty obscure myth*—I study the two figures to see if I can tell the two sisters apart and decide which one is depicted in the Lady window. They look too much alike though. As in the photo Christine showed in her lecture the only difference is their hair. Iole's flows freely down her back, while Dryope's hair is drawn back tightly—as if snatched by the clawlike fingers of the branches and yanked and twisted into an uncomfortable-looking chignon of bark and twigs.

I turn to Falco to put him out of his misery but he holds a finger up to his lips and signals for me to be quiet. He hasn't, after all, spent the last few minutes pondering over mythological references. He's listening to the conversation occurring behind the screens in Gavin's office.

CHAPTER TWENTY-TWO

"And I told you, the bill will be paid by the end of the week. I have a small liquidity problem at the moment due to a fund transfer from the family estate. If you don't wish to wait I can always suggest that the college look elsewhere for its landscaping needs next year . . ."

There's a pause during which I raise my eyebrows at Falco and he, in turn, mouths the words *small liquidity problem* with such mock gravity that I nearly burst out laughing. He's managed, without uttering a sound, to mimic Gavin Penrose's upper-class inflections to a tee.

"Yes, I realize the flowers for the party aren't a college expense and I certainly never meant to imply that they were—"

I look down at the narrow canal of water that feeds into the fountain in the central courtyard. It's clogged with fragrant white gardenias. The marble urns that line the hallway are filled with the same assortment of white lilies, lilacs, and roses as the urns in the courtyard. The air is thick with the sweet smell of so many flowers, some of which, like the white lilacs and lilies, must cost a fortune because they're out of season.

"No, I never told your girl that they should go on the college account. This is a private party—which I should be attending to at this very moment so if you'd please . . ."

I miss the last few words because Falco waves with one hand to guide me back down the hall to the courtyard while keeping one finger to his lips. I take one step and he cringes at the slap of my sandals on the tile floor so I slip out of them and walk the rest of the way barefoot and silent like some penitent nun. What I'm thinking of is Gavin's phrase *your girl*. The landscape company that has the contract for the college grounds is Minelli and Sons. Dominic Minelli is Annemarie's husband's uncle. Uncle Dom. A sweet potbellied man who always gave Bea a daisy or a miniature potted cactus (Bea's favorite) when we'd go into the nursery to buy flats of geraniums and impatiens for my father's flower boxes. The *girl* Gavin is referring to could only be Dom's unmarried daughter, Angela, who graduated top in her class at Hunter College and gave up a job at one of the top eight accounting firms to help in the family business when her mother died five years ago. She does my taxes every year and she's one of the smartest people I know. If Angela was under the impression that Gavin was charging the flowers for this party to the college it could only be because that's what he told her.

When we get to the courtyard I start to explain all this to Daniel Falco, but he shushes me again and hurries me through the dining room and out onto the terrace. A light rain has chased most of the guests inside, but still he guides me under a pergola at the far end of the terrace, which gives some protection from the rain and makes us nearly invisible from the house. Falco leans back against the balustrade, nearly knocking over one of the frosted glass luminaria (shaped like a gardenia, I notice) that have been set up all along the length of the terrace and along the garden paths—and I rest my arms on the cool marble and look out at the formal rose garden below us—its perfectly manicured hedges and flourishing roses a testament to the care of Minelli and Sons. I know the rose garden is Dominic Minelli's favorite part of the grounds because of its Italianate formality—a leftover from the previous estate that had been on this property before the Penroses came. The rest of the grounds are landscaped in a more naturalistic manner that harmonizes with the Arts & Crafts style of the buildings.

"I know Dom and Angela Minelli," Falco tells me when I begin my defense of Angela, "and I couldn't agree more. Angela would never make a mistake like that."

"So Gavin must have tried to get the college to pay for the flowers, and when he got called on it he didn't have the money to pay for them himself. I've always thought he was so wealthy—he's always driven expensive cars, traveled in Europe, and he's got an apartment in the city and a house in the Hamptons." *And this beautiful house to live in rent free*, I think, gazing at the manicured box hedge maze and the marble statues glowing dimly in the greenery, some of which, I notice when a piece of marble drapery seems to move in the breeze, have been draped in the same tulle as the picture frames in the dining room.

"So what he's got," Falco says, "is an expensive lifestyle on a college president's salary—which would probably be plenty for you or me but might fall short of the image he likes to present."

"I guess I just assumed he was wealthy because he's a Penrose, but actually, Augustus Penrose gave most of his money and all of his property on this side of the river, except for the glass factory, to the college—"

"—and the glass factory went bankrupt in the sixties," Falco adds.

"There's still all that land on the west side of the river where Astolat used to be."

Falco shakes his head. "It can't be developed. Augustus Penrose stipulated that in his will. The Land Conservancy has been trying to gain control of it, but I've heard that it can't even be sold until a specified number of years after Augustus's death—I forget how many."

"So Gavin might actually have very little other than his salary to live on." I think of the figure the young Gavin Penrose had cut all those years ago when he'd pull up in front of our dorm—the smart, preppy clothes, the out-of-season tan. It would never have occurred to me that he didn't have all the money he could possibly need—but then I suppose that someone who grew up in the shadow of a once-wealthy family might have needs more extensive than anything I could imagine. For instance, I can't imagine needing that apartment in the city and a vacation home when he lives here. It's like Arcadia, I think, gazing at a grouping of statues of three girls with their arms clasped around each other's waists. The Three Graces, I suppose, although I can't remember them being there.

"I guess his financial situation will change when he marries Joan Shelley," I say, "but I bet you she has no idea that he has any money problems."

"No, I'm sure Mr. Penrose has been careful to create the impression that he's at least comfortably well-off. I imagine a woman like Joan Shelley—"

"Shh," I touch his arm and shake my head. "I think that's Joan down in the garden. Look . . ."

The statues I'd been admiring at the far end of the garden have for some time looked oddly lifelike—an effect I'd attributed to the flickering candlelight from the luminaria, their tulle wraps, and the two mojitos I had drunk. But now two of the three graces—a tall one and a short one—have undeniably detached themselves from the grouping and are wending their way through the box hedge maze, giggling as they trip over their wispy drapery. The third grace stands frozen and lonely and I remember now that she's not a grace; she's a statue of my namesake, Juno.

Before the two women in white reach us, they're joined by a third figure who appears out of the shrubbery just below the pergola.

"Did you get it, Fay?" the tall grace, whom I recognize now as Regula Howell, asks.

"Did we look like statues?" the short grace, Joan Shelley, chimes in. "Do you think it will come out? Do you have the right film for night pictures—" and then seeing Falco and me standing above them on the terrace, calls out, "Reg and I have been playing statues. We did it all the time in college and Fay offered to take our pictures. Did you get it, Fay?" Joan asks, repeating Regula's initial question.

Fay is looking down at the settings on her camera—a large 35 millimeter Nikon. She looks up, not at Joan and Regula, but at me and Daniel Falco. "Yes," she says, "I got everything. I was in the perfect location."

JOAN AND REGULA COME UP THE STEPS TO THE TERRACE holding up their damp skirts. Fay trails behind like the forgotten third grace.

"I didn't know you were a photographer," I say to Fay, hoping that when she's forced to look at me I'll be able to guess if she overheard our conversation about Gavin.

She does look annoyed when she looks at me, but then she looks down again and mutters something about the film being stuck. "It's just a hobby," she says. "I started taking pictures at college functions for the alumnae magazine and Mr. Penrose liked them so much he asked me to take the pictures for his engagement party."

"That's just like Gavin," Joan says, "always bringing out people's hidden talents." I glance down at Joan, who's leaning against the balustrade, balanced on one foot while she puts her sandals back on—a pose that reminds me of a classical statue at the Met. She looks younger and more girlish than I remember her from four weeks ago at

Christine's lecture—she looks like a woman in love. If she suspects that Gavin might have another reason for getting Fay to act as unpaid photographer she certainly doesn't show it.

Regula is also ready to sing Gavin's praises. "I haven't seen so many gardenias since I went to Joan's cotillion in Charleston! And look at *this*," she says, lifting Joan's hand and angling it so we can all see the chunky diamond on her left ring finger—six carats at least, I estimate, recalling a gemology class I took a few years back when I started incorporating cut crystals into my glass designs.

Joan pulls her hand free and swats her friend on the arm playfully—all with her wrist flexed so that the diamond catches the candlelight from the luminaria and shines to its best advantage. "Reg! As if I cared about how big a ring I got! What I love is how thoughtful Gav is. He chose gardenias for the party's theme because I'm from the South." She picks up one of the votive candleholders to show to Detective Falco as an example of her fiance's thoughtfulness. "Isn't it darling? And wait till you see the cake—it's shaped like a giant gardenia. He had it done up by this sweet little Italian bakery called Gal's that he's been going to since he was a little boy."

"Cafe Galatea," I say, "my mother's cousin runs it. In fact, I think I'll go back to the kitchen to see if her daughter's helping with the catering—" I notice that Falco is glaring at me as I back away from the group, no doubt because he's dreading being left alone to hear Regula and Joan's tales of cotillions and gardenia blossoms, but I wink at him and mouth the word *bill* as I turn to flee. From the confused look on his face I gather he thinks I'm talking about someone named Bill. *But he's a detective,* I think, threading myself through the partyers in the dining room, *he'll figure out that I mean to find out if Gavin has paid up for all these cannolis and biscotti.*

I cut through the central courtyard and into the butler's pantry and kitchen on the north side of the house. I'm familiar with the layout because I helped cater a few parties myself back when I went here—and for a couple of years after as well—whenever Annemarie needed the help or she guessed I needed the extra money. She always made sure I worked in the kitchen doing setup and cleanup instead of serving so I could be spared the awkwardness of handing out canapés to my rich classmates. I'm not surprised that she's got Portia working back here or that she's put Portia's friend—the industrious Latin scholar, Scott Heeley—to work washing dishes. Unfortunately, neither of them had anticipated my appearance; I find them kissing over a tray of half-filled cannolis.

"*Zia* Juno! What are you doing here?" Portia pushes away from Scott, who turns and plunges his hands into the huge sink full of soapy water (from the color of his face I'd wager he'd like to dive in headfirst and swim away), takes up a pastry tube, and hurriedly resumes stuffing cheese filling into the cannolis. I notice that both of them are liberally sprinkled with the confectioner's sugar meant to dust the pastries. The whole scene reminds me of Francesca's account in *The Inferno* of the courtship between herself and Paolo—how their book was interrupted by a kiss so "that day we read no further." Without my sudden intrusion Portia and Scott might one day be saying, "that day we stuffed no cannolis further."

"I just wanted to see if you needed any help back here—but it looks like you have everything under control." Scott's ears and the back of his neck turn an even brighter pink. I turn away from him to look at the cake that Annemarie was working on when I came by earlier today. Sitting on a linen-covered serving cart strewn with real gardenia leaves, the flower-shaped cake gleams like polished ivory. Annemarie has outdone herself; it must have taken her all day to create this masterpiece. "Is your mother here?" I ask.

"She had to run down to the cafe for more ricotta for the filling. I hope she's back in time to serve the cake so she can get the credit for it. Isn't it beautiful?"

"*Multo bello*. I hope this crowd appreciates it—and I hope your mother charged enough for it. She's always underselling herself."

"Uh-uh. She told me no more—*finito*—she's putting away every penny for my tuition to Penrose in the fall." Portia raises her head and licks a dab of cheese filling off her finger and grins.

"Penrose? You heard?"

"Yep. I'm in—plus I've gotten a partial scholarship that pays half my tuition, but we'll need the money from these catering jobs to pay for the rest—"

I step around the counter and hug Portia. Her apron is damp and she smells like vanilla and lemon dishwashing soap. When I step back I realize I've gotten confectioner's sugar all over my dress. "—so we'd better get back to work," Portia continues, trying to repress the grin on her face. "Mom says she's owed on two other jobs she did for Mr. Penrose and she wants to make sure we do a super job on this one so we can collect for all three this week."

SINCE ANNEMARIE ISN'T BACK YET, PORTIA ASKS ME TO HELP her bring the cake out. I send Scott ahead to tell Gavin Penrose to assemble the guests in the dining room and to make sure we've got a clear path through the courtyard. As we push the serving trolley across the uneven tiled floor I keep my eyes on the cake, which trembles gently, like a real gardenia blossom on a wind-swept branch. I have to stop myself from reaching out with my hand to steady it and spoiling the glossy buttercream icing.

I hear the little oohs and aahs from the assembled guests before looking up to see them gathered in a semicircle around the dining room table. Gavin Penrose and Joan Shelley are standing in the front on either side of the table. Green porcelain plates shaped like leaves—no paper plates for this occasion!—have been arranged across the table in a deceptively haphazard manner so that it looks as if they had been blown there by a summer storm. Real gardenia leaves and petals have been scattered on the white linen tablecloth.

When Scott and another young man have finished filling champagne glasses Gavin lifts his glass and holds it aloft toward his fiancée.

"To my southern belle, my sweet gardenia blossom,

fairer than that bloom because you will never fade. *She cannot fade, though thou hast not thy bliss, for ever wilt thou love and she be fair!"*

The guests raise their glasses and drink. I hand plates to Portia while she cleverly cuts the cake so that each slice looks like a petal. I hand the first plates to Gavin and Joan, who proceed to feed each other mouthfuls of cake.

"You ready to go?" asks Falco, who's sidled up to me, hands stuffed deep in his pockets.

"Aren't you going to have some cake?"

"I've lost my appetite," he says, looking toward Gavin and Joan, who have managed to get cake crumbs and icing all over their faces.

"Yeah, feeding each other cake has always been right up there with 'where's the garter' as my least favorite wedding tradition—and it's not even their wedding!" I lower my voice but still I'm surprised at my own crankiness. Am I becoming a bitter divorcée carping at the happiness of others? Or is it the fact that Gavin chose the same poem—Keats's "Ode on a Grecian Urn"—to toast his new fiancée that he used to eulogize Christine a week ago that's left me with a bitter taste in my mouth?

CHAPTER TWENTY-THREE

WHEN HE PULLS UP IN FRONT OF THE FACTORY, DETECTIVE Falco—I'm still having trouble thinking of him as *Daniel*—puts his car in park but doesn't turn off the engine. Although I hadn't exactly been thinking about asking him in, something about his assumption that I won't irks me. Or maybe I'm just still in a bad mood from the sight of Gavin and Joan enjoying their engagement cake.

"Are you sure Gavin Penrose's alibi is airtight?" I ask.

Falco turns to face me. "*Airtight?* I think you've been watching too much *Law & Order* . . ."

"You know what I mean."

"Well, he says he drove Joan Shelley home to Manhattan and then drove out to his house in the Hamptons. His E-ZPass account clocks him crossing the Triboro Bridge at 12:53 AM—"

"Someone else could have been driving the car . . ."

"—and we have a video record of an ATM withdrawal in Riverhead at 2:33 AM and a credit card purchase the following morning of some expensive garden knickknacks at a nursery in Sagaponack. So unless Mr. Penrose had an accomplice—and no, it can't be Joan Shelley because she was at a co-op meeting at nine AM on the Upper East Side—with his taste in Mongolian sixth-century jardinieres, I'm afraid he's not our man. Why do you want him to be so much?"

I look past Falco at the dark factory that I call home. "I guess I was spinning a little romance between him and Christine when I saw them together after the lecture and it bothers me that he was actually already engaged to Joan Shelley. Maybe he really liked Christine, but he needed to marry Joan for her money . . . it just doesn't seem fair to Christine."

"Look, I'm asking for blood samples from Penrose, Nathan Bell, and your ex, Neil Buchwald. If any one of them turns out to be the father of Christine's child, I'll let you know."

"Okay." I readjust my shawl over my shoulders and turn to get out of the car, but Daniel puts his hand on my arm.

"Do you want me to walk you in? It looks pretty dark in there."

"No, thanks, I've got the dogs."

I LET PAOLO AND FRANCESCA OUT IN THE COURTYARD FOR A brief run and then crawl into bed. As exhausted as this long day has left me, though, I know it will be a while before I can sleep. I take out the entry from Eugenie's journal that I had started reading earlier today in the doctor's office and pick up where I'd left off, with Eugenie's little speech on interior decorating.

> *Think of how a mood is changed by our surroundings—how more harmonious is the life lived among beautiful things.*

I think of the house I just left, Forest Hall, where Eugenie lived out her life in the shadow of all those paintings of her and her sister whom she never saw again even though she was just up the river living in her own tower room, surrounded by paintings of a lonely pool that must have reminded her of that spot where the great painter Augustus Penrose first painted her. Had either woman found solace or comfort in their surroundings?

> *Clare remained unpersuaded by my reasoning and angry with me for bringing up Mr. Penrose's penury. "You and Papa, all you ever care about are livings and interest on investments," she said, walking on ahead of me.*
> *Poor Clare. It's hard on her that Papa has settled a comfortable income on me, but not on her. Of course, Papa doesn't mean to play favorites but, as he's explained to me, if he gave Clare an independent income then her father might reappear and attempt to influence Clare. We both know how generous Clare is, how susceptible to impressions. When I asked if I could make a small gift to her from my own income he showed me how that, too, would be rash.*

"Think of how your future husband might regard such an arrangement," he counseled me.

I replied that any man I would consider marrying would not begrudge my sister a share in my fortune. To which Papa answered that in that case I could wait until I was married to make whatever arrangements my husband and I found suitable.

I could hardly argue with that line of reasoning and, besides, I found all this talk of an imaginary husband disconcerting. I have, until of late, dismissed the thought of marriage as something belonging to natures other than mine. Clare has always been the romantic one, the one enamored of old-fashioned tales of knights and ladies. Lately, though, I've begun to envision a kind of marriage removed from those fairy tales of love—a marriage based on mutual interest and dedication to honest work.

But perhaps that is as much a fairy tale as the old stories of knights and ladies. I beguile myself with these foolish fancies when I should be sleeping. I remember how I used to laugh at Clare's notions of love as a sickness that could rob one of sleep and even sanity, and now I'm the one . . .

Well, best to put my pen down and call it a night before the light at my window makes me a liar and calls it day.

I let the journal pages drop onto the floor with the rest that have fallen there and close my eyes. Eugenie's timid intimations of love have much the same effect on me as

Gavin's toast to his fiancée—I would be touched if the shadow of a third person wasn't thrown over the sentiments. Could Eugenie not have known that Clare was falling in love with Augustus Penrose? Even from my vantage point—over a hundred years later—her feelings are clear to me. I can imagine, as well, that Augustus returned her feelings, but courted Eugenie because she was the heiress and he needed her father's money to save his family's glass business and provide the funds to start a new business in America. I wonder if it was Augustus's proposal to Eugenie that tipped Clare over into madness.

I picture the two sisters in the Dryope paintings—the one reaching over the water to pluck a forbidden flower and the other safe on shore, watching with horror as her sister draws back a bloody hand. The last thought I have before falling asleep is that the painting should be the other way around. It should be Clare reaching for the bloody lotus, and Clare who turns into the tree while her sister watches in horror.

In my dream I'm wheeling the serving trolley across the courtyard in Forest Hall—only the president's house has become a real forest. I can sense the trees looming above me and hear the water falling into a deep pool and feel the rough ground beneath my feet, but I have to keep my eyes on the cake to keep it steady. I come to a clearing in the forest where everyone has gathered: Gavin and Joan and Regula Howell and Fay, and also Neil and Dr. Horace and, cutting the cake instead of Portia, Christine. She sinks a silver knife into the cake and I see that beneath the white frosting the filling is a deep carmine red.

"It's a new recipe," Christine tells me, laying a slice of the red and white cake on a plate. "I call it Lotus Cake. For forgetting."

I pass out the plates and watch as not just Gavin and Joan, but everyone begins to feed each other mouthfuls of cake. Dr. Horace and Neil, Fay and Regula, Detective Falco and a woman in white whom I realize, after a moment, isn't a woman. She's the statue of Juno from the garden. I turn back to Christine, who's holding a forkful of cake out to me. I watch as a drop of the filling splatters the ground. I look back at the crowd and see that all their mouths are stained with blood.

I wake up with a metallic taste in my mouth and a pounding in my head. When I stumble into the bathroom and scoop water from the faucet to drink, a drop of blood falls from my lip. Even though I know that I must have bitten my lip in my sleep I can't help but feel like the girl in Ovid's story—that I've crossed some forbidden line and my cells have already begun to wreak some irrevocable transformation to my flesh.

I TRY IN THE NEXT FEW DAYS TO PRETEND THAT I'M NOT waiting for Neil to call but even the dogs have taken to flinching when the phone rings in anticipation of my lunges to pick it up. On one such mad dash I knock over and break a lancet window that Robbie had just finished cleaning for a church in Rhinebeck.

Fortunately, everyone assumes that it's Bea I'm waiting to hear from.

"You're just like your mother," my father says to me on Tuesday—three days since I saw Neil at the gallery opening. "When you went on an overnight with the Girl Scouts she couldn't sleep a wink. She made me drive all the way out to the Frost Valley YMCA camp and sit in a pickup outside your bunk till the next morning. The camp director thought I was a child molester and snuck up on me with a six-gauge shotgun. We ended up sharing a six-pack and playing pinochle until sunrise."

My father chuckles to himself, the sound muted by the face mask he's wearing to filter the fumes of solder and flux. While Robbie and I have already finished resoldering the figure of the lady, he and Ernesto are still working on the landscape section. Because the work on the landscape is too complex for Robbie, I've given him the task of developing the pictures that he's taken to document the restoration. I could chip in myself, but since my dream the smell of metal—either from the lead solder when it's melting or from my hands after I've handled the lead—makes me nauseous. I've spent the last three days—when I'm not leaping to answer the phone—drafting a letter to Gavin Penrose explaining why we've chosen to reassemble the window differently from how it was originally assembled.

"I should have run it by him," I say, not for the first time this week. "We might have to take it apart and redo the whole thing if he doesn't approve the reconstruction."

"There's nobody who's going to look at this window and not see this was the way it was meant to be," Ernesto says. "And you've got Eugenie's notebook to back you up."

I have found sketches in Eugenie's design notebook that support our reconfiguration of the glass. Her sketches of the landscape clearly resemble the picture created by the dichroic pattern in the glass that had been obscured by the previous arrangement of the panes. What I can't figure out is why the window was assembled incorrectly in the first place. Each time Ernesto and my father finish another layer of the reconstruction Ernesto calls Robbie and me over, first turning the light table off, and then switching the light on so we can see the hidden stream of water spring to life and pour into the pool, which ripples now with colors and patterns that had been invisible before. I'm peering into the layers of glass at a pattern that seems to be emerging when the phone rings and for once I let Robbie answer it.

"It's for you," Robbie says, handing me the cordless phone.

For a moment the voice on the other end seems to be underwater, but then I realize it's because my ears are ringing. I've given myself a slight touch of vertigo by staring too long into the rippled layers of glass. I walk away from the window and from the three men in the studio and shake my head to clear the ringing sound, and when I hear that it's Neil, I keep walking with the phone, up the spiral staircase and out onto the roof.

"Hey, sorry, I couldn't hear you down in the studio, someone was running the glass grinder."

"If you're busy . . ."

"No, no, I've been waiting to hear from you."

"Yeah, I'm sorry about that. I had my session with Dr.

Horace on Monday and . . . well, he wasn't exactly enthusiastic about me seeing you."

I can't think of anything to say—both because I'm oddly hurt that Dr. Horace might consider me an impediment to Neil's recovery and because I'm amazed that Neil would be so receptive to that kind of authoritative input.

"Shit," Neil says after a long period of silence, "maybe I shouldn't have told you that."

"No, it's okay. I don't want anything to interfere with how well you're doing. If Dr. Horace thinks—"

"Oh, to hell with Dr. Horace," Neil breaks in. "I want to see you. What are you doing tonight?"

I tell Neil the truth, that I'm not doing anything tonight. I'm relieved that he's suggested night so I don't have to worry about him running into my father and I'm also relieved—and maybe a little alarmed—at how much, in his dismissal of his doctor's advice, he suddenly sounded like his old self.

WHEN I COME DOWN THE SPIRAL STAIRS FIVE SETS OF EYES LOOK up at me—the three men and both greyhounds.

"Who was that?" my father asks. From the way Robbie and Ernesto quickly look away I guess that the three of them have been talking about me. For a minute I think my dad knows it was Neil on the phone, but then I realize that he'd have no way of knowing that I'm back in touch with him. My jittery nerves have no doubt affected him and he's worried that it's bad news about Bea.

"It was Annemarie—" I remember midsentence that

Robbie picked up the phone and heard a man's voice, "—Annemarie's husband, Ray," I clumsily amend. I feel like I'm fifteen again, making up some story about going to the library when I'm really planning to meet Carl Ventimiglio down behind the boathouse. "He had some questions about financial aid. You know Portia got into Penrose."

"No kidding. That's great." He looks genuinely pleased and relieved. I wonder if it's just that he's worried about Bea or if he has something else on his mind.

"Yeah, Ray wanted to know if I'd help her with some of the forms. I thought I'd take a walk over to Gal's." At the word *walk* Paolo and Francesca's ears perk up. Poor things. Since Bea's been gone they've gotten most of their exercise in the courtyard. "I'll take the dogs," I say clicking my tongue for them to come, "and I'll bring back some coffees and pastries."

I run back upstairs to get the leashes with the dogs close at my heels. On my way down I overhear my father saying "that policeman" and Ernesto answering something about the party at the college. So that's what's gotten my father worked up—not worrying over Bea—someone told him I went to Gavin's engagement party with Daniel Falco and he's worried that . . . what? That I'm in trouble with the police? That I'm having an affair with the detective? It must be the latter. Most fathers would be happy that their unmarried thirty-seven-year-old daughter was dating a clean-cut, gainfully employed guy like Daniel Falco, but given my past history in choosing men I guess I can't blame my father for being leery of my judgment.

* * *

WHEN I GET OUTSIDE THE DOGS STRAIN ON THEIR LEADS TOWARD the riverside park and the boathouse—an area I've been avoiding since Kyle came over the night I found Christine's body or, as I've come to think of it, the night of the seaweed incident. I can't avoid him forever, I think, letting the dogs pull me toward the water. And besides, he's probably out on the water.

When we get to the park I unleash the dogs and let them run along the shoreline. Trailing behind them I think about the little lie I've just told my father and realize how hard it will be to tell him that I'm back in touch with Neil. No matter how I think of ways to introduce the subject—*Bea's been asking about her father* or *I hear they've got some great new antipsychotic drugs*—I keep picturing my father's face the night he came to the police station to collect Bea and me after "the accident." That's what he thought it was: an accident. When the police officer explained that Neil was being held on charges of assault I saw the look of fear on his face turn into pure horror.

It was my fault that Neil's mental instability came as such a surprise to him. I'd done everything I could to hide Neil's deteriorating mental state from him. It hadn't been hard. My father had been drinking heavily since my mother's death. By the time I'd gotten pregnant and married Neil he spent most of his day down at Flannery's bar. The joke in town was that Gil McKay broke more windows than he fixed. If he'd continued going the way he was going I have no doubt that he'd be dead by now, but the night he brought Bea and me back to his house he'd poured every ounce of alcohol down the drain.

"It's not your fault," I'd said, watching him pour a fifth of Jameson's into the sink. "I didn't want you to know how bad he was."

"My daughter and granddaughter are living with a homicidal maniac and I don't know a thing about it?" he said. "Your mother would have my head. Besides, if you two are going to stay here I've got to set a better example for little Bea."

And he had. He'd joined AA and hadn't taken a drink since that night. How in the world, I wonder now, was I going to tell him that Neil was better now. And what if we started seeing each other . . . ?

I stop abruptly and stare out at the river, dazzled by the late afternoon light on the water. *What in the world are you thinking?* I ask myself. I can't actually be thinking of *seeing* Neil or entering into a relationship with him. "You must be crazier than he is," I say aloud to the dogs, who, hearing my voice, come bounding over, wet and muddy, both of them holding the same stick.

"Than who is?" The voice startles me so much I turn around and take two steps backward into the shallow water. It's Kyle. The dogs, obviously remembering him, lay their stick down at his feet and prance around him.

"Shit, Kyle, you scared the hell out of me. I didn't hear you." I look down and notice he's barefoot. I also notice that I'm standing in two inches of water.

"Sorry, this is my place of work—such as it is." He

gestures to the boathouse, which looks as empty and forlorn as it did back in my high school days.

"Business slow?" I ask. "I'd have thought you'd be out on a day this nice."

"Yeah, funny how a drowning and a police investigation can dampen the public's ardor for kayaking." He smiles with his mouth but not his eyes and pushes his loose hair out of his face. It looks a little grayer than I remember it.

"But it wasn't like Christine was a client. She stole your kayak—"

"Yeah, well, word gets around that the police are asking you questions and then someone must have got a hold of the story about the boy in Colorado. Here, look at this." Kyle takes out a folded piece of paper from the pocket of his fleece vest. I unfold it and see that it's a newspaper article downloaded from the Internet about the white-water rafting accident in Steamboat Springs.

"I found this tacked to the boathouse door last week. The same article was forwarded to my whole mailing list. Two tour groups canceled this week."

"Oh, Kyle, I'm so sorry. I swear I didn't tell anyone."

"I didn't say I thought it was you, Juno. Someone must have done a Google search on my name and came up with this. Anyone could have done that, but hacking into my mailing list would require a little more expertise. As I remember, you're not exactly a computer whiz."

Kyle smiles again—this time it's a smile that does reach his eyes—and I find myself smiling back. Bea had told him a few months ago that I was going to hire someone to design a Web site for McKay Glass, and Kyle, because he'd worked for a computer company back in Colorado, had offered to do it himself for free.

What a nice man, I think to myself after we've said good-bye and I'm heading toward Gal's with my two damp greyhounds, *Who could be trying to do him harm?*

CHAPTER TWENTY-FOUR

AS IF TO SUBSTANTIATE MY LIE TO MY FATHER, I FIND PORTIA slumped over a stack of papers that I deduce from the pained expression on her face can only be financial aid forms. Annemarie is standing behind her polishing the cappuccino maker. She's rubbing so hard it's as if she believed the copper machine was a magic lantern that might produce enough money to send Portia to Penrose.

"You mean because we own our own house you're not eligible for certain kinds of aid?" she's asking as I come in.

"They assume we could borrow on the house—"

"Well, then, we'll borrow on the house."

"No, Mama, you worked so long to pay off the mortgage. We'll think of something else. Here's Aunt Juno; she'll have an idea."

Annemarie turns around and both women look at me with the same kind of beseeching gaze the dogs gave me when I tied them up on the porch outside.

"Let me take a look at those," I offer even though I seriously doubt I'll be able to find some hidden source of money in the labyrinth of financial language. Annemarie comes around the counter and bustles me over to a table while telling Portia to get me coffee and biscotti and whatever else I want. *Some panini? A little minestrone?*

I take an almond biscotti and an amaretto cappuccino and turn to the forms. A half an hour and two refills later I've managed to scare up a few extra hundred dollars and thought of a few scholarship suggestions—she's already gotten one from the Rotary Club and one from the Sons of Columbus—but it's clear that she's still thousands short of making even the first semester's tuition.

"I think we can clear about five thousand dollars if we take on more catering jobs this summer. We've gotten three calls already from people who were at Gavin Penrose's engagement party. Thanks for helping with the cake, by the way. When I got back here I discovered that the power was out so I had to move all the perishables to our refrigerator at home."

"No problem. Everyone loved the cake—" Instead of remembering Annemarie's lovely cake, though, I suddenly see the bleeding cake of my dreams. "Has Gavin Penrose paid up your bill yet?" I ask, trying to drive the image from my mind. "Portia told me he owed you for two jobs."

"Three including last night," Annemarie says. She nods at Portia—which Portia takes as a cue to go back to the counter—and then she looks back at me and, lowering her voice, asks, "Why? Have you heard of any problems with other people getting paid?"

I think of the phone call I overheard between Gavin and Dominic Minelli. Although I can hardly tell Annemarie that I've been eavesdropping on private conversations I feel I have to give her some warning. I take a look around to see who's in the cafe, but it's mostly old Italian-American men. The lunch crowd from the Heights hasn't turned up yet. Only two women customers in casual khakis and T-shirts, but expensive-looking loafers and handbags, are having salads on the other side of the room too far away to overhear.

"Look, I don't know anything for sure, but why don't you ask Ray's uncle, Dom, if he knows anything, okay? And maybe you should ask for cash up front for any other jobs for *him*." I look over toward the two women in khakis to let Annemarie know why I'm not pronouncing Gavin's name. "Are you doing their wedding?"

"Yes, in August. I could ask for a fifty percent deposit, but if I get him angry he might tell his friends that he wasn't happy with us . . ." Annemarie shrugs her elegant shoulders and rolls her eyes heavenward as if to indicate the disapproval that might emanate from the celestial beings on high. It's ridiculous, I think, as if we were medieval serfs living at the whim and pleasure of the landed gentry. I know it's not *that* bad, but it's true that many of the town's businesses—Gal's and Minelli and Sons and McKay Glass—are dependent on the money and goodwill of the people who live in the Heights, on people like Gavin Penrose.

"I'll see if I can find out anything else. Meanwhile, why don't you try dealing directly with Joan Shelley? I'm pretty sure *she's* loaded."

Annemarie gives my hand a squeeze and tells me to

wait a moment—she'll get me some food for lunch. Do I want anything else?

"Well, I am making dinner for a friend tonight. Could I buy one of your tiramisu cakes?"

"Buy? After all your help, *cara*? Don't insult me."

Annemarie disappears into the kitchen and I finish my coffee. A group of young women come in wearing the same khakis-loafers-Louis-Vuitton-handbag uniform as the first pair and take the table next to me. They talk about the relative merits of several nursery schools and the competition to get into the best ones. Portia comes over and they order salads *with dressing on the side* and mineral water with *extra lemon*, slowly pronouncing their special requests as if Portia were a deaf-mute. After they order the conversation turns to nannies. One woman mentions that she's had to fire hers because she wanted a month off to go home to Jamaica to visit her children.

"I've been a corporate lawyer for twelve years and I only get two weeks off," she says.

By the time Annemarie comes back with two shopping bags full of food I'm wondering if it's really so important that Bea finish out high school in Rosedale. I've stuck it out here for all these years, first because of my dad, and then because of the good schools and, I suppose, a sense of nostalgia, but I'm beginning to wonder if it's really such a healthy environment.

IN ADDITION TO SANDWICHES, COFFEES, AND PASTRIES *FOR THE guys*, Annemarie has given me enough food to serve an elegant dinner for a party of twelve. Salad, thinly sliced prosciutto, a whole melon, fresh mozzarella, a huge chunk of imported parmesan, hand-rolled spaghetti, a loaf of sour dough, and a tiramisu cake. I unpack it all into the refrigerator and spend the rest of the afternoon cleaning the loft. Before my father can get too nosy our daily thundershower rolls in with such fury that it knocks the power out.

"Are you sure you'll be all right here all alone in the dark?" my father asks before leaving.

"I've got plenty of candles," I tell him.

When they've finally gone I light the candles. I've got dozens from the crafts shows I used to sell at—hand-dipped tapers and scented votives, enormous squat pillars and ones shaped like flowers that float in water. When I finish lighting them all the loft with its high-pitched roof looks like a cathedral—the panes in the skylight misted over by the rain, the pattern of interlaced vines and leaves in the glass a dark tracery of shadows.

I slice the honeydew into thin crescents that I fan out on a willowware platter and then drape with a sheer layer of pink prosciutto. I go out onto the roof and pick some tomatoes and basil and make another platter with the fresh mozzarella. Then I pour a glass of wine and, taking one of the votive candles with me, go into the bathroom and fill up the tub.

It's not until I step in that I remember that the hot water heater is electric. The water isn't exactly frigid— there must have been some hot water left in the tank—but it's cool enough to shock me. Still, I'm sweaty from all that cleaning so I force myself in and once I'm in it feels kind of good. I dip my head back until the water touches my forehead and my hair fans out behind me—I can make out a dim reflection of myself in the misty skylight above me—and it reminds me of Millais's painting of drowned Ophelia. All I need are flowers. Then I remember Christine's experiment to see how long she could stay in a tub filled with cold water and instantly I feel the chill of the water seeping into my bones—an insistent pressure pushing all the warmth out of my veins. I pull myself out of the tub and grab the towel hanging next to the bathroom mirror, where I meet my own gaze. The face that looks back at me in the candlelit half light is drained of blood, lips blue, eyes cavernous—the face of someone drowning. "What in the world are you thinking?" I ask myself for the second time today. "What do you think you're doing?"

AFTER THAT I PUT ON JEANS AND A T-SHIRT—NOT THE GAUZY little summer dress I'd laid out on my bed—and blow out about half the candles. I pour my glass of wine down the drain. My cold bath has done nothing for my tangled mess of hair, but at least it's cleared my head.

I'm making dinner for my ex-husband, I say to myself as I chop onions and lay bacon strips in the cast-iron skillet—my daughter's father. Lots of divorced women I know have amicable relationships with their exes. It'll be good for Bea to see that we get along—but that's it. It would not be good for Bea for me to become romantically involved with an ex-mental patient—the man who tried to drown us both fourteen years ago.

The buzzer from the front door sounds when the last of the bacon is fried. I turn off the burner, wipe my hands on the back of my jeans, and head down to the front door, taking with me the faint smell of onions and bacon through the factory, past the doors to the furnaces where Penrose's iridescent glass used to be blown, past the rooms where the stained-glass windows were assembled and the loading docks where the crated windows once waited to be taken down to the city by train. Sometimes when I imagine the factory in full swing it's hard to understand why it couldn't be like that again.

When I open the door no one's there. I'd forgotten to mention that it takes about five minutes for me to get down from the loft to the front entrance, but surely Neil wouldn't just leave. I step out into the wet street—the rain's stopped, but water is still running in the gutters, and the air is saturated with moisture—and look right and left. There's an old VW Bug with a sticker for Greenpeace on it that I suspect is Neil's, but it's empty. I'm going back in when I hear a voice from above.

"Vito's is brief," the voice says in a deep, rumbly bass, "but Art's is longer."

He's sitting on the ledge beneath the inscription, about fifteen feet above the sidewalk, dangling his legs over the side. I can see the soles of his red canvas high-tops.

"So who would you rather date?"

"Very funny. You never were very good at Latin."

"No, I'm far better at the Romance languages." He

turns around and starts climbing down, his fingers finding handholds between the old, cracked bricks until he's five or six feet off the ground. Then he pushes off the wall and lands, knees slightly bent, light as a cat by my side. He's got all his grace back. The last time I saw him at Briarwood—thirteen years ago—he was so dosed up on lithium he could barely walk down the hall without falling on his face.

"Hey," he says, shaking brick dust off his hands, "I like your place so far."

"Well, do you want to go in the traditional route," I ask, indicating the door, "or are you planning to scale the battlements?"

"Not if the lady of the keep is willing to let down the drawbridge." He sweeps down into a deep bow with a flourish of his hand and I try to keep from laughing.

"It's hardly a castle, but wipe your feet," I say walking in ahead of him. "These floor are hell to clean."

I can hear him stop behind me at just the same spot where Christine paused when I brought her here—in the middle of the room in front of the wall of windows facing west. The sky is still overcast out on the street, but to the west a thin band of sunlight has appeared above the hills, enough to light up the heavy blue-gray clouds as if from inside. Furrowed with bands of copper, they look like another set of ridges above the Hudson Highlands. When I turn to Neil I see that his face is bathed in that eerie after-rain glow.

"It's as if the room were a vessel to hold the light," he says. "It should be a museum."

"Penrose wanted only natural light in his studios and workshops. Come on, I'll show you the rest."

When I open the door to the annex the dogs are waiting there. They take one look at Neil and lift up their long, thin noses and howl.

"They're a little skittish," I explain, although truthfully I've never heard them howl before. "They were trained to race and kept in these awful cramped crates. They're still not used to being loose."

"Yeah, I know how they feel." Neil puts out his hand, palm up and the dogs stretch their long necks toward him without taking a step forward. He scratches Francesca behind the ear and she leans her whole head into his hand, rolling her eyes back. Paolo still eyes him suspiciously.

"Something smells great," Neil says.

"I'm making spaghetti carbonara. I hope you haven't become a vegetarian."

"Nope, still a meat eater . . . is this your studio?"

"This is McKay Glass. I'd show you the Lady window but the power is out so I can't turn on the light table." Neil doesn't seem interested in the window, though; he's squinting at the spiral staircase and looking up at the skylights in the loft above as if trying to remember something. "Hey, didn't we break in here once?"

"I was wondering if you'd remember." Neil and I—and sometimes Christine—had broken into several old abandoned mansions along the Hudson and a couple of old warehouses and factories. It was a sort of hobby of Neil's. We'd seen far more spectacular places—ruined ballrooms with grass growing up in between the marble

floors and indoor pools turned into underground lakes—
than this little factory and so I'd thought he might have
forgotten it. "We didn't get far and this area looked
different. It was originally Penrose's private office and
studio, but then it was used for storage after his death—"

"And there was broken glass all over the place." Neil
reaches out, takes my hand, and turns it over. I hope he
doesn't feel the tremor that runs through me when he
traces the little crescent-shaped scar at the base of my
right thumb. "You cut yourself on some broken glass that
was on the floor. . . ."

His voice trails off and I know he's remembering how I
cut my hand. We'd been making love and I had reached
out across the floor—for what? to grab onto something? I
can't remember, only that I'd felt something slice into my
hand and screamed, but Neil hadn't realized I was hurt
until later.

"Come upstairs," I say, wishing my voice didn't sound
so gravelly. "I'll show you something."

On the window ledges the shards of glass are glowing
in the last sunlight, copper and violet, citrine green and
gold-flecked rose—like peacock feathers or dragonfly
wings.

"They're from Penrose's opalescent vases done during
his art nouveau stage when he was copying Tiffany's
Favrile glass. I found shattered pieces all over the floor in
here, as if someone had smashed a hundred vases. We're
lucky we didn't get torn to shreds."

Neil's looking around the loft. Of all the guests I've had
here recently—Christine, Kyle, Detective Falco—none of

them saw it the way Neil can, with the image of the present loft superimposed on how it looked that night when we climbed up to the roof from the railroad tracks and came in through a broken skylight that had been overgrown with vines. The moonlight cast the shadows of the vines onto the floor, turning the loft into a shadow jungle, and lit up the crushed iridescent glass like sand from a tropical beach. Neil looks up at the stained-glass panels in the skylight—at the pattern of leaf and vine I've set into them—and then down at the tiles on the floor, which I glazed in a swirl of iridescent colors that I copied from the glass shards I found here.

"You've made it the way it looked that night," he says.

"Remember what you said? That you wanted us to live in a ruin—"

"And you said only if there was adequate plumbing and heating. You've done it, Juno, you've made a livable ruin." He smiles the way I remember—an upward lift of the left corner of his mouth that seems to tug at some corresponding muscle deep inside me.

I turn away and pull out the plates of food and put them on the counter for him to snack on while I cook, then turn on the burner underneath the iron skillet (which still has a little bacon fat in it) and under the pot of water. Neil nibbles at the the prosciutto and melon while wandering around the loft, stopping to look at pictures of Bea and asking me how old she is in each one and the occasion of the photo. Fifth grade graduation, third grade play, her bunkmates at the Adirondack camp she went to for five years—a compendium of life events he's missed. It must get depressing for him because he stops asking until he gets to a shot of Bea and Christine taken last year in front of the Christmas tree at Rockefeller Center.

"Christine said she was grateful for the time she got to spend with Bea," he says, "that it made up a little for not having her own child."

"Really?" I look up from the bowl of eggs I'm beating. "I never realized until the last time we talked that she missed not having a kid. She was always so independent."

Neil comes over to the counter and picks up the knife from the chopping board and starts mincing the onions that I've already cut into finer pieces. When we used to cook together he always did the chopping because he thought I wasn't thorough enough. I'd have to stop him sometimes from pulverizing the vegetables.

"I think she had always been afraid of having a kid because of the bouts she'd had with depression. She thought it would make her a bad mother. I think she was afraid, too, that there was something wrong with her that she'd pass on."

I think of how horrible it must have been for her to find out that her baby had Tay-Sachs. "She was pregnant when she died," I say, turning to Neil to take the onions from him so that he can't help but meet my gaze. His eyes widen, but whether from surprise or the onion fumes I'm not sure. I slide the onions into the skillet. The crackle they make in the hot grease is the only sound for a few minutes.

"I thought maybe there was something like that going

on," Neil finally says, "from the questions she asked me." He picks up a chunk of parmesan and grates it into the eggs while I sauté the onions. *How easily we've fallen into the old patterns*, I think, watching the white flesh of the onions turn translucent in the skillet. This was a dish we often cooked together. Neil loved that it was a recipe that I'd gotten from my mother and the story that it was a dish that coal carriers ate in Rome.

"I thought you said she mostly asked you questions about Clare Barovier?"

"Should I put the pasta in?" he asks because the water's come to a boil. I tell him yes and he adds a pinch of salt without asking whether I've salted the water yet because I'd told him once that it was an old Italian superstition that it was bad luck to salt the water before it boiled. "It was the kind of questions she asked about Clare," he continues, stirring the spaghetti noodles into the boiling water. "Had she recovered her sanity in her last years? Could she have done all those paintings if she were still crazy? And then she started asking about my recovery. How long had I been taking the Pieridine? Were there any side effects? How widely had it been tested? What would I do if the drug stopped working? Mostly she seemed interested in figuring out if a person could truly recover from mental illness. I thought she might be asking for herself. It was her biggest fear I think—that she was unbalanced and she might someday go insane."

"And what were your answers?"

"To which questions? The ones about Clare or the ones about me?"

The pot of boiling water I'm carrying to the sink is heavy, but still I pause for a moment. I'm not sure myself what I want to know anymore. My interest has shifted suddenly from Christine to Neil.

"The questions about your recovery. I want to know how you're doing." I pour the water and pasta into a colander and step back as a wave of steam rises from the sink.

"I told her the truth—that the Pieridine has been a miracle for me, but that there were no guarantees. It hasn't cleared Phase II testing yet and it's only been field tested at less than a dozen facilities. Since it's a new drug there aren't any long-range studies on its effectiveness over time. I told her I was trying to make the most of the clarity it's given me while I can."

I pour the drained pasta back in the large pot and put it back on the stove on a low light. Neil pours the sautéed onions into it and then holds the bowl of eggs and cheese over the pot. This is the tricky part of making carbonara. Getting the eggs to cook just enough so that the sauce clings to the pasta without clumping or curdling. I nod for him to start pouring. I stir.

"What about her last question?" I ask, keeping my eyes on the yellow sauce as it thickens around the thin, nearly transparent noodles.

"You mean what would I do if it stopped working?"

I nod. I hear Neil sigh, but I don't look up.

"I told her I couldn't go back. That I'd rather die than go back to how I was before."

CHAPTER TWENTY-FIVE

WE EAT OUT ON THE ROOFTOP, THE FOOD LAID OUT ON A TABLE made from an old Rose Glass packing crate, a dozen candles lining the railing. Francesca lies under Neil's chair with her head resting on his foot, but Paolo roams back and forth restlessly, disdainful of the bacon treats Neil offers him.

"You know we've got a Gatsby-Daisy thing going on," he says, gesturing with his wineglass toward the dark hills across the river. (Another miracle of Pieridine, I've learned, is its compatibility with moderate alcohol consumption.) "The place where I'm living is almost directly across the river from here only it's just below that hill. If I climbed straight up from my back door I could put out a green light and signal to you."

"I thought all that land belonged to Astolat," I say, deliberately choosing not to enlarge on his reference to Fitzgerald's star-crossed lovers. What amuses me, actually, is that he's made himself Daisy in the analogy.

"The Beeches is the old gatehouse. Penrose donated it

to Briarwood before he died to be used an an outpatient facility—a sort of halfway house for us recovering loonies. We're not allowed to wander around the estate—"

"I bet that hasn't stopped you."

"Actually, Astolat is sealed off behind another wall beyond the gatehouse. A fifteen-foot stone wall with iron spikes and broken glass on top. The only person who goes onto the estate is Gavin Penrose. Some of the older residents of The Beeches say he roams the grounds at night looking for buried treasure."

"Buried treasure?" I ask skeptically.

"Yeah, well, these are mental patients telling these stories. The caretaker told me that Penrose did in fact shoot at something he thought was a trespasser once, only it turned out to be a raccoon. Makes you wonder who's crazy."

I smile at the image of Gavin nervously prowling his grandfather's estate. "Why do you think he's so anxious to keep people off the grounds?"

"The caretaker says it's to avoid lawsuits—you know, someone stumbles into an old basement, breaks a leg, and sues—but it does seem a little paranoid. Christine said she thought Penrose was a little crazy himself near the end of his life. The disposition of the estate was bizarre. Besides leaving The Beeches to Briarwood he stipulated that the rest of Astolat couldn't be sold or open to the public until fifty years after his death. Christine had tried to get permission to tour the grounds, but she said Gavin Penrose refused."

"I guess that's why she was so intrigued when she

heard Bea say you could get onto the grounds from the water. I wonder what she wanted to see so badly that she'd risk crossing the river in a kayak in the middle of the night."

Neil shrugs and gets up, dislodging Francesca's head from his foot. She follows him to the railing, where he moves a few candles aside so he can sit on the top rail. It makes me nervous to see him balanced above the sheer drop to the train tracks, but I resist saying anything. It's the type of warning that always used to make him angry and would push him toward doing something even more reckless.

"She probably just wanted to see the ruins of Astolat. I would, too. You say you can paddle right up the Wicomico?"

"Uh-huh. We didn't get very far the day we found Christine, but Bea says there's a spot farther upstream where you can beach and get out to walk around."

There's an awkward pause during which I wonder if I should suggest we do just that. Somehow we've managed to get through most of the evening without reference to the future. To our future. I guess a kayaking trip would be a neutral enough outing for us to take, but the thought of it opens up so many potentially uncomfortable situations—renting the kayaks from Kyle, my dad hearing about it, not to mention actually being out on the water with Neil again and revisiting the scene of Christine's death. So instead of suggesting we make the trip I ask if he wants another slice of tiramisu.

Immediately, something in his face that had been open

closes. It's the way he used to look at the end of my visits to Briarwood when he realized that I hadn't come to take him home.

"No thanks," he says, sliding off the railing, "actually I'd better get going. We sort of have curfew—a voluntary curfew, they call it, whatever that means."

I walk him down the side stairs and around to the front of the factory. Francesca comes with us, but Paolo stays on the stairs howling. It's the first time I've seen the dogs more than six feet apart from each other.

"I'd better go back up," I say, "before he wakes up the whole neighborhood."

Neil looks up and down the deserted street, at the abandoned storefronts and disreputable-looking boardinghouses, the only sign of life the neon shamrock over Flannery's bar across from the train station. It doesn't look like a neighborhood that is easily disturbed.

"Thanks for dinner, Juno. I thought I'd never taste anything as good as your carbonara again."

It's such a simple compliment that I immediately regret not asking to see him again—for missing that moment. "Maybe we could do it again sometime . . ." I say weakly, ashamed at how my voice trails off.

"Look," he says, "I understand that you can't just open up your life and let me in after all these years. And you shouldn't have to deal with people talking about us . . . but there is something I wanted to do with you . . . a favor I wanted to ask you and it wouldn't involve being here, so we could get used to each other before dealing with other people's opinions . . ."

He takes a step forward and touches my face. His wording has reminded me of the Latin poem I translated for Portia, the one where Catullus tells his girlfriend that they shouldn't care about the opinions of others and then asks her for a thousand kisses, so many that no evil person would ever be able to count their number.

"We could do it at The Beeches," he says. "There's plenty of room and light . . ."

"Do what?" I manage to ask, my voice so trembly that Francesca, who's wedged herself in between us, looks up at me and whimpers.

"Pose for me," he says. "I want to paint you one more time, only this time not as some character from a story, but as yourself."

I drop my hand onto Francesca's head and rub one of her silky ears in between my fingers. "Okay," I tell him, "I can do that."

THE NEXT DAY, THOUGH, WHEN I COME DOWNSTAIRS INTO THE studio, I don't have the slightest idea how I'm going to explain to my father and my crew why I need to be gone two or three mornings a week. But then my father presents me with a perfect solution, albeit a solution caused by the misfortune of others.

"I got a call early this morning from Brother Michael up at St. Eustace's. They had a fire last night."

"Oh no, was anyone hurt?" McKay Glass had restored the windows at the Chapel of St. Eustace's, a girls' school on the northeast shore of Lake Champlain, two years ago.

I could still picture the twelve lancets depicting St. Eustace hunting a stag, and a rose window modeled on the one at Chartres. Brother Michael and I had had many long conversations about medieval stained glass and about handling troubled teenaged girls—St. Eustace's was a reform school for girls so incorrigible that the school's nickname was St. Useless.

"No, it was only in the chapel and in the middle of the night. They got it out before there was too much damage to the walls and roof, but the windows started cracking an hour later. He's afraid they're going to fall to pieces. I told him the fact that they'd been recently restored would help—"

"But they should be stabilized right away."

"I told him he should shore them up with plywood on both sides and that I'd get back to him. I warned him, though, that we were in the middle of a job and I wasn't sure how soon we could get up there, but that even if we couldn't do it we'd call with a referral by noon today." My father pauses for breath and then adds, "He thanked me and said he hoped we could do the repair since we already had a feel for the windows."

He pushes his hair back, takes a sip of coffee, and waits for what I'm going to say. Looking at him—at his neatly pressed khakis and blue work shirt and his trim gray hair—I'm impressed with how well he's handled the situation. Years ago, when he was still drinking, he would have either agreed to take the job before looking at the rest of his workload or said no because he was too hungover to make the drive.

"Well, let's figure out how much longer we've got on the Lady and whether we can fit in a trip to St. Eustace's," I say. "It would be a great experience for Robbie."

We spend the next hour looking at all stages of the restoration of the Lady window and estimating the work left to be done. The window is reassembled except for some of the plating behind the glass in the lily pool and in the upper branches of the weeping beech, all of which should take only another week or so. Then we map out a plan for handling the fire-damaged windows at St. Eustace's. It seems like we've got plenty of time to handle that job and still have most of August to finish and reinstall the Lady window.

"I think I should stay here, though," I say, "to take care of the dogs and answer any questions Gavin might have about the progress we've made on the Lady window. Maybe I can work up the nerve to show him the dichroic pattern and how we've altered the assemblage of the window."

"Are you sure, honey?" my dad asks. "Won't you be lonely without us?"

"I'll survive," I say, putting my arm around my dad's shoulder. "I've got Paolo and Francesca."

AND SO I START SITTING FOR NEIL A COUPLE OF HOURS EACH morning. "I might as well take advantage of the break," I tell him the first day I come to The Beeches. "Once the guys come back we'll be busy reinstalling the window."

"And once I get started I know I won't want to stop," he

says, setting out his paints, "and I only want the early morning light for this painting."

Before climbing the hill behind The Beeches—so named for the copse of ancient copper beeches that stand behind the old gatehouse—Neil gave me a tour of the house, which has none of the dreariness one might associate with the term "halfway house." Its rooms are spacious and airy, each resident has his or her own sitting room fitted out with handsome mission-styled furniture and thick, Persian rugs, and the meals are served in a glassed-in sunroom facing the magnificent violet-leaved trees. There is, though, something *marginal* about the house in the way it straddles the entrance to the estate and how its stone walls merge into the estate walls—all hewn out of the same blue-gray fieldstone. "It's not a real gateway, though," Neil explains as he sets up his easel on the crest of the hill just above the second stone wall. "The outside walls enclose the inner wall around Astolat."

"Like a moat," I say.

"A moat of trees," Neil says. "These beeches are my favorite, especially in the early morning when the sun comes through them from the east. Look at the colors— in the center of the tree and at the crown the leaves are mostly green with just a faint purple mottling, but on the outer branches at the bottom the new leaves are deep violet and when the sun shines through them there's this halo of crimson—" He's squeezing purple and red paint onto his palette. "—that reminds me of your hair."

"My hair? I know it's pretty unmanageable, but I

thought I'd gotten it a little neater than these shaggy old trees." It's always been a bit of a sore point to me, my wild kinky mass of hair that resists combs and conditioners and seems to weave itself into tangles and knots while I sleep as if it had a will of its own.

"The color," he says, "the way it turns red when you stand with the sun at your back, but then it's this dark eggplanty purple in the dark. That's why I want to paint you here, with the beeches behind you, and the sun coming through the leaves just touching you around the edges . . . like that," he says, looking up and then, moving forward, touching me lightly on the chin to tilt my face a little to the left and on my shoulder to angle my body slightly to the right. He's already gotten that abstracted look he gets when he starts to paint, his eyes moving rapidly over the surface of things, charting the play of light over their contours the way a sailor studies the surface of water to gauge depth and wind direction. I'd noticed, long ago, that his eyes would change colors rapidly while he was painting, as if the pigments on his brush seeped down the thin stalk of his paintbrush, though his veins, and into his irises. Today they're dark blue, almost violet, like the copper beech leaves in the shadows.

"Like that?" I ask when he's given me the last adjustment and stepped back.

"Like that," he says stepping behind his easel. "Now don't move a muscle."

When I first sat for Neil the commandment to stay still had driven me crazy. Instantly, every nerve in my body had rebelled, every pore itched, the blood had ceased to flow to my extremities, and currents of electricity had flared up in my hands and feet. Eventually, though, I had learned to let the stillness settle over me and how to sit so as not to cut off circulation to my limbs. I'd come to enjoy being the object of attention while, at the same time, nothing was demanded of me.

Now I find these hours we spend together in the mornings while he paints and I sit in the cool, dusky shadows of the beech trees oddly soothing. We don't talk. I'm not supposed to move my mouth; he's too engrossed in what he's doing. He looks at me, I look at him and sometimes, after many hours, our eyes meet as if we'd just come upon each other on the street and we both smile. That's when we take a break.

I join him on his side of the easel and he pours me some coffee from a thermos and takes out sandwiches and fruit while I look at what he's painted so far. Another change. He used to never let me see a painting before it was finished.

"It doesn't bother me now," he says after the first couple of days. "I'd like to know what you think."

"It's beautiful," I say truthfully. "It looks like I'm part of the forest, like my face is rising up out of the trees and I'm a part of everything around me because it's all connected by the light."

"That's exactly what I wanted," he says, biting into an apple. "That's just how I pictured it."

We stop when the light reaches the top branches of the trees—a little before noon each day. Sometimes we take a walk then, through the woods and around the inner perimeter wall. He hasn't brought up the idea of kayaking into Astolat again and neither have I, but I have to admit that taking these walks has made me curious about what's on the other side of the wall.

"Did you walk here with Christine?" I ask during the second week of sittings.

"Yeah, she wanted to see if there was any way into Astolat. I think she was disappointed that I hadn't found a way to get over the wall, but I told her I drew the line at crossing iron spikes and broken glass."

I don't tell him that I'm also surprised at his caution— he'd scaled far more imposing and treacherous barriers back in college—nor do I ask him if he would draw the line at crossing the river with her in a kayak in the middle of the night. I don't ask because although I can believe he would have made the trip across the river with her I can't believe he would have left her there to drown. Even when he purposely capsized our boat all those years ago—when he was out of his mind—he hadn't, in the end, left. He'd held one of my hands to the side of the capsized boat while I'd kept Bea's head above water with the other hand. It was only after the Coast Guard fished us out that he'd disappeared beneath the surface of the river.

In the evenings I stand out on my roof and look across the river to the crest of the hill where the sun, just as it sets, lights the tops of the beeches into flares of bright copper. Not Daisy's green light, perhaps, but a beacon of sorts, a signal in the night sky.

In bed I read Eugenie's journal, finding in her accounts of posing for Augustus an unsettling parallel to my days with Neil.

> It is a curious experience, posing for a painting. To be looked at but not have one's gaze met, as if one were invisible or one's spirit had left one's body.
>
> One one one
>
> I say one, but the sensation is of being two.
>
> After I have sat for many hours (Augustus is anxious to have the series done for Sir R—and collect his fee so that he can finance a certain event—and so he has asked me to sit for as long as I can manage it) and after I have passed through a not altogether unpleasant tingling sensation in my limbs and into a numbness (a bit like getting used to cold water) there comes a moment when I can feel my spirit lifting away from my flesh—departing my body right out the top of my head, where it hovers, attached only by a gossamer thread finer than my embroidery silk—looking down at its cast-off shell. I can see not only myself but Augustus and Clare.
>
> Poor Clare. Since she is only a part of the background in the second painting of the Dryope series Augustus has told her she needn't bother to pose, so instead she endeavors to capture Augustus's attention by drawing and he, kind as he is, heaps praise on her pretty little landscapes and encourages her to continue drawing the same scene over and over until she gets it exactly right. Of course he has no idea how literally she takes his assignment. How hour after hour she sketches the same

*weeping beech, the same lily pond, and the same hills in
the distance. Augustus tells her what she's got right and
what she's got wrong until their voices begin to sound
like insects and I feel myself drifting farther away. I feel
a great longing to just go—just leave my body behind—
but I know that if I did the slender thread that connects
spirit to flesh might snap . . .*

I let the page slip onto the floor with the others that
have fallen there and look for the continuation of that
particular entry but there isn't any—the next entry is
dated several weeks later and Eugenie has resumed her
usual crisp, practical tone. Already she's making an
inventory of dresses and underclothes and shawls—
winter and summer—as if preparing for a long voyage. Has
Augustus proposed? Have they made their plan to go to
America? Have they told Clare? And what about those
landscape drawings of Clare's? Is she still trying to please
her soon-to-be brother-in-law with those drawings of the
same scene—the same scene she would one day be
painting again and again in a sequestered room on the
other side of the ocean, the tower room of the mental
institution where she'd live out the rest of her life? No
wonder Augustus's last portrait of her was in the role of
the Lady of Shalott: a woman doomed to see the world
through the distorted lens of a mirror and fruitlessly copy
what she saw there until the mirror cracked. How fitting
that he chose to paint her on glass, sitting in front of the
very landscape that so haunted her.

As I fall asleep that night I can almost feel, as Eugenie

described, my spirit slipping free of my body, shrugging off the burden of flesh like one of Eugenie's winter shawls, the thread connecting spirit to body stretched thin as the coil of copper wire Augustus used to weld together his portrait of glass.

CHAPTER TWENTY-SIX

"Eugenie Penrose seemed to have had out-of-body experiences while posing for Augustus," I tell Neil the next day when we take a break in the beech clearing. We're sitting on a large, flat rock with our picnic lunch spread out between us. Neil looks up from the apple he's peeling and laughs.

"No kidding? Stodgy old Eugenie? I always thought she sounded like an old prude—all that reforming zeal, organizing the factory girls into improvement circles . . ."

"She did a lot of good work for women," I counter, even though I know what Neil means. Penrose College was still hobbled when I went there with Eugenie's antiquated notions of what constituted a hygienic, well-balanced regimen for young ladies: mandatory Latin and Home Economics, early curfews, no off-campus housing, no visitors of the opposite sex in the dorms beyond the lounges. For a woman whose mission was establishing meaningful work for women, she seemed to have very little faith in her sex's ability to make choices for themselves.

"Maybe it was seeing her younger sister Clare fall apart over love for a man that made her so strict," I suggest, taking a slice of the apple Neil has neatly pared.

"What makes you think Clare fell apart over a man?" he asks, starting to peel another apple.

"Eugenie's journal. It's obvious that Clare was falling in love with Augustus Penrose at the same time that Eugenie and he were getting engaged."

"And you think that unrequited love made her go crazy?"

"Well, she seemed kind of high-strung before that—"

"According to whom? Her big sister, Eugenie?" Neil gouges a chunk out of the apple, which falls to the ground. I remember suddenly that when Neil was committed to Briarwood his sister Sarah had told the intake committee that her little brother had always been volatile and hypersensitive to criticism. It had seemed unfair at the time because Sarah had always been hypercritical herself. When he'd married me she'd referred to me as his little upstate shiksa.

"True," I say, trying to smooth over the argument, "I imagine Clare would tell another version of the story."

Neil puts down the apple and the knife and stands up, wiping his hands on his jeans. "Christine thought that Eugenie had her committed because she was sleeping with Augustus."

"Oh. Did she tell you why she thought that?"

"I didn't spend enough time with her to hear all her theories, Juno, although I know you think I did. Why don't you just ask me what's really on your mind?"

He looks down at me for a moment, but when I don't immediately answer he looks off through the beech grove toward the river. The sun has already reached the tops of the trees while we've been talking and the trees' long purple shadows stretch across the clearing. The light's already too far gone for him to paint any more today. When he turns toward me I notice, looking up at him, shadows beneath his eyes that match the deep purple shadows of the trees.

"Ask what?" I finally say. "I don't know what you mean."

"How many times I saw Christine. Whether I slept with her. Was it my baby?"

"You told me before you saw her in May, five weeks before she died. She was almost three months pregnant by then."

"I see you've done the math. Unfortunately your friend Detective Falco isn't so good with numbers—or else he doesn't believe that I only saw Christine that once. He came yesterday to ask for some blood."

Neil lifts his right arm and turns it over to show me the bruised skin in the crook of his elbow just above where his shirtsleeve has been rolled. "Damned police medical technicians aren't very good at taking blood. Took them three tries to find a vein."

"I'm sorry, Neil, but I don't know what you think it has to do with me—Detective Falco isn't exactly my friend."

"That's funny—Reg said he was your date at Penrose's engagement party." He smiles while rolling down his sleeve and buttoning his cuff. It occurs to me that he's always in long-sleeved shirts even though the days have been hot. Before I can stop myself my eyes travel to his other arm, where his sleeve is still rolled above the elbow. The bruising there is worse, the puncture marks visible as a thin line of raised red dots. Of course, I realize, he's in a drug trial. They must have to monitor his blood regularly.

I look up from his arm and when our eyes meet I feel my own blood heating my face, not, as he must think, because of his reference to the detective but because I realize how strongly I want to reach out and stroke his bruised flesh. And so, before I can explain why I went to that party with Daniel Falco, he's turning around and walking down the hill, his long stride taking him deep into the violet-shadowed woods.

WHEN I GET HOME I CALL FALCO. WHILE IT RINGS I REALIZE I'M close to hyperventilating I'm so angry, so I take the cordless phone out on the roof, hoping the fresh air will calm me down. When he answers, though, I'm hardly calm.

"When you went over to The Beeches to take Neil's blood, just exactly what did you say to him?" I ask.

"Juno McKay, how nice of you to call. I was just thinking of you."

"Did you tell him he was a suspect? Did you interrogate him while your butchers were stabbing him with their hypodermic needles? Do you realize that he's in a delicate stage of recovery—"

"Whoa, missy, I'm perfectly aware of Mr. Buchwald's psychological and medical profile. His psychiatrist, Dr.

Horace, was present and advised his patient to cooperate fully with our investigation. If his DNA doesn't match that of Christine Webb's unborn child, that information will speak in his favor."

"He says he only saw her that one time five weeks before she died so he can't be the father."

"Juno, you can't expect me to just take his word on that and not pursue the possibility that he could be the father of Christine's child when so many other factors make him a prime suspect in this case."

"What other factors?"

"Well, for one thing he lives within a mile of where Christine died."

I stop pacing and face the opposite shore across the river. Although I can't see the mouth of the Wicomico, I know it's there, somewhere in the fold of green hills just below where I can make out the deep violet treetops of the copper beeches. "The house where he lives is separated from the estate by a fifteen-foot stone wall topped with metal spikes and broken glass—"

"According to Dr. Horace, Neil was quite the avid rock climber back in college. He could easily have gotten over that wall."

"But you said the other kayak was found on the east side of the river, which means that whoever was with Christine left by water. So the fact that Neil happens to live nearby is irrelevant."

"I can't ignore it any more than I can ignore Neil's prior history. After all, he attempted to drown you and your baby."

"That was years ago. He was very sick, but he's better now."

"I hope that's true, Juno, for your sake. I really do."

His voice sounds so full of genuine compassion that for a moment my anger is deflected, replaced by a suspicion I've been trying to ignore these last few weeks, that the need to believe Neil is better is because I've fallen in love with him all over again. I take a deep breath and try to steady my voice.

"What does Dr. Horace say? Doesn't he think Neil is better?"

"Dr. Horace believes that Neil has been cured by the miracle of modern psychopharmacology, that this new wonder drug is the hottest thing since penicillin, but even he has to admit that the drug is too new to rule out the possibility of unforeseen side effects. Prozac, for instance, has been known to cause incidents of violent rage in some patients—"

I picture Neil striding off into the beech forest today, his back rigid with anger. Above those trees, now, storm clouds are gathering that are the same livid purple as the beeches, as if the trees had breathed some poisonous miasma into the atmosphere.

"—and no drug is effective if the patient doesn't take it," Falco continues, "and Neil has a history of going off his medication."

"But the staff at The Beeches is monitoring his dosage, right?" Although I don't know this for sure, it's what I guessed from the track marks I saw on Neil's arm today.

"Yes," Falco admits, "they have to. He's part of an FDA

trial so his dosage has to be carefully monitored and recorded."

I feel a small thrill of vindication that I've won at least this point. Falco seems willing to concede me this momentary victory. "You may be completely right about Neil," he says. "There's nothing in Christine's personal effects to indicate that she was seeing him. Some of the stuff I found in her home office indicates that she was more interested in our friend Gavin Penrose—"

"I knew it! Something's not right with his financial situation—"

"There may be more to it than just a few unpaid bills, but I can't make out exactly why Christine was so interested in him. The notes in her calendar and diary are somewhat cryptic. Perhaps you could help me interpret them."

"Of course, I'd be more than happy to help." I walk inside to look at my own calendar and because it has started to rain. "Do you want me to come to the station—"

"Well, actually I was planning to go down to her apartment again to have another look at her desk—"

"You mean her things haven't been cleared out yet?" I ask, guiltily remembering that I'd told Amy, at the beginning of July, that I'd help when she went down to the city and now there are only three days left to the month.

"The desk is covered with Post-it notes, file cards, books with little slips of paper in them, art postcards . . . like a diorama of her last few months of research. I want to have one more look at the whole thing and I'd like you there with me to see if any of it means something to you. Do you think you could come into the city with me?"

"Sure," I say, staring at my blank calendar. Who knows if Neil will even want me to keep posing for him after today. "When?"

"How about tomorrow? The last month's rent is up on Thursday and I told Christine's aunt she could get in on Wednesday so if you wanted you could stay over and help her . . . but if you're too busy sitting for your portrait—"

"I'll go," I say quickly.

"Great. I'd like an early start—can I pick you up at nine thirty?"

"Sure," I say, and then before he can get off I ask, feeling like a teenager pumping her best friend for details about a boy she likes, "Hey, did Neil tell you I was sitting for him?"

"He didn't have to," he says. "I saw the painting. I'm no art expert, but if you ask me, I don't think it does you justice."

AFTER I GET OFF THE PHONE I GO INTO THE BATHROOM AND start filling the tub. Between my argument with Neil and conversation with Falco my nerves are stretched taut to the snapping point. The rain pounding on the skylight seems to be beating into my head. How could I have let myself fall in love with Neil again? How could I let him back in my life—a man who almost killed not just me, but our daughter?

"No," I say aloud as I slip into the scalding-hot water. "No, no, no." I'm not even sure what I'm saying *no* to, whether I'm denying that Neil could have killed Christine or trying to excise my feelings for him. I sink back into the bath and watch the steam rise toward the skylight, where it seems to melt into the water pooling on the other side of the glass. Water seeking water, as streams find their way to rivers and rivers find their way to the sea. All these years I've thought that the way I felt about Neil died that day on the river but every night there he was in my dreams, a sodden ghost demanding not to be forgotten, not to be dead. Not Neil, but my love for Neil, not drowned yet, but forever drowning in front of my eyes.

I close my eyes and lean my head back until the water laps up against the crown of my head and something seems to let go inside of me. Just as Eugenie felt her spirit rise out of her body through the top of her head I feel something go out of me and twist up with the steam, twining itself into a shape like a howl—

It is a howl, a sound that turns my flesh cold even in the hot bath. I grip the sides of the tub with both hands and listen.

One of the dogs—Paolo, I think—is howling in the loft. It must be the rain that's frightened him . . . but then I hear glass breaking.

I rise out of the tub as if pushed out by the water and wrap myself in a towel.

"Paolo?" I call. "Francesca?" I wait to hear the click of their nails on the tile floor, but there's nothing. Only the rain.

I walk into the living room, holding the towel against my chest and head straight for the kitchen counter where I left the cordless phone after talking to Detective Falco. I pick it up and then turn around to check both doors—the one to the roof and the one to the side stairs. Both are closed, but one of the glass panels in the roof door is broken and Paolo is standing with his nose in the jagged opening, his body rigid, the hair on his long neck standing straight up and a barely audible growl rumbling from his taut throat. Francesca, by his side, is not as tense, but she's also riveted to the glass door.

I hit redial as I cross the room. Francesca hears my approach and half turns, starts toward me, and then dances back to Paolo, then to me again, her long body twisting in an agony of indecision. "Good girl," I croon, tapping my hand against my bare leg, "come here." I'm listening to the phone but I don't hear a ringing. I turn the phone off, then on again, and wait for a dial tone, but there's none. The phone's dead.

"It's just the storm," I say to Francesca when she dances close enough so that I can loop my fingers around her collar. I let her pull me over to the door. Otherwise I might just stand frozen in the middle of the floor. The tile near the door is damp from the rain that's coming in through the broken glass and I feel something sharp under my bare foot, but ignore it. The unbroken glass panels are fogged over so I wipe my hand against the pane to clear a spot to see and uncover my own reflection: staring eyes, sunken shadows beneath. It's only when he lifts his hand to knock on the glass that I realize I'm looking not at my own reflection but at Neil.

Francesca's tail thumps against my leg; Paolo growls.

I let go of Francesca's collar and grab Paolo's instead as

I unlock the door, thinking as I do that it's too late to lock him out.

As Neil steps over the doorway Paolo growls and lunges forward, taking me with him. The phone, which I'm still holding up against my chest, clatters to the floor, and the towel comes loose. Neil catches me, one hand steadying my elbow, the other moving as if to tuck the towel more firmly around my chest but then straying aimlessly in the air. I yell *down* at Paolo until he crouches and whines.

"I knocked," he says, "on the side door, but when you didn't answer I climbed up to the roof. I didn't realize those panels were so thin." He holds up his hand to show me the gash across his knuckles. I take his hand in mine and start to pick out the glass splinters, but my hands are shaking so much that all I accomplish is to cut my own fingers, the glass sliding from under his skin into mine.

He pulls my hand away and the sleeve of his shirt brushes against my arm like a layer of ice clinging to his skin. His hair is soaking and when I brush it back from his brow the drops that fall are cold as river water. He's come back to me just as he always does in my dreams—a drowning man—only now when I step up against him I can feel, through his clothes and my damp towel, the warmth of his skin and the heat of his breath as he rests his head against my neck.

Not drowned. Not drowned.

After the Coast Guard had gotten me and Bea into their boat they had to dive for Neil. By the time they found him he was unconscious—the body they hauled up into the boat as gray and lifeless as the leaden sky and the surface of the water. While they pounded his chest and tried to breathe life into him I watched his lifeless body and remembered Halcyone—how when she found her husband's drowned body her grief had turned them both into seabirds and granted them eternal life together. I saw then how grief could do this—turn you into a tree or a stone or a bird—and I thought, *if he's dead, I want to be dead*, too. I stood up, meaning to throw myself into the water, only I'd forgotten I was still holding Bea. Out of everything that happened that day, that's what frightened me the most—that I'd been ready to join him—in death, in madness, whatever it took. I gasped out loud when I realized what I'd been about to do and as I did Neil took in a harsh rasping breath, a breath that sounded as if he begrudged it space in his lungs.

Now his breath travels down my neck and over my breasts, warming the flesh with his mouth, drawing a trail of heat across my body the way a soldering iron draws a bead of melted lead along the seams between two pieces of glass to seal them together.

I touch my mouth to his skin, unbuttoning his shirt, his pants, peeling the wet clothes off him to find the warmth underneath, the living part of him underneath the drowning man. The part that's still him. In my dreams I always knew it was still there underneath the drowned apparition that came to me. The real Neil, not drowned, not crazy.

He wraps himself around me, a vine around a tree, and I press myself into him, Salmacis clutching Hermaphroditus in her sacred pool until her flesh sank into his and they became two spirits in one body. We sink onto the floor as if drifting down through water, our bodies weightless as they press against each other, each taking the weight of the other so that even when we move into the bedroom, it's as if we're making love in a still, clear pool of water.

CHAPTER TWENTY-SEVEN

WHEN I WAKE UP IN THE MORNING I'M ALONE. FOR A MOMENT, lying on my back and staring up at the flawless blue square of skylight, I think it was just another one of my dreams, but when I hold my hands up in the sunlight I see the cuts on my fingertips from when I tried to take the glass out of Neil's hand. I remember then that he'd woken me up at four to tell me he had to be back at The Beeches before morning or he'd get kicked out of the trial.

"No trial, no Pieridine," he said, picking up his damp clothes from the living room floor and shaking bits of glass out of them. "But you can still come and sit for me later, right?"

"I have to go into the city," I told him. I considered lying but I didn't want that to be the way we started out—or started over again—whatever it was we were starting. "Detective Falco wants me to look at Christine's desk before her apartment's packed up."

I thought I saw a muscle twitch in his face when I said Falco's name but he kept buttoning his shirt and when he was dressed he came over to me, drew my hair away from my neck, and brushed his lips against my throat.

"Should I come back here tonight?" he asked.

I told him yes, forgetting Falco's suggestion that I spend the night in the city and help Amy clean out the apartment.

Oh well, I think, stretching lazily in the sun streaming into the loft from the skylight, I'll just take the train back tonight and catch the early train into the city tomorrow. I won't even have to mention it to Falco.

At the thought of the detective I realize I should be getting up and ready for him, but I stay in bed another few minutes, basking in the sun. I lift my arms up over my head and twirl my hands in a light that is stained emerald and violet from the grapevine pattern in the glass. The green light snakes around my arms and, when I look down, I see it has wrapped around the length of my body. Like one of Ovid's nymphs, I seem to be turning into a tree.

Although I'm down on the street by 9:20, Falco's already there, leaning against his car and sipping from a blue and white paper coffee cup, looking fresh in neatly pressed khakis and a blue cotton shirt. I've showered and put on a nice linen dress but I feel rumpled in comparison, bleary from lack of sleep and unreasonably covetous of his coffee. Before I can build up too much resentment, though, he hands me my own cup and a cinnamon brioche.

"Gosh, Annemarie only makes these by special request. How'd you rate one?"

"I happened to ask Gavin Penrose a few questions

about some unpaid bills with local businesspeople and the next day he paid up all his accounts. I have no idea how your cousin decided I was the one to thank but she loaded me down with so many baked goods that I'm afraid I'll be accused of graft." Falco brushes some powdered sugar from his shirt and grins. "As you can see I've been trying to eat the evidence."

"And you want to make me an accessory to the cover-up?" I ask, biting into the warm, sweet bread. Annemarie's version of a brioche contains pine nuts and currants and, she once confessed, a hint of pepper.

Falco shrugs and opens the passenger side door for me. The whole car is so fragrant with coffee, fresh baked bread, and cinnamon that I feel suddenly light-headed and unreasonably happy. Maybe it's the night I spent with Neil or just the way the sun reflects off the Hudson as we head south toward the city that makes me feel like I'm back in college on a road trip and that the day offers endless possibilities.

Falco seems in a pretty good mood, too. Maybe the trip reminds him of college as well because instead of talking about the case he spends most of the time reminiscing about his years at John Jay: his classes, some of his more memorable professors, and the friends he made there. It's only when a few too many of his stories end in a too early death—one in a drug bust in the South Bronx, two heart attacks, and a classmate who died in uniform at the World Trade Center—that his mood shifts. As we cross over the Henry Hudson Bridge into Manhattan we both lapse into silence.

We pass near the entrance to the Cloisters and I remember the winter day Christine and I walked through the snow toward the medieval monastery and I felt like a pilgrim looking for sanctuary. I found Neil instead.

Falco exits the highway on 95th Street and we head south on Riverside Drive. Riverside Park is full of flowers and dog walkers and bicyclists—a bright panorama of city life that fails to revive my mood. When we pull up in front of Christine's apartment—into a spot that says NO PARKING—Falco turns to me before turning off the engine, his face still full of regret not, as it turns out, for his fallen comrades, but for me.

"I didn't want to point this out to you, but I guess I'd better since I'm not sure you made the connection."

"What connection?"

"Gavin paying off his debts so quickly. It looks like he mustn't have real money problems—he just doesn't bother to pay his bills on time." He pauses another moment to turn the car off and reach across me to take a laminated permit of some kind out of the glove compartment. "It kind of kills the theory that he needed to marry Joan Shelley for money."

RUTH WEBB HAS GIVEN FALCO THE KEYS TO HER DAUGHTER'S apartment—and permission for me to stay overnight—so after showing the doorman his search warrant we ride the elevator up to the fourteenth floor. As he opens the Yale lock and dead bolt on Christine's door I still can't help but feel that I'm somehow invading Christine's privacy. I've only been to the apartment a couple of times in the six years Christine has lived here. It's so small that whenever I came into the city Christine would usually suggest we meet at a restaurant or a museum. I'd thought that she was embarrassed by living in such a tiny, modest apartment, but now, when I step into the narrow entry hall—made narrower by bookshelves lining both walls— it occurs to me that Christine had become more and more reclusive over the years and that the apartment, with its copious artifacts of her studies, had become a too private manifestation of her obsessions for her to enjoy sharing it with even her best friend.

At the end of the hallway, though, is a reminder that I still had a place in her world. It's a three-quarter oil portrait of Christine wearing a green Indian kurta and jeans, leaning against a tree. When I pause in front of it Falco says, "Yeah, I keep looking at that, too. I always like to look at pictures of a homicide victim so I picture them alive and not as the corpse I see in the morgue . . . but this . . . the girl in this picture looks so young it's hard to believe she'll ever grow old, let alone die at thirty-seven. I looked to see who did the painting but there's only this green stamp in the corner. Some kind of stylized bird. It's on a bunch of paintings in the apartment. I wondered if they were done by your ex."

I shake my head. "Neil did use a Japanese style stamp on his paintings, but his was a tree—because he thought his name meant beech forest." I don't bother to explain that I've also heard that Buchwald means "book forest." "He made the peacock stamp for me," I say, lightly touching the green square in the corner and tracing the corona of feathers surrounding the long-necked bird, "because it's an attribute of Juno."

"You painted this?" he asks, looking genuinely surprised. I nod. "And these other ones in here?"

I follow him into the tiny living room. Every inch of wall space that hasn't been taken up by bookshelves has been filled with pictures: watercolors, prints, sketches, oil paintings. Some are reproductions from museums of Christine's favorite artists but intermixed with the Pre-Raphaelites and medieval tapestries are dozens of pieces I did—from careless rough charcoal sketches I'd torn out of my sketch pad to throw away to the larger oil paintings I did in my last year of college and that I'd given to Christine when Bea and I moved back in with my father.

I don't have room for these at my dad's, I told her, although we'd both known I just couldn't live with them anymore. Most of them are of Neil.

"These are really good," Falco says, pausing in front of an oil painting of several people standing in a rose garden. "Do you still paint?"

I shake my head and turn away from the detective's gaze. "Christine's desk is in her bedroom, right?" Without waiting for an answer I turn on my heel and go into an even smaller room, most of which is taken up by a queen-sized platform bed. Christine's desk—a mission library table that we'd found together at the Poughkeepsie Salvation Army—is fitted into an arched alcove on the wall opposite the foot of the bed.

Immediately I see what Falco meant by the desk being

a kind of diorama. The arched alcove frames the desk like a proscenium stage. The stacks of books on either side and leaning against the back wall are like stage sets; the domed glass lamp, when Falco switches it on, reveals a bucolic scene of shepherds and milkmaids that could be a painted scrim for an eighteenth-century farce, the array of postcards thumbtacked to the wall over the desk background scenery.

I look at the postcards first. When I was last here two years ago the postcards were confined to the bulletin board above her desk, but now they've spread over the entire wall so that it's hard to tell where the bulletin board ends and the wall begins. Many are art postcards that Christine collected over the years and reflect the progression of her taste from swooning Pre-Raphaelite beauties to chaste medieval maidens carved in ivory or stitched in silk. Many are reproductions of Penrose's paintings—the same wan nymphs that decorated her childhood bedroom—although I notice more of the wood nymph variety than the water nymph. Along the top of the wall she's arranged the pictures that line Forest Hall— all those figures turning into trees: Baucis and Philemon, Daphne, the three paintings of Iole and Dryope, and then the unnamed girl leaning over a pool with her hair hanging in the water, the tips of her hair just beginning to turn into trailing beech leaves, incipient bark creeping up her legs.

"Do you mind if I untack one to look at the back?" I call, thinking Detective Falco's still in the other room, but when he answers I'm startled to find he's just behind me.

"Go ahead."

I take down the one of the girl leaning over the pool and turn it over. *Penrose Collection*, it reads, *The Drowning Tree, Augustus Penrose, 1893.* And then underneath, a note in Christine's handwriting: *Same year as Iole and Dryope? Part of the same series?*

"Something wrong?" Falco asks. He's standing next to me looking down at the card. I try to give it to him, but he takes my hand instead and lowers it so the card is in the light of the desk lamp. The gesture brings to mind the way Neil took my hand last night when I was plucking glass from his knuckles and that image stirs a fleeting ache that makes me shift my weight and brings a flush to my face. Falco turns my hand over so he can see the picture. "Yet another one of those Greek girls turning into a tree. What did this one do wrong—or was she trying to get away from some lecherous god?"

I shake my head. "No one knows what myth it depicts, but from the note on the back it sounds like Christine thought it might be part of the Iole and Dryope series."

"You mean that one with the two sisters and the baby?"

"Uh-huh."

"Why would she think that?" Falco asks.

"Well, it does hang next to the ones of Iole and Dryope in Forest Hall."

"I don't remember it."

"No, it's been taken down for cleaning."

Falco angles the desk lamp to get a better look at the postcard. Unfortunately, it's not a great reproduction, so it's hard to see details. "I don't know," he says. "If it's part of that series where's the sister? Where's the baby?"

"Maybe this one is of Dryope after her sister takes the baby away. It's her all alone, mourning." I shrug and slide the card into his hand, forcing him to take it, and try to pull my hand away, but he holds onto it.

"What happened to your fingers?" he asks, pulling my hand back into the light. The red scratches look particularly garish under the lamplight.

"Occupational hazard," I tell him, "of working with glass." I take my hand back and cross my arms over my chest, tucking my right hand underneath my left arm. "Is this why you thought Christine was interested in Gavin Penrose," I ask, "because she has all these Augustus Penrose paintings?"

"No, I expected that because of her research on the window. It's this—"

He takes a folder off the desk and hands it to me. Inside are color Xeroxes of paintings that look vaguely like Penroses or someone imitating Penrose. I don't recognize any of them. I turn one over and see in Christine's handwriting, "*Untitled work by Gavin Penrose, date?*"

"Did you know Gavin Penrose painted?" Falco asks.

"Actually I just found that out a few weeks ago. He said he'd spent a year in Paris studying painting but that he gave it up . . . how did Christine get these?"

"I was hoping you could tell me. Here's another thing—"

He opens another folder and takes from it a piece of heavy drawing paper with rough edges—as if torn from a notebook—on which is a sketch of a woman at a loom. It takes me only a moment to recognize the figure as the lady in the library window.

"Fay was right," I admit reluctantly. "Christine did tear a page out of Eugenie's notebook. I could have sworn she wouldn't have done anything like that—" But how well, I wonder, did I really know Christine? "—I wonder what was so important about this sketch."

I look at the drawing more closely and notice that the cloth on the loom, which is blank in the window, is woven with a finely detailed rendering of the landscape in the window only—

"It's not the same," I tell Falco. "Look, the tree is weird, almost—"

"Like a person. Yeah, I see what you mean. And it looks like there's something, or someone, in the water. Hey, look at this." Falco lays the postcard of *The Drowning Tree* next to Eugenie's sketch. "The picture in the loom looks just like the one in this postcard."

"You're right. Christine mentioned in her lecture that the original glass panels for the loom were broken and that's why they were blank. But I wonder why she didn't mention this sketch."

"Maybe she wanted to find out more about it before going public with the information. There's also a letter in the folder."

He hands me a sheet of cream-colored stationery embossed with the gold monogram EBP. *Eugenie Barovier Penrose.*

"This is an original letter from Eugenie Penrose," I

say. "Fay Morgan would have a fit if she knew where it was."

"I know. My guess is that Christine found it in one of those notebooks she borrowed and held onto it. Read it. It's to a lawyer in Albany."

Even when the ink was fresh it would have been hard to make out this thin spidery handwriting (which I recognize from Eugenie's diary and notebook) so I sit down and place the paper under the lamp so that I can see it better. Falco sits on the edge of the desk.

Dear Mr. Arnot,

In answer to your letter of June the twelfth, I must insist once again that you honor the letter of my husband's will. Although it's possible, as you believe, that he did not intend to leave the persons in question quite so destitute, we must remember that my husband and I have dedicated our lives to the institutions we've founded and that my husband's will—although some might call it harsh— reflects that dedication. I must repeat that all of my husband's paintings were left to the college. That includes the one to which your clients have claimed ownership.

In closing, let me point out that I have no complaint living out the remainder of my life in modest cir- cumstances. Your clients will simply have to content themselves with the same.

Yours truly,
Eugenie Penrose

"Wow, she sounds like a bitch in this. I wonder if Christine showed this to Gavin."

"From these notes, I think she might have." Falco turns over the folder that held the letter. On the back Christine had written: *Arnot's clients? Gavin's father? Gavin himself? Ask Gavin exactly what he did inherit from estate—which paintings? Who else inherited? Did anyone else inherit paintings?* And written in boldfaced caps and underlined: *Ask about* The Drowning Tree?

I look up and catch Falco still staring at my injured fingertips. "If she asked Gavin these questions he would have thought she was pretty interested in his financial situation," I say, trying to meet Falco's gaze without looking away.

"Right. Of course, we don't know for sure that she did ask—"

"Christine wasn't one to leave a question unasked when it came to her research."

"But she never mentioned this to you? She didn't ask you what you knew about Penrose's financial situation?"

"No—" I finally look away because what I think I see in those calm, gray eyes is sympathy—as if he knows how much I want to make Gavin the one responsible for Christine's death, and why. As if he can see every touch of Neil's hands on my flesh as easily as he can see the scratches on my fingertips. I pick up a glass paperweight just to feel its cool roundness in my palm and smooth out the folded newspaper that it had been weighing down—a section from the *Times* listing gallery shows with one at the Queen Gallery on Arts & Crafts painters circled in red.

384 • CAROL GOODMAN

"You don't really think it's Gavin, do you? You don't think
he's the one responsible for Christine's death?"

"I haven't made up my mind yet. If she were having an
affair with him I think she'd have his picture up there."
Falco points to the wall behind me—the right inner wall of
the alcove, which is plastered with photographs. A lot of
them, I notice right away, are of me—some from college
and some with Beatrice. Some of the ones from college
have Neil in them, but these aren't the only pictures of
Neil. When Christine helped me move out of the apartment
I lived in with Neil I'd given her a box of pictures I had of
Neil. *I'll burn these if I keep them*, I told her, *and Bea might
want them some day. Will you keep them for me?* I never
expected her to hang them up though.

"This is what you really wanted me to see, isn't it?"

"I just want you to be careful," he says.

"It doesn't prove they were seeing each other. She
might have felt something for him—" *Love, which absolves
no one beloved from loving*, she'd said at the train station
that last night. Had she been talking about Neil? Did she
think if she loved him long enough he'd have to love her
back? "—but that doesn't mean he reciprocated the
feeling."

Falco's eyes darken from pale gray to slate, like the
river just before a storm. "I think you should look at this."
He turns around and takes down a calendar from the left-
hand wall of the alcove. It's the Tiffany calendar that I
bought at the Met and gave Christine for Christmas. He
opens it to May. On the third Saturday Christine has
drawn a little tree.

"You said Neil used a stamp with a beech tree to sign his paintings. Does that look like the same symbol?"

"It's just a tree . . . I mean, it might be—" I look closer at the little drawing. There's no point in lying because it would be easy enough for Falco to find one of Neil's old paintings and compare the stamp he used to this design. "Okay, yeah, it looks like the design Neil used, but this is in May. We know they saw each other in May."

Falco flips the page back to April. There are five trees. Then he turns back to March. There are too many trees for me to count at first glance—a whole forest of trees that starts to blur as if a mist had risen from the forest floor.

"I'm sorry, Juno," Falco says, covering my hand with his, "but I thought you'd better know. I got the lab results back today. The baby was Neil's."

CHAPTER TWENTY-EIGHT

"It doesn't mean he killed her."

"I didn't say it did."

"It still could have been Gavin Penrose. Maybe he didn't like being asked all these questions about his family history and his finances. Maybe he had something else to hide. Maybe she was sleeping with him, too—"

On that last conjecture—my third *maybe*—my voice cracks and I press my fingertips into my eyelids to keep the tears back. They come anyway, seeping into the little cuts until my fingertips burn. Falco looks sadly toward the scene on the lamp, as if gravely disapproving of the shepherds and milkmaids' antics. When the worst is over, he hands me a clean white handkerchief, neatly folded in quarters.

"I'm sorry," he says when I have dried my eyes, "that you had to learn about it here in your friend's apartment, but I wanted you to realize that this wasn't a onetime thing—"

Falco gestures at the pictures of Neil and the calendar

with its swelling grove of trees. They were seeing each other every couple of days in March. Christine must have taken the train past the factory each and every time—unless she drove.

"How was she getting over there to see him?" I ask, sniffling into my handkerchief. "She didn't have a car and the train only runs on the east side of the river."

"Why do you assume she went there?" Falco asks, his voice soft and reluctant.

The notion startles me out of my chair. I turn around to face the bed and the sight of it propels me into the living room, Falco so close on my heels that when I wheel around he nearly collides with me.

"How could you have brought me here? Did you really think I could stay here after learning about . . . them?"

"I'll drive you back."

I look around at my own paintings of Neil, done fifteen years ago and stamped with the little green bird that he designed. "You knew the paintings were mine, didn't you? You just wanted me to tell you about Neil's tree stamp so I couldn't deny it was his sign in Christine's calendar. What you said about having information on Gavin Penrose's involvement was just a lie to get me here to confirm your hunch."

"No, Juno, I still consider Gavin a suspect, but I thought you ought to know about Neil and Christine for your own sake." He reaches for my hand and grazes the cuts on my fingertips ever so lightly, but I can feel his touch travel through my broken skin and pour into my veins like molten glass. I look up at him and then look away, unable to bear the look of pity in his eyes. It's clear from the way he looks at me that he knows everything—not just that Neil and I are lovers but how much I've allowed myself to fall in love with him again.

"I have to get out of here," I tell him, turning in a full circle as if I'd forgotten where the front door was.

"I'll take you back. I can leave the key with the doorman for Amy—"

I'd forgotten about Amy.

"No. Why should she have to suffer for my stupidity? I'll stay. I'll start packing tonight." I look around the room as if I can't wait to start peeling the paintings off the wall. Yes, that's what I'll do. I'll stay here all night until the walls are bare and all traces of Christine's life are erased from inside these rooms and then I'll start erasing all traces of her from inside my heart.

"If you're sure that's what you want," he says, handing me the keys to the apartment, "maybe it would be safer for you to stay here tonight."

"Why? Because you think Neil might hurt me?" I'm about to say that he'd never do such a thing when I realize the absurdity of making that statement about a man who once tried to drown me. "He's better now," I say instead.

"Maybe," Falco says. "You have to admit that sleeping with your best friend and then lying about it doesn't speak all that well for his stability. And he seemed awfully excitable when I spoke with him at The Beeches. This drug he's on, Prozine—"

"Pieridine," I correct him, "it's named for the Greek muses."

"I don't care if it's named for Zeus himself, it's still in trial. It might have side effects we don't know anything about yet . . ."

"Do you have any reason to believe that?" I ask.

I can see him hesitate, as if trying to decide whether or not to tell me something. "Look," he says finally, "all I'm suggesting is that you take the night to absorb what you've learned before going back—" He hesitates again and then finishes, "before going back home. Okay?"

I nod, mostly because I'm tired of the argument and scared of what else he might say. I guess that instead of "back home" he'd been about to say "before you go back to Neil." I suspect that he's giving me this night in the city to absorb what I've learned and store up a little self-control because even with all I've learned I may not be able to resist seeing Neil again. Mostly I quit arguing because I can't tell him the night away isn't necessary. I'm more afraid that one night won't be enough.

I WAIT TEN MINUTES AFTER FALCO LEAVES AND THEN LEAVE, too. Although I'm determined to spend the night in the apartment I need a break. Some air and a brisk walk. Walking on crowded city streets, though, fails to release all the rage and grief I'm feeling so I head east toward Central Park and enter the park on 86th Street near the Great Lawn. I walk south, glad of the shade and privacy the wooded paths offer; not so glad of the memories that the carefully landscaped terrain sparks.

During our last year at Penrose, after Neil had gone

back to Columbia, Christine and I rode the train down almost every weekend to visit him in the apartment he shared with four other students on 104th and Broadway. We slept on couches or the floor and during the day we'd escape the overcrowded apartment by heading over to the park. Always the three of us. Looking back, I'm amazed at how much I took Christine's presence for granted. I'd never asked for more time alone with Neil or resented her being with us. Instead I remember feeling that Christine's company somehow steadied us—like the third leg on a tripod.

We'd often end up in the Ramble, that jumble of boulders and meandering paths that feels like a miniature woodland within the larger park. We'd wander there for hours and then settle into a secluded spot. Neil loved to sketch the trees, many of which twisted into improbable shapes or were so covered by vines and creepers that they'd been transformed into shaggy beasts and looming specters. While Neil drew the trees, I drew him. Christine read, sometimes reading aloud bits of Ovid and Dante to us.

As I follow the web of paths my thoughts twist back on themselves as often as the paths do. I keep picturing the three of us together back in college and then imagining Neil and Christine together these last few months. Every time I approach this picture in my mind I step back from it, but no matter what direction I take in my thoughts it's what I return to. Neil and Christine walking through the beech woods at Astolat, or here in Central Park—if he came to visit her in the city, why not?—or rowing up the

Wicomico to the pool underneath the weeping beech. It's as if I'm executing the steps of some complicated courtly dance in which the two of them shadow my every step.

And it's not just the three of us that I see in the dance. I can't help but think how much we resemble another threesome: Augustus Penrose and the two Barovier sisters. Two women and a man, both women in love with the man, one pushed aside. I picture the three of us—Neil, Christine and I—lined up across from Penrose and the two sisters. Who would stand across from whom? Neil and Penrose, Eugenie and I. . . . I wonder if Christine noticed the resemblance while researching the window. If so, maybe she'd identified with Clare as the one pushed aside by the two lovers.

I've been wandering in the maze so engrossed in my thoughts that I've lost track of where I am, when I come out suddenly at the bridge that crosses the lake. Lovely Bow Bridge, unfurling like a ribbon over the green water, designed by Calvert Vaux, the same landscape architect who designed the grounds of Briarwood. Who knew when we wandered these paths all those years ago that Neil would end up following ones laid out by the same designer—only for mental patients instead of urban recreationists?

The position of the dancers in my head shifts. Now instead of Clare and Christine standing across from each other I imagine Neil and Clare—the two who ended up in the same psychiatric hospital. And who's my partner in this new dance? Who do I see as I walk across the bridge to the other side of the lake? Augustus, who loved Clare and kept visiting her? Or Eugenie, who abandoned her sister and left her to live out her life in an insane asylum?

Coming out of the woods I find myself at Bethesda Terrace. I cross to the fountain and look up at the bronze angel who holds her hands above the fountain—the Angel of Waters she's called, carved by Emma Stebbins in 1873. Vaux's original idea for the fountain was that it be dedicated to love, but Stebbins chose the biblical angel whose touch turns the pool of Bethesda into healing waters, perhaps because the woman she loved was dying of breast cancer and they'd tried water cures to heal her. What better token of love than the power to make whole again? How many times had I lain next to Neil while he slept, stroking his brow, willing my touch to banish the bad dreams I knew roiled below the surface, willing my fingers to leach out the madness inside him?

But eventually I gave up. *I'm not Augustus*, I think. *He's not the partner I see standing across from me.* He kept visiting Clare until he died, he still loved her, just as Christine still believed in Neil and loved him so much that she hoped one day he'd have no choice but to return her love.

And he had.

Standing beneath the outspread hands of the angel, I wish it were Christine that I'm crying for and not my own selfish loss. That I wasn't like spiteful Eugenie, so jealous of her sister's hold on her husband that she broke the panes that filled the loom when she saw that the story they told was of her sister's descent into madness. She must have known that Augustus visited Clare and still loved her and that the window was a tribute to her and she couldn't bear for the world to see it.

I think of Christine on the train platform. Did she want to tell me about what had happened between her and Neil? That he was better and that they loved each other? But then I told her that I hadn't been able to love anyone since Neil and she changed her mind. How could she take the one man I'd ever loved away from me just when he was well again? I imagine her taking the kayak and crossing the river, paddling across the dark water to the weeping beech and swallowing the pills until she fell asleep and tipped into the water. Could she have killed herself because Neil had rejected her or was she leaving him free to be with me?

I stir the water in the pool with the tips of my fingers. The cold water stings the cuts on my hand but I also feel something knitting together, some tear deeper than the ones on my fingers beginning to heal.

I walk out of the park on the East Side and wander over to Madison to find a place to eat. I haven't eaten anything since that cinnamon brioche Falco gave me and it's nearly dinnertime. I see a coffee shop on the next corner heading south, but before I get to it my attention is caught by something in a gallery window—just a flicker of green that I catch out of the corner of my eye, like a flash of green water. I stop and look through the window, past my own reflection and toward the painting on the rear wall of the gallery and for a moment I feel the same horror that the figure in the painting of the *The Drowning Tree* must feel when she sees herself transformed. My face in the window appears to be superimposed on the tree in the painting, my body encased in bark. I stand frozen on the sidewalk—as if my body had actually turned to wood and my legs had grown roots—while pedestrians surge around me as unmindful of me as though I had indeed become one of the ornamental shade trees planted behind metal gates along the avenue.

What pulls me out of my stupor is the name on the window: The Queen Gallery. This is the gallery show on Arts & Crafts painters that Christine had circled in the *Times*.

I open the door and the air inside the gallery is so cold on my damp skin that I immediately begin to shiver. Still, I walk straight toward the painting on the back wall, ignoring the forced smile of the slim young woman dressed in a pink knit suit behind the reception desk. I stop a few feet away from the painting so I can take it all in. The canvas is huge, much bigger than the other paintings in Forest Hall, but I do remember it now from my college days. I can even hear Christine's voice in my ear—my own personal art history audio tour—telling me about it.

This was one of Penrose's first paintings of a woman turning into a tree. Critics believe it's what started him on the series of Ovid-inspired paintings, only no one's been able to identify the myth it's based on.

"Extraordinary, isn't it? It's by Augustus Penrose, a second-generation Pre-Raphaelite who was later associated with the Arts and Crafts movement." Christine's voice is replaced by the modulated tones of the woman in pink. She fingers a long rope of pearls as she talks, balancing daintily on a pair of high-heeled navy sandals emblazoned with interlocking C's that match the interlocking C's dangling from her ears. A flamingo in Chanel.

"Notice the anthropomorphic handling of the tree and the way her hair, as it turns into the cascading branches of the weeping beech, intertwines with the reeds in an organic Art Nouveau motif . . ."

"Is this painting for sale?" I ask, so abruptly that she stops midsentence and teeters on her heels, clutching her pearls as if for support. "And if so, who's the seller?"

"The owner wishes to remain anonymous but any offers can be tendered through the gallery." She flicks her eyes over me, either trying to assess my spending power by my wardrobe (clearly my J. Crew sundress and flat sandals aren't earning me many points) or looking for a concealed weapon. I must be staring at the painting as if I'd like to slash it.

"Is the gallery owner here?" I ask.

"She's in a meeting, but if you leave your number—"

"Look," I say, "I'm a trustee of Penrose College—" *One of those starchy blue bloods who happens to have an eccentric liking for inexpensive catalog clothing.* "—and this painting is, I believe, the property of the college, which means it shouldn't be for sale at all. Unless you'd like me to call the police—"

"I'm afraid you must be mistaken," Ms. Flamingo says, shifting her weight from foot to foot as if she suddenly had to go to the bathroom. "The owner of the gallery is herself a trustee of the college—"

"Is there a problem, CeCe?"

CeCe. No wonder she's so fond of the Chanel logo!

I turn to see who's spoken and find myself facing Regula Howell, looking cool and stately in another one of her striking folkloric ensembles—a sleeveless black knit dress embroidered with gold passementerie scrolls and matching gold spirals encircling her wrists, neck, and upper arm. She looks, actually, more like an Etruscan priestess than a gallery owner—and then I get it. Regula—Queen.

"Ms. Howell," I say, hoping she didn't hear my lie about being a Penrose trustee, "I didn't realize that this was your gallery. I came in because I recognized this painting by Penrose, *The Drowning Tree*. I'm just surprised to see it here on sale. Doesn't it belong to the college?"

"Miss McKay, isn't it? You've made a very understandable mistake. Not all of Augustus Penrose's paintings were left to the college. Some were left to the family—"

"So Gavin's the owner?"

"I didn't say that; the owner wishes to remain anonymous."

"Oh," I say, taking another step toward the painting. The two reproductions I've seen recently—the print in Christine's old bedroom and the postcard in her apartment—failed to do the painting justice. Unlike the frail nymphs Penrose usually favors, this figure is monumental. Her torso, emerging from its sheath of bark, is powerful, stomach muscles tensed as she leans over the pool, her arms breaking free from the stranglehold of branches to balance herself above the water. The painting doesn't show, I suddenly realize, a woman turning into a tree, but one breaking free of the imprisoning bark. I follow the sweep of hair into the water and find the face of a girl hidden in the ripples. The girl's look of horror and fear does not seem to match the aggressive posture of the woman above her. In fact, the figure in the water, I can see now, is lifting her arms up, while the arms of the tree-woman are held back. The figure in the water isn't a reflection at all. It reminds me of something—the hand reaching up . . . I close my eyes and see, instead of the beech tree's branches trailing in the water, Christine's hair swaying in the clear water, a white marble hand reaching up from the bottom of the pool.

"Of course," I say aloud, "the statue in the water."

"What statue in the water?" Regula asks.

"Nothing," I say, taking a step backward toward the exit. "I'm sorry I misunderstood who owned the painting. Of course if you say it's owned by Gavin . . ."

"I didn't," she begins, turning as pink as CeCe's suit. "I tried to explain that to Christine . . ."

"So she did come here," I say. "I see. Well, that's all I really need to know for now." I hold out my hand to shake Regula's but she seems to be too busy hating herself for giving away that last little bit of information to notice. So I give a little wave to her—and to CeCe—and step out onto the street, where I hail a cab to take me back to Christine's apartment.

CHAPTER TWENTY-NINE

THE CAB TAKES ME BACK THROUGH CENTRAL PARK, THROUGH a tunnel of late summer greenery. Staring at the reflection of leaves on the cab window, I picture the face under the water in the painting, looking up through the water at the looming specter of that terrifying tree-woman. When I get to Christine's apartment I go straight to her desk, where I've left the postcard of *The Drowning Tree*. Although it's hard to make out the details in the poor-quality reproduction, the original is seared into my brain.

Clearly the scene depicts some kind of horrible encounter between two women. Although I still don't understand it completely, I suspect that the painting holds the key to what happened between Clare and Eugenie and that Christine thought so, too. I imagine that after she tracked the painting down to Regula's gallery she would have met with Gavin. Perhaps that's what they argued about before her lecture—either over the impropriety of selling a piece of college property or over what Christine thought the painting revealed about Augustus and the two sisters. Either way, Gavin would have felt threatened by what Christine had learned. All Christine would have wanted, though, would have been to learn more.

I close my eyes and again I picture Christine as I saw her last, suspended in the water above the submerged marble statue. That must be what she wanted to see. She must have guessed that the statue would reveal what happened between Eugenie and Clare. So she used what she already knew to bribe Gavin to take her across the river.

Poor Christine, I think, *so obsessed with her research that she couldn't see any danger to herself.*

I pause in my packing—I've decided to take some of Christine's files and pictures back with me—surprised that all my anger at Christine has faded. A few hours ago I was ready to rip her apartment apart in my rage over her sleeping with Neil and now all I feel is pity. I look down at my fingers, half expecting that those wounds, too, will have been healed by the water in Bethesda fountain, but the scratches, of course, are still there. I run my thumb along my fingertips, testing for pain, but all I feel is a little tingle on the surface and a stone-cold reservoir of intent under my skin to find out what happened to Christine.

I'll take the train back tonight and first thing in the morning I'll ask Kyle to take me across the river. I'm certain that Christine would only have gone across the river with Gavin if she believed that the statue submerged in the pool below the weeping beech would tell her what happened among Eugenie, Penrose, and Clare. If I can find what she was looking for I might understand why she went with

Gavin and then I'll be able to explain it all to Falco. If I can find some link between the scene in the painting that Gavin is selling—perhaps illegally—at the gallery and the real-life scene of Christine's death, he'll have to believe that it was Gavin and not Neil who killed her.

I SPEND THE NEXT FEW HOURS GOING THROUGH CHRISTINE'S papers, searching for something else that might implicate Gavin in Christine's death, but find nothing. What I do find are all the letters I wrote to her when she was at Oxford in a file labeled "Juno" and another file labeled "Beatrice" with every drawing that Bea had ever given her over the years. Although I'm anxious to get back home I find it hard, when it comes time, to leave the apartment. It's the last time I'll see it; the last time I'll be surrounded by Christine's things. When I finally do leave I stand in the hall a moment and then go back in, go into the living room, and take down the painting I'd done of Christine and me and Neil together in the Rose Garden. I'd copied it from a photo that was taken the day Neil and I were married. With the canvas tucked under my arm, I head down to Grand Central.

By the time I get a taxi, and the taxi makes it through traffic to the station, I just barely make the 6:29 train. When the train comes out of the tunnel the sun is already low in the sky, the buildings casting long shadows, and I'm reminded of those Sundays when Christine and I would come back late from the city and I would dash to the library to finish my schoolwork. It makes me want to be doing something, so I take out Eugenie's journal pages from my overnight bag and read the last few entries. All but the very last one are curiously brief.

> *Today Augustus asked me to share with him the labors of his life. "We share a vision," he said to me, "and will do great things together." Since he'd already sought and received Papa's consent it only remained for us to tell Clare . . .*

I puzzle over Eugenie's tone, which seems cool for a woman who's received a proposal from a man she obviously loved. Was it only Victorian reserve? Or was there something in Penrose's proposal that disappointed her—some lack of ardor or a too-stolid pragmatism? Or was she afraid of Clare's reaction?

> *Clare took the news with all appearance of calm, only asking what would become of her. I told her what Augustus and I had discussed and how generous and resourceful he'd been in using his connections to obtain for her a teaching position . . .*

Teaching position? So the original plan had not been to bring Clare along with them to America. I wonder whose idea the teaching position had really been. Apparently Clare wondered, too.

> *I've just had a very distressing talk with Clare in which she accused me of poisoning Augustus against her*

*and of stealing his affections. She appears to be under the
delusion that he'd been courting her all along. I begin to
fear for her reason.*

Looking out the window at the river under a darkening
sky, I wonder how far to trust Eugenie's assessment. Was
Clare really losing her mind or was it just easier to believe
that Clare was mad than to suspect that her fiancé was
only marrying her for her money when he really loved her
penniless sister? Apparently it was Augustus, after all,
who chose to bring Clare with them to America.

*Augustus suggests that we bring Clare to America
with us in the hope that a change of scene will restore her
reason. I'm afraid that he doesn't know her as well as I
do—after all, he hasn't lived through her variations in
mood and episodic fancies as I have. He believes her
present agitation to be an aberration and the sunny,
cheerful disposition he encountered when we first made
his acquaintance to be her "true self." What he doesn't
understand is that the girl he saw at first is but a
reflection of the one he sees now and no more substantial
than a shimmer on the water's surface. The real girl
lurks below the water's surface, a shadow wraith,
waiting to drag her unsuspecting victims into the depths.*

I look away from the page, chilled by this last image
Eugenie has drawn. It's an eerie rendering of the manic-
depressive: charming and sparkling when she's in her
manic stage, but capable of sucking the world around her

into her own shadows when she descends into depression. But what also strikes me is how Eugenie's luridly fanciful image of Clare as a water-demon waiting to drag her unsuspecting lovers to a watery death echoes the image in *The Drowning Tree*.

In the second-to-last entry, written on the eve of her wedding day, Eugenie tried one last time to reconcile her sister to her marriage.

> I took her to the pool below the weeping beech because I thought the pastoral setting with its fond associations might soothe her nerves. It seemed at first to be working. She let down her hair and allowed me to comb it as I had when she was little while she told me one of the fanciful tales she so loves.
>
> "Here's a story," she said, bowing her head so that I could work my comb into the tangles at the base of her neck. "Once upon a time there was a beautiful wood nymph who lived by a pool in the forest in a grove of trees that were sacred to her. One day she saw a mortal youth sitting by the pool drawing pictures of the trees and because he seemed to love the trees that were sacred to her she fell in love with him. But before she could reveal herself to him, he saw her sister, and she put a spell on him and forced him to believe himself in love with her. Together the youth and the wicked sister prepared to leave the grove. The wood nymph, in her grief, let down her hair and leaned over the pool knowing that the weight of her hair would drag her to the bottom of the pool, but at the very moment she dived into the water the gods of

404 • CAROL GOODMAN

the woods took pity on her and turned her into one of the trees she so loved—a weeping beech tree that forever trails its branches in the water like the drowning girl. So you see, she's always drowning but never wholly drowned. The tree, from that day on, was called the drowning tree."

"That's a pretty story," I told Clare, working my fingers into one of the knots at the nape of her neck. "Is it from Ovid?"

She looked out at me from under her hair and it gave me a start—she looked like a girl who's been strangled in the grasses that grow beneath the water. Like the drowning girl in her story. "Not everything's from a book, Eugenie," she said, clutching her hands over her stomach as if she were in physical pain. "Here's life," she cried, "whether you see it or not."

She tried to stand up then but my ring—the ring dear Augustus had given me—caught in her hair and she let out a cry when the hair tore away in my hand. I tried to soothe her, but she looked at me as if I were a stranger— oh, it was a look to chill the bones! I'll never forget it if I live to be a hundred—and then she turned from me and, lifting her skirts as if she were alighting from a carriage, stepped into the pool.

It happened so quickly I couldn't move. I stood on the bank, frozen to the spot, as if I had become the tree in Clare's story. I could see, beneath the clear water, Clare's face as she sank deeper into the pool and she— awful to say!—could see me. I think it was her look that kept me rooted to the spot. Those blue eyes of hers! How *they burned! I believe that I was mesmerized by them into a kind of waking sleep. Why else would I not have lifted a hand to help my own sister? She had put a spell on me to render me helpless to save her so she could accomplish her purpose—to drown herself!*

And then something brushed past me. I thought for a moment it was some enormous black bird swooping down out of the beech tree to skim the surface of the pool, but it was Augustus. He told me later that he heard Clare's cry—from when my hand got stuck in her hair—and came running. Thank goodness he did because he was able to drag Clare's drenched and bleeding body out of the water onto the shore and breathe life back into her. I shudder to think what might have happened if he hadn't been nearby.

The conductor calls the stop that's right before Rosedale, so I fold up the journal pages and tuck them into one of Christine's file folders. There's only one more page and it seems to be about making arrangements to leave for America. It must have been clear after the incident under the beech tree that Clare would have to go to America with them. I don't envy Eugenie's position—forced to be a caretaker to an unstable sister infatuated with her new husband, but neither can I trust her explanation of her failure to prevent Clare's suicide attempt. Maybe she was paralyzed with fear while her sister struggled in the water, but surely to Clare it looked as if her sister stood coldly by while she drowned. And wouldn't it have looked that way to Augustus as well? Perhaps that was why Eugenie decided to hide these pages in the stone grooves of the window. The wonder is that she didn't destroy them altogether. Who would want a reminder of that moment? How must she have felt, then, when her husband chose that very scene to depict in the window that was supposed to honor her?

I remember that Christine said in her lecture that the reason the glass panes in the lady's loom didn't match the ones in the landscape scene in the window was because they'd been broken at the last minute. By whom? Could it have been Eugenie herself who broke them because they too clearly re-created that scene between her and Clare?

I pull out the pages that Christine had torn from Eugenie's notebook and find the sketches Eugenie did of the window. There on the loom is the scene from *The Drowning Tree*—the tree-woman hovering over the lily pool as another figure struggles in the water. I look up from the picture and meet my own gaze in the glass window—reflective now that it's fully dark outside—and realize what Augustus meant by designing the window as he did. The Lady of Shalott looks away from the shadows and sees the truth for the first time. He wanted Eugenie to acknowledge what she—and he, by not stopping her— had done all those years ago. They'd condemned Clare to a life of madness and then locked her up so they wouldn't have to live with the reminder of their sins. Only Augustus hadn't been able to forget Clare and he wouldn't let Eugenie forget either.

It's not a pretty story. And not a story Gavin Penrose would have wanted Christine to tell in her lecture. No wonder he agreed to take her across the river in exchange for leaving it out of her lecture.

As the train stops the lights in my car flicker and then go out. My reflection in the window is replaced by a clear view of the Rosedale Station, the figures on the platform emerging behind the dark glass like faces rising out of dark water. I remember that for Christine, too, the lights had briefly gone out before the train left. She would have looked for me and seen. . . .

Gavin Penrose.

For a moment I think I've conjured him up out of my speculations, but there he is—in the flesh—-standing on the platform.

Although there are half a dozen explanations for what Gavin might be doing at the station, what I suddenly fear is that Regula called and told him about my appearance at the gallery and that I'd accused him of stealing *The Drowning Tree* and then blurted out something about "the statue in the water." He knows I must have put the pieces together and he's waiting for me—just as he must have waited on the platform for Christine after I saw her off. I have no intention, however, of meeting him on the platform.

I PICK UP MY BAGS AND WALK THROUGH THE CARS, HEADING south until I've reached the last one. When I get off I immediately walk behind the train, crossing two sets of tracks and ducking behind the raised platform on the west side of the station.

I stop there, my heart beating so hard I think for a moment it's the vibration of an oncoming train. I used to walk the tracks all the time when I was in high school, but it's been years since I've done it and I've spent so much time lecturing Bea against the practice that I'm amazed that I'm still breathing at all.

Although I know that I should leave while the north-bound train is still obstructing the view from the opposite platform I'm curious to see if Gavin's still there and whether he's met anyone getting off the train. When the train pulls out I flatten myself against the edge of the platform and peer cautiously around the corner. At first I think the opposite platform is empty but then I see him, standing directly across from me, looking over the tracks and toward the riverfront park. The only reason he can't see me is because I'm in the shadow of the platform.

He takes out a cell phone and punches in a number. Maybe he was meeting someone who's missed the train, but then why would he be looking toward the park? How many of the people whom Gavin would be meeting are likely to have vanished into the park between the station and the glass factory? The answer is one: me.

The realization that my improbable suspicion may not be so improbable after all sets my heart to pounding once again. I'm trembling so hard now I'd like a Halcion myself, but then I realize that it's not me that's trembling, it's the ground. The southbound train is pulling into the station.

Whatever Gavin's doing at the station, I have no intention of running into him. As soon as the train stops I head toward the park, hoping that Kyle has stayed late at the boathouse. The building, though, is dark. Even the light on the landing is out. Kyle's often complained that the local teenagers use the park street lamps for target practice—much in the same way that kids threw stones at the factory windows when I was in high school.

I try the boathouse door—hoping that the lock's still broken from the break-in weeks ago—but the door won't budge. I notice that the fanlight above the door is broken and remember that once when I was in high school Carl and I got in that way, but I'd needed Carl to give me a boost up. I'm not getting in there on my own.

I start back toward the factory, figuring that I'll go in the side door, but when I approach the side of the building I can see that there's a car parked at the end of the alleyway between the station parking lot and the factory. It's hard to tell for sure, but it looks a lot like Gavin's Jaguar.

I quickly duck back into the shadows of the park and follow a narrow path that leads up to the train tracks directly behind the factory. There's a hole in the fence here that I discovered once when Paolo and Francesca took off after a squirrel and squirmed through, nearly giving me a heart attack when I saw them on the tracks. I'm not quite as slim as a greyhound but I suspect the hole was made by the same teenagers who like to break streetlights and I'm betting I'm not too much wider than they are.

This section of the park is just a narrow strip between the train tracks and the river. I can hear the water moving against the muddy banks as I work my way along the fence, feeling with my feet for the hole. The smell of the river is strong here, the ground beneath my sandals soft and damp. A vine, clammy with the day's humidity, brushes against my face and I'm reminded of the fat, swollen seaweed that Kyle tried to get me to eat weeks ago. The same dead-fish, low-tide smell fills the air, coating my throat and lungs, a smell that could drown you on dry land.

I'm tapping my foot against the fence when suddenly it goes through empty space and I trip, landing on both knees in the mud. It would be easy, I think, to sink into this mud and just cry but then I think of Bea and take a deep breath, holding it in while I press my face and chest into the mud and slither through the narrow opening in the chain-link fence.

I wipe the mud off my hands onto the back of my dress and listen for trains. When I'm sure that all I hear is the river, I cross over to the back of the factory, scanning the area first for any sign of Gavin, but there's no one. The loading dock is on this side, raised so that the crated glassware and windows could be loaded right onto the train beds. I climb up onto this first and then look up at the brick wall, trying to imagine where Neil found the handholds to scale the sheer surface.

After a few minutes of staring at the blank wall I realize how foolish I'd been to think that just because Neil found a way up to the roof I could, too. Especially in the dark. I'll have to chance going around to the front.

First, though, I sit down, my back to the loading platform wall and try to gather my strength. I look out through the trees toward the river, but it's so dark that I can't tell the water from the hills or the hills from the sky. Then, as I watch, a thin band of silver appears on the water, travels across the river and touches the opposite shore at just the spot where there's a break between the hills. The moonlight seems to cleave the hills in two and light up a winding stream between them just as the stream in the Lady window appears when the light shines through the glass.

I look back at the brick wall. Now that the moon has risen above the factory I can make out the pattern in the brick: a simple chevron motif created by a pattern of slightly protruding bricks. Leave it to Penrose never to leave well enough alone. Even the back wall of his factory had to have a decorative touch. Fortunately for me, it makes a perfect ladder. I climb it quickly, without giving myself time to think about the drop or the likelihood of crumbling brick, and pull myself over the railing onto my rooftop garden. The French doors are locked, but I put my hand carefully through the panel that Neil broke last night and open the door.

The loft is perfectly quiet. Too quiet I realize. There's no sign of the dogs. I'm trying to remember if I could have possibly left them out in the courtyard—surely not in this heat—when a shaft of moonlight comes through the skylight, brightening the room and glancing off the face of the man sitting at my kitchen counter.

CHAPTER THIRTY

"Neil! My God, you scared me half to death. What are you doing here?"

"We had a date, which I guess you've forgotten. I thought I'd surprise you by cooking dinner." He strikes a match to light one of my long, tapered candles and I see that the table is set for two. "Instead you surprise me by coming in through the roof." He looks at me and I can see his eyes widen as he takes in the mud on my dress.

"Where are the dogs?" I ask, crossing the room to the sink to wash my hands.

"I let them out in the courtyard. I figured they'd let me know when you came home. Juno, tell me what's happened. You're shaking like a leaf."

Instead of answering I splash water on my face and then, leaning over the sink, I lift my hair up and pour water down the back of my neck. I'd like to hold my head under the tap and run the cold water until the low-tide smell of the river is gone, but then Neil lays his hands on my shoulders and starts kneading the tensed muscles. I turn around so quickly his hands fly off my back like leaves whipped by a sudden wind.

"I know," I tell him, "about you and Christine. That you saw her all those times and you were sleeping with her. The baby was yours."

Neil bows his head—a quick duck that is almost like a man nodding off—and shuts his eyes.

"How did you think I wouldn't find out once the DNA test was done?"

"Slept with," he says, "I wasn't sleeping with her, I slept with her once. She told me that she was seeing someone else so I thought the baby was probably his."

"So you thought you might get away with lying to me. You still think you can lie to me."

"I'm not lying, Juno. It only happened that once. It's true we did see each other a lot back in March."

"But I thought Dr. Horace didn't give you her number until May?"

"He didn't, but I'd gotten in touch with her before that. I wanted to find out about you and Bea so she came up to The Beeches—and then she told me she was writing about the window and we started talking about Clare Barovier's paintings and the drug trial—"

"The drug trial?"

"Yeah. At first I thought she was asking because she wanted to know if I was really cured and whether I was going to stay cured or not. I got the idea she was . . . you know . . . interested in me. I knew she kind of liked me back in college."

Neil looks so bashful saying this that I nearly soften

toward him, but then remind myself of what happened next.

"So you were happy to reciprocate? I guess it's flattering to have an old flame come calling."

"Juno, I'd been in a mental hospital for fourteen years. It was flattering to have *anyone* come calling. Being with Christine reminded me of you—"

"Oh please, don't give me that crap. Like sleeping with my best friend was the next best thing to sleeping with me. That's not fair to me and it's not even fair to Christine."

Neil nods—again with that heavy dip of the head that looks as if he's having trouble keeping his eyes open. In the candlelight the dark circles under his eyes look cavernous. A man haunted. "No, it wasn't fair to her and I told her so right away—well, the next time I saw her anyway. I told her I didn't think we should see each other anymore because I still loved you and I still believed that you might love me again someday if I was really better. I had this silly idea that you couldn't be so beloved and be absolved from returning that love—"

"Wait, you said it just like that? In those exact words?"

Neil laughs. "What difference—?"

"Just tell me. What did you say to her exactly?"

"Well, it's embarrassing, but I quoted that line we liked so much in Dante class—what Francesca says: 'Love, which absolves no one beloved from loving.' I know it sounds stupid, but it always gave me hope."

"And what did she say?" My voice comes out hoarsely, barely a whisper.

"She said she thought I was right, that you and I had

been meant to be together from that first day we met at the Cloisters and that was what she'd always been jealous of—finding someone you were meant to spend your whole life with—because it had never happened to her. I think she realized then that it wasn't *me* she wanted but *us*. She wanted what the two of us had. She insisted that we could go on being friends without any physical relationship between us. She even said she'd try to find out the next time she saw you if you still felt anything for me. I guess she didn't have time."

"No, she did in a way. She asked me if I believed that line from Dante."

"And what was your answer?" Neil asks, lifting his hand to push away a strand of damp hair clinging to my neck.

"I told her I couldn't answer a question like that so quickly. I said I needed time to figure that one out."

"And did you?"

I remember full well the answer that came to me as her train pulled out of the station, but before I can tell Neil a low moaning wail cleaves the air around us. Even when I realize that it's one of the dogs I'm still chilled by the sound.

"Expecting anyone?" He says it with a smile that doesn't quite reach his eyes. In fact, his eyes, I notice now, have that same glazed look they used to get when he stopped sleeping. I recognize, too, the look of suspicion from his manic stages. He thinks it's Falco who's in the courtyard. I wish he were right.

"I saw Gavin Penrose at the train station and I had an

idea he might be waiting for me. I wanted to avoid him, but I didn't think he'd break into the factory. I don't know who else it could be though. Ernesto and my father are the only ones with keys and they're all the way up on Lake Champlain." I reach past him to the phone. "I think I'd better call the police."

"It's dead," he says as I lift up the handset. "I tried it while I was waiting for you."

I depress the on/off button, remembering that the line had gone down during the storm last night. I had assumed, though, that it would have been fixed by now, but Neil's right. The phone's dead.

"What would Gavin want with you?" Neil asks, following me over to the top of the spiral staircase.

"I went to Regula's gallery today and saw one of Penrose's paintings that I think Gavin is selling illegally—" I'm trying to find a way to see the door to the courtyard from the top of the stairs, but I can see only as far as the light table, where the partially assembled Lady window lies in shadow. Neil's so close behind me that I can feel his breath on the back of my neck as I lean over the iron railing.

"*The Drowning Tree?*" Neil asks. "Was that the painting?"

"How do you know?"

"Christine asked if I'd seen it at Briarwood. She said it was missing from the college. You think Gavin would have killed her because she found out he had stolen it from the college?"

"I don't know, maybe she just asked too many

questions about the painting and Gavin thought she was threatening him, while all she was trying to do was find out what happened among Augustus, Eugenie, and Clare a hundred years ago. There's a figure in the water in the painting and I saw a statue in the pool where Christine was drowned—"

"Under the weeping beech? Christine told me she read something in Eugenie's notebook about a statue in the sunken gardens at Astolat. She thought it was a re-creation of the scene from *The Drowning Tree* and she wanted to know if I'd ever seen it on the sketching trips I took with Dr. Horace, but we never went up the Wicomico to Astolat."

As if summoned into being by his mention of the stream, a bar of light lengthens over the the table, traveling up the rippled surface of the glass stream in the window. I take a step back and lose my balance when I bump into Neil. I nearly topple down the stairs but his hand catches in my hair and pulls me back. Something hard and cold grazes my shoulder and I see he's holding one of my large carving knives. In the darkness I can see his eyes glittering. He's ready to take on whoever's down there.

"Come on," I hiss, untwining his hand from my hair and pulling him toward the side door. Neil hesitates for a moment and then we both hear a sound like sandpaper as whoever is down below walks across a floor gritty with glass particles. It's a sound to set your teeth on edge and it seems to release Neil from his stasis, propelling him across the room and out the side door. On the landing outside he stops for a moment and slides the knife into his back pocket. Then he grabs my hand and pulls me down the stairs so quickly that the old rusted-out metal frame shakes and groans with our weight. When we hit the ground I start for the street, but Neil pushes me back against the wall and points toward the street.

The green Jaguar is still there. The windows are tinted, though, so I can't see if anyone's inside.

"That's Gavin's car," I whisper.

Neil nods and looks behind him toward the riverfront park.

"We'll be trapped if we go that way," I tell him. "No one's at the boathouse."

"Can we get into the boathouse?"

"It's locked, but I think you could get in through the fanlight if you could get up to it."

Of course any mention of a difficult height to scale only serves to inflame Neil's ardor to scale it. He sets off running toward the park and it's all I can do to keep up with him. It's not until we're at the boathouse that I can afford the breath to remonstrate with him.

"Neil, this is crazy. There are half a dozen better ways to get away from Gavin than taking to the water."

"But how many ways to prove he killed Christine? You think Christine went with him to find the statue under the beech tree, so if we find it we'll know why he was willing to kill her."

"But why do we have to do it tonight?" I ask. "Why not wait until the morning?"

"Because if Gavin gets there first he might destroy the statue."

I try to argue with him again, but he's already scrambling up the doorway and hoisting himself through the broken fanlight. I'm waiting to hear a crash as he hits the floor on the other side but instead there's only the click of the door unlocking. I push it open into empty space; Neil has already vanished into the shadows of the stacked kayaks.

There's an old metal desk a few feet from the doorway. I slide open the top drawer and feel around for the flashlight I know Kyle keeps there. When I switch it on I see the white underbelly of a canoe floating toward me.

"This one looks big enough for the two of us," Neil says, his voice echoing in the hollow hull.

"It's Kyle's two-man outrigger canoe," I tell him. "He brought it here from Hawaii." It's also named *Kingfisher* and it's Kyle's favorite boat, but I don't mention any of that to Neil; I'm too horrified at the thought of taking to the water in any boat with him. He's moving forward so quickly, though, that all I can do is follow—grabbing two life vests just in case I can't talk him out of it.

When was I ever able to talk Neil out of anything? I wonder, trailing him down to the sandy beach.

He's already got the canoe flipped over with the prow facing out into the river. He reaches for the life vest in my hand, but I hold it back.

"I can't, Neil. I can't get in that boat."

Neil's eyes meet mine—they have a glassy shine in the moonlight—and he nods. "I can understand," he says, "but unless you're more afraid of me than Gavin Penrose, you don't have any other choice."

I turn to look over my shoulder and see a figure approaching from the factory—the vague silhouette of a man who may or may not be Gavin Penrose. Who else could it be, though?

I turn back and look at Neil, his eyes holding mine. Although they still have that glassy shine I can see how much he loves me. "Okay," I say, handing Neil his life jacket. I slip mine on and stuff the flashlight into a zippered pocket. Neil pushes the boat into the water and waves for me to climb in. *He couldn't look at me with so much love and still hurt me,* I think as I wade into the river. But as the cold water washes over my ankles I remember that he'd looked at me much the same way the last time we were on the water—just before he'd tried to drown us both.

I'M GLAD AT LEAST THAT WE'RE IN THE OUTRIGGER CANOE because I know it's less likely to tip. The only problem with the *Kingfisher*, though, is that it's white, making us a visible target from the shore. I risk a look back, but the motion sets the boat rocking and I quickly face forward again.

"Anyone following us?"

"Not that I could see."

"Good. He might try to drive across the bridge and onto the estate, but it's a good forty-minute trip that way. If we paddle fast we should be able to get across the river in ten minutes. How far upstream was the beech tree?"

"Not far."

Neil picks up the pace and I have to concentrate to

keep up. I lock my eyes on the blade of his paddle as it dips into the water and try to imitate the exact motion. I'm surprised at how good he is at this and then I remember that he's had practice on those trips with Dr. Horace. He rotates his body just right to get the farthest reach on each stroke, burying the paddle blade deep into the water and pulling us smoothly across the river. Although I struggle to keep up with him I feel as if he's doing most of the work and that my stroke is only a faint echo of his—like I'm a bird soaring in his tailwind, moving easily in a current he's cleared for me. I relax a little and let the rhythmic push and pull of paddling calm my nerves.

Just put the water behind you, Kyle always tells his beginning kayakers, and I do. I feel the river sweeping under my paddle and out to the sea. I even take a moment to notice how beautiful it is to be out on the river in the moonlight, the path we're following lit up by white ripples on the water. It seems like no time at all before we've reached the other shore. Neil lifts up his paddle and holds it parallel to the water, letting us drift with the current while we scan the shore for the mouth of the Wicomico.

"Have you got that flashlight?" he asks.

I take the flashlight out of my life vest pocket and shine it over the water toward the shore. The beam of light picks up a steep, rocky bank and catches particles of quartz glittering on the rock face. A dead end. Could we have overshot the creek?

Just when I'm about to suggest we paddle upstream there's a break in the rock wall and the light vanishes under an arched canopy of weeping willows dark as an underground tunnel. I hadn't noticed during the day how overgrown the creek's mouth was or how narrow a passage it makes through the steep hills and overhanging trees.

"Don't worry about paddling," Neil says, steering the canoe into the narrow passageway, "just hold the light on the right side of the bank."

It's darker under the trees than out on the river in the moonlight. The beam of my flashlight briefly spotlights patches of river grass and thick-stalked irises that sway with the rhythm of Neil's paddle. I glimpse something black and oily slipping into the water and nearly drop the flashlight. Instead its beam pierces the dark water and glances off something white beneath the surface: a face looking up through the water with blind eyes.

I'd forgotten about the other statues. We pass the one of the crouching boy—Narcissus—and I realize we must be close. Still I'm not prepared for the yet deeper darkness as we pass under the branches of the weeping beech.

Neil backpaddles to keep us steady. "Is this it?" he whispers in a voice hushed with awe, as if we'd entered some medieval cathedral.

"This is where I found her." I shine the flashlight down into the water, sweeping the beam through the silty depths like a paddle. The illuminated water casts up rippling strips of light onto the branches above our head and for a moment the effect is so dazzling I forget why we've come. It's as if we're in an underwater cavern looking up through a streaming forest of phosphorescent seaweed.

"I think I see it," Neil says. "It looks like a statue that's toppled over into the water."

I hold the light steady on the white marble hand that had been threaded through Christine's hair when I found her.

"It looks like there's some kind of brass plaque attached to it," Neil says.

"There's something about a plaque in Eugenie's notebook," I say. "That might tell us what we need to know."

I look toward the shore, trying to see past the curtain of leaves, wondering how long it's been since we left the boathouse. As if reading my thoughts, Neil says, "We still have time. I'm going to try diving for it."

He takes off his life jacket and strips off his T-shirt, handing me the soft bundle of cloth.

"Hold the light on it," he tells me. He slips out of the boat and into the water as smoothly as that animal I saw on the shore a few minutes ago, but still the boat rocks and it takes me a moment to steady myself and aim the flashlight back on the statue. I can see Neil's face pressed close up to the plaque, his cheeks distended with held breath so that he looks like a personification of the wind in some Renaissance painting. When he comes up I breathe in and realize I'd been holding my breath, too.

"I can't read it," he gasps, "but it feels loose. I think the piece of statue it's attached to isn't that big. We could probably get it up if we did it together."

"Together?"

"The water's not cold at all," he says, splashing a little of it onto my leg. "And I can tie the towline around one of

these branches so the canoe won't drift. But if you don't
want to—"

"No, it's all right. It's not even that deep, right?"

Neil smiles. "That's my girl."

I take off my life jacket and stick the flashlight back in
its pocket but don't bother zipping it. Getting out of a
floating canoe is no easy feat. I swing my legs around and
dangle them into the water—which feels pretty damn
cold to me—but when I try to push myself off, the whole
boat tips and topples me ungracefully into the water along
with the life jackets and flashlight.

Neil dives and retrieves the flashlight and sticks it into
the waistband of his jeans, lit end up. Thankfully, it's an
underwater model so it's still working. The life jackets,
though, have drifted too far downstream to reach. He ties
the canoe to one of the branches of the beech tree that has
snaked over the brick wall and into the water.

"Okay?" Neil asks.

I nod, trying to conserve my breath.

"We'll dive on three," Neil says.

I take in a large breath on "two" and dive down,
following the beam of light coming from the flashlight. I
can see Neil's fingers working their way under the marble
and I plunge my hands into the muck, trying not to think
about what could be under there. We both pull up at the
same time and, amazingly, the lump of marble comes free.
We haul it up onto one of the submerged rocks from the
stone wall and come up for air.

"Okay, let's try to stand on this rock and get it onto the
bank," Neil says.

The rock is coated with algae and moss, making the footing treacherous. I slip the first time and stub my toe on the wall, but the second time we're able to get the slab of marble and bronze up onto the bank. We stand there for a moment, waist-deep in the water, panting. Then Neil pulls himself up onto the wall and, turning, offers me a hand up.

"The secret to eternal life better be inscribed on this plaque after all that trouble," Neil says, pulling the flashlight out of the waistband of his jeans. "I think it gave me a hernia."

"I'm so sorry to hear that," a male voice says, "but I thank you for retrieving my property."

I look up to an opening in the tree. Gavin Penrose is holding the branches back with one hand. In the other hand he's holding a gun aimed at us.

CHAPTER THIRTY-ONE

OUT OF THE CORNER OF MY EYE I SEE NEIL REACHING AROUND TO his back pocket where, I remember, he hid the carving knife. Gavin notices, too.

"Keep your hands where I can see them, Buchwald," he says, pointing the gun toward Neil. "I don't want to have to use this, although I'd certainly be within my rights shooting two trespassers."

"I don't think Detective Falco would see it that way," I say, inching a little closer to Neil. "I think he would find it a little suspicious that three people have died on your property."

"Three?" Gavin looks behind us toward the water.

"I mean Christine."

Gavin shrugs. "It's not my fault she came out here in the middle of the night to look at some chunk of marble. Is that it?" He points the gun toward the fragment of statue lying on the grass between us. I feel a little easier with the gun pointed away from me, but still I don't like the way he's waving it around.

He takes out a handkerchief and tosses it to me. "You're the restorer, Juno, why don't you have a go at cleaning off that plaque while your assistant here holds the flashlight for you and we'll see what Christine wanted to see so badly that she got herself drowned."

"Didn't she tell you what it was?" I ask, picking up the cloth and scrubbing at the mud-and-algae-covered plaque.

Gavin shakes his head. "She told me some ridiculous story about my grandfather and grandmother—how Augustus was really in love with Eugenie's sister all along, but he married Eugenie because she was the one with the money. As if that would be such a crime. She actually thought I'd care about her telling the world my grandfather married for money."

"But you argued with her about something before the lecture."

"She had some crazy ideas about my great-aunt Clare," he says. "I couldn't very well let her ravings get around. Haven't you finished with that yet?" he asks, impatiently waving the gun toward the plaque. I feel Neil, crouched beside me, tense up when Gavin directs the gun to me and I'm afraid that he'll try to rush Gavin and get himself killed. I vainly try to decipher the imprint of lettering engraved in the bronze, hoping now that it reveals nothing incriminating about Gavin's family and that Gavin will let us go. He hasn't, after all, confessed to killing Christine although everything he's said so far seems to be leading to that. I rub at the plaque harder, hoping that we'll be able to read it.

"I think I can make out something," I say, "a name."

Gavin steps closer and motions with his gun for Neil to aim the flashlight closer to the plaque.

"*For Clare*," I read. "It's just a commemorative plaque," I say, my voice shaking with relief. "Augustus only wanted to remember your great-aunt—"

"There's more," Gavin says, "another line."

I rub away the mud and algae and read the single word on the line below Clare's name. "*Beloved.*"

I look up at Gavin, his face an ugly mask in the glow of the flashlight. "So she was right after all," he says, "he did love her."

"I can't see how it matters now," I say, surprised at the tone of my voice. Who would have believed I'd end the night trying to comfort Gavin Penrose?

"It doesn't," he says, his voice hard again. "The rest of it is crazy. She came to me with this insane idea that not only had Augustus loved Clare in the beginning—when they first met in Kelmscott—but that he'd loved her all along. Even after she was locked away in Briarwood. That he visited her and took her here to Astolat and then—this is the craziest part—she had his child. Only the child was given away—"

"To the Webbs," I can't help myself from finishing. "Who worked at Briarwood. The little boy whom Augustus and Clare took on their boat trips to a 'palace on the river.' It was Christine's father."

"She was insane." Gavin is practically screaming now. At first I think he's still talking about Clare, but then I realize he's talking about Christine. All his rage seems to be directed toward her, but it's me he's screaming at, waving the gun in my face. I can feel every muscle in Neil's body tighten as he stares at the gun in Gavin's hand.

"She came to me with this story about missing babies and drowning statues and thought I'd open up my arms and welcome her into the family. Well, obviously I couldn't allow her to go around saying those things—"

I have no warning when Neil finally springs forward. One minute he's by my side, the next he's airborne, hurtling toward Gavin.

I pick up the flashlight Neil dropped and aim it at the two men struggling in the dirt, trying to make out which one's Neil and where the gun is, but then they roll under the heavy curtain of beech branches and out of my sight. As I get up to follow them I hear an explosion. The gun going off.

I part the branches, terrified at what I'll find on the other side, and breathe a sigh of relief. Gavin is crouched in the dirt and Neil's standing over him holding the gun.

"I should shoot the bastard," Neil says as I edge around a frightened, but unharmed, Gavin, "for threatening you."

When I'm close enough I put my hand on Neil's arm. "No, don't hurt him, we'll call the police."

"How? Neither of us has a phone."

Gavin moves his hand toward his jacket pocket and Neil lunges forward, pressing the gun into his temple. Even in the lurid glow of the flashlight I can tell that all the blood rushes out of Gavin's face. "I was just going to offer you the use of my phone," he says, his voice shaking.

Neil uses the muzzle of the gun to push Gavin's jacket open and nods when he sees the plastic cell phone sticking out of his shirt pocket. "Okay, give it to Juno," he says.

I take the phone from Gavin's hand—which is shaking so badly he nearly drops it.

"Call your friend Detective Falco," Neil says to me.

It's only after I've made the call that I wonder how he knew I'd know the number.

BY THE TIME NEIL AND I HAVE FINISHED GIVING OUR statements at the police station it's after three in the morning. Falco assures Neil and me that he's going to question Gavin further after we leave.

"But aren't you going to arrest him?" I ask. "He broke into the factory."

"Well, technically, since you're leasing your studio space from him he's legally within his rights to inspect the property if he thinks it's in danger. He claims he smelled smoke coming from the furnaces."

"Right," I say. "Then why was he coming into my studio? It's in a whole different part of the building."

"He says he only wanted to talk to you about some 'misapprehension' you were laboring under."

"And that's why he followed us to the estate?" Neil asks.

"It's his property," Falco answers, dragging a hand over his face. He looks almost as tired as Neil.

"He practically admitted to killing Christine," I tell Falco.

"Unfortunately it's your word against his and he claims he was only protecting his property."

"Does protecting his property include holding us at gunpoint while forcing Juno to clean that statue?" Neil asks. "He was raving like a lunatic." Neil smiles at me, a tired smile that barely creases his face. "And I should know what one sounds like. That gun could have gone off at any minute. I couldn't take that chance."

Falco shakes his head and puts his hand on Neil's shoulder. "No, you couldn't. You did the right thing." Neil shrugs but I can tell he's actually pleased with the commendation and I find myself absurdly grateful that Falco has realized that this is what Neil needed. "I promise I'll do all I can to get a confession out of him, but first I think I'd better get Juno home. She should get out of those damp clothes before she gets sick and you—" He bends down and looks closely into Neil's face. "—you look like you *are* sick. Can I get someone to take you back to The Beeches? Get a doctor to examine you?"

Neil does look horrible. The energy that sustained him through the night has evaporated, leaving a frail shell. His skin, under the station's fluorescent lights, looks positively yellow.

"I think he'd better come back with me," I tell Falco, "if he wants to, that is."

Neil nods and smiles—a weak smile that fades into a grimace. Falco looks away.

"All right, then, I'll give you both a lift back."

I thank Falco and then ask him one more favor. "The canoe we took from the boathouse was Kyle's favorite and we left it tied up on the creek beneath the beech tree. Do you think you could return it to him?"

WHEN WE GET BACK TO THE FACTORY THE FIRST THING I DO IS let the dogs out of the courtyard. I notice that as they head up the spiral stairs Francesca is limping and holding her front left paw up.

"That bastard Penrose, I bet he kicked her. I'll have to take her to the vet in the morning—" I stop when I notice that Neil has slumped into a chair and is shivering. "Why don't I draw you a hot bath," I say, realizing that I've got more to worry about than a hurt greyhound. Besides, the dogs have curled up together on the couch and Paolo is licking Francesca's paw. They look like they're taking care of each other.

When Neil gets into the tub I start to leave to put a kettle on for some hot tea, but he grabs hold of my hand and pulls me toward him.

"Don't go," he says. "You look like you could use a good soaking yourself."

He's right. I smell like mud and river water. I take off my dress and climb in. It's a big tub. I bought it from an old hotel up in Saratoga that was going out of business, which I suspected had once been a brothel. Neil moves over to one side so I can stretch out next to him. I dip my head back in the water and then rest my cheek on his shoulder. When the water starts to cool, I adjust the hot water faucet to a trickle and let the overflow drain pull out the excess water. I close my eyes and, lulled by the gurgle of the water and the warmth of Neil's skin, nearly fall asleep. Just as I'm drifting off, though, I feel water lapping against my face and it startles me awake. We could both drown in here, I realize, an ironic end to our adventures tonight.

I can't help but wonder what it was like for Christine in the end. Did she know that Gavin had given her an overdose of drugs? Was she frightened? How could she have gone with him when the things she had found out—about the illegal sale of the painting and the affair between Augustus and Clare—would be damaging to him if they got out?

"Why would she trust Gavin to take her across the river?" I say aloud to Neil.

He doesn't answer for a moment and I think he's asleep, but then he says, with his eyes still closed, "She thought she had found her real family. She thought Gavin would be as excited as she was to find out they were related."

"Do you think they were?" I ask. "I mean, do you really think Clare had a baby in the asylum that was adopted by the Webbs and it was Christine's father?"

"I don't know, but now I understand why she wanted to see Clare's file so badly."

"She did?"

"Yeah, she told me she'd found a way to get to Clare's file . . ." Neil half opens his eyes, uncovering a narrow slit of blue iris and yellowed whites. "She told me the last time we met . . ." His voice fades out and his eyes flutter closed. I sit upright so quickly that water sloshes over the rim of the tub and onto the floor.

"Neil? Are you okay?"

Again he takes a long time to answer and when he does his voice sounds as if it's coming from under the water. "Fine . . . just need to rest . . ."

Despite the infusion of hot water the tub has grown chilly. "I think we'd better get out," I tell him.

I get out first, put on a robe, and then help him, handing him a towel and leading him straight to the bed. He keeps his eyes closed until he's lying down and then his lids briefly flutter upward. The whites of his eyes are as yellow as the silver stain used in medieval windows. I have a sudden image of my mother toward the end of her life when the cancer had moved into her liver. Her skin and eyes had taken on the same yellow hue.

"Neil," I say, trying to keep my voice calm, "those blood tests you get every day. Do they test for liver damage?"

"Sure . . . and for 'medication compliance' . . . you know, to check that we're not tonguing the tablets."

"Uh-huh. And you've checked out okay?"

"Yeah, I guess. I'd have been taken off the trial if I didn't . . . like Daria . . ."

"Daria?"

"Daria Cohen. She was in the trial but she got sick . . . Dr. Horace said it was an . . . an . . . anomaly." Neil stutters on the word and is quiet again for so long I think he's gone back to sleep, but then he finishes in a barely audible voice, "He suggested she remove herself voluntarily . . . poor Daria."

I remember now where I've heard her name. She's the patient who killed herself the night before Christine's funeral. "Look," I say, "I think we should call someone—one of your doctors at The Beeches maybe."

Neil rolls his head back and forth on the pillow. "Dr. Horace always says to notify him if anything's wrong."

"It's four in the morning."

"That's okay . . . he says anytime . . . the number's in my wallet."

I find Neil's wallet in the pocket of his damp jeans, which lie crumpled on the bathroom floor. The nylon and velcro billfold is so slim I think for a moment that some things must have fallen out when he was in the water, but then I remember that this is the wallet of a man who up to a few months ago was in a mental hospital. He has a driver's license but no credit cards, no library card, no gym membership, or any of the normal accoutrements of modern life. Aside from his license there are only two pictures—a third grade class picture of Bea that I remember sending to Essie and a picture taken of me on our wedding day—and Dr. Horace's business card. The doctor's cell phone number has been written on the back.

As soon as I've got the card I remember that my phone is still dead.

I go back in the bedroom to pull on gym shorts, T-shirt, and sneakers, and to tell Neil that I've got to run up the street to Gal's to use the phone (I know that Annemarie comes in at four to start baking the bread for the day), but I can't rouse him. I can see the shallow rise and fall of his chest but instead of reassuring me the slight motion accentuates how his ribs show through the skin and how slight a dent he makes in the bed. As the slimness of his wallet suggested, he doesn't seem to have much invested in this world. I'm pretty much it.

I run all the way to Gal's and circle around to the back door. Annemarie's humming to a recording of Madame Butterfly—her favorite opera—and kneading a ball of buttery yellow dough. She's startled when she sees me, but she doesn't ask any questions as I reach for the phone and dial Dr. Horace's number.

He answers on the third ring, sounding surprisingly alert for this time in the morning. I tell him that Neil's at my place, that he seems very weak, and that his skin looks yellowish to me.

"I see," Dr. Horace says in the calm, objective therapeutic voice that always drives me crazy. I half expect that he's going to ask me how I feel about Neil turning yellow as a daffodil, but after a short pause he asks instead, "Are you at the factory?"

I answer yes, not wanting to go into the details of my phone being dead and the idiocy of not owning a cell phone.

"I'll be there in fifteen minutes," he tells me.

"Should I call an ambulance?"

"No, Juno, please stay calm. There's nothing to be alarmed about. Pieridine sometimes causes slight weakness and jaundice, but I've got something that will fix him right up. Just keep him warm and don't say anything to agitate him."

Although I'd normally resent Dr. Horace's paternalistic tone I find it reassuring that he's not more alarmed about Neil's condition. When I hang up, Annemarie, who's brushed the flour off her hands, asks if there's anything she can do. I'm tempted to ask her to pray, but I don't want to sound melodramatic. Besides, I know it's not necessary to ask.

I run back to the factory and up the outside stairs to the side door, which I'd left open. Neil's still asleep. He's breathing, but it seems to me that his breath is even shallower. Francesca has crawled up into the bed with him and lain her head across Neil's legs. Poor Paolo follows me as I pace back and forth between the bedroom and the open side door, which is where I told Dr. Horace to come. He cleaves to my side as tightly as if I were Francesca. Twice, when I turn too quickly, he stumbles for lack of ballast and whimpers in a way that tears at my heart, but also sets my nerves on edge. It occurs to me that Francesca will be in Dr. Horace's way, so I decide to take both dogs back down to the courtyard even though I feel bad making Francesca walk on her injured paw. When I've gotten them settled I turn back at the door and see that Francesca has lain down, but Paolo is making a lonely circuit of the courtyard in an off-balanced lope. I can't help thinking that if Neil doesn't survive I'll be no better off than Paolo—alone and leaning into the void.

CHAPTER THIRTY-TWO

WHEN I GET BACK UPSTAIRS DR. HORACE IS STANDING NEXT TO the bed, taking Neil's pulse. He shakes his head at me when I start to ask him a question. I sink down onto the bed in a spot still warm from Francesca. I'd like to lay my head across Neil's feet like she had, but instead I clasp my hands in my lap, pressing my thumb into my left wrist and counting my own pulse beats.

"How is he?" I ask as soon as Dr. Horace drops Neil's wrist.

In true Freudian analyst style, he answers my question with a question. "What on earth has he been doing to get him into this exhausted state?"

Dr. Horace is looking at me as if I'd taken out an old horse and beaten him into a gallop until he dropped. I look toward Neil as I explain, as briefly as I can, the events of the last few hours. I leave out lots of details but still I cringe as I realize the enormous physical exertion Neil had undertaken in my behalf.

"—and then he tackled Gavin Penrose and got the gun away from him—"

Dr. Horace shakes his head and clicks his tongue against the roof of his mouth. I'm surprised his first comment is not a reprimand for leading Neil on this wild escapade. "And the police think Gavin Penrose killed Christine?"

"Well, there's not enough evidence yet," I say hurriedly, far more interested at this point in Neil's prognosis than in who killed Christine. "But there's no doubt that Gavin was angry about Christine's claim that she was related to him."

Dr. Horace shakes his head and opens up a leather satchel he's brought with him. "I'm afraid that's probably a delusional fixation of Christine's. Clare Barovier couldn't have had a baby while residing at Briarwood—the very idea is preposterous. I'm only sorry that you dragged Neil into this wild-goose chase of hers." He takes out a syringe and a glass ampule filled with an amber-colored liquid. "I'm going to give him a mild stimulant to boost his circulation and purge the toxins from his system. He should be fine given some rest, but I'm afraid this will mean he's out of the trial—"

"Well, obviously the drug's not agreeing with him."

"The Pieridine requires a regimen of rest and proper diet to work properly. Neil signed an agreement to follow certain guidelines in order to be in this trial and now he's disqualified himself. You can blame the drug if you like, but I blame you and Miss Webb. If she hadn't stolen Clare Barovier's file—"

"How did you know she stole the file?" I ask, hoping to avoid a lecture on my "bad behavior." My question is more effective in staunching his tirade than I'd expected.

In fact, he's so startled by it that the ampule he's holding slips from his fingers and rolls under the bed.

"Damn," I say, getting down on my hands and knees and sticking my head under the bed to look for it. "Was that the only one you had?"

"No, I have plenty."

"Good, because I can't find—" I pull my head out from under the bed and look up to find Dr. Horace holding not another drug ampule, but a gun. It's the second time I've had a gun pointed at me tonight, but I find I haven't gotten used to it at all.

"What's going on?" I ask, as if imagining that this sudden intrusion of a firearm will have some medicinal explanation.

"Do you have any tape?" he asks, ignoring my question.

"Tape?"

"You must use it in packing your windows."

"Uh, yeah . . . I've got some down in the studio."

"Good, let's go." He waves the gun in no particular direction, but I realize he means that I should head out of the bedroom and down the spiral stairs.

"I don't understand," I say as he follows me down the stairs, "what did I say?" And then I know. Clare's file. In my recounting of the night's events I hadn't mentioned Neil's suspicion that Christine had stolen Clare Barovier's file.

I try to think a little more carefully about what to say next as I rummage through the supply drawers for tape, deliberately choosing for last the drawer I know it's in.

I open the last drawer and hand him a roll of thread-reinforced packing tape and ask him the only question I can think of: "Why are you doing this? What could have been so important in Clare's file?"

"It's not Clare's file I'm worried about," he says, taking the tape with one hand and waving me back to the stairs with the gun held in the other. "That wasn't the only file she took. She could never leave well enough alone. It was part of her obsessive-compulsive behavior . . ." Dr. Horace continues his analysis of Christine's psychological flaws as he follows me up the stairs. "When she kept coming back to the hospital I thought it was just her obsession with the paper she was writing on the window. I gave her most of Clare Barovier's records and let her spend hours in the tower suite looking at her paintings, but that wasn't enough. She got into the records room by stealing her aunt's key—I don't blame Amy, she didn't seem to know anything about it—and stole private papers that belonged to the hospital. I thought they were all from Clare Barovier's files, but then I realized she'd also tampered with Neil's files. At first I thought that was just part of her romantic obsession with Neil—oh yes, don't act surprised." I've only paused because we've gotten to the foot of the bed and what I'm surprised at is that Neil—although he's still lying with his eyes closed—seems to have moved a good foot to the right. Dr. Horace is too busy ranting to notice, only interrupting his story long enough to order me to tape Neil's hands together, which I do, being careful not to disturb the metal nail file that Neil has managed to get off my nightstand and hide in the palm of his hand.

"The disgusting thing I realized after years of listening to Neil talk about the three of you is how you pushed them together. Did it validate your own feelings for Neil to see Christine's attraction for him? Or were you sublimating your own homoerotic attraction for Christine?" Dr. Horace pauses and looks up from Neil's bound hands. He actually seems to expect an answer.

"We were friends," I say. "They were—are—the two people I care most about in the world. I just wanted them to like each other."

Dr. Horace laughs. "My dear, if we had time we could explore the Oedipal family drama you so elaborately created, but I'm afraid your hour's up." He switches the gun to his left hand and takes out another syringe and ampule.

"That's not really fair," I say, wondering how he plans to fill the syringe with one hand. "You've done most of the talking."

He manages to stick the syringe into the ampule and fill it while still aiming the gun at me. I look away only when he jabs the needle into Neil's arm. I hate to admit it, but I'm relieved the needle wasn't for me.

"Another stimulant," he informs me. "This should get him going."

"Are you sure it's not too much—" I stop, realizing how stupid the question is. Clearly Neil's health is no longer Dr. Horace's prime concern. And that's when the pieces all fall together.

"The trial," I say, knowing I'm only digging a deeper hole for myself, but knowing, too, that's it's too late to feign ignorance. "That's what Christine found in Neil's files. His blood tests would have shown that his liver enzymes were elevated unless—"

"Unless I tampered with the results? Well, yes, of course. But let me tell you this, Juno, aside from Neil and Daria Cohen only a few other patients have had significant liver damage. It's enough to prevent the FDA from approving the drug even though thousands of mentally ill patients will probably tolerate the drug perfectly well and benefit enormously from it. You've seen the change in Neil—would you have denied him the lucidity he's had this last year because a few people can't handle the drug?"

I've never been a big fan of the "sacrificing the individual for the common good" credo, but it occurs to me that this might not be the ideal time to debate ideological differences with the doctor. "So what you're saying is that Neil could voluntarily drop out of the trial so as not to skew the results. That's what Daria did, right? Only she was so distraught that she killed herself." I'm talking quickly, hoping that I've got it right and that Daria won't turn out to be another victim of Dr. Horace's. "Okay. That makes sense to me. So Neil drops out."

Dr. Horace smiles. "I'm glad you see it my way, Juno, but I'm afraid it's too late for that. I can't expect you both to stay quiet about my role in Christine's death. I'm afraid that Neil will be dropping out of the trial in a far more dramatic fashion."

Neil's eyelids have begun to flutter open. Dr. Horace

nudges him with the muzzle of the gun. "Come on, Neil," he says in a surprisingly gentle voice, "we're going to take a little boat trip."

DR. HORACE LINKS HIS LEFT HAND THROUGH NEIL'S BOUND arms and has me lead the way to the boathouse. The sky is still dark, but I guess from the sounds of the birds that it's almost dawn. I try to look over my shoulder to the eastern sky, but Dr. Horace barks angrily at me, "No looking back" and does something to Neil that makes him cry out.

I stare straight ahead, feeling like Orpheus leading Eurydice up from the gates of hell, only we're going in the wrong direction: into hell itself. A thick fog is rising from the river, making it look like the boiling waters of the Styx. Even if the sun rises when we're out on the water, the fog will cover us from view. No one will see us. Dr. Horace will make it look as if Neil finally achieved what he tried to do fourteen years ago: drowning us both in the river. The worst part of it is that Bea will be left believing that her father killed her mother and then took his own life. It would be better, I think, to force Horace to shoot us here. He might still try to make it look like Neil shot me, but I'd be leaving Detective Falco with a little more to work with.

I can't make myself do it, though. I trudge on, trying to make myself believe I'm buying us more time—that there will be some way to escape when we're on the water—but when Dr. Horace opens the boathouse and orders me to drag out an old wooden rowboat I have to admit that it's plain cowardice that keeps me from bolting.

As if reading my thoughts Dr. Horace tells me, once we're in the boat with him and Neil seated in the stern, and me rowing, that I've got nothing to worry about. "I've prepared a sedative for both of you so you'll be unconscious when you go in the water, just like Christine was. You won't feel a thing. Poor Neil here will hardly need much of a shot at all." In spite of the injection Dr. Horace gave him, Neil hardly seems able to keep his eyes open.

"Won't the drugs show up in our autopsies?"

"Yes, that's why I'm using a common sedative that Neil had access to at The Beeches. I'll have to hurry on back there and break into one of the meds cabinets, but since Neil had a history of using intravenous drugs—"

"No, he doesn't! Neil never shot up."

"He does now, my dear. According to his chief psychologist."

"Is that how you got the drugs into Christine?" I ask. I can just make out through the fog the dim outline of the shore as a faint light creeps over the water from the eastern bank. Maybe if I can keep Dr. Horace talking a little bit longer the sun will burn off the fog and some early morning fisherman or kayaker might see us. "Did you inject her with the same drugs you knew she had prescriptions for?"

"No, I put them in her coffee. When I met her at the station—yes, I was right behind you but you never noticed me or Christine when she got off at the far end of the track—I had a thermos of her favorite coffee from Gal's with plenty of amaretto to mask the taste of the drugs. She never suspected a thing. In fact, she would have drunk the whole thermos before we got in the kayaks and passed out before we got across the river if I hadn't made her save some for later."

"But then she must not have thought you knew that she'd found out anything about the trial, or she wouldn't have gone with you—" A thought occurs to me. "Are you sure she did know?"

"She stole a page from Neil's file with his blood test records on it. It was one of the early records when his liver enzyme levels were just beginning to elevate and I hadn't bothered to change anything, but I know she would have put it together eventually. And then when I heard her lecture—no, of course you didn't see me, I was in one of the upper galleries behind the shelves—I saw how she paused when she mentioned Briarwood."

I remember that I thought she had paused to spare me the reminder of Neil's institutionalization and that later Gavin told me he thought the pause meant that she had acceded to his request to leave out certain details about his great-aunt's madness. We had all read our own shameful secrets into that pause—but only one of us was crazy enough to commit a murder on the strength of that suspicion.

As Dr. Horace loads a syringe with liquid—this time the fluid is clear as glass—I realize that he's insane. How hard would it be, I wonder, to lunge across this short space and overpower him? I start to slide one of the oars out of its lock, but as I do I see Neil looking straight at me, his eyes clear and alert. He silently mouths a word that I can't make out.

"Ladies first," Dr. Horace says, rising slightly on bent knees and leaning toward me with the syringe poised above my left arm. As soon as he's moved in front of him, Neil raises his taped hands and brings them down over Dr. Horace's head, jerking his bound hands into his sternum so sharply the syringe flies out of his hands. The gun fires into the bottom of the boat, releasing a fountain of splinters and water. I fall backward into the prow and when I open my eyes an instant later I'm looking straight into the barrel of the gun. I lift my eyes from the gun to Neil, who's trying to stab the doctor's hand with the nail file, but he's not able to make Dr. Horace drop the gun. The minute our eyes meet Neil throws his body to the right, taking him and Horace over the side and into the water.

I lean over the side but there's nothing but a series of concentric circles to mark where they went down. I aim for the center of the circles and dive, holding my eyes open even though the salt water stings them. For a moment all I see is blackness and then, as the morning light pierces the water, I see them, so wrapped around each other that they look like one body with two heads. A horrible monster sinking into the abyss.

Part of that creature is Neil, though. I surface briefly to fill my lungs and then plunge down again, arrowing my body toward the bottom of the river. And just as I'm running out of air a hand reaches out of the gloom and grabs me by the hand.

It's Dr. Horace. I clasp his arm with my other hand and start pulling back to lift him and Neil up to the surface but he pulls me down. I'm looking straight into his eyes and I can see he's completely out of his mind. Neil's eyes, though, which look out at me from behind Dr. Horace, look completely sane. He knows exactly what he's doing when he corkscrews his body with such force that the water rushes around me like a whirlpool and I see them both sinking down into the depths of the river as I'm pushed back to the surface.

I gulp air and dive down again, but no matter how deep I go I see only blackness. I rise to the surface and dive again . . . and again, and again, but I can't find them. Even when I mean to keep on going down into the dark something leads me back into the air and light. After a while I can't tell the difference. The dark water is lit with stars and explosions like fireworks, and the sky above is fretted with dark bands that ripple and wave across the silver skin of the river like banners in a medieval pageant. They're coming for me across the river on silver boats. Neil and Christine and Eugenie and Clare and Augustus— coming to tell me that there's no difference at all. Above the water or below. The surface of the water is a silver mirror reflecting the silver window of the sky. It's all silver light spreading as far as the eye can see, a mirror reflecting a window. What difference does it make which side I'm on?

Still I wait. All but one of the boats has vanished and now I can see that it's not a boat at all, but a pure white bird skimming the surface of the waves, its wings tilting first to one side and then to the other. I have only to wait for its touch to transform me into a bird as well and then we'll ride the waves together forever on a sea becalmed by the transformation of our undying love.

CHAPTER THIRTY-THREE

I STAYED IN BED FOR A WEEK AFTER THEY BROUGHT ME HOME from the hospital and I would have stayed longer if I hadn't awoken one morning to the sound of hammering. I'd been dreaming that Ernesto and my father were building me a coffin out of glass—like Snow White's—and when I opened my eyes I could look out through the clear lid and see Bea standing over me crying. That got me out of bed and down the spiral stairs into the studio.

I found that the coffin they were making wasn't for me, but for the lady. While I'd lain in bed, my father, Ernesto, and Robbie had finished the restoration without me and now they were crating the window to take it back to the college. The window would be reinstalled in time for the dedication ceremony the day after Labor Day.

"Good riddance," I say to the wooden pallet covering the Lady's face. I've developed a real animosity toward the lady in the window. If I hadn't gotten Christine the lecture appointment, she wouldn't have gone up to Briarwood to research the lady's antecedents and she and Neil would still be alive. I wish I'd never seen her face.

Ernesto and my father exchange looks while Robbie busies himself drawing arrows on the crate to indicate which side is up.

"I talked to Beatrice yesterday," my father says with studied casualness. "She's coming home on Tuesday." I feel a pang of reproach that manages to pierce through the general malaise of guilt that hovers around me like a noxious gas. I'd let my father make the call to Bea explaining that Neil was dead. I hadn't even remembered when she was coming home.

"She has a lot of questions that I didn't really know how to answer," my father says.

"And you think I do?" I glare at my father, daring him to tell me how to explain to Bea that her father was killed by the very man who'd been entrusted with his health and well-being all these years.

"That nice Italian police officer came by yesterday," he says, looking away. "He said that when you were ready he had some things to tell you. Maybe he can give you an idea what to tell Bea . . ."

My father's holding out one of Falco's business cards, but I don't take it. I don't have to. I still remember the number.

WHEN I CALL, FALCO SAYS HE'LL PICK ME UP. "WE CAN TALK IN my car on the way."

"On the way where?"

"I'll explain that on the way, too."

He hangs up before I can object. I agreed to meet with him to get my father off my back, but I hadn't bargained on a road trip, which means actually getting dressed and leaving the factory. I consider calling back and telling him not to come, but aside from the fact that he probably wouldn't listen, I have to admit I owe him. If he and Kyle hadn't come for me in the outrigger canoe, I would have drowned.

When he came to see me in the hospital he told me that after he'd dropped Neil and me off at the factory he'd gone back across the river to retrieve Kyle's outrigger canoe from the Penrose estate. On his way to the boathouse, though, he'd stopped to pick up a cup of coffee at Gal's. Annemarie had told him that I'd been in to call Dr. Horace because Neil was sick, so he'd gone by the factory. When he couldn't find us there he went to the boathouse, where he met Kyle—just coming in for an early morning tour he was giving to a singles group from the 92nd Street Y. He'd asked Kyle if he'd seen me or Neil or Dr. Horace.

"When I mentioned Horace's name, Kyle turned as white as a dead fish. He spilled his guts—that he'd been trading stock for Dr. Horace in a drug company and he was afraid it might have something to do with Christine's death. When he saw that the rowboat was gone he had that canoe in the water so quick it was all I could do to hop aboard. My arms still ache from trying to keep up with his paddling."

Falco told me that Kyle had cut a deal with the SEC in exchange for providing information on the transactions and that his efforts to rescue me would be taken into consideration at his hearing. He'd even dived for Neil and Dr. Horace, but without any luck. Their bodies, still wrapped together, were found a week later in a cove just south of the Tappan Zee Bridge. Falco had come to see me when they found the bodies.

I'm waiting outside the main door when he pulls up in front of the factory. I'd just as soon get right in the air-conditioned car to get out of the heat—the erratic stormy weather of July has settled into the kind of hot, humid August weather that makes one long for the crispness of autumn—but he parks and gets out. He's dressed more casually than I've seen him before—in jeans and a yellow Polo shirt—so I guess he must consider this an off-duty call. Then I notice that he's carrying a soft black leather messenger bag and I remind myself that this is a man who's never completely off duty.

"I thought we'd have coffee at Gal's first," he says. "I have some things I want to show you."

I turn without comment and start walking toward the cafe. I half suspect this whole outing is part of a scheme he's cooked up with my father to get me back into the routines of daily life. I remember that after Neil was put in Briarwood, Christine would come up here from the city with little made-up errands: looking for old furniture at the Salvation Army or going to an old church to look at some window she was writing a paper on. My father kept losing workers and needing "a hand" on one job or another. And of course, there had been Bea, only a toddler at the time, needing so much.

Eventually the demands of daily life had filled in the cracks Neil's absence had left behind, just as my dad and Ernesto had poured epoxy into the fire-damaged windows up at St. Eustace's to keep them from falling apart. But the cracks were still there and it was unlikely that those windows would survive another disaster. The question was, could I?

As soon as I walk into Gal's, Portia comes out from behind the counter and throws her soft, damp arms around my neck. She smells like almonds and hot milk.

"*Zia*, we're all so sorry about Uncle Neil." *Uncle Neil?* I can't remember anyone in my family calling him that before. "Is it true he saved your life?"

I look into Portia's wide brown eyes and past her to her friend, Scott, who's sitting at a little metal table, writing in a notebook between sips of espresso. In his black jeans and black T-shirt all he needs is a beret to complete the picture of Hemingway-writing-in-a-cafe. He steals a look up at me and blushes. They've talked about me, I realize, and about what happened on the river. Neil and I have become for them one of the romantic stories they read about, like Francesca and Paolo or Halcyone and Ceyx. The only difference is that those lovers always died together or at least transformed into some shape that bound them together for eternity. What am I still doing here?

Fortunately, Annemarie comes out and rescues me from Portia's well-meaning, but unnerving, adulation. She seats us at an out-of-the-way table and brings us cappuccinos (I ask for a plain one—I've lost my taste for amaretto) and biscotti. When she leaves us, she smiles at Falco and calls him *Danieli*.

"Wow, I'm impressed," I tell him. "Annemarie doesn't warm up to just anyone like that."

Falco shrugs and takes a sip of his coffee, which leaves a mustache of foam on his upper lip. *What nice lips*, I find myself thinking, and then blush just like Portia's teenaged boyfriend.

Falco wipes his mouth with his napkin and lays the leather bag on the table between us. "Recognize this?"

It's a plain leather bag—good quality, a little fancier than what I'd expect a police detective to carry, and while it doesn't look exactly feminine, it's the kind of item that could be worn equally well by a stylish man or woman. When he unzips it, though, I recognize the silk jacquard lining embossed with the logo of an Italian luggage maker.

"It's Christine's," I say. "She had it with her when I put her on the train."

"Yes. We found it locked in one of Dr. Horace's file cabinets. Apparently he hadn't figured out yet how to dispose of it safely."

He takes out a manila file folder and slides a sheet of paper across the table. It appears to be a page taken from some kind of medical report—a badly Xeroxed form with spaces for dosage amounts and blood counts, a series of numbers and dates that mean nothing to me. I realize, though, that this must be the page of blood results that Horace failed to alter and that Christine stole from Neil's file. On the bottom of the page is a larger blank left for "comments." Scribbled here, in handwriting I recognize as Dr. Horace's, is a progress report on Neil's condition.

> *Patient has shown tremendous improvement under drug therapy. He no longer represents a threat to himself or others. It's recommended that he be placed in a less-supervised setting, with the expectation that he will someday resume a normal life.*

I lay the page down and push it back toward him carelessly into a puddle of spilled coffee. "Thanks, but I don't see what good this is to me now." It's like getting an invitation after the party's over.

"I thought you'd want to know why Christine stole the file in the first place."

He unpeels a bright yellow Post-it note from the inside of the folder and hands it to me. *Show Juno,* it says. "She wanted you to know that Neil was better."

"She almost did show it to me," I say, remembering that she'd reached into her bag at the station, "but then she changed her mind."

"Do you know why?"

"I think because I told her I never wanted to feel for anyone what I had felt for Neil." I look away from him because my eyes have filled with tears. "She stole this page from Neil's file so she could show me that Neil was better. Neil had told her that he still loved me. She was trying to give us a second chance . . . Damn . . ."

I cover my face with my hands. I hear the scrape of Falco's chair and when I uncover my face he's got a glass of water for me and a clean white linen napkin that's been soaked in cold water and wrung out like the cold compresses my mother would press to my forehead during childhood fevers.

"And that's why Horace killed her. Because she stole that page from Neil's files and it has the original blood work on it before he tampered with the results."

Falco nods. "Amy Webb says that she misplaced her keys a few months ago when Christine was visiting and then they showed up a few hours later. Christine must have had copies made."

"She was always an overzealous researcher," I say, trying to smile, but the effort of moving my lips makes me sob again.

"Her interest in Clare Barovier wasn't merely academic. I had a long talk with Gavin Penrose—"

"About Christine thinking she was related to him? Gavin said something about that at Astolat, but I wasn't sure if it was true or not. It sounded kind of crazy . . ."

"Well, I think I understand how she came to the idea. Here—this is the page she took from Clare Barovier's file."

He takes out another piece of paper and hands it to me. It's another patient progress report, only this one is much older—a yellowed page of typescript dated December 18, 1923 and signed by a Dr. Peabody, who, I remember, was Dr. Horace's predecessor at Briarwood. I read the comments written on the bottom of the page.

Clare Barovier has made an excellent and unforeseen recovery since her surgery. I attribute this improvement

to the removal of her uterus. Patient has seemed quite
logical and calm since the operation, and has finally
given over her long-held obsession with her lost baby

"Lost baby?"

"That's what led Christine to believe that Clare had had
a baby—Augustus's baby—in the asylum and that it had
been adopted by the Webbs. It makes sense when you
remember the stories Christine's father told about taking
those boat trips as a boy. And then when Christine found
out she was pregnant—"

"Amy said that Christine was asking a lot of questions
about the family history. She thought it was because
Christine was pregnant."

"It was. When she found out she had Tay-Sachs she
wanted to know how the Protestant, English Webbs came
by an Eastern European hereditary disease. She thought
that maybe Clare's father was Jewish."

"The drawing teacher that Eugenie and Clare's mother
eloped with. And was he?"

Falco shrugs. "I have no idea. Nor do the Webbs have
any idea where the gene could have come from."

"So after all Christine's efforts the whole thing is still a
mystery."

"That part, yes, but there's a piece I think I've figured
out. Only I need your help."

"My help?"

"Yes, it's right up your alley—a little restoration job
I've been working on with a friend of yours."

We drive across the river and head south on Route 9W.

It doesn't take me long to realize where we're going and the knowledge breaks the fragile thread of interest revived in me by Falco's revelations. When we turn into the main gate at The Beeches, the color of the copper-red trees is almost too painful to look at. I feel as if it's my blood draining out from my body and seeping into the humid, hazy air. I slump down in my seat and close my eyes while Falco asks the groundskeeper to unlock the inner gate to the estate.

"Gavin's been most cooperative," he says, as we drive through the gate. "He's hoping the local police will put in a good word for him when his case comes up for trial. And he'll need it. Aside from *The Drowning Tree*, he sold a Rubens and two Hudson River school landscapes. When Joan Shelley found out she called off the engagement. You know he's resigned the presidency of the college."

"No," I say, half opening my eyes to sneak a look at the woods we're driving through. We've passed the copper beech grove and are driving on a wide, curving road lined with sycamores. "I didn't know that."

"Yep, I hear that Professor Umberto Da Silva is going to act as interim president while the Board of Trustees conducts a search."

"The college could do a lot worse than to keep him; he'd be a fine president," I say, thinking of Professor Da Silva's regal Roman bearing and his kindness.

"I hear he's going to preside at the dedication of the window in September."

I turn toward Falco, whose profile against the dappled green of the sycamores is pretty regal itself. "You hear quite a bit, don't you? Since when are you so involved in the affairs of the college?"

He half turns his head toward me and smiles. "This case has given me a new interest in the town . . ." He seems like he's going to say something else, but a sudden jolt draws his attention back to the road. The drive has come to an abrupt end at a bare, grassy rise above the river. Falco brakes and turns off the engine and we both stare ahead for a moment at the scattered stones and crumbling walls that mark the ruins of the old estate.

"Astolat," Falco says. "There's not much left is there?"

I shake my head.

We get out and Falco leads me down the hill, through the crumbling terraces populated by broken urns and overgrown garden beds, toward the stream and the weeping beech tree. Approaching it from higher ground, the tree looks like a giant shaggy animal grazing at the water, a saber-toothed tiger, perhaps, come to drink at a primeval watering hole, the bank of which is littered with the bleached white bones of its prey. Not bones, I see as we get closer, but pieces of marble laid out on the bank. Two men are bending over them.

One of the men straightens up and waves and I recognize Nathan Bell. He shakes Falco's hand and then, when I put my hand out, pulls me into an awkward hug. "I'm so glad you convinced her to come," he says to Falco. "We found another piece of the second figure today and it works to link the two together. It's beginning to make sense."

"The second figure?" I ask.

"Come look," Nathan says.

The marble pieces have been arranged on the grass like pieces of a jigsaw puzzle. It's like looking at a stained-glass window before the pieces are soldered together, only because the final project here is three-dimensional it's harder to read. Nathan crouches in the grass and touches each piece, explaining how they fit together, until slowly a picture of the two statues emerges.

The first figure half stands, half crouches, her arms thrown back as if to catch her balance. Her hair falls over her head, covering her face. In among the strands are leaves.

"What are these ridges?" I ask, fingering the rough surface of the marble.

"Bark," Nathan says. "She's turning into a tree, just like Bernini's Daphne."

"Or like the figure in *The Drowning Tree*."

"Right. We think it stood on the wall, right at the edge of the water above the second statue. It's exactly like the scene in *The Drowning Tree*. Two women, one turning into a tree, the other below her in the water."

"It re-creates the moment Eugenie told Clare that she was going to marry Augustus and she tried to drown herself," I tell Nathan and Falco. "I read about it in Eugenie's diary."

Nathan nods. "That may be, but I don't think the one in the water is trying to drown herself. Look—"

Nathan points to another group of fragments. There's only a piece left of the face: a sliver of nose and eye, half a mouth opened in midscream. The expression in the one eye is of terror and . . . something else . . . pleading, I think. One arm is extended, the fingers splayed, as if reaching toward the figure on the shore for help. The other arm is wrapped around a piece of the statue's torso, clutching loose folds of drapery that fall over her stomach. The gesture reminds me of something from Eugenie's diary.

"When Clare finished telling her story about the drowning tree," I say, "Eugenie asked if the story was from Ovid."

"Another woman fond of her myths," Falco says, shaking his head.

"Yes, Clare sounded impatient, too. She told Eugenie, 'Not everything's from a book' and then she said . . ." I close my eyes, trying to remember the words from the diary and picture instead the scene it described. Clare, crouched at the edge of the water below her sister, holding one hand over her belly—"She said, 'Here's life, whether you see it or not.' She was telling Eugenie that she was pregnant and that it was Augustus's child. God, it must have killed Eugenie."

"Enough to make her push her sister in the water," Falco says.

I shake my head. "No . . . I don't know . . . I think Clare did step into the water herself, but she must have thought Eugenie would save her. She was her big sister, always looking out for her, even if she was sometimes a little overbearing. But then Eugenie just stood there. She did nothing to save Clare. If Augustus hadn't come along—I bet he was hiding someplace nearby to see how the interview went—she might have drowned. By the time he got her out of the water, though, she was having a miscarriage. Eugenie's diary says her body was *drenched and bleeding.*"

"Poor Clare," Nathan says, looking down at the fragments of marble scattered on the grass. We're all silent for a few moments, gazing on the white stones glistening in the sun like bones left over from some awful carnage.

I WAS LATE FOR THE LECTURE.

I almost didn't go.

I had sworn that I'd never look at the lady in the window again, but I felt I owed it to Christine to look at the window one more time, now that it had been put back together the way it was meant to be. Besides, Bea wanted to go and I didn't want her to go alone.

The day was overcast. I was glad for that. I didn't want to see the light shining through the glass and casting lozenges of bright color onto the speaker the way it had for Christine. Professor Da Silva's speech was brief and subdued. He alluded to a striking new interpretation of the window that we'd all be reading soon when Christine's research (edited by Nathan Bell) was published. It might challenge some of our preconceived ideas about the college, and about ourselves, but that's what real scholarship is about, he said, having the vision to see things anew.

When the lecture is over I stay in my seat while the rest

of the audience filters out. Sometime during the talk I'd felt Bea's head rest on my shoulder. I didn't want to move. How many years, I wondered, did we have left of this kind of physical closeness? I didn't know. My own mother had died when I was not much older than Bea. I didn't have a script for the rest of our lives together.

After a few moments, when everyone has left, Bea rises and walks up to the window. I watch her as I've been watching her since she came home last week, amazed at the transformation that eight weeks away has wrought in her. When she'd left at the beginning of the summer she'd been hovering on the edge between childhood and adulthood, but now the gawkiness of her long limbs is gone. There's a grace and assurance in the way she holds herself that I've never seen before, a confidence in what her body and mind are capable of. She looks like a person who has settled into her own bones. What takes my breath away is how much she looks like Neil. All her life I've feared what she might inherit from Neil, but now I can see how much of what is good and strong in her comes from Neil: her willingness to confront life, the way she pushes herself into the current.

I can only hope that whatever she's inherited from me serves her half as well. Last week, when I'd finally summoned up the nerve to go back to Dr. Irini Pearlman, the genetic counselor, she told me that I didn't have the breast cancer gene. "At least not the two we've identified," she'd cautioned after telling me the good news. "You should, of course, continue monthly self-exams and yearly mammograms and encourage your daughter to do the same when she's older. Even if there's no genetic propensity in the family, all it means is that you're in the general risk pool—which is risky enough."

Bea touches the plaque beneath the window and reads aloud the line of poetry that comes after Christine's name and life span, "'Here with her face doth memory sit.' You know, the lady really does look a lot like Aunt Christine. Are you sure they weren't related?"

"I don't think so, honey."

She turns, the look of disappointment on her face making her look like a child again. She would like, I know, to make sense out of Christine's death. She has been able, at least, to take some comfort in the fact that her father died saving my life—but Christine seems to have died for nothing. "It just seems like such a waste," Bea says. "That she died trying to find out something that turned out to be untrue."

"I think she started out looking through those files to prove she was Clare's granddaughter," I say. "Her own family had given her so little that she wanted to belong to something else. But then when she found your father's file and learned he was doing so much better she wanted me to know. She thought that maybe we—me and your dad and you—could be a family again. So, in a way, that's what she died trying to do. In the end, I think we were the people she really loved—we were her family."

WHEN BEA LEAVES TO FIND PORTIA AT THE RECEPTION, I STAY a little longer, sitting below the window in just about the

466 • CAROL GOODMAN

same spot where I met Christine for the first time. I close my eyes and pray for inspiration.

"I hear that anyone who studies under this window gets an A on their paper," a voice says. "I'm hoping for a little inspiration on a report I'm writing." I open my eyes and look up into Daniel Falco's clear, gray eyes. "What are you working on?" he asks.

"A question," I answer.

"Just one?"

"A hard one," I say. "It's something Christine asked me on the train platform. She asked if I agreed with this line from Dante."

"Oh, Dante, my favorite. Such good punishments. The criminal justice system could learn a lot from him. Which line?"

"'Love, which absolves no one beloved from loving' . . ."

"Oh yeah, that one. Francesca, right?"

"Yes." I've ceased being surprised at the detective's command of literature. "What do you think? Do you agree with her that when you're loved you have no choice but to love back?"

He shrugs and looks up at the window. The cloud cover must be lifting outside because the window is now full of late afternoon light. The light opens up a path in the mountains and releases a stream that tumbles into the pool beneath the weeping beech and churns up the water. As the light flickers behind the tree you can make out the form of a woman trapped within the bark. Any moment she will free herself from her long imprisonment. The figure below her in the water holds both arms up toward her as if beckoning her sister to join her in the pool. Just before the light fades I catch the look in her eyes and I'm almost sure, this time, that what I see is forgiveness.

"What did you say?" I ask. I'd been so busy looking at the window that I'd missed Falco's answer.

"I said there's plenty of unrequited love around."

I sigh. "Yeah, that's what I was going to say to Christine." I don't mention that I'd thought of another answer before she got on the train.

"But then, you know," Falco continues, looking down at me, "all Dante's saying is that once you're beloved you've got to love someone. He doesn't say who you've got to love. It could mean that when you've been loved once, you'll love again, because . . . you know . . . you've been taught how." He turns back to the window and goes on, his voice sounding suddenly shy. "I guess that sounds pretty silly."

"No," I say. What I don't tell him is that it's exactly the answer I'd thought of when the train pulled out. "I don't think it sounds silly at all." I look up at Falco's back, framed against the darkening window. When he turns and looks at me the only light in the room seems to be coming from his eyes.

The Lake of Dead Languages

Carol Goodman

Jane Hudson never thought she would return to Heart Lake. Her years there as a scholarship girl ended in a double tragedy: the drownings of her two roommates.

Now she is back, struggling to adjust to her new life teaching Latin and as a single mother. But the events that haunted her memories for so many years begin to recur in front of her eyes. It seems she alone can see what is happening, and only she will be able to prevent a second catastrophe . . .

Surrounded by the lake that gives the school its name, steeped in history and overflowing with the emotions of teenage girls, Heart Lake guards its past – but cannot keep it hidden.

'Fulfilling . . . Miss Jean Brodie meets Donna Tartt . . . a good read, promising much for the future'
Daily Express

arrow books

The Seduction of Water

Carol Goodman

Many years ago, Iris Greenfeder's mother disappeared. They were living at Hotel Equinox where Iris's father was the manager and where Iris's mother wrote delicate, powerful fantasies. Then she took a train and never returned, dying in a hotel fire in Brooklyn where she was registered as another man's wife.

Returning to Hotel Equinox, now an established English professor, Iris needs to find the truth about her mother; some keys are held in those fantastical writings and others in the memories of those who knew her. Kay Greenfeder, it seems, was a woman without a past. But as Iris begins to untangle the secrets of years before, she realises that the past was very different to what she had believed, and much more dangerous . . .

'A gripping, well-written psychological thriller, rich in atmospheric detail'
Family Circle

arrow books

Judus Child

Carol O'Connell

When Sadie Green's bicycle is discovered abandoned at a bus stop, coinciding with the disappearance of her friend Gwen, police inform the press of their runaway theory suspicions. But State Police Investigator Rouge Kendall isn't convinced. He remembers all too clearly his own mother, begging for the life of his twin sister.

It has been fifteen years since a man was imprisoned for the murder of Kendall's sister. The man was Father Paul Marie, a priest, barely in his twenties, who had continued to proclaim his innocence.

Rouge Kendall must now struggle with the reality that the priest could have been telling the truth all along, and that the real killer may well have struck again . . .

'A menacing and unsettling thriller . . . more shocking surprises than a nail-biting horror film . . . O'Connell is a consummate story-teller . . . a unique talent who deserves to be a household name. The *Judas Child* is a scary monster of a book that should do just that'

Val McDermid *Express*

arrow books

Blindsighted

Karin Slaughter

The sleepy town of Heartsdale, Georgia, is jolted into panic when Sara Linton, paediatrician and medical examiner, finds Sibyl Adams dead in the local diner. As well as being viciously raped, Sibyl has been cut: two deep knife wounds form a lethal cross over her stomach. But it's only once Sara starts to perform the post-mortem that the full extent of the killer's brutality becomes clear.

Police chief Jeffrey Tolliver – Sara's ex-husband – is in charge of the investigation, and when a second victim is found, crucified, only a few days later, both Jeffrey and Sara have to face the fact that Sibyl's murder wasn't a one-off attack. What they're dealing with is a seasoned sexual predator. A violent serial killer . . .

'Don't read this alone. Don't read this after dark. But do read it.'
The Mirror

'Wildly readable . . . deftly crafted, damnably suspenseful and, in the end, deadly serious. Slaughter's plotting is brilliant, her suspense relentless.'
Washington Post

arrow books

Order further Arrow titles
from your local bookshop, or have them delivered direct to your door by Bookpost

☐ **The Lake of Dead Languages**		
Carol Goodman	0 09 943559 4	£6.99
☐ **The Seduction of Water**		
Carol Goodman	0 09 943562 4	£6.99
☐ **Judas Child** Carol O'Connell	0 09 924452 7	£5.99
☐ **Blindsighted** Karin Slaughter	0 09 942177 1	£6.99
☐ **Kisscut** Karin Slaughter	0 09 942178 X	£6.99
☐ **A Faint Cold Fear** Karin Slaughter	0 09 944532 8	£6.99

Free post and packing
Overseas customers allow £2 per paperback

Phone: 01624 677237

Post: Random House Books
c/o Bookpost, PO Box 29, Douglas, Isle of Man IM99 1BQ

Fax: 01624 670923

email: bookshop@enterprise.net

Cheques (payable to Bookpost) and credit cards accepted

Prices and availability subject to change without notice.
Allow 28 days for delivery.
When placing your order, please state if you do not wish to receive any
additional information.

www.randomhouse.co.uk/arrowbooks

arrow books